I Remember
Paris

Lucy Diamond

I Remember Paris

QUERCUS

First published in Great Britain in 2023 by

QUERCUS

Quercus Editions Ltd
Carmelite House
50 Victoria Embankment
London EC4Y 0DZ

An Hachette UK company

A CIP catalogue record for this book is available
from the British Library

HB ISBN 978 1 52943 293 0
TPB ISBN 978 1 52943 294 7
EB ISBN 978 1 52943 296 1

10 9 8 7 6 5 4 3 2 1

Typeset by CC Book Production
Printed and bound in Great Britain by Clays Ltd, Elcograf S.p.A.

Lovely Hannah, this one's for you –
see you in Le Mélange

PART ONE

Chapter One

Is it him again? Adelaide wonders, seeing a figure approach the building. The floor-length windows are on the grimy side but even so, there's no mistaking his height, his gait, the way his head twists on his neck as he looks up towards her. She feels a lurch inside, nausea rising. How did he know where to find her? And why won't he leave her alone?

She hears him try the door – it's unlocked – and now he's in; easy as that. What should she do? This has all escalated at unnerving speed. A couple of months earlier the man was merely a face in the crowd, someone she noticed staring at her in the Prince of Wales from a few tables away. Then she kept seeing him: a lone figure waiting on the same Tube platform, browsing the shops outside her studio, loitering near the bakery where she always buys bread. Coincidence, she told herself, the first time it dawned on her that he seemed to be everywhere she was. Or maybe he was a shy fan, hovering as he built up the confidence to say he admired her work. She did get them, after all. But as time passed and she kept on noticing him – outside a gallery or a theatre, in the same train carriage as her – a creeping sense of dread set in. A conviction that this would surely only get worse.

So it has proved. Last week, she was upstairs closing the bedroom curtains when she saw him perched on the wall of the house opposite, staring intently in her direction. It felt as if a boundary had been crossed. What does he want with her? 'That man's there again,' she said to Remy, but he merely flung back the bedcovers, revealing his naked body, and said, 'The only man you need to think about, baby, is right here.' Adelaide is not a woman given easily to scares but it proved hard to sleep that night, wondering who her watcher was, and what he might do next.

'Speak to the police,' Margie urged when Adelaide confided in her, but the suggestion seemed too far-fetched to take seriously.

'And say what? They'll laugh in my face. He hasn't done anything,' she protested.

'Yet,' Margie replied darkly. 'You be careful, Ads. Promise me.'

That 'yet' rings round Adelaide's head with horrible prescience because now he's here, at remote Little Bower, the place she has always come to get away from everything. Formerly a farm building, it's become a home from home for her and her closest friends, with this particular room used as shared studio space. It's a peaceful spot, surrounded by fields and hedgerows, with a meandering stretch of river nearby where she likes to swim on hot days. At night there are owls and bats, the sky darker than she's ever known it, punctured by the glitter of stars. But the tranquillity of being here alone has now been shattered and her adrenalin surges as she hears footsteps on the stairs. She glances around the room – dusty and messy, paints and brushes littering the surfaces, the radio tootling jazz – and wonders what will happen. How this will end.

Her heart is beating faster. Take control, she tells herself. Interviewers always describe her as fierce, as if she's some kind of wild animal; let's see if she can use that in her favour. Then he appears in the doorway, and a hot rush of fury courses through her.

'What on *earth*,' she shouts, striding across the room towards him, 'do you think you are doing here? Answer me immediately!'

He stops and stares, one hand reaching behind him for the solidity of the door frame as if he has lost his nerve. *Good.*

'Miss Fox,' he says, then breaks off. She has never heard him speak until now, she realises. Never been so close to him either; he's always lurked in her peripheral vision, a shadowy figure on the sidelines. He's in his thirties, she guesses, taking in his rumpled brown hair, the wide-spaced eyes and large nose, the pockmarked skin on his face. There's something shabby about him, unkempt. He's a loser.

'*What?*' Her eyes blaze. 'What's this all about? Because I'm sick of seeing you wherever I go. And I refuse to put up with it any more, do you hear me? This is private property; you are trespassing.'

'I . . .' He is still staring and the effect is unsettling.

'Well?'

He takes a step towards her. Her instinct is to move back, keep her distance, but she forces herself to hold her ground.

'Don't you remember me?' he asks.

She has absolutely no idea who he is, what he means. 'I would like you to leave,' she commands. 'Before I telephone the police.' This last is a bluff, of course. There is no phone here, no means of communication whatsoever when it comes to the rest of the world. This is the way they've always preferred it, the way she's been able to work best. Until today, anyway.

'But it's *me*,' he says plaintively. 'From the gallery.'

'What gallery? What are you talking about?' Her hands curl and uncurl by her sides, adrenalin spiking. She doesn't like this at all.

'We love each other,' he says simply. He's even blushing a little as he says the words, his eyes shifting away from hers. 'Adelaide, you know we do.'

He's deluded, then. And dangerous with it? she wonders, feeling a prickle of vulnerability. Is it too late to grab something as a makeshift weapon?

'I'm afraid you're mistaken,' she replies as frostily as she can muster. 'Now, I'm a very busy person as I'm sure you know, so if you don't mind—'

'I just want to be with you,' he says, edging closer. His eyes are wet and so is his big red mouth. He's not going to try and kiss her, is he? She takes an involuntary step back. He wouldn't actually put his hands on her or hurt her. Would he?

'Go away,' she orders, but he continues towards her. He's smiling, he looks happy, he's reaching his hands out, his gaze locked on hers. Now she's really frightened. 'GO AWAY!' she yells, and then—

6

Adelaide wakes up with a jerk. The nightmare again. She blinks, registering that Jean-Paul, her squat brown Staffie, is standing on the pillow beside her, his warm breath on her face. The room takes shape around her – early morning, soft pink light outlining the shutters – and she reaches out to pet his compact muscular body, her heart rate gradually subsiding from its frantic gallop. 'Thank you, darling,' she murmurs, taking comfort from his loyalty. She has been plagued by this same nightmare for years now, and it never gets any less terrifying. It's partly why she wants to get that awful day written down, in the hope that she can finally let it go. What she'd give to be rid of this particular ghost once and for all.

A short while later, she and Jean-Paul set out for their usual walk. It's a golden summer's morning in Paris, the light glittering from the windows of Place des Vosges as they stump along beneath the linden trees. So much for the image of Adelaide being a tough old bird; the public would soon change their minds if they knew what a soft touch she is with Jean-Paul. He has an excellent diet of choice cuts from the local *boucherie*, plus he is allowed to sleep on her bed every night (she has had a small ramp made for him to climb up there, now that his ageing legs are less springy than they once were). But he's worth all of it. She had no idea it was possible to love a dog quite so much.

This is their daily constitutional: a diagonal stride across the centre of the square, so that Jean-Paul can make use of the grass there, followed by a slow circuit around the edges. The waiters at the brasserie respectfully bow their heads towards her, occasionally appearing with a sausage for Jean-Paul, or trying to tempt her to take a seat and enjoy an espresso. 'Our gift to you, Madame!' they wheedle even though she always turns them down. She passes the fancy hotel and the galleries, Victor Hugo's house and all the tourists queuing with their oversized backpacks and loud voices. Sometimes – not so much these days – she might hear her name mentioned. *Hey! Isn't that Adelaide Fox? Look! It* is *her, right?* She has also – less flatteringly – heard the follow-up comments: *Wait, she's still* alive? *I thought she was dead!*

'Not yet, dear,' she enjoys replying tartly whenever this happens, just to see their expressions afterwards: sometimes awkward and apologetic, other times thrilled.

No, not yet, she repeats to herself now. Although sometimes she wonders why she bothers to stay alive. Old age – she'll be eighty before she knows it – is no place for weaklings. For her, the last few years have felt like the Badlands of a life – bleak territory, with precious little to get out of bed for. If it wasn't for her dog, then … She glances down at Jean-Paul, who has stopped to sniff around a bench with unerring optimism. He once found the remnants of a ham baguette at this particular spot and always makes a point of returning, despite having been disappointed every time since. At least one of them still has a positive outlook on life, she supposes.

A small girl sidles up. Jean-Paul is something of a magnet for small girls, not least because Adelaide has made him a sparkly collar fashioned with pieces of colourful clear plastic that look like jewels. It is ridiculous but it makes her smile. The girl is dressed in cheap-looking pink leggings, a T-shirt with a pattern of yellow flowers and those unattractive white trainers that have flashing lights in the heel. Dreadful.

'What is your dog called?' the child asks in French.

Adelaide gives the girl a terrifying glower. 'He is called "I eat children",' she replies sternly and stalks past, but not before she has seen the child's face crumple. Serves her right. Maybe she'll think twice about talking to a stranger next time.

A wail goes up behind her but Adelaide does not look back. She is an artist, this is what she has always done: create a moment, impact, drama. Over the years, her work has forced others to see the world in a different light – and if her memoir ever gets off the ground, she'll one day be doing that in print too.

She frowns at the thought of this seemingly doomed project. There have been many publishers over the years sniffing around for her stories but she has perpetuated a haughty silence – a woman has her secrets after all. But then six months ago, there came a savage article in *Le Monde*, in which the journalist basically rubbished her life's work as infantile and narcissistic. Feeling bruised, she didn't immediately delete the persuasive email that arrived the same day, by chance, from yet another commissioning editor. *We'd love to help you recount your story in your own words*, the editor had coaxed. *Remy told his side of the tale, but what about yours? Wouldn't you love to set the record straight?*

Later, as she set about furiously sketching the *Le Monde* journalist on a torture rack with pencils jabbed into his eyeballs – not so smug now, are you, dear? – she found herself reflecting on the many other revenge fantasies she's captured in paints or charcoal over the years, how cathartic it has been to dish out vengeance with her brushes. Maybe there could be something in this memoir business after all. A new weapon with which to take down her assailants. The Art of Revenge, she's calling it in her head, and the title feels satisfyingly apt.

Her nephew Lucas, a corporate lawyer, has been very helpful with the contract and paperwork so far, and, following a recent redundancy, has rented a flat nearby, so that he can assist with hiring a suitable ghostwriter, as well as sorting through her neglected archive of paintings and associated paperwork. With a bit of luck, they can organise a new exhibition to coincide with the book's publication – or so they originally hoped. Alas, neither task has proved straightforward. What a lot of Moaning Minnies they have met and discarded so far in the hunt for a decent writer. Carping on about working conditions, disagreeing with her about content and focus . . . Good riddance, frankly. They barely deserve to say her name aloud, let alone be entrusted to tell her life story to the waiting world. As for the archive, let's just say that Lucas has his work cut out for him. A methodical, punctilious person by nature, he couldn't actually speak for several minutes when first presented with the Belleville rooms stuffed haphazardly with decades' worth of her art plus heaps of correspondence and other documents. 'It'll keep you busy,' she told him bracingly, kicking a pile of canvases only for them both to start coughing at the resulting dust cloud that swirled into their faces.

She passes the brasserie – almost home – and Jean-Paul stops to drink, with his usual splashy gusto, from the metal dog bowl the waiters always leave there. Her bothersome knee is starting to ache, her hip too; this body of hers protesting with each step. 'Hurry up now,' she tells the dog, because sometimes she feels as if she will seize up like a rusty old machine if she stops moving for too long. 'Let's go home, come along.'

Home to the quiet apartment, with her memories and her secrets, and the grudges that silently smoulder. But not for much longer, she tells herself, reaching the door and fumbling for her key. Once she has settled on a writer who can actually stay the course, out will come all of those stories, scorching the pages on which they're told. And after that, nobody will have any doubts about whether or not she is still alive. Because her life – and those who have crossed her – will be all the world is able to talk about.

Chapter Two

Sitting on the Eurostar as it starts to glide out of the station – next stop, Paris! – Jess Bright can't help the feeling that any minute now, a heavy hand will clamp on her shoulder – a train guard, a police officer, even – and she'll hear the gruff words, 'Excuse me, madam. You seem to be in the wrong life here.'

Forty-seven, and impostor syndrome is still deeply entrenched within her. Cut her in half and you'd probably see the words 'Not That Good Really' printed all the way through, as if she's a stick of Margate rock. She's a freelance journalist and frazzled single mum of three teenage daughters, nothing special. But today, to everyone's surprise, Jess is on her way to Paris to meet famous artist Adelaide Fox in the hope of writing her memoir. It's the job of her dreams. Can it really be happening? Astonishingly, it appears so.

Her lips purse as she remembers her ex-husband's reaction to the news last week. 'No offence, but why do you think she's asked you?' he'd mused aloud, when she mentioned the opportunity.

No offence, David, but why do you think I don't want to be married to you any more? she'd felt like retaliating. (She didn't. See how far she has evolved! Besides, she needed to keep him on side so that he'd have the girls while she's away.) Instead she calmly reminded him how, years earlier, back when Mia was still a twinkle in the womb, Jess had interviewed the reclusive artist for the Sunday newspaper where she worked at the time. 'And now that she wants a memoir writing, her nephew got in touch to ask if I'd be interested,' she said. Put that in your pipe and smoke it, David.

God, she had loved that old job. As a journalist on the Culture team, her life had been a whirl of gallery openings, author interviews and film premieres. She'd had clout, she was making a name for herself. But then she became a mum – first to Mia, then Edie, then Polly – and has been freelance ever since, picking up bits and pieces of work wherever she can. She's written an advice column in one of the Kent newspapers for years ('Look on the Bright Side') plus a parenting column for *Glorious*, a monthly glossy ('Mum's the Word! Dispatches from the Frontline of Motherhood'). Okay, so the Press Industry Awards committee hasn't exactly been beating a path to her door, but she's made it work this far. Until a month ago, anyway, when *Glorious* magazine decided to move to a digital-only model, shucking off a handful of faithful columnists along the way. No more motherhood dispatches from Jess. ('Thank *God*,' Mia had exclaimed theatrically when Jess broke the news over dinner. 'I'm sick of people finding that nits story online and calling me Lice Girl.')

Her daughters might have complained about Jess parcelling up their antics as humorous content on a monthly basis but the column had covered much of the household expenses which, in this post-separation landscape, was not to be sniffed at. And to be fair, most of her columns were complete confections anyway. She never mentioned Mia's run of panic attacks before her exams last summer, nor the miserable toxic friendships Edie keeps finding herself trapped in, nor indeed the unpleasant revelation that Polly had been stealing classmates' belongings for two whole terms back in year six. Whatever – since losing this tent pole of income, she's profoundly grateful for the serendipity of one Lucas Brockes, nephew of Adelaide, emailing about the memoir, and hopefully saving them all from imminent destitution. Would Jess be willing to come to Paris, accommodation provided, to work with Adelaide on a memoir, initially on a week's trial, with the possibility of returning for a month? Hell yes, Lucas.

It feels as if Fate has given her a lucky break for once. That's if she's up to the job, anyway. Writing a serious biography is something of a leap from her mum column and agony aunt page, isn't it? She can't help feeling a bit ... well, rusty, for one thing. Intimidated for another.

'Here's an idea,' David had said, all those years earlier when she first went on maternity leave. 'I put my career first, while you take some time out, say for a couple of years, then you can do the same when you're ready to go back to work, and I'll support whatever dreams you have.' He's a sports journalist, and at the time of this suggestion, was keen to shadow a senior colleague on an Ashes tour in Australia. Keen to bugger off for four weeks while Jess slaved alone for a grizzly three-month-old who hated sleeping, more like, but the offer of being able to call in a similar favour for her own ambitions had kept her going. One day she would be able to cash in her promised time, guilt-free, and work on something really meaningful, she fantasised. A stirring, highbrow novel, perhaps, in contention for numerous literary prizes. An incredible screenplay that would see her wooed by Hollywood directors and mingling with the beautiful people. Or a searing set of journalistic investigations that would change society for the better; her own legacy bequeathed to the world.

Only it never happened like that. There was always something else more pressing that prevented them from putting Jess's career front and centre – various issues with the girls, David's parents becoming ill one after another, the cricket tours abroad he was contractually obliged to go on as his star rose. *It's just not the right time*, he would say apologetically, and she'd started to believe, following their separation, that this elusive, mystical 'right time' would never happen now. But might this be Jess's time at last? What if this is the job that turns everything around for her?

Sipping her coffee as the Kent countryside rushes past the window, she finds herself remembering the promotion she'd once applied for back at the Sunday newspaper, how she'd walked down the corridor after the interview thinking it had gone pretty well only to then remember in a fluster that she'd left her bag behind. Back she'd gone, reaching the interview room just in time to hear her boss Lucinda and the HR woman Maxine discussing her. *The thing about Jess*, Lucinda had said, *is that she's very lowbrow. Does she have the gravitas to be credible with our readers?*

These words have long since been branded across Jess's mind, impossible to forget. Imagine, though, if she gets the nod to write Adelaide's memoir and it's published as a gorgeous, upmarket hardback book. The first chance she gets, she'll be marching into the Culture office with a personal copy for her old boss. *That enough gravitas for you, love?* she'll say, letting it drop from her hands on to Lucinda's desk with a thud. God, that will be a good, good moment!

She glances down at her notes, filled with renewed determination. Jess is a grafter: she will work her socks off to make a success of this opportunity. 'Hard work is your ticket to a good life,' she is fond of telling her daughters, although, alas, none of them seem to have taken this advice to their hearts yet. Mia would rather be out with a gang of noisy friends ('her squad'), Edie can (and does) spend hours, literally hours, lying in bed watching YouTube videos, whereas Polly is smart and quick, coasting through homework with the least amount of effort she can get away with. 'Done!' she carols, snapping the exercise book shut and tossing it to the floor with evident relief each time.

Retrieving a pen from her bag, Jess underlines a couple of words in the notes she's made. 'Adelaide Fox? She's that wild feminist one who was part of a really cool set of female artists, right? Didn't she smash up her husband's exhibition in Berlin or something too?' her friend Becky had summarised when Jess told her about the offer of work.

There's so much more to her than that, though. According to Jess's research, the young Adelaide left home and school at sixteen, and moved into a squat with a group of friends, before making a name for herself in her twenties with a groundbreaking show called Work. She went on to become a key figure in the so-called London Bohemian movement, a collective of women at the forefront of the sixties' wave of counterculture who became noted conceptual artists, designers and sculptors, mixing in radical underground circles.

Then come a few gaps in the online versions of her biography. Jess remembers, from her previous interview research, coming across various rumours about Adelaide – tempestuous love affairs, a mysterious child, addictions of one kind or another, and some kind of rift with Margie Flint, a fellow artist; the two of them still apparently estranged all these years later. There's also a spell in Berlin (a nervous breakdown?) plus the mysterious suicide of a man at a rural house used as a studio by the Bohemians.

Adelaide's been an enigma for decades. Despite the numerous articles and interviews, she's somehow managed to flit between questions without ever revealing too much. When Jess met her before, she was interesting, sparky company, but very much there to talk about her Tate exhibition and little else. She was initially a little prickly too, upon discovering that the interview would be conducted by a junior writer (Jess) rather than the newspaper's lead arts correspondent, as promised (Lucinda, who had unfortunately come down with a bout of gastro-enteritis). Full disclosure: Jess had used the words 'coming out of both ends' when trying to explain why her boss really *really* couldn't be there. (In hindsight, this was perhaps rather unsisterly of her, but Lucinda would never know, at least.)

'Wow, what a life,' Becky said, on hearing the stories. 'You've got to do this, Jess. A work trip to Paris, you lucky cow! Watch out, because I might start hating you if this gets any better.'

Despite Becky's encouragement, Jess has had a few qualms about going away for so long – what with that boy Zach appearing unexpectedly out of seventeen-year-old Mia's bedroom the other morning ('God, Mum, we're just *friends*, don't look at me like that!'), and the fact that she recently found a small gold anklet in Polly's skirt pocket that definitely wasn't her daughter's ('Someone *gave* it to me, Mum, I'm not lying!'). Strangely enough though, now that she's on the train, the qualms are melting away, like butter into toast. It will be like revisiting the gap year she spent in Paris post-university, she thinks happily: the wonderful freedom of doing exactly what she wants in her spare time. Long evening walks through the old streets as the brasseries fill with diners, Sacré-Coeur gleaming like a beautiful pearl from the dark hillside, lights spangling the Eiffel Tower for a million tourist photos ...

And everyone will manage perfectly well without her for a few days, she reminds herself. Becky has promised to feed Albertine the cat, while the girls will be fine with David. Besides, he's gone abroad for work enough times, leaving her to cope single-handedly. She finds herself thinking again of the slog of those weeks alone with a tiny not-sleeping baby, while he lived his best life in Brisbane. *Having an amazing time!* he would message periodically and she would feel like throwing her phone out the window. He owes her big-style.

Mesdames et messieurs, the train announcer says at that moment. *Nous arrivons à Paris maintenant*, and a thrill sweeps through her entire body. This is happening. This is really happening!

Of course, Jess has been to Paris with David and the girls at various times over the years — weekend trips, a Euro Disney break, stopping off for a few days en route to campsites further south — but she's always been looking after other people on these occasions. Their wants and needs have taken priority — Mickey Mouse winning out over a leisurely Louvre wander, for instance. David's insistence on them slogging up the steps of the Eiffel Tower in protest against the lift prices, when her preference would have been not only to take said lift, but also to splash out on an overpriced glass of champagne at the top.

Now look at her, arriving alone in the city, wheeling her case along the platform with a fizz of sheer joy pinballing inside her. Breezing through the ticket barriers and into the station like she's never been away, images of her twenty-two-year-old self striding alongside her. That had been such a happy period of her life, fresh out of university, determined to enjoy some time abroad before she had to think about anything too grown-up like finding a proper job. She'd worked a stint in an ice cream shop (who knew it was possible to get sick of ice cream?) then took a job chambermaiding at a glamorous hotel in the chi-chi 6th arrondissement, close to the Jardin du Luxembourg. She'd fallen in love with Georges, a handsome older man who educated her in all sorts of interesting ways — sexual ways first and foremost, but also by taking her to see opera and ballet at the Palais Garnier, and teaching her about French wine. She'd also hung out in grungy bars with her new friend Pascale, mastered cycling along cobblestoned streets and perfected her French, complete with shrugs and hand gestures.

As well as having her sign a contract and confidentiality agreement, Adelaide's nephew Lucas has also arranged hotel accommodation for Jess in the Marais district, and she navigates the metro system to emerge at Saint-Paul. Stepping out from the station, the warmth of the city settles upon her skin as she gazes around to orient herself. It feels like a dream as she takes in the elegant, ivory-coloured buildings with their shutters and balconies, the canopied cafés and tobacconists, the children's carousel turning with jaunty music on a central paved area right in front of her. A couple are drinking champagne in long-stemmed glasses at a bar across the road; cyclists skim by, legs scissoring; women wearing chic trouser suits and sunglasses glide past her, leaving wafts of tuberose perfume in their wake.

Hello, Paris, you beauty, Jess thinks, momentarily overcome. Even if this only turns out to be a week-long gig, it feels like the best kind of gift, one she didn't know she needed until now. Checking the map on her phone, she turns and starts walking.

The hotel is a charming old building on a quiet street, ten minutes from the metro. There are sprays of pink cherry blossom around the front door – fake ones, obviously, but the effect is very pretty nonetheless. Her room, it turns out, is on the top floor. 'Madame, I apologise, but the lift, he is not working today,' the man behind the reception desk says, handing over the key with an expressive flex of his dark eyebrows. He seems determined to speak to her in heavily accented English, even though she has so far spoken only in French to him, and with decent fluency as well, she thought. Also she's unquestionably a 'Madame' now, she realises, and can't help feeling a pang for her 'Mademoiselle' days before telling herself she's being ridiculous.

Heaving her case up five flights of ageing, well-trodden stairs, Jess has broken into a sweat by the time she reaches her room. But then she opens the door, sees the sweet white-painted attic space with its original oak beams across the ceiling, shutters at the window and tiny en-suite bathroom, and she forgets her tiredness. She drops her case and hurries to the window, through which she can see a small cobbled square with trees and benches in its centre, plus what looks like a *crêperie*, *boulangerie* and brasserie set around its sides. There are Orangina umbrellas outside a café, and she can hear music and voices, children's laughter, the buzz of a moped nearby ... It's perfect, she thinks, almost tearful with a sudden rush of happiness.

Arrived safely – here's my view! she messages the girls with a photo from the window. *Everything all right back home? Surviving without me?*

BONJOUR PARIS! she messages Becky along with emojis of the French flag, a croissant, baguette, wine bottle and the Eiffel Tower. *I made it!*

Then, unable to resist, she sends the photo to her mum, Samantha, as well. *Back in Paris for a week-long commission, interviewing a famous artist!* she reports with studied nonchalance. She presses 'Send', trying not to cringe at her own neediness.

What does it say about her, that she's in her forties and still angling for approval from her mother? On second thoughts, she'd rather not get into that.

'Oh dear,' Samantha had clucked down the phone when Jess told her she'd lost the 'Mum's the Word' column. 'It's such a *fickle* profession, isn't it? So precarious!'

Yes. So fickle and so precarious compared to – ooh, let's see – medicine: Jess's brother Owen's chosen career. 'My son – he's a doctor, you know' has long been Samantha Stanton's catchphrase; it's surprising she hasn't got the words printed on a T-shirt by now. Golden boy Owen studied for his medicine degree in Newcastle, where he's been living ever since. Now Dr Stanton, an orthopaedic specialist, he's married to Deanna, a geriatrician, and they have two little boys. Practically the minute Deanna announced she was pregnant, Jess's mum was clearing out the house in Gravesend where Owen and Jess had grown up, then putting it on the market in order to follow them up north.

These days, she lives five minutes from their posh road of big houses, full of doctors and lawyers, on a new-build estate, where one of the spotless bedrooms is set up as 'the boys' room' and the mantelpiece is a parade of photographs featuring Jake and Ollie, the stars around which her world now orbits. 'Those little boys have given me a whole new lease of life!' she's fond of saying, even to Jess, whose three wonderful daughters barely get a look-in from Grandma Stanton. Jess is always left feeling as if she's seven again, and jealous of the shiny bike her brother was given for Christmas. Meanwhile, she'd received a plastic doll with springy nylon hair, and one eye that never closed properly, so that it looked drunk, or as if it was winking sarcastically. *Yeah*, the wink seemed to say. *Bum deal. We both know it, kiddo.*

The girls haven't replied – maybe David has taken them out for Nando's and the cinema for the latest Marvel film, and they're all wishing they lived with him year-round, rather than boring old Mum. They are still collectively finding their way as a family with separated parents, and it hasn't been easy. After the whole Bella business, Jess tried her hardest to make the broken marriage work, to keep them together, but in doing so, felt her own self-respect leaking away. She couldn't sleep, felt like she was going mad, burst into tears at regular intervals. Then, last May, two weeks short of them having been together for twenty years, she made the decision that their relationship had malingered for so long, it was now beyond resuscitation. David had cried into his hands and promised he would change but they both knew he wasn't capable. The girls still resent her for breaking up the family – 'God, Mum, sabotage my GCSEs, why don't you?' Mia had griped bitterly at the time, while Edie responded to every nag or criticism with a shrill 'I'm from a broken home, back off!' for what felt like months on end. It wracks Jess with guilt every single day but she stands by her decision nevertheless. It's better this way.

Perched on the bed, staring at an unchanged phone screen, she has a sudden moment of clarity. This isn't what her Paris trip is about, is it? It's four in the afternoon and she isn't due to meet Adelaide until tomorrow morning; the rest of the day is entirely her own. First on the agenda: a quick wash to freshen up, she decides. A change of clothes. And then she will redo her lipstick, spritz her wrists with perfume, and venture into the sunny streets she'll be calling home for the next week. Longer, if she plays her cards right. She'll sip an espresso and watch the world go by, while enjoying some leisurely deliberation over which restaurant to dine in later on.

That's more like it. The Paris adventure starts here.

Chapter Three

Adelaide waits in the living room of her apartment, seated on her damson-coloured velvet Louis XVI-style sofa. This room overlooks the square, with two huge windows that allow the morning light to stream in, and it's a grand space, designed to impress, with its marble fireplace, crystal chandeliers, antique furniture and large gilded mirrors.

The doorbell rings at ten o'clock exactly, followed by the heavy tread of Marie-Thérèse, the housekeeper, as she trudges to answer it. Marie-Thérèse is a dreary sort of person, with bad skin and a permanent cold. If she was named in homage to Picasso's charismatic, athletic muse, then it has been the most disastrous misnomer of all time. She has been with Adelaide six weeks so far and her presence is slightly repellent, but she cleans fastidiously (even the light bulbs have been dusted) and she is yet to break anything, which is more than can be said for some of her predecessors. For the time being, she's staying.

A knock sounds at the living room door moments later, and Jean-Paul's small triangular ears prick up from where he is curled up on the floor near her feet.

'*Entrez,*' says Adelaide. Here we go.

Please let this one work out, she thinks as the door opens. Adelaide approves of very few people as a rule, but she approved highly of Jessica when they originally met, finding her a serious, thoughtful person who knew a great deal about art. Not one of the many idiot writers she has come across since then who only have banal questions for her, and who fixate on Adelaide's relationship with Remy. Is it any wonder she has shunned the press for so long?

In comes Marie-Thérèse mumbling an introduction, and Adelaide asks for a tray of coffee to be brought. Behind her comes another woman, wearing a rather cheap-looking olive green belted shirt dress and wedge sandals, toting a large black bag on her shoulder. But this isn't Jessica Martindale, the eloquent, fiercely intelligent former *New Yorker* writer, Adelaide registers, frowning uncertainly. Not unless she has had dramatic corrective surgery, anyway. Which begs the question: who *is* this?

'Hello again,' says the new arrival, sounding nervous but determined. She has long brown hair tied back in a ponytail, and her eyes shine as she gazes around. Adelaide's heart sinks as she pictures Jessica Martindale with her silver pixie-cut, the piercing blue eyes behind rimless glasses, the multitude of knuckle-duster rings on every finger. This woman before her is a gauche schoolgirl by comparison. Could she be Jessica's assistant who has arrived before her, perhaps? It's not a stretch to imagine Martindale with an entourage, she supposes.

'Gosh,' the creature is saying, slack-jawed, 'what a beautiful room this—'

She gets no further because Jean-Paul is up on his feet, barking. He sometimes takes violent dislikes to people for no apparent reason, although on the whole he is a good judge of character. Maybe he was expecting Jessica Martindale too.

'Thank you,' Adelaide tells him sternly. This is generally enough to silence him, although not today – on he continues, charging towards the woman, who stumbles back in alarm with a nervous cry, one ankle twisting in those ridiculous sandals. Oh dear. She is not a dog person, then – this gets worse by the minute. By contrast, Adelaide remembers Jessica Martindale, two glasses of champagne down in their previous interview, getting out her phone to show pictures of her whippet. But this woman said 'Hello again', didn't she? she realises belatedly. So they *have* met on some occasion, presumably – but when?

'Jean-Paul, that is *enough*!' Adelaide tells him, frustrated both by the dog and her own slow-churning brain. 'Come here this *minute.*'

He gives a final defiant bark before reluctantly turning back towards her. The woman meanwhile hovers at a distance, no longer quite so smiley. 'Sorry, I—'

'Are you scared of dogs? He's never bitten anyone,' Adelaide interrupts, unable to resist adding, 'Not yet, anyway.' It's the badness in her, she is fully aware of it; the dark streak in her that responds gleefully to other people's discomfort. *Can't you just be nice?* her mother would plead despairingly when Adelaide was a little girl. But *is* there a nice way to ask, *I'm sorry but who are you?* Because heaven help her, she can't come up with one.

27

'It's not that I'm *scared* of dogs,' the wrong Jessica is saying now, without a great deal of conviction. 'More that . . . Well, I've always had cats, so . . .' She trails off, possibly because of the contempt on Adelaide's face. Bloody cat people. Picasso, Warhol, Dalí . . . all renowned cat-lovers, and, if the stories are to be believed, absolute arseholes, the lot of them. And you can quote her on that, she thinks, patting Jean-Paul as he sinks to the floor beside her once more, huffing a sigh.

Adelaide beckons the other woman over. 'Come and sit down. And take no notice of Jean-Paul, he's a big softie really, like all Staffies.'

With a wary glance at the big softie, Jessica lowers herself on to the armchair Adelaide is indicating. Then in tramps adenoidal Marie-Thérèse, thud thud thud, with a tray of tea and coffee things, and there is some fussing around of pouring, and stirring in milk, giving Adelaide time to think. If this woman *was* Martindale's assistant, you'd think she'd have mentioned her boss by now. She'd have said *Jessica will be joining us in twenty minutes* or something, wouldn't she? Besides, she isn't glamorous enough to be working for Jessica Martindale. So they're back to the old question – who is she? Feeling increasingly desperate, Adelaide hunts through her memory, back to the conversation when she and Lucas had discussed which writer to try next.

'It's a long shot because she'll no doubt be busy, but there was that Jessica woman who wrote a piece when I was promoting the Darkness show,' she'd said. It was early evening, the weekend before last, and Lucas had come over, bearing boxes of Vietnamese takeaway food, so that they could plan a new strategy.

'Jessica . . .' he muttered, typing quickly into his laptop. 'You mean the feature in—'

Her memory stutters a little at this point because now she's wondering if he did really say the *New Yorker* or if she just assumed he did, because that was what she was expecting. She was feeling tired, she remembers. Somewhat dull around the edges because the wretched tremors in her hands had started up again and she'd knocked back a large brandy in the hope that it might help. (Wishful thinking, sadly.) She was possibly distracted too because they were in the dining room and Jean-Paul always has a good old roll on his favourite scratchy rug there, his tan back arching with delight. There is precious little to smile about in the world most days, Adelaide feels, but a joyfully rolling dog gets her every time.

Is this the mistake? she wonders now, hysteria rising. That they've inadvertently invited the wrong Jessica here to Paris because Adelaide was too busy gazing fondly at her dog's contortions to pay proper attention to the conversation? Oh dear.

By now, the two of them are settled with their drinks and the other woman – the mysterious wrong Jessica – is waiting expectantly.

'So – welcome,' Adelaide says eventually. She'll have to go through the motions for the time being, she supposes. Although there *is* something vaguely familiar about her, now that she looks again. Those earnest brown eyes, the apple cheeks . . . a bell is ringing in her distant memory although she can't quite locate any further details. But presumably Jessica has written about her in the past (*Hello again*), and done a good enough job that she is on Lucas's database.

'Jessica, isn't it?' she ventures, gambling that her guesswork is correct. 'Your journey was all right yesterday, I take it? The hotel suitable?'

She's only asking to be polite, not particularly caring either way, but Jessica – who doesn't dispute the name – is suddenly falling over herself to praise the hotel and how generous Adelaide has been, her cheeks flushing pink as if chastising herself for not saying so already. Oh heavens, she does seem jittery, fiddling with a bangle on her wrist, crossing and uncrossing her legs at the ankle. The bell continues to ring in a dim corner of Adelaide's brain – yes, she did this before, didn't she? An initial nervousness – there was some problem at the start of the interview, she recalls. Something that put the younger woman on edge for a while. It'll come to her.

She holds up her hand because Jessica is still wittering. 'That's fine. I'm glad everything's all right. Now – shall we begin?' The minutes are slipping by, and she has neither the time nor the patience for small talk. Just wait until she speaks to Lucas about this.

'Of course.' Jessica digs into her bag, retrieving a laptop, notebook and pen. She also gets out her phone and holds it in mid-air. 'Are you all right with me recording these sessions?'

'Absolutely,' Adelaide replies. 'As I will be too.' She narrows her eyes at the woman to underline her point. You might seem a sweet little thing, but you are still a journalist, and I know better than to trust your sort. She fumbles to set her

30

own phone recording, her hands starting their usual trembling in the process. Damn it.

Jessica doesn't seem to notice at least. She appears more confident now that she has the accoutrements of work around her; more at ease. Adelaide was always the same. Put her in front of a microphone and she'd freeze; give her a paintbrush and it was like a piece of armour behind which she was safe. Not that there's been much paintbrush-holding since her stupid ageing body started playing tricks on her.

'So. How would you like to do this?' Jessica asks. 'I'm imagining you have ideas about structure and tone ... We could construct the narrative around particularly significant works of yours, perhaps, or places you've lived or worked, or ...'

'As this is a trial period,' Adelaide interrupts, 'I suggest I talk to you about my early years, then you can write that up as your sample chapter. Yes?' Chances are, Wrong Jessica won't have to bother her head about the book's structure because she won't be writing it, she thinks, wondering how quickly they can get Jessica Martindale over here instead.

Jessica nods meekly. 'Yes, of course.' Then her face changes from one of earnestness to beaming warmth. 'Really – thank you for asking me here. This is my dream job,' she goes on, 'and I'm ready to give my absolute all to make this book a massive success for you. I know that last time we met, it was to talk about the Tate exhibition, and it was pretty much business only, so it's a complete thrill to be trusted with your life story. Consider me on board with whatever works best for you!' She stops herself, blushes. 'That's if I pass the trial period, of course.'

31

The Tate exhibition – ahh yes. Adelaide's last launch in London. She had a whole week of exhausting TV, radio and press interviews in the run-up to the grand opening – never again, she vowed at the time. She vaguely remembers meeting Jessica now, in a chilly hotel, all overstuffed couches and obsequious waiting staff. In fact, the memories are rushing back with gratifying fullness, not least Jessica's rather shady tale-telling, regarding her boss suffering some revolting gastric complaint. The resulting write-up was pretty nice though. No tricks, no behind-the-hand bitching, as there has been so many times before, especially if the writer in question is a jealous, insecure man.

'Thank you,' she says stiffly. 'If you're ready, then let's make a start. My childhood. Well . . .' She pauses as a series of images flash through her mind. The East End bomb sites she and her brothers played amidst. The rural Pickering summers, collecting warm eggs from her grandmother's softly clucking hens. The chalk-smelling schoolroom, the hot itchy misery of measles, the thrill of leaving home, finding her tribe, the art school years. Plus other, secret things she has never publicly divulged: the flush of her little brother's hurt face as he turned away from her that final time. Her dad walloping her mum so hard she ricocheted off the door and back. The sensation of her fingers curling around a matchbox, with the devil in her ear, urging her to wreak revenge . . .

Oh Lord. Something awful has just come back to her. Her launch at the Tate: a big glamorous affair, with camera flashes and foaming champagne and head-cocked critics scribbling notes as they gazed at the canvases. Also the pale, skinny

32

woman in a cream trouser suit hurrying up to introduce herself, the correspondent from the Sunday newspaper who had originally been rostered in to interview her. Lindsay something? Louisa? Full of grovelling apologies she had been, anyway, the most dreadful kind of arse-kisser. And Adelaide . . . Oh goodness. She'd been several sheets to the wind by then, giddy on the gorgeousness of the exhibition, flattered by the compliments that had rung so gloriously in her ears all night. There was no excuse for what she'd said though.

There's a small, polite cough from Jessica at that moment. 'It must be hard to know where to begin,' she says. 'But your stories don't have to be in any kind of chronological order at this point – I can work that out when I edit. Maybe start by telling me about your parents?'

Adelaide reaches down to pat Jean-Paul, trying to reorient herself here, in this room, rather than back in the Tate, needlessly humiliating Jess's boss. 'Ahh yes, I heard you had come down with something ghastly,' she had replied to her (Lilian? Lorraine?). Something in the woman's pretty, simpering face had reminded her of Coco, which perhaps explained the cruelty behind her next words. 'I'm surprised you're wearing cream, to be honest, given what I was told,' she'd gone on. 'Exploding out of both ends, wasn't it?'

The woman (Lucille? *Lucinda*, that's it) had gulped in a shocked breath before pasting on an artificial smile, eyes glittering with embarrassment, or anger perhaps. Tears, even, now that Adelaide thinks back. She hopes – belatedly – that there were no repercussions for the writer now sitting in front of her. Oops. Is this karma, finally coming to punish her for her sins? Has Jessica arrived gunning for a hatchet job out of revenge?

'My parents, yes,' she says hastily. 'Robert and Geraldine Brockes.' And then she's off, her composure gradually returning as she skims light-heartedly over her dad's fiery temper and her mum's monumental mood swings, retelling the funniest, most charming stories about her brothers. With one thing and another, she hasn't yet made up her mind about this Jessica, even though, given what she's just remembered, she probably owes her one. Nevertheless, Adelaide won't be revealing anything remotely personal yet. Her secrets will have to wait.

Chapter Four

That afternoon, as Jess leaves Adelaide's intimidatingly grand apartment, it feels nigh on impossible to give herself a 'Look on the Bright Side' pep talk. She can't think of a single positive to take from the experience. First there was the dog rushing at her, and her embarrassing, startled reaction, and then – worse – the 'who the hell are you?' look on Adelaide's face that greeted her. It wasn't as if Jess had been expecting a matey reunion or anything, but the total blankness was unnerving, to say the least. Plus there was Adelaide herself – stand-offish and hard to warm to. Her hair, now the colour of pewter, is cut in a forbidding crop, and her very nature seems forbidding. Several times when Jess dared to probe a little deeper into an anecdote, it was as if the older woman closed right up, a mask appearing on her face. *None of your business*, the mask said.

Fine, if this was an interview, 1,500 words to feature online or in print. They could stick to paddling in the shallow waters, avoid any murkier depths. But for a memoir, surely the whole point is to elaborate, to reveal more of oneself? And yet Jess feels as if she spent the entire day trying in vain to weasel out further information. 'Can you tell me about a couple of objects in your childhood bedroom?' she'd asked, hoping for some background details with which she could conjure a scene. 'What did the kitchen look like? Is there a smell you associate with that time? What did you wear for school? Did you have a best friend? Did you already love drawing by then?'

It proved hard work, the proverbial blood from a stone. But it begs the question: what is Adelaide keeping from her? It's not as if Jess can go spilling any confidentialities, what with the stringent contract she had to sign. Maybe Adelaide'll loosen up over the coming days, once they've re-established a connection. Christ, she hopes so.

Still, silver lining: it's only just two o'clock and she's already been released for the day. She should type up the morning's recordings while everything is fresh in her head, she supposes. Only ... Her footsteps slow as she approaches the hotel and she reflects on how roasting her sweet little attic room will be right now. Then she recalls the small square in the street beyond, how cheering it had been to explore the night before; the very nice glass of wine she'd treated herself to in the brasserie, the delicious *moules frites*. Sod it, it's been ages since breakfast and Adelaide didn't offer her lunch. She's starving and dispirited, and willing to bet that the brasserie does a knockout *croque-monsieur*, one that doesn't skimp on the cheese. Work can wait.

Brasserie Les Amours is pretty busy when she arrives, but she's pleased to see a couple of outdoor tables are still free, and makes a beeline for one with a good view of the square.

Sinking into her seat, enjoying the sunshine on her face and arms, she is greeted moments later by a white-aproned waiter who sets down a basket of delicious-looking bread and a tall glass bottle of cold water with a murmured 'Madame'. She can already feel the incremental return of her equilibrium, the lessening of the morning's disappointments. Any new job has its challenges on a first day, she reminds herself. And she can surely cope with a barking dog and a rude boss if this is the flipside: late lunch in a gorgeous Parisian square, sparrows twittering about through the dappled light, the city at her fingertips. She exhales slowly and nibbles a piece of bread. Of course she can manage, she tells herself bracingly. Especially when the bread tastes this good.

'Madame? You are ready to order?' The waiter is back by her table, insanely handsome with his slicked-back dark hair, humorous brown eyes and white even teeth. He's half her age sadly, but it's still nice to admire another's beauty.

She orders a *croque-monsieur* in French, although, like the hotel manager the day before, the waiter replies in English. 'A salad with that, Madame? Some fries?' He notices her hesitation and winks. 'They are very good fries,' he murmurs, as if they are in league together. 'Famously good.'

It's silly but she's blushing like a twenty-year-old. 'Well, in that case,' she hears herself reply. 'I'm absolutely saying yes to famously good fries. *Les frites célèbres!*' she adds. '*Merci, monsieur.*'

She settles back in her seat, sunglasses on, and watches the world go by, like just another cool Frenchwoman with her life under control. Two young women – students? – sail past on bikes with folders and books stuffed into their baskets, legs lean and tanned beneath denim shorts. A white-haired man in a tired brown suit drinks coffee outside the nearby *crêperie*, raising a gnarled hand in greeting when he catches Jess's gaze. A wasp buzzes around, perhaps lured in by the soft drinks on the neighbouring table where a woman is trying to placate the baby on her shoulder while two small children bicker peevishly.

The wasp buzzes closer and she swats at it, only to swipe too vigorously and accidentally knock her glass of water to the ground, where it explodes in a smash of glittering shards. Oh God! So much for being a cool Frenchwoman, she groans, scrabbling around trying to pick up the larger pieces of broken glass, her sunglasses falling off her face and clattering to the cobbles in the process. As if that's not enough, she hears a male voice saying her name in the next moment – 'What do you mean, the wrong Jessica?' – and promptly bangs her head against the table leg, turning to see who it is.

She just catches a glimpse of a tall dark-haired man striding past, phone to his ear, before registering a strange wetness on her hand. Dizziness engulfs her as she sees two crimson splats on the cobbles below; she's never been good with blood.

Do not faint, she tells herself, cringing as she notices that the older man across the road is rising to his feet, apparently in concern for her. She's somehow managed to turn the calm moment into a drama, gifting herself a starring role that is about as unchic and unsophisticated as you can get. This is not the Jess-in-Paris scenario of her daydreams.

'Madame? You are okay?'

She's not sure what's more mortifying – that she's trashed the brasserie's glassware, forced an octogenarian from his seat in alarm, or that the sexy waiter is now crouching beside her, so close she can smell his peppery cologne.

'I am so sorry – *je suis désolée!*' she cries as he presses a clean napkin to her bleeding hand and helps her back into her chair.

'Not at all! It was an accident, I am sure.' He has brought a dustpan and brush and sweeps up the broken pieces, then glances her way with a humorously waggling eyebrow. 'I think? Or maybe you hate that glass and want to destroy it? Stupid, bad glass!'

Despite everything, she laughs. 'Stupid, bad person,' she corrects him, pointing at herself.

'Not at all, Madame. Not at *all.*' He gestures to where she has taken over pressing the napkin to her bloodied hand. 'One moment and I will be back to look at that.'

She sits there trying to gather herself, then thinks to glance across at the *crêperie*, where she sees the man in the brown suit still gazing in her direction. Even at this distance, the tilt of his head conveys worry. Seeing her look, he holds up a thumb with a questioning expression, and she smiles weakly, nodding. Honestly, she should just accept that she will never pass as a cool person, full stop. The only consolation is that she is far from home and won't ever have to see any of these people again.

The waiter reappears, complete with first aid kit, and sits at the table opposite her. 'May I?' he asks, pointing at her hand.

She nods, taking a deep breath as he peels away the bloody napkin and begins to gently clean it. 'You will not die,' he informs her solemnly and she gulps a laugh that's almost a sob. 'No hospital for you today, Madame.'

'Thank you,' she says, feeling like a child again as he tears open a plaster then sticks it carefully into place.

'*Voilà*. Okay? Ahh, and look, here is your food arriving.'

A second waiter has appeared, setting down a bronze, oozing *croque-monsieur*, along with a metal beaker of golden fries. The first waiter takes another glass from an empty table nearby and fills it with water. 'Everything will be okay now, I think, yes?' he says, one of his gorgeous eyebrows raised. She nods appreciatively, breathing in the smell of her lunch, and he gives a little bow, before leaving her to it.

The *croque* is fantastically cheesy, the chips perfectly cooked. For a few moments, she refuses to think about anything else while she tucks in. *Everything will be okay now, I think, yes?* she hears the waiter say in her head once more, his conviction touching. And for the moment at least, he's right. She's in Paris, after all. The sun is shining. The elderly man in the brown suit gets up from his table, waving at her before embarking on a slow trudge across the square. She waves back, already feeling better. She's the luckiest woman in the world, she tells herself.

Chapter Five

After her restorative cheese toastie and chips – somehow it sounds way more sophisticated when you call it *croque-monsieur et frites* – Jess spends the rest of the afternoon back at the hotel, transcribing her recorded conversation. Even now, with many interviews under her belt, the sound of her own voice makes her cringe, and especially so this time, hearing the nervous wobble in her first few questions. It's dissatisfying too, listening again to how Adelaide parries any difficult subjects with a practised air, closing the door time after time. Meanwhile, there's Jess politely accepting the conversational dead ends instead of challenging them. A better journalist would have pushed harder at the brick wall, she tells herself with a sigh. A better journalist wouldn't have let herself get so rattled by the glamour, the dog, Adelaide's perma-frown.

There's also the fact that they have completely different personalities. Unlike Jess, Adelaide seems . . . well, pretty dour, to be frank. Bitter. On hearing about her rambunctious, noisy East End childhood, Jess had thought wistfully of her own quieter upbringing and said, 'That must have been lovely and cosy, so many of you in the family,' only for Adelaide to stare at her as if she were mad. 'Cosy?' she repeated witheringly. 'There was no central heating back then, Jessica. We couldn't even afford firewood half the time.' Jess had gulped, feeling misunderstood. 'I just meant . . .' but Adelaide was shaking her head. 'It wasn't cosy,' she said flatly, as if that was the end of it.

Still, there's plenty of time for them to get to know each other better, she reminds herself. They have sessions together every weekday, and then, on Friday afternoon, Jess will go home, finish her sample chapter and deliver it by the close of this weekend. Hopefully she can write something that's good enough to clinch her the gig – and if that means avoiding romanticising Adelaide's life with words like 'cosy', then game on.

When she next looks up from her laptop and notepad, it's seven o'clock and her eyes are starting to ache. She needs some fresh air and sustenance, she thinks, stretching as she rises from her small desk. Having changed into a pretty top and cropped trousers, she heads down the many flights of stairs once more.

'*Bonsoir, monsieur,*' she calls to the man on reception in passing, only for him to reply with 'Good evening, Madame.' She'll keep working on him, she vows, smiling to herself.

Outside in the Marais, the tropical afternoon has become a balmy evening. The buildings are the colour of pale honey as the sun sinks lower in the sky, and the streets are bustling with couples, families, and groups of friends seeking out bars and restaurants, entertainment for the night ahead. Jess feels her worries lift as she wends her way towards the river and absorbs the light-hearted mood around her. She crosses Pont des Arts then strolls along the Left Bank beneath the trees, remembering an evening when she'd walked hand in hand down here with Georges. He had taken her first to an exhibition at the Palais des expositions des Beaux-Arts, followed by dinner at Les Deux Magots, a former hangout for luminaries such as Joyce, Sartre and Picasso. 'And now – us, too!' he'd said, raising his glass of red wine with a wink, apparently enjoying her starstruck expression.

Oh, Georges. Tall handsome Georges, with his sculpted jaw and sexy accent. Aged twenty-eight to her unworldly twenty-two, he had seemed like a real man compared to the immature student-types she'd dated before. Of all the iconic places to meet a gorgeous Frenchman, they'd first struck up conversation while browsing the shelves of Shakespeare and Company, the famous bookshop, not far from here. A good-tempered discussion about whether or not Hemingway was a dick (conclusion: yes) led to his suggestion of a drink, and then . . . Well, by then she was already hooked, and drowning in his expressive brown eyes.

Like an idiot, she glances around hopefully, on the off-chance that he might be walking towards her now, their destinies colliding once more. In all the years since, she has never dated anyone as cultured or as attractive or as plain old masculine as Georges. Is he still here in the city? she wonders, with a pang for her youth, and his too. He has probably married a stunning Frenchwoman who gives him blow jobs whenever he tilts an eyebrow at her. Jess can imagine their chic flat in an achingly cool district, with art on the walls and masses of bohemian friends who drop in for intellectual conversation. Well, good luck to him.

By now she's in the grand Faubourg Saint-Germain area of the city and she crosses the road to cut through the Esplanade des Invalides, the lush lawns full of tourists taking sunset Eiffel Tower photos. The hotel where she worked as a chambermaid was near here and her hand flies up to her throat suddenly, as if seeking out the cheap friendship necklace she'd worn for months on end then, the golden half of a heart nestled in the soft space between her collarbones. Pascale, her best friend at the time, had bought the necklaces – one each, the halves interlocking when put together. Jess must have her necklace somewhere at home, it's not something she would have thrown away. As for Pascale and her half . . .

She stops abruptly, then turns so that the hotel and its surrounding streets are behind her once more. The blood beats around her body as she walks quickly away. So many years have passed but she's never quite got over the shock of how her time in Paris ended, she thinks, tears suddenly blurring her eyes. A dark space opened up in her afterwards, a space filled with sadness and regret. Don't think about it, she orders herself, increasing her pace.

Once she's a safe distance away, she takes a seat at a riverside bar with pavement tables and a Stevie Nicks song playing, and orders a glass of red wine. Then, to distract herself from her memories of Pascale, she types Georges' name into her phone, and sifts through the results until she lands upon his social media profiles. As she begins piecing together his life in the intervening decades, she can't help but experience a delicious fluttery feeling. *Hello, you.*

He's still handsome, she decides, lingering over a picture of him with some mates in a bar. His hair is streaked with grey these days but his eyes smoulder from the screen, his mouth quirked in amusement as if he's smiling at her. Even when he's a digital image, it's impossible not to smile right back. Theirs had only ever been a summer's fling – it had never developed into a more rounded, serious relationship with arguments, compromises or irritations. Perhaps because of this, he's always been a fond memory to her; a high bar set at an impressionable age. When Jess first started seeing David a few years later, it was Georges' effortless style that came to mind upon encountering David's black bed linen and that awful bath towel with the word 'FACE' printed on one side, and 'ARSE' on the other. In hindsight, the clues that her ex-husband would always be a man-child were there from the start, she thinks now.

As for Georges, he was a post-grad when she knew him, working on his doctorate, but according to her internet sleuthing, he's since left academia and currently practises as an architect. In fact – her heart quickens as she reads on – in fact, the company seems to be based in Bastille, just down the road from her hotel. Could Fate be making this any easier for her? *Oh là là*, she imagines Pascale saying in her head, because her friend always had strong views about living life to the max. *Time has been good to this one. What are you waiting for?*

She gulps another mouthful of wine, feeling unexpectedly jangled. Curious, too. Would it be very forward of her to send him a message, say a friendly hello? It wouldn't do any harm, would it? It's not as if she's still married – and as for him … Well, she hasn't seen any pictures of a wife or girlfriend in his social media accounts, but even if he *is* happily settled, it's not as if she's trying to muscle in on him. Or at least, not immediately, she concedes, her mouth twitching as further reminiscences come to mind. Mainly, admittedly, about how he always made her feel so womanly. So desirable. They could hardly keep their hands off one another sometimes.

Hi Georges, she types. *This is a blast from the past but I'm over in Paris for work* – yes, that sounds impressive, like she's some kind of high-flier – *and wondered if by any chance you're free in the next few days to catch up? All the best, Jess.*

She reads through the scant message once more, then presses 'Send'. She'd regret it if she went home without at least *trying*, she reasons. Besides, there's something about being here that makes her feel different, as if she's having a holiday from ordinary life. What happens in Paris, stays in Paris, and all that.

'Hotel California' starts playing and goosebumps spring up on Jess's arms because this was a song Pascale loved, and it feels uncanny to hear it so soon after thinking about her. Jess can picture her now, dimpling with a smile at the sound of the opening chords, changing the lyrics to those about the hotel where they worked, bawling them at the top of her voice. *Welcome to the Hotel d'Or in Paris! Such a shitty place, look at my miserable face.*

Oh Pascale. Jess would give anything to see her old friend again, with those dimples and laughing eyes, even with that terrible singing voice of hers. What happened to you, Pascale?

Then her phone pings and her breath seizes. Is it Georges already? Are the girls okay? No, it's Becky, replying to Jess's rather miserable voice note of earlier. *I believe in you!* she has written. *You've got this, Jess! PS Dog treats in your handbag tomorrow = your secret weapon.*

It's exactly what she needs to snap out of her melancholic mood and she smiles. Becky's right – she's got this. Of course she has! Tomorrow is another day.

The following morning, Jess heads downstairs for breakfast, wondering where she might be able to buy dog treats around Le Marais. Behind the reception desk today, there's a chic Black woman around her own age, wearing a crisp white linen shift dress on which a name badge reads Beatrice.

'*Bonjour,*' Jess says politely. 'Can I ask you something?' she goes on in French. 'Do you know anywhere around here I can buy ...' She hesitates, stumped on how to say 'dog treats', then resorts to English. 'Uhh ... dog food? Treats?'

'*Dog* food?' Beatrice repeats, looking confused. 'You have a dog here?'

'No!' Jess says, imagining herself getting thrown out of the hotel on suspicion of smuggling in a canine companion. 'Um ... I'm here working for a woman – Adelaide Fox, have you heard of her?'

'The artist? But of course!' says Beatrice, then frowns. 'She asks you to buy dog food?'

'No – but she has a dog, who is very ...' Jess bares her teeth and growls, and Beatrice, startled, takes a step back as if concerned for Jess's mental well-being. Jess ploughs on. 'I want the dog to like me. I want to buy something tasty – *délicieux!* – for the dog so that he thinks, *mon Dieu!* This woman is the greatest.'

She says all of this in a garbled mix of English and French, unsure whether or not she is making any sense, but thankfully Beatrice smiles then puts a finger in the air.

'Aha! I have the answer. Follow me.' She walks through to the small breakfast room with Jess in tow. It's an informal space, with six or seven tables, and a help-yourself counter that has a coffee machine, jugs of juice and a selection of pastries and fruit. Beatrice heads to the counter, picks up a napkin and uses tongs to select two fat slices of ham from the plate of cold meats. '*Voilà*,' she says, putting the ham into the napkin and holding it out to Jess. 'The dog eats the ham and . . .' She kisses the fingers of her other hand theatrically. 'He loves you for ever. Simple!'

Jess bursts out laughing as she accepts the proffered napkin. 'Beatrice, you're a genius,' she says. 'And this is okay? You don't mind?'

Beatrice glances around conspiratorially and taps her nose. 'It is our secret,' she says. 'We will never tell, no?'

'We will never tell,' Jess assures her. 'Thank you so much. You might have just saved the day.'

By ten o'clock that morning, she is pressing Adelaide's doorbell with her game face on. Professional writer, reporting for duty! She's wearing her second-favourite dress (mustard yellow) and a power-red lipstick, and she has a napkin of juicy ham nestled at the top of her bag. The sun is shining, and she, Adelaide and Jean-Paul will all be firm friends in no time, she's certain of it.

'Good morning,' she greets Adelaide when shown in by the housekeeper. They're in the same room as yesterday but Jess is prepared for the grandeur this time, and doesn't allow herself to be intimidated. 'Gosh, it's a lovely day already out there,' she continues chattily, gesturing towards the window. 'Absolutely gorgeous!'

Adelaide gives her a suspicious look but doesn't immediately reply, probably because Jean-Paul has leapt up from where he was snoozing to rush over, barking ferociously.

Channelling her new friend Beatrice, Jess reaches into her bag. 'And *bonjour* to you too, Jean-Paul,' she says, trying to keep the shake from her voice. 'I have a gift for him,' she tells Adelaide, having to speak louder above the barking. 'Shameless bribery, I'm afraid.' She holds up the napkin. 'Some ham from the breakfast buffet. May I?'

She's half expecting Adelaide to disapprove – maybe even to snap that her precious dog is on a special diet and can't have anything so fatty – but to her great relief, the other woman's eyes are a little less steely all of a sudden. Is that even a twinkle?

'Oh my, Jean-Paul,' she says. 'You're about to be a very happy boy. Now SIT!'

Jean-Paul, it turns out, is an absolute pushover when it comes to shreds of *jambon*. He will sit, turn around, lie down, give a paw – pretty much anything Jess asks him to – for this highly desirable reward. His soulful brown eyes are fastened to her the entire time there is ham between her fingers, as if ready to leap up and perform at a second's notice. If only people were so easy to get on side.

'Are we friends now?' Jess says, scratching behind his ears when he's scoffed the lot. 'Are we going to be pals, mm?'

'For the love of God, don't tell any passing burglars how easy it is to win him over,' Adelaide says drily but she's not pulling disparaging faces about cat people like yesterday, at least.

They start work, with Adelaide now recounting her early teenage years, describing the secondary-school art teacher who taught her perspective and encouraged her creativity, before Adelaide moved on to her rebellious period: the rejection of her mother's Christianity and refusal to attend church services ('It was scandalous within the family at the time,' Adelaide reports with a certain relish), followed by the smoking and underage drinking, the subversive older friends she took up with.

'And your brothers?' Jess interrupts. She's heard these stories before, in other interviews, and is keen to excavate deeper for readers. 'What did they make of this? Were the four of you still close then, or were you breaking away from them too?'

'They . . .' Until this point, Adelaide has been in full flow but Jess's questions cause her to falter. 'Well . . . my older brothers did not approve, put it like that. They were sensible, cautious characters. Very different from me.'

'And William?' Jess presses, mentioning Adelaide's favourite sibling. 'Was he more sympathetic to the person you were becoming?'

The older woman's eyes flash. 'He was dead,' she snaps. 'I don't want to discuss him.'

'Oh!' Jess's head spins. William died? Despite her copious research of Adelaide's life and career, this is a gap in her knowledge, and she can tell from the other woman's face that she's struck a note that still jars, decades on. 'I'm sorry,' she says humbly, then hesitates. It's not enough for a reader – nor for her, the writer – simply to gloss over what must have been an important and traumatic moment in her subject's childhood. She remembers her feeble voice on yesterday's recording and how she wishes she'd been tougher, pushed harder.

'That must have been awful,' she adds, then girds her loins. *Be brave. Keep going.* 'Was it a catalyst for the change in your behaviour, would you say? What happened to the girl who loved art class, who never wanted to stop drawing?'

Adelaide's jaw visibly clenches. 'I *said* I didn't want to discuss it. Are you deaf or just stupid?'

Jess gulps, her face flaming with the other woman's rudeness, and it takes a few seconds before she can reply. 'I understand, and we don't have to talk about his actual death' – not today, anyway, although you bet she'll do her damnedest to winkle out the story – 'but I'm interested in you as a girl, a young woman. The impact his loss had on you. How this might have featured in your early work, even.' She's heard enough artist interviews to know that art can be a means of processing personal experiences and emotions, and there's often a particular trigger behind significant pieces. It's a perfectly reasonable question.

But Adelaide lowers her gaze, her gnarled fingers knotting

together in her lap, her lips seemingly sealed shut. Jess holds
her breath, wondering if she's gone too far, if she's upset her
by pressing on a bruise. Yet for the sake of the memoir, surely
she has to? Nobody wants to read a completely safe, sanitised
life story, do they?

'Well,' says Adelaide eventually, her voice gruff and low,
as if the words are an effort to force out. 'The impact was
devastating. We were all ... lost.'

Jess remains silent. This has often proved the most effective
tool in her journalistic box: leaving a vacuum in conversation that an interviewee can't help but fill. Sure enough,
after several weighty seconds, Adelaide continues, her head
bowed, apparently lost in memories. 'He was an anchor for
me,' she says. 'A steady, still point in my life, around which my
creativity – and my chaos – could flow. Everything changed
after his death.'

Had this been a conversation with a friend, Jess would have
been making sympathetic noises by now, an arm around the
shoulders, but she forces herself to keep quiet. She is not a
friend; if anything, she feels more like a hunter watching prey.
Any sudden moves, any inane remarks, and Adelaide will snap
out of the moment, become guarded once more.

'And yes, you're right, I think there was a correlation. Losing
him left me ... untethered. My mother became obsessed with
housework and the church. My brothers were busy with their
own lives. Suddenly I had space and freedom that had not
been there before. And I was consumed by this terrible rage
and g—'

She breaks off, the word unfinished, because something

awful has happened: Jess's phone has just sounded a cheery little notification, breaking the spell. Jess's face blooms with mortification – in the thrill of Jean-Paul not savaging her earlier, she completely forgot to switch on her Do Not Disturb. And now the sombre confessional atmosphere has shattered, and it's all her stupid fault. She could kick herself!

'For heaven's sake!' Adelaide snaps, her face like thunder.

'Sorry,' Jess says, muting her phone shamefacedly. Damn! Just as they were getting somewhere, too. Just as she was easing her way beneath the older woman's carapace. But then Jess sees what's on the screen, and finds it impossible not to react. Georges has replied!

'What is it?' Adelaide asks. So much for Jess's game face. She's always been atrocious at hiding her feelings.

'It's— Nothing. I'm sorry to have interrupted you,' she says, swiping the screen to dismiss the notification. But the blood pounds in her ears nonetheless and warmth spreads through her, a gathering excitement in her body. What has he *said*? No, stop. She needs to concentrate. 'Where were we?'

Adelaide purses her lips. 'Perhaps you could make sure we're not interrupted again. It's very distracting to have silly noises when I'm trying to think.'

'Of course,' Jess replies contritely. She pushes Georges from her thoughts. 'You were telling me about feeling angry and—' She pauses because Adelaide had broken off without finishing her sentence; she'll have to listen back to that moment, to see if she can guess what the woman was about to say. 'About the turbulent time you were going through,' she says instead. 'Can we pick up there?'

'I think I've said everything I need to about that,' Adelaide replies, resisting being drawn. 'Perhaps we should move on now, to when I left home?'

Jess sighs. Obviously she would much rather find out what happened to William, and spend longer circling around Adelaide's corresponding emotions, but she feels powerless to protest. Her priority in these early days has to be to keep Adelaide sweet, show that she can be trusted.

'Sure,' she says. 'Take me back to how that happened. How were you feeling at the time? Talk me through the run-up to you leaving.'

And so Adelaide launches into a story that Jess already knows, detailing the packing of the small yellow suitcase, the filching of twenty pounds from her dad's wallet while he's drunk, and then the semi-derelict, mouse-infested squat in Poland Street, Soho, that becomes home to herself and various other future luminaries of the new art and culture movement.

'So after you move into Poland Street,' says Jess, leaving her earlier frustration to one side. This, she knows, is where Adelaide's narrative starts to take a turn. 'What happens next?'

Chapter Six

The squat on Poland Street was a dive, no question. The kitchen was permanently damp, however many smoky fires they lit in its grate. The window in the back bedroom was broken, allowing freezing winter air to poke through like a knife; ice crystals formed glittering patterns either side of the glass on cold mornings. Mould colonised the walls with alien blue blotches, clothes became mildewed if you left them in one place for too long, and the bathroom always smelled so bad they all became experts in speedy strip washes. But to Adelaide, it marked a clear delineation from her old life and this new exciting one, where there were no rules, where you could do what you liked.

The housemates were a varied bunch – there was Esme, Adelaide's friend from school, plus Esme's brother Bob and a few of his mates, all united in their desire to escape from their parents and make a go of life themselves. Like Adelaide, Esme was good at art, whereas one of the boys, Tony, wanted to act and his girlfriend Jeanette loved fashion and made clothes for everyone. They had friends who formed guitar bands and sang, others who played piano in pubs.

Heady times. Happy times. Soho was buzzing, the pill was newly available, and the world seemed to be opening up before Adelaide's eyes. She and Esme managed to blag occasional work helping to paint theatre backdrops, and Adelaide also took shifts as a machinist in the rag trade, like her mother before her, although her mind teemed with bigger ideas. She would amuse her colleagues in tea breaks by making lightning sketches of their supervisors, and soon was being commissioned by her co-workers to draw caricatures of themselves and loved ones. But still she wanted more.

Spotting a new opportunity, she began squirrelling away fabric ends from the factory in order to make her own items at home. Aprons were easy to run up on her machine and were popular everyday items – this was a time when self-regarding housewives donned an apron each morning like a uniform. Soon she had enough stock to chance her arm with a stall at the Saturday market, where her aprons sold at gratifying speed. But, conflicted about creating more domestic wear and further enslaving her own kind, it wasn't long before she began making secret additions. *NO THANKS*, she stitched in pale thread along the inside hem of one apron. *NOT FOR ME*. She liked the idea of women wearing her aprons with their subversive messages and unwittingly becoming part of a secret resistance group. *YOU CAN DO BETTER THAN THIS*, she encouraged them in embroidery thread.

Soon her imagination was pushing her further, the rebel voice inside her growing louder. She used brighter threads, put her slogans in more prominent places. *I'D RATHER BE READING* claimed one. *DO IT YOURSELF*. Young

56

women giggled together when they saw her designs in the stall, although there would also be pursed lips and tuts from the older matriarchs who noticed them. Adelaide didn't let that stop her. She embroidered pretty flowers along the bottom of some aprons, stitching the word *FIGHT* inside the top hem so it would only be visible to the wearer.

It was such a great time, all in all. She was painting, making, falling in and out of love . . . truly *living* for what seemed like the first time ever. Best of all, it felt as if she was sidestepping the guilt and confusion that had strangled her since William's death – at last she could breathe again. Not that she articulates this last aspect to her eager writer, obviously.

Jessica appears to be enjoying the tale nonetheless. 'And it was in that particular market – Berwick Street, right? – that life took an unexpected turn, I believe,' she says, smiling in the way of someone who already knows the happy ending to a story.

Oh yes. And what a transformative turn it proved! Egged on by Esme, Adelaide had run up some new aprons that merely said *FUCK THIS* on the front pocket in large crimson letters.

'For context, this was the early 1960s, when swearing was seen as outrageous and offensive,' she says, able to visualise even now the shocked expressions of the marketgoers when she hung up the aprons in full view. One elderly woman actually put a gloved hand in front of her eyes as if the sight might permanently blind her.

And then in stepped Ursula, an unlikely fairy godmother at first glance – tall and beak-nosed, hands behind her back as she approached the stall like a visiting vicar. 'My mother bought one of your aprons last week,' she began sternly, without preamble. 'She was very upset to discover the words "YOU DON'T HAVE TO SERVE ANYONE" stitched on the rear side.'

Adelaide was sticking out her chin, about to say that she couldn't give a fig how this woman's mother felt, when Ursula went on. 'But I love it. And I love *that*,' she said, gesturing at the *FUCK THIS* apron. 'I absolutely fucking love it, in fact.'

That was Ursula for you. A kindred spirit. 'And I was wondering,' she continued, smirking a little at Adelaide's expression of stunned delight, 'are you ... trained? Is there other work you could show me, a portfolio?'

'A *portfolio*?' Adelaide repeated because she wasn't entirely sure what the word even meant. Was this some sort of wind-up?

'Are you an art student?' Ursula clarified. 'Can you paint and draw?'

'Unfortunately, I didn't have time to answer her questions,' Adelaide tells Jess now, 'because at that moment, a policeman arrived and told me I had to pack up and leave the market, saying I was contravening public decency laws. Thankfully, that didn't put Ursula off her stride. She bunged the copper a few quid, helped me pack up my stock and then whisked me off to the nearest pub. And then—'

Annoyingly, there's someone ringing the doorbell, just as she's approaching the punchline of the story. The punchline that everyone knows, the catapulting of Adelaide from apron-stitching nobody to art school superstar. There goes the heavy thump of Marie-Thérèse's feet as she trudges to answer it. Meanwhile, Jessica's eyes are shining.

'I've always thought Ursula sounded a total legend,' she gushes. 'What a woman. Is it true that the pair of you sat there in the pub wearing the "FUCK THIS" aprons after a few gins?'

Despite herself, Adelaide chuckles, because the image still tickles her. 'Absolutely. I was all for wearing mine like a cape about my shoulders' – she mimes putting it on and Jessica hoots with laughter – 'but Ursula was worried I would be arrested, and so—' There's a knock and then the door opens, and it's Lucas.

Jean-Paul goes berserk with joy, rushing around to find his most disgusting old tennis ball as a gift for this arriving prince. It was Lucas who first suggested Adelaide think about getting a dog when she was going through an especially dark time, and although Jean-Paul can't possibly know this, he always acts as if he's ecstatically grateful towards Lucas for coming up with such an excellent idea. Meanwhile, Jessica, who's been lolling in the chair, immersed in the narrative, sits up and switches off the recording.

Adelaide catches Lucas's eye and he gives her a tiny shake of his head. Bugger. Does that mean what she thinks it means?

Then she remembers herself. 'Jessica – this is Lucas, my nephew. Lucas, Jessica ... er, sorry, remind me of your sur-name again?'

'It's Bright,' she says. 'Jess Bright. Nice to meet you, Lucas, I've been having a wonderful time listening to your aunt's stories.'

Adelaide can tell Lucas feels bad about the whole business because his smile is brief and apologetic as he mumbles hello.

Then he gestures towards the door. 'Should we ... ? Excuse us, Jess, but I need to speak to Adelaide for a moment.'

'Of course,' says Jessica politely. She probably wants to get back to her phone, Adelaide thinks, so that she can check the message that got her all hot and bothered earlier. It must be a man, surely.

Adelaide drains her coffee, then she and Lucas retreat to the dining room. 'Well?' she asks, sitting down at the table.

'She's not interested,' he says flatly.

'Not *interested*?' Adelaide can hardly speak for indignation. 'What do you mean? Why not?' After ringing Lucas in a fury yesterday to tell him about the farcical situation, he had promised to track down Jessica Martindale and fly her over. His exact words were 'I'll sort this, don't worry. We'll be laughing about it in a few days.'

Well, she's not laughing now. How dare Jessica Martindale spurn her memoir when they're offering such a good fee – and such a plum job, moreover? The chance to work with Adelaide Fox herself! How has Lucas managed to mess this up so badly?

Lucas sighs and sinks into a chair opposite her. When she first moved into this apartment, shortly after Remy died, when everything seemed bleak, she held out hope that one day life would become fun again, envisaging this as the room where they'd entertain the great and good of Paris together. She had the walls painted aubergine and has them hung with her own work; she picked out the long cherrywood dining table and elegant matching chairs, faithfully dusted by Marie-Thérèse each week. In a cupboard somewhere are starched white tablecloths and boxed champagne glasses, a set of fine china serving dishes with gilded edges. Never used, any of them. She dines here alone every night, and feels the space mock her with its emptiness.

'She's good friends with Elin Burling,' Lucas replies, referring to the last journalist they'd asked to try out for the job. 'Reading between the lines, Burling must have said something ... um ... less than flattering about her time here.'

Adelaide pulls a face as she remembers the humourless, shrill-voiced woman who had complained the whole time. It's not a stretch to imagine her still carping about the experience. 'So who's next on our list?' she asks crossly.

Lucas's expression is strained. 'I think we might need to draw up a new list,' he says. 'Unless this other Jessica is working out, of course.'

'Well—' In truth, Adelaide has already written her off. She looked up some of her work last night only to find an agony aunt column and a series of very pedestrian pieces about motherhood. (Of course she is an agony aunt, Adelaide thinks to herself now, rolling her eyes. Of *course*.) 'I mean, she's hardly Joan Didion,' she sniffs after a moment.

'Was *she* on our list?' Lucas asks and Adelaide's about to take him to task on his ignorance until she registers his deadpan tone. 'Seriously though, Jess Bright did write a great piece on you last time,' he goes on. 'That's why I assumed she was the person you intended.'

'Yes, but ... Look, she's perfectly *nice*' – this is not necessarily a compliment – 'but is there anything else *to* her?' Adelaide doesn't want her memoir to be 'nice'. She intends it to be a dagger to the heart of everyone who has wronged her. 'I just don't think she's my kind of person,' she adds.

'But ...' He breaks off, presses his lips together for a moment. 'But who *is* your kind of person? Because, no offence, we seem to be struggling to find them.'

Her kind of person? It's a fair question. In truth, there have only ever been a few in her lifetime, and they're all lost to her now. She traces the grain in the table with her finger, suddenly disconsolate. Will this surface ever be covered by a gleaming white tablecloth and fancy serving plates? she wonders. Will the room ever be full of people, her people? The chances, she realises, are slim.

'You're only saying that because you want this job over and done with, you want to go back to London,' she replies, stung.

'All we need is one good writer who can represent you and your story faithfully,' he says, ignoring her barb. He's fed up with her, she can tell. He's regretting offering to help out in the first place. 'We might as well let Jess write the chapter, see what we think, take it from there. Yes?'

Adelaide is about to argue but then her hands start trembling and she has to hide them under the table before he notices.

'Are you okay?' he asks when she doesn't reply.

This feeble body of hers, and the tricks it plays on her! She saw her mum deteriorate dreadfully with Parkinson's, and is convinced the same affliction is now coming for her too. Getting old is to live in a permanent state of dread, wondering which part will give up on you next.

'Yes, I'm fine,' she snaps, clutching her hands together in

the hope of stilling them. 'Very well,' she goes on, defeated. 'Let's see the week out.' Jessica did at least bring some ham for Jean-Paul that morning, she remembers, which is a tick in her favour. But what's the point of any of this, if the woman doesn't have it in her to twist the knife on Adelaide's behalf?

Chapter Seven

Jess frowns to herself as soon as the door closes on them. She was expecting Adelaide's nephew to be much older after his businesslike emails – a suited stiff, all fusty and proper. But she's been surprised twice over on meeting him – first that he looks about her age, and actually pretty approachable in his indigo shirt, jeans and Vans. Second, that she has the strangest feeling their paths have crossed before. But how can that be?

While she waits for Adelaide to reappear, she busies herself by rereading Georges' message (he wants to meet!), before a string of unhappy texts comes in from Edie. *Mum, can I call you?* is the final one. Jess immediately dials her number – it must be break time at school – to find her middle daughter tearful and needing sympathy in the wake of some ongoing toxic-friend drama. Jess listens, making all the right noises on cue and loyally saying 'What an absolute cow' at intervals, knowing this is the one-sided partisan content her daughter needs from her. 'What a total bitch.'

But then she hears a sound behind her and turns to see Lucas standing there, staring in what looks like shocked disapproval. Oh no. He doesn't think she was referring to *Adelaide*, does he?

'I've got to go,' she mumbles to Edie, cheeks burning. 'That was my daughter, she's fallen out with a friend,' she blusters to Lucas. 'That's who I was talking about. Not—'

Lucas doesn't seem to be listening. He has the air of a man at the end of his tether. 'Adelaide is tired, she's had enough for today,' is all he says, before calling the dog. 'Shall we go for a walk, Jean-Paul?'

'Did you hear me?' Jess asks, scrabbling her belongings back into her bag and hurrying out of the apartment after him. 'Lucas!' she calls. 'I wasn't talking about Adelaide when I said that, okay?'

They're in the stairwell, cool and dim, and he pushes a hand through his dark hair and shrugs. He'd probably be good-looking if he smiled a bit more, she thinks. 'Sure,' he says, heading off down the stone steps with the dog.

Does he even believe her? She does not want him getting the wrong idea. 'My daughter's having a hard time, all right?' she persists, clattering after him. Really, she would like to speak to the pastoral head at school and have a professional wade in, but Edie is immovable on this. *Snitches get stitches, Mum,* she says, like a world-weary prisoner whenever Jess suggests telling a teacher. 'I was trying to show some solidarity, that's all,' she goes on. 'Trying to make her feel better!'

She's so agitated, her voice rises as they reach the ground floor. Jean-Paul gazes up at her in alarm and Lucas too seems taken aback. 'Sorry to hear that,' he says, stopping by the huge front door. They're in the vestibule, which has a wooden pigeonhole arrangement for post, and somebody's bike propped against the wall. 'Is she okay?'

'She's . . . I don't know,' Jess admits, sagging a little as she pictures her daughter's pale, unhappy face. 'She's only fifteen. It's a tough age. I'm usually at home all the time so she might be finding this as weird as I am.'

'Do you want to go back?' he asks, his brown eyes searching her face. He has very good eyebrows, she notices, wondering if he gets them waxed. Then the impact of his question hits her.

'No! Not at all!' she cries hurriedly, only to remember the hush-hush chat Adelaide and Lucas just had. What was that about, anyway? 'Does *Adelaide* want me to go back?' she blurts out, suddenly paranoid.

His poker face isn't much better than hers. 'No! Absolutely not,' he replies unconvincingly. 'She'll see you at the usual time tomorrow.' He opens the front door and the light from outside pours in. 'Good to meet you,' he says, stepping out with the dog in tow.

It's then, seeing him stride away, that she realises where she has seen him before: back when she was crouching on the ground at the brasserie yesterday, having smashed her glass. He'd said her name on the phone too, that was why she noticed him in the first place. But what was it he said?

Annoyingly, his exact words escape her, despite her searching her memory for them. What a frustrating end to the morning it's been, she thinks, not least having been dismissed from work, just as Adelaide was reaching a critical turning point in her narrative, when Ursula Fontaine, influential lecturer at

Goldsmiths College, was about to take her on as a protégée. This is not turning out to be the most straightforward job, she thinks, weaving her way through the busy streets of the Marais.

'Madame! Your usual table?' she hears a few minutes later, having reached the square nearest her hotel. The lovely brasserie waiter from yesterday is waving and calling out to her, and she's so charmed to be recognised, so delighted at the thought of having a 'usual table' here in Paris, that she can't help but beam in reply and head over. And talk about déjà vu – because there's the elderly man again too, seated outside the *crêperie*. He mimes doffing a cap to her and she smiles back. Less than forty-eight hours here and she practically feels like a local. This is more like it.

'*Bonjour*! I promise I won't break anything today,' she assures the waiter as he makes a fuss, drawing out the chair for her and straightening the salt and pepper pots with enjoyable flamboyance.

He cocks his head, feigning confusion. 'No,' he says after a moment. 'I don't know what you mean, Madame. I don't remember any breaking or smashing.' His mouth quirks briefly, you can tell he's loving his little game. 'But your hand, Madame – it is still there, I see. I am pleased. Shall I bring you wine to celebrate?'

She laughs at his outrageous upselling. She should say no, really, especially when she has so much work to do this afternoon, but she's still ruffled after that exchange with Lucas and unable to resist the thought of a glass of delicious, chilled Sauvignon Blanc. Oh sod it, she thinks, ordering herself one in the next breath.

'I'm Jess, by the way,' she says, as the waiter is about to depart. 'And you are ...?'

'I am Valentin,' he tells her, then gravely offers her a hand. 'I am honoured to meet you, Jess.'

'You too, Valentin,' she says, twinkling at him as they shake.

'Now I will bring you wine and then you will tell me what you would like to eat. One moment, please,' he says, before making a small bow and vanishing again.

The white apron tied around his middle makes Jess think about Adelaide's groundbreaking first collection, entitled simply Work, that launched her into the mid-1960s art world with such a bang. By then, she was painting more than creating textile art, but the original marketplace aprons featured within the seminal collection, which became a standard-bearer for what was to follow, her interest in subverting the domestic through art. Jess is already looking forward to tomorrow's session, for the next instalment.

Valentin returns, setting down her wine, the glass misted with cold, and Jess orders a mushroom omelette and salad. Then she indulges herself by reading the message from Georges for a third time, experiencing a delicious throb of anticipation. *Jess! Good to hear from you!* he's written, before suggesting dinner at some bar or other on Thursday evening. She looks up the venue only to see 'a romantic riverside bistro' in the first line of the description. Tingles ripple through her at once. Does this mean ...? What does this mean? It's probably simply a nice bar, styling itself as romantic for tourists, she reminds herself, but all the same, she's excited. This will definitely warrant some FaceTiming with Becky to discuss possible outfits – and possible outcomes too.

She can't actually remember when she last had a night like this on her horizon: a date with a sexy man, and maybe the whiff of romance in the air ... Before she was married, certainly.

She has a slight wobble, thinking of David moving out to that bland new-build house he's renting, wondering how the girls are getting on there this week. The one and only time she has been inside, he had made her a coffee in the soulless kitchen, and it cracked her heart a little when he opened the cupboard to reveal four solitary mugs there in the darkness. One box of teabags. One jar of instant coffee. You'd look at that cupboard and know at once you were in the house of a newly separated man. Or possibly a serial killer.

In the next moment, though, an image comes to mind of the first time she saw Bella's picture on David's phone: the long red hair, porcelain skin, her laughing, lipsticked mouth. It felt at the time as if the other woman was laughing about dumb trusting Jess. Boring, middle-aged, getting-fat-around-the-waist Jess. She evicts Bella from her thoughts with a gulp of cold wine. Be gone, demon. David can fuck off as well. Bring on the epic summer romance 2.0, she thinks.

While waiting for her lunch to arrive, she flicks through her notebook, reading back through the scribbles she's made over the last two days. The conversations with Adelaide have all been recorded and downloaded for safekeeping, but often she jots down reminders, questions she can't always ask at the time. WHAT HAPPENED TO WILLIAM??? is the first one that leaps out at her and she bites her lip. There must be a way she can find out more about him, she figures – the register of deaths, perhaps local news items.

Other question marks litter her notes where she needs to check – somehow – the veracity of what Adelaide has told her. Did her dad *really* cook and serve up the children's pet rabbit for Sunday dinner as a punishment when they'd been playing up? Was Adelaide's head teacher genuinely put in prison for having sex with minors? Or are these sly traps set for Jess to fall into, a means to prove that she hasn't done her investigatory homework properly?

Who knows, but the few glimpses of Adelaide's life Jess has had so far have only whetted her appetite for more. Maybe Adelaide, like Jean-Paul, simply needs coaxing out a little. Probably not with slices of ham from a handbag, but there must be a way Jess can get through to her, right?

Chapter Eight

'The art world,' intones Fiona Bruce dramatically. 'A place of outrageous fortune. But beneath the surface lurks danger ...'

Lying back on her overstuffed teal chaise longue, Adelaide lets out a contented sigh as the opening titles to *Fake or Fortune* play on her TV screen. She's watching an early episode of this art history detective show, set in Paris, where Fiona and her sidekick Philip try to establish the provenance of a pretty Degas painting. Is it a fake, or the real thing? The one upside to her ageing memory is that she often forgets the ending to these programmes; it's always a thrill to find out the result, however many times she watches. 'This case will be one of the most challenging we've ever faced,' Fiona declares from the screen, and Adelaide folds her hands across her chest in happy anticipation. She doesn't doubt it for a moment.

The show begins with a few teasers for what's to come, and Adelaide allows her mind to drift. Talking to Jessica this morning was surprisingly enjoyable, all things considered. Compared to the other writers who have tried out for the job, Jessica is less pushy; she doesn't interrupt every two minutes or attempt to make everything about her – even if she does keep asking 'And how did that make you *feel?*' like some kind of pound-shop psychiatrist.

It reminds Adelaide of being in that awful hospital in Berlin, the incessant, over-the-notebook questions about her feelings, her bloody feelings. In truth, they'd dosed her up with so many sedatives, she'd barely been able to feel a thing. All those quiet afternoons where she had watched the slanted rays of the sun slide across the room, her mind chemically blank. The intermittent screams and yells of patients from along the corridor like ghosts she never saw. 'An episode,' was what the press coyly termed Adelaide's very public disintegration in the Berlinische Galerie, although Monica, her then manager, was blunter. 'Your little breakdown,' she called it, but there was nothing little about it, in Adelaide's opinion – certainly not the gallery bill that came through for the cleaning costs after she'd defaced Remy's painting there. Her former manager is dead now, of course, like most of the key characters in her life, who once loomed so large: Esme, Ursula, Colin ... No, she corrects herself as his face floats into her mind. Not Colin. He was nobody; nothing.

She focuses back on the TV screen, and becomes engrossed in the quest to verify the painting's provenance. Degas was born and lived in Paris, and Adelaide brightens when Fiona and her co-presenter wander through the Musée d'Orsay together. Goodness, and look at his self-portrait, aged twenty-one – he was already so talented, she marvels, peering forward to see his youthful, pout-lipped face, the hint of uncertainty – apprehension? – in his gaze.

She finds herself thinking again of her own youth, and that life-changing meeting with Ursula. Did Degas have an Ursula, some eagle-eyed stranger who saw his potential and swooped? It had been Ursula who suggested that Adelaide register for the new term at Goldsmiths, who said she didn't care that Adelaide had no qualifications to show for herself, she hadn't been so excited at the promise of an emerging artist in years. It takes Adelaide's breath away even now to wonder how her life might have played out, had Ursula's mother not bought an apron from Adelaide that fateful day, had Ursula not taken a closer look and been intrigued. 'I'm sticking my neck out here, because it's obvious you've never had any proper instruction, but there's something raw and intuitive about your work that I really like,' she'd said, sitting there in that grotty old pub, flicking through the little sketchpad that Adelaide always carried, filled with drawings of factory workers and the occasional street scene. She'd jotted down a number on a beer mat and pressed it into Adelaide's hand. 'Ring this number on Monday – ask for Carole on the admissions desk, tell her I want you on my course.'

'But . . .' Adelaide hesitated, feeling flattered but dismayed, because Ursula seemed to be making all sorts of assumptions. Could she even trust this woman and her grand declarations? 'What about my job?' she asked eventually, suspicion getting the better of her. 'I don't have much money. I can't afford equipment or anything. Why do you think I'm selling aprons in the market?'

'We can make it work. There are grants available, and – look, we'll make it work, I promise.' Ursula tapped the beer mat, still sitting there on Adelaide's palm. 'Ring Carole. And I'll see you next week, I hope. Please try not to get yourself arrested in the meantime.' She tossed the rest of her drink down her throat, rising to her feet. 'Good to meet you, Adelaide. I'm excited about getting to know you and your work.'

As it turned out, Carole ended up playing more important a part than either of them could have predicted. When Adelaide rang her the following Monday, encouraged by her curious housemates ('What have you got to lose?'), a terrible phone line proved to be the making of Adelaide's new identity. 'Adelaide what, dear? Adelaide Box?' 'No, *Brockes*. Adelaide *Brockes*.' 'Sorry, you keep cutting out – Adelaide Fox, was that?' In the end, Adelaide, who still had her doubts over Ursula's artistic expectations, lied and said yes, her name was Adelaide Fox. Moments later, her money ran out, the line went dead and she replaced the handset, feeling stunned that this might actually be happening.

Because, wonder of all wonders, Ursula seemed to be legit – Carole was expecting her call and had already been tasked with arranging a set of grant forms for her to complete. Wheels were turning with exhilarating speed. What was more, Adelaide liked the name Adelaide Fox – it sounded more elegant, more urbane than plain old Brockes. She emerged from the phone box letting the new name – and her new prospects – settle upon her like Cinderella's ball gown. Watch out, London, she thought. Adelaide Fox has arrived and she's going places.

Despite everything, she's rather looking forward to telling Jessica the next part of her story tomorrow.

★

The following morning when Jessica arrives, Jean-Paul, the little pushover, greets her like his long-lost best buddy, yelping with excitement and even rolling over to have his tummy rubbed.

'Honestly, Jean-Paul, where is your dignity?' Adelaide tuts, but she can't help smiling indulgently as Jessica produces another thick slice of ham and proceeds to have the idiot dog put through all kinds of tricks for the privilege of it.

Picking up from yesterday, Adelaide recounts the weeks preceding her enrolment at art school. Carole's incredible ability to wring out every last penny available from the council, by means of grants and special dispensation, was a revelation to Adelaide's friends, who had no idea such funds were available, and galvanised them into finding similar college courses and their own grant applications. Esme pulled together a portfolio of work and wangled a place at Camberwell. Jeanette made a beeline for the London College of Fashion with an armful of designs. They ripped down the greying curtains in their empty attic room and turned it into their very own studio, daring to take themselves seriously.

'And what about you, starting at Goldsmiths?' Jessica asks. 'Please give me as much detail as you can remember of your early weeks and months there, I think this will be a really fascinating section for readers.'

It's odd to think of her life being parcelled up into chunks for readers to find fascinating or not, but Adelaide continues, recounting tales about her first forays into painting, the textile art module she adored, the women she befriended. Goldsmiths life was rich and hedonistic, with favourite new pubs to discover and parties full of fascinating people. But above all else was the work itself. How willingly she had thrown herself into learning – determined to improve, to impress, to absorb everything she could.

'It sounds as if you were really happy during this time,' Jessica comments.

'Happy?' Adelaide snorts. 'Well, I was raped by a fellow student in my second year and broke my ankle falling from a window on a bad acid trip, but apart from that . . .'

She blurts these things out without meaning to, purely to contradict Jessica, to put her in her place. More fool her, though, because Jessica immediately leans closer, eyes a mixture of concern but also interest. No doubt she thinks this will be *really* fascinating for the readers ghoulishly picking over her worst, most terrifying moments. But while Simon Dunster will definitely feature in her memoir – may he rot in hell – Adelaide isn't yet willing to hand the story over to sweet-faced Jessica. Let's face it, she'd probably only try to tack a happy ending on to it, and there definitely wasn't one of those.

'Gosh, Adelaide, I'm so sorry,' the younger woman says, before employing that annoying hack trick of falling maddeningly silent in the hope of luring further confidences.

She can forget it. 'In the summer after my first year, I saved up and went to Italy with my friends Esme and Margie,' Adelaide continues instead, enjoying the flash of frustration that flickers across Jessica's face. 'We went to Florence, Siena and Rome, to see for ourselves the frescoes and architecture our teachers had talked so much about. I returned to the Uffizi Gallery three days on the trot because I couldn't get enough.'

'It must have been incredibly inspiring,' Jessica prompts. 'And fun too, I bet. Who doesn't love a girls' trip?'

Adelaide snorts at such a cheesy comment. Would Jessica Martindale or any other heavyweight journalist refer to that pivotal summer as 'a girls' trip'? Never in a million years. Adelaide can't imagine it even *occurring* to serious, gravel-voiced Martindale to put the words together as a concept, let alone say them aloud. She'd be grilling Adelaide about the art, wanting to hear about the trip purely on an intellectual level, how it developed the three friends as artists and creators.

And yet, she realises in the next moment, what's strange is that this Jessica actually has a point. 'Nobody has ever put it *quite* like that to me before,' she says slowly, 'but you're right. We had so much fun. It was the first time any of us had been abroad. We felt free, unbridled. The world seemed to stretch out before us, and for once, nobody was standing in our way.'

She's lost in nostalgia now, revisiting moments she hasn't thought about for years. The three of them setting themselves up with sketchpads and charcoal in the most touristy spots to earn a few lire drawing portraits for holidaymakers. Busking, too, in the hope of boosting their meagre funds, singing Beatles' songs in the Piazza della Signoria, admittedly with more enthusiasm than talent but having an absolute hoot in the process. Clambering on the backs of mopeds with handsome Italian boys, squealing as they zipped around city corners at thrilling speeds.

'It was wonderful,' she says eventually with a little laugh. *Wish you were here*, they'd written on postcards to Jeanette, Rita and other friends, but in truth, they had not wished for anything when their days were so rich. 'And yes,' she adds as a sop to her upbeat interviewer, 'we were all very happy.'

'There you were in beautiful Italian cities – young, gorgeous, talented, carefree . . .' Jess prompts, clearly wanting more.

But Adelaide can't say anything immediately because something peculiar is happening inside her. Emotions have surged within like a river bursting its banks. She is thinking about Esme and Margie, the best of women, the finest of friends, and can't help a longing to revisit that time, for a day – even an hour – so that she could see their bright, smiling faces once more in a sunny Italian piazza; so that they could drink cheap red wine and dream big dreams together, catch the eye of sexy passing men and giggle behind their hands. Back then, their friendship had been everything.

'Oh Adelaide,' she hears Jessica say, and it's only then that she realises tears are skidding down her face. Idiot woman! Ridiculous old fool! 'Let me find you a tissue,' Jessica murmurs, rifling through her massive handbag – which immediately gets Jean-Paul excited, thinking he's in for more ham. So much for canine loyalty, Adelaide thinks, amidst her tumultuous emotions. Completely ignore your weeping mistress, why don't you?

'Would you like to take a break?' Jessica asks, still delving in her bag. 'Can I get you some water?'

To Adelaide's great embarrassment, a sob emerges from her throat. Whatever has come over her? At least by now Jean-Paul has tuned into her distress and presses his head against her leg in solidarity, gazing up at her with his liquid brown eyes.

'Here – take these,' Jessica says, putting a battered packet of tissues on the table in front of her. 'I'll get you a glass of water, okay? Do you want anything else?'

Adelaide shakes her head, not trusting herself to speak. Small mercies though – there wasn't an attempt to hug her, or anything awful like that, she reflects as Jessica departs, closing the door quietly behind her. Thank goodness, also, that the other woman has the sensitivity to leave her alone to compose herself in private rather than hanging around in an awkward fluster. Adelaide hears Margie's amused voice in her head – *Bloody hell, Ads, what are you like? I feel like I'm back at the Trevi Fountain, with you waterworking everywhere, girl!* – along with one of her customary cigarette-husky chuckles, but this imaginary commentary only makes her feel worse.

Oh shut up, Margie, she thinks wearily, wiping her eyes. She fondles Jean-Paul's soft ears, exhaling slowly. Silly woman. Not like her to lose her composure. She's known all along that she'd have to talk about Margie but she wasn't expecting to be ambushed by old feelings quite so soon – and so strongly. Jessica innocently asking about the fun they had . . . it caught her off guard, that's all. Usually she forbids herself to think about that side of things; it's easier to be angry.

The press has always shown interest in the collective of artists Adelaide belonged to – their mutual exhibitions, the houseshares and messy interweaving of relationships. Jeanette and Esme made the front pages of the tabloids in the seventies when they swapped husbands as part of a performance piece about modern marriage, and this still gets referenced, breathlessly, pruriently, whenever the group are written about. Rumours swirled back then about betrayal, back-stabbing and bitching between members, all playing to a tired old trope of women at each other's throats in the jostle for glory. Nobody has ever asked about the fun they had, the camaraderie, until now. Jessica's directness, while naïve, is rather refreshing. People can be too reverent around artists – fawning over her, fake and simpering. They forget that she was once young and carefree too.

There's a soft knock at the door, then Jessica returns holding a glass of iced water. 'Are you all right?'

'Yes, perfectly,' Adelaide replies firmly. 'Thank you.' But she no longer trusts her own steeliness in the face of Jessica's disarming responses. 'I wonder if we should leave it there,' she says, making the decision on the spur of the moment. 'You must have plenty of material for your sample chapter. Perhaps it's best if you get on with writing, so that Lucas and I can make a decision about ... about next steps. Yes?'

It's obvious by the way her face falls that Jessica was not expecting to be dismissed so early.

'Oh. Right. Yes, of course,' she says. She's trying to sound upbeat and professional but there's no disguising the disappointment in her slumping shoulders. 'Yes, absolutely. Well – thank you for your hospitality. It's been great to spend the last few days with you. I appreciate the opportunity and ...' She's wrangling with something, Adelaide can tell. Wondering if she can stay for the rest of the week in the hotel, maybe? 'And ... well, it's none of my business, but I'm sure if you wanted to see Margie again, you could do that? Wouldn't it be ... you know, worth the effort to make up?'

The change of direction is so unexpected, it takes Adelaide

a moment to process the stupid girl's comments. Who does she think she is? 'I *beg* your pardon?' she asks, her voice so icy the very air around them seems to plunge in temperature.

Jessica swallows, but is apparently undeterred by Adelaide's frostiness. 'I could see how upset you were, talking about Margie – and I know you're a proud person but it might ... help?' she says. 'If you just tried to set things right with her? Then you might not be so ... you know, so lonely and ...' She's faltering, seemingly losing her nerve as Adelaide's expression becomes increasingly severe. Nevertheless, on she goes, like a foolhardy kamikaze bomber on one final mission. '... So unhappy?'

Adelaide can hardly speak because she is bristling all over with indignation. Fury too, at the brazen cheek of this upstart before her. '*Unhappy?*' she repeats, incredulous. 'You think I'm unhappy, do you? And *lonely*? What the *hell*' – Jean-Paul whimpers as her voice rises – 'are you basing that on? A few lurid headlines you've read? An idea for your problem page? You know nothing about me – and nothing about what happened with Margie, do you understand?'

And yet that's still not enough to deter Jessica. 'But that's the point, isn't it?' she parries, face flushed. 'I thought I was here so that I could find out more about you, tell your story with all the detail and nuance and ... and the *honesty* it deserves. But at every turn you close up, you push me away. You tell me I know nothing. So then explain it to me! Describe what I don't know! Because I'm here for you, remember, for your memoir!'

Adelaide does not appreciate being lectured, not by

anyone – least of all someone who, by rights, shouldn't even be in this room. How dare she?

'You're only here because Lucas made a *mistake*,' she corrects her contemptuously. 'You're the wrong Jessica – wrong on every level. And now I would like you to leave.' Her heart is pounding, adrenalin roaring through her. If only Jean-Paul wasn't such a greedy little ham-guzzler, she would set him on this wretched woman, she really would. The nerve of her!

Jessica gulps, looking stricken. 'Adelaide, I'm sorry, I—'

'Get out, or I'll throw you out. And God help me, I will, with my own bare hands, so don't tempt me,' she shouts, pointing at the door for good measure. 'Out! Now! Go!'

With an anguished expression, Jessica bows her head and scoops up her phone, notepad and bag. 'I really am—'

'I'm not interested,' Adelaide snaps. 'Just go.'

She sits rigid in her chair, not even looking as the younger woman makes her way across the room and out of the door. Only when she hears the front door close, does she allow her body to go limp against the upholstery. She puts a hand to her heart where it's thumping so violently she almost fears it might leap out of her chest. Damn it. Damn and blast.

Jean-Paul whines and leans against her – he hates raised voices – and she strokes him gently, her fingers trembling against his fur. 'Sorry, darling,' she croons, feeling breathless. 'Don't worry. Another one bites the dust, eh, Jean-Paul?' She's trying her best but her voice doesn't sound anywhere near as bold as her words. 'We didn't like her anyway, did we? Good riddance!'

Chapter Nine

'What a total psychopath,' Becky rages down the phone when Jess, shaken and tearful, rings to tell her what has happened. 'What, and she just threw you out, there and then? That is outrageous! Of all the ... Well, it's her loss, Jess. Her massive, craterous loss. Bloody prima donna arsehole!'

Jess feels so desolate she can't raise a smile, let alone be cheered by Becky's fury. The wrong Jessica, she keeps thinking to herself, as if she's slapping her own face with the words. The moment of her scrabbling around under the table at the brasserie has come back to her in full now: *What do you mean, the wrong Jessica?* the man on the phone had said. Lucas speaking to Adelaide, at a guess, with her haranguing him for whatever mistake had been made.

She closes her eyes with a groan. And what a mistake. She wasn't even meant to be there in the first place! Her old boss Lucinda was right – she's simply not good enough for the world of high culture. She's been out of her depth this whole time. But how crushing to fall so spectacularly. To have your nose rubbed in it before being booted out the door! *An idea for your problem page*, Adelaide had sneered, as if to rubbish her. God, it feels awful.

'And by the way,' Becky goes on, warming to her theme, 'before you leave town, make sure you rack up the most gargantuan room service bill at that hotel. Champagne, oysters, the works. That'll teach her. Vile old cow.'

'I'm so gutted, Becks,' Jess wails, stumbling along the pavement. 'I felt such an *adult* coming here. Like a proper grown-up career woman – as if everything was about to turn around for me. I worked so hard to make her like me, as well, even when she was being rude. But she's just thrown everything back in my face. When I was only t-t-trying' – her voice cracks – 'to help!'

'She doesn't deserve your help, babe. You're a million times better than her. A billion times!'

'And now I've got to slink home early and admit that it didn't work out ...' Fresh tears prick her eyes because this is almost the worst element about her dismissal, imagining David's smug oh-dear face. Fuck! He's going to be so patronising, isn't he? He's going to bloody love it. 'I'm mortified.'

'Don't be! If anyone should be mortified, it's her, for behaving like a toddler throwing toys out of the pram, when she's nearly eighty, for crying out loud. You're well shot of her. Lucky escape, I reckon.'

It stings too much to feel like a lucky escape yet though, that's the problem. Her pride is in tatters at having such a great piece of work snatched away before she's even had the chance to prove herself. The thought of an enforced return to ordinary life – the mothering, the cooking, the laundry – without

84

having this other gilded mirror to glance into admiringly . . . she's unable to see any positives in her loss.

'Silver lining though.' Becky, as ever, is heroically trying to find one for her. 'You're not coming back until Friday, right? So you've basically got a day and a half to yourself now. In Paris. And before you say anything, I absolutely forbid you to bail out and come home earlier. The kids are fine. Albertine is living her best moggy life with the place to herself, and me waiting on her hand and foot. Plus you've got your date tomorrow night, haven't you? So—'

'It's not a *date*, it's only—'

'So you stay where you are and have a great time. There will be other jobs. Let David manage a full week of childcare for once, and then swan back on Friday with bags of duty-free and a secret post-date smile on your face. Albertine and I *insist*.'

Becky might have a point, Jess thinks as she hangs up, feeling a tiny bit better. Her hotel room is paid for until Friday morning, which is when her train ticket is booked for too. For the rest of her stay, she can be a tourist and Adelaide can go to hell.

The phone call has taken her halfway along Rue de Rivoli and she decides to keep walking, towards the Louvre and Jardin des Tuileries. Forget great culture, forget high art; she's going to be her lowbrow normal-person self and take a spin on the Ferris wheel there, enjoy the views across the city and remind herself that there's more to life than one petulant artist and her temper tantrums.

From that moment on, Jess's day improves considerably. A Ferris wheel ride kicks things off, followed by a forget-the-diet cheeseburger and chips from a nearby café. She buys some souvenirs for the girls – a pretty silk scarf each and a box of pastel-coloured macarons to share – and sends a photo of herself modelling an orange beret to Polly. *Too much?* she writes with a winking face. (Polly is the fashionista of the three and has strong opinions.) Then she indulges herself with a boat trip along the river to the Eiffel Tower, where she splashes out on a lift to the top and orders a flute of champagne at the swanky bar there, just like she's always wanted to. It's extortionate, of course, and far more than she should be spending on a drink under current circumstances, but you only live once, she decides. She's earned this. Exhaling until her shoulders inch lower, she tries to savour the moment, taking a mental snapshot of herself. Here I am, having a great time in Paris, she thinks, and whatever else happens, look at me now with my glass of Moët and spectacular view. This is *good*.

Her phone rings in the next moment, an unknown number on the screen, and her heart thumps.

'Hello? Jess Bright speaking,' she says, praying that a miracle has happened and Adelaide is calling her to apologise.

'Hi. Um . . . Jessica? This is Lucas Brockes,' she hears instead.

'Oh.' She feels herself sag. He's probably going to ask her to leave the hotel, sling her hook, isn't he? Or bollock her for upsetting his neurotic old aunty. 'Hi,' she adds unhappily. Go on, then. Let's hear it. Only watch out, mate, because she's had half a glass of fizz by now, and might well fight back with a few home truths of her own.

'I gather there was a bit of a falling-out this morning,' he begins.

That's one way of putting it. No doubt Adelaide has slagged her to the absolute death. It's a miracle Jess's ears haven't burst into flames by now, what with all the vitriol she imagines has been slung about. 'Yes,' she replies.

'For what it's worth . . . I'm sorry,' he says. 'She's family and I'm used to her ways but I appreciate she can be . . .' There's a pause, where she imagines him trying to find a tactful way to say 'a nightmare'. 'Well . . . strong-minded, let's be honest,' he eventually manages. 'She's not the easiest person to work with.'

'No,' Jess agrees. Understatement of the year, she thinks, remembering Adelaide's imperious voice ordering her to leave. But why's he ringing up to tell her stuff she already knows?

'Listen . . . are you at the hotel?' he asks. 'It might be easier if we chat face to face.'

At the hotel? No, love, she's necking champagne at the top of the Eiffel Tower. But he doesn't need to know that. 'No,' she says. 'I'm . . .' She can't quite bring herself to reveal her exact location, because she has the horrible feeling he will look down on her. The Eiffel Tower? What a tourist! 'I'm in Faubourg Saint-Germain,' she continues, citing the area instead. What business is it of his anyway?

'Okay,' he says. 'I could be there in twenty minutes, would that work for you?'

She rolls her eyes, exasperated because he is totally ruining her moment here. And if he thinks she's about to slug back her pricey champers on his behalf, after the way his aunt behaved earlier, he can absolutely jog on. 'Can we say forty?' she asks through gritted teeth.

He says yes, then suggests a coffee shop nearby where they

can meet. Jess hangs up and inadvertently groans aloud, with such frustration that two suited men on the table next to hers turn and gaze at her, eyebrows raised in bemusement. She raises her glass at them, feeling vaguely hysterical. Should she even drink the rest of this when she's due to meet stiff-neck Lucas in less than an hour? Wouldn't it be sensible to keep her wits about her at this point? Too late for sensible, she decides, taking a sip in defiance. Nobody, but nobody, is going to take her Eiffel Tower champagne away from her, and that's that.

'Hello again,' says Lucas, when Jess arrives at the café, having crunched two Polos and splashed some cold water on her face in the top-level Eiffel Tower loos. 'I'm sorry that we're meeting under these circumstances. What can I get you?'

His brown eyes are steady and reassuring rather than combative, and Jess finds her tension dissipating, as he goes to order her a flat white. Maybe he's not about to totally roast her in public, then. Or if he is, at least he's paying for her coffee first.

She checks her phone to see that a message has come in from Polly. *That colour is terrible on you!!! But would look so good on me?* There's a praying hands emoji and a love-heart, and Jess snorts back a laugh as she spots Lucas returning with her drink.

'So, do you want to tell me what happened?' he asks, sitting down opposite her. 'I mean, Adelaide's already given me her side of the story, but I appreciate that doesn't mean I've heard a balanced version of events.'

Perhaps it's the champagne talking but Jess finds herself unable to hold back. 'She said you'd made a mistake in hiring

88

me,' she blurts out, still feeling the sting from this revelation. 'That I was, and I quote, "the wrong Jessica". Is that true?' She's ready to add that she overheard him on the phone that day if he tries to deflect but he merely stares down at the table, which is all the answer she needs.

'Oh, right. Wonderful,' she says sarcastically, and all of a sudden she has the horrible feeling that she's about to cry. The disappointment, the humiliation … it's too much.

'It's not as bad as it sounds,' he tells her. 'When we were discussing who to approach next, and Adelaide said "Jessica", I assumed she meant you because I'd read your great interview with her. As far as I was concerned, you were a credible candidate.'

Jess is not loving the use of past tense in regards to her being credible. 'But in actual fact she meant … ?'

He fiddles with a teaspoon, delaying the knockout punch. 'Well … not that it's relevant, but … okay. Jessica Martindale,' he replies, which is when Jess groans and puts her head in her hands. There it is. *Now* she understands why Adelaide looked at her like that on the first day. Now she knows why the older woman could hardly shoo her out of the door fast enough. Because Jessica Martindale is an intellectual powerhouse, an American writer always popping up on culture shows with her opinions, writing op-ed pieces for broadsheet newspapers, not to mention the well-received biographies to her name. Of *course* Adelaide wanted Jessica fucking Martindale to write her memoir. Who wouldn't?

'I wish I hadn't asked,' she mutters. Just when she thought today had already hit rock bottom, as well. Wrong!

'She doesn't want the job, if that makes you feel any better,' Lucas tells her with a resigned expression. 'The memoir is not exactly having the smoothest of journeys, to be honest.'

Jess snorts. 'I wonder why,' she says. 'When Adelaide is such a delight to work with.'

It's unprofessional of her but she no longer cares. Why is she even wasting her time having this conversation – that so far has only made her feel worse – when she is in Paris, footloose and fancy-free? When there are a million other things she could be doing right now? She should have ordered another glass of Moët at the Eiffel Tower when she had the chance, told Lucas she was too busy to meet him.

'Fair point,' he concedes. 'But I'm not here to talk about other writers. I'm here to see if there's any way back for you. If I could persuade you to at least write the sample chapter, as originally planned.'

She laughs in his face. 'Are you kidding me? Because I don't think that's what your aunt wants, not for a minute.'

He sighs but doesn't look surprised by her response. 'You know, when we realised on Monday what had happened – the whole "wrong Jessica" debacle,' he says, which makes her cringe all over again. 'Sorry – but hear me out. By then, I had already been in touch with the publisher we're working with, and mentioned your name. They said – and I promise I'm not bullshitting you – they said they were really pleased at our choice, calling you "a safe pair of hands" and saying you had a good reputation in the industry.'

Jess narrows her eyes, wondering if this is a massive buttering-up exercise, but he seems sincere enough. 'Hmm.' If his words are true, she can't deny that they are extremely nice to hear. Perhaps somebody at the publisher remembers her from her Culture correspondent days, although her pride prevents her from asking for further details.

'Whereas some other writers, who think they're big cheeses in the arts world – naming no names, obviously – are total divas who miss every deadline, don't bother putting in the effort and piss everyone off,' he goes on.

'You don't need to tell *me* that,' she replies, thinking back to the so-called star columnists she's worked with in the past, some of whom have been so unanimously loathed that you could practically hear a low hiss sweeping around the office whenever their names were mentioned.

'Anyway, what I'm saying is, if you come back with a brilliant first chapter that makes the publishers happy, then . . . Well, Adelaide might change her mind.'

Yeah, right. 'I'm pretty sure Adelaide doesn't want me to write her memoir,' Jess says. 'And newsflash, I don't want that either, now that I've had a taste of the experience. So . . .' She shrugs, not bothering to finish the sentence.

'Well, updated newsflash,' he retaliates, 'it's in your contract that you have to write the first chapter before we pay you the rest of the week's trial fee. So . . .' He shrugs right back at her and she feels the colour surge in her cheeks.

'What? No, it isn't,' she argues, but even as she's saying the words, she has a sinking feeling, remembering who drew up the document in the first place. 'Anyway, even if it *is*,' she goes on, rallying quickly, 'then newsflash, maybe I'll ignore that and not get paid. Because what's the point when I won't get the job anyway?' Today is not doing much for her blood pressure, she reflects, instantly realising that, actually, she needs that pay; she has already factored it into her budget. Bollocks.

'It's certainly a busy afternoon for breaking news,' he comments drily and she blushes even harder.

'Sorry,' she mutters. 'It's been a trying sort of day. Disappointing.'

'I can imagine. I've been on the receiving end of Adelaide's temper before,' he replies. 'But if it makes you feel any better, she did seem sorry for how things turned out.'

'Right,' Jess says darkly, not believing it for a second. He's trying to paper over the cracks, she thinks. But surely the cracks are already too big? 'Tell me about you, anyway,' she goes on, suddenly sick of them dwelling on her failings. 'You're working on Adelaide's archive, right? How's that going, have you come across anything really juicy?'

'Well—' Oh wow, is he actually about to divulge some secrets? she wonders, trying to mask her eagerness as he leaves a tantalising pause. 'If you get the commission, you'll be able to look at everything for yourself, won't you?' is all he gives her, discretion obviously getting the better of him.

She groans in frustration and he smiles at her, the first proper smile she's seen from him. It's nice. 'What if I need to be tempted a bit more to write the chapter, with a hint at things to come?' she counters, raising a hopeful eyebrow.

He laughs but doesn't take the bait. 'It's all there and waiting for the writer who gets the commission,' he says.

'So when you say "it's all there" – are you referring

specifically to the years with Remy? What happened with William? The fallout with Margie?'

'It's all there,' he repeats, annoyingly inscrutable. Then he wrinkles his nose. 'I haven't got very far, truth be told,' he confesses. 'It's a huge job, especially with the haphazard state of her document-keeping. We're talking boxes and boxes of stuff, randomly chucked in together.'

Despite everything, Jess feels prickles of intrigue at the thought of having permission to leaf through Adelaide's sketchpads, letters and diaries. There must be so much treasure in those boxes, some of it no doubt material that has been sealed up and stored away for years, decades. It's every nosey writer's dream.

'How come you're doing this anyway?' she asks. 'I mean – have you had to put your real job on hold, or are you managing to combine the two? What *do* you do, out of interest?'

'I've always worked in corporate law,' he says. That makes sense, she thinks, remembering the overzealous contract. 'And ... well, I've been through some upheavals over the last few years, personally and career-wise, so back in the spring, Adelaide suggested I come and work for her for a few months.'

'Sorry to hear that,' Jess says, her eyes flicking to his hand and noting the absence of a wedding ring. She falls silent, hoping he'll supply her with more information. He doesn't.

'Oh – I meant to say, I can change your ticket home,' he replies instead, tapping his phone back to life and finding the Eurostar website. 'Would tomorrow morning suit you? Eleven o'clock?'

It takes Jess a moment to reply because all she can think about (shamefully) is her date with Georges tomorrow evening – not a date, she corrects herself immediately – and how she'll have to cancel it if she leaves in the morning. 'Um . . .'

'If you want?' he prompts when she advances no further. 'I just assumed you'd want to be back with your kids sooner?'

Of course she wants to be back with her kids sooner. Of course they are far more important than Georges. Absolutely. 'Yes, that's right, I would,' she says, while her brain races, wondering if they can rearrange tomorrow's meetup to tonight. If there's any way she can salvage this? 'Eleven sounds perfect.'

'No problem,' he says, typing away. 'There. All done. I'll forward you the new ticket and confirmation.' He puts his phone down and drains his coffee. 'So – you're going to do it, then?'

'Do what?' She's still thinking about Georges and it takes her a moment to rewind. 'Oh – the chapter.' Annoyingly, it feels as if he's rather got her over a barrel. She needs the money, for one thing, but all his talk of the archive and its secrets have piqued her interest considerably too. And if it's true, about her not having *completely* lost the job yet, then shouldn't she at least give it her best shot? 'I suppose so,' she agrees through gritted teeth.

Chapter Ten

It's Thursday morning, and Adelaide and Jean-Paul are making their slow way around Place des Vosges as usual, although Adelaide's thoughts are very far from the summer scene before her. Ever since she first agreed to the memoir, Simon Dunster has been lurking at the back of her mind, waiting for his moment to reappear like a cartoon villain. She met him at art school — a quiff-haired pretty boy from the Home Counties who thought he was something special because his dad was a big deal in politics. Adelaide wasn't particularly bothered about him or his dad, but as her second year began, their paths kept crossing and not in a good way. Before then, she'd knuckled down and worked hard, learning everything she could in order to catch up with the other students, and it had taken her a while to gain confidence, to feel that maybe she did belong there after all. But as the autumn term got underway, she could feel herself accelerating beyond her classmates, as if powered by rocket fuel. She was producing good work, everyone kept saying. Agents started sniffing around her. A disparaging piece about the radical nature of her aprons appeared in *The Times*, which drove dozens more women to seek out her Berwick Street stall and buy up her stock like never before.

Simon Dunster didn't seem to like her getting so much attention. The first thing she remembers him saying to her was 'You're not that good,' standing looking at one of her still-life paintings with his hands in his pockets. This was after class had finished one day, when the teacher had already left, and everyone was packing up their things.

She glanced back at him, unfazed. 'I know,' she said. 'That's why I'm here. Studying how to *be* good.'

Her reply was entirely sincere – she didn't care whether or not he liked her work – but he interpreted her response as sarcasm. 'Think you're better than everyone else, don't you?' he sneered.

'Not really,' she said, before taking in his peevish expression, the look of someone not used to having a woman answer him back. 'Although I think I'm better than you,' she added coolly.

A couple of his mates in the vicinity laughed at that, jostling him as he pushed past them, face rigid with fury. Others tittered as they continued cleaning their brushes and putting paints away. Simon acted like a big shot but he wasn't especially well liked. But then a girl with long flaxen plaits – Heidi, everyone called her, although her real name was Pam – said in a low voice, 'Watch yourself with him, won't you? He's got a nasty streak.'

Adelaide did not take kindly to being told what to do, not even by sweet, well-meaning Heidi. She'd faced down her drunk, belligerent dad enough times, and she'd seen off a would-be burglar at the squat with a poker in her hand; she certainly wasn't scared of a spoilt brat like Simon Dunster trying to throw his weight around. He seemed determined to get a rise out of her though, frequently criticising her work and muttering coded remarks about her to his cronies whenever she was in earshot. 'Ignore him,' said Margie, when Adelaide complained about the situation in the pub after college. 'Sounds to me like he fancies you,' Jeanette reckoned. 'Although he's got a funny way of showing it.'

Adelaide was too busy with her aprons, her coursework and the college social events to lose much sleep over him. But then came a Christmas party thrown by a popular group in their year, held in a disused warehouse in Deptford. There were lit candles everywhere, gallons of punch, and somebody's Dansette record player rigged up to a small generator to provide music. Everyone was dancing, and Adelaide felt happy, truly happy. She had found her people; she knew what she wanted to do for the rest of her life. It was 1964 and London seemed like the centre of the world, pulsating with change; a place where anything was possible.

Later that evening, there came a point when she was stumbling around in the darkness outside, trying to find the outdoor lav in the yard. Her breath was steaming in the wintry air when somebody's hand suddenly caught hold of her arm, and gripped so tightly she'd have a circlet of bruises there the next day. 'What are you—?' she yelped as she was yanked against a brick wall and held there. The moon was full, but not bright enough to reveal the identity of the shadowy person who'd grabbed her. 'Hey!' she cried, trying to wrestle free.

'Shut up,' came a voice she recognised all too well, the

weight of him pressing her against the wall so that she couldn't move.

'Simon, what are you—?'

'I *said* shut UP!'

She shudders now to remember this exchange, even under the bright July sunshine, sixty or so years later. Loathsome, big-lipped Simon, ripping at her clothes and pounding away at her there in the freezing darkness, because in his limited imagination it was the only way he could best her. Afterwards she spat full in his face and he slapped her. 'Dirty bitch,' he said, doing up his trousers as she stood there trembling.

He thought that was it, he'd won, but he was wrong. Boy, was he ever wrong.

'Come along, Jean-Paul,' Adelaide says, tugging at his lead where he has ground to a determined halt in his attempt to reach a couple of dropped frites under one of the brasserie tables. When Jean-Paul is pursuing a delicacy as high value to him as a pavement chip, it's astonishing how heavy he can make himself.

Her eye falls on a used match on the ground and it's enough to send her back in time, to the night when she was standing outside Simon Dunster's New Cross flat with a matchbox in her hand, a few weeks after that party. The rasping strike of a match under cover of darkness, the quick orange flare of light that soon became a leaping, engulfing fire, rampaging through Simon's home and belongings. Sometimes it turns out that revenge is best served hot, after all.

In her defence, she'd assumed he wouldn't be there at the time; it was New Year's Eve, he was sure to be at some party or other, she told herself. How was she to know he'd come down with flu, and taken to his bed for an early night instead? He didn't die, although his pretty face was never the same again. He dropped out of college and the last she heard, he was working for his dad, doing some office work behind closed doors where he wouldn't frighten the public with his burns. Couldn't happen to a nicer person, in Adelaide's mind. No, she's not sorry. Why should she be?

'Come *on*,' she orders Jean-Paul, who finally submits, looking defeated. Adelaide empathises. It's not been a great week, all in all. Talking about the past has stirred up some unpleasant memories that are yet to settle back into the mud. And Lucas is annoyed with her for having dispatched Jessica so hastily, even chasing after her across town when he heard what had happened. 'I'm starting to think you don't want this memoir to be written at all,' he'd fumed, barely able to disguise his impatience. 'Has the whole thing been some kind of vanity project for you? Should I bother with your archive when there will be nobody to look at it, at this rate? Because I do have a life of my own back home, remember.'

It's not like him to be so cross. He's always been calm and even-tempered, right from boyhood. She knows he has a lot on his mind, and that his own concerns have been somewhat sidelined recently. She's been asking a lot of him. Perhaps too much? Oh, why does everything have to be so complicated?

Chapter Eleven

As Paris slips away through the train window later that morning, Jess feels a tangle of emotions. She also has a merciless, thumping headache after drinking far too much wine the night before, drowning her sorrows at the brasserie. Thank goodness for Valentin, her new friend, who not only recommended the salmon tartare for one final delicious dinner (good shout), but who called his boyfriend Nicolas to come out and keep her company when work became too busy for him to do so. Nicolas is fun, but possibly a bit too much fun, Jess thinks now, flashing back to the cocktails he ordered them after the first bottle of wine was empty. Not to mention the shots of Pernod he insisted on buying when she started to flag.

Her stomach roils at the memory and she leans her head against the side of the train, closing her eyes. *Don't think about the Pernod. Do not even imagine the smell of it, Jess, for the love of God!*

Her new friend from last night, Nicolas, was tall and handsome with rumpled brown hair, perfectly groomed eyebrows complete with slits at each end, and a gold cross in one ear. He proved to be highly skilled in the art of extracting secrets from others. 'You should be a journalist yourself,' Jess told him, half aghast, half admiring, after spilling the story of her marriage breakdown at his prompting. 'Or a spy. Or an interrogator.'

Worse, despite having recognised this in him, she was still apparently powerless to withhold anything, because in the next moment, she was confessing all about Georges, including the fact that she'd had to cancel the date when he wasn't able to rearrange meeting earlier. *If you're ever in London . . .* she had messaged with a smiley face to cover up her disappointment, but it felt very much as if she was clutching at straws. 'Look how gorgeous he is,' she wailed to Nicolas, showing him Georges' Facebook page, and Nicolas whistled approvingly. 'But he is so handsome, no? This is a tragedy! Fate, you are killing us here!' he cried, shaking a fist at the sky. 'Why are you doing this to Jess?'

She smiles ruefully now, remembering his passionate cry, and feels only too glad she wasn't quite drunk enough to go along with Nicolas's insane suggestion later on of calling him and inviting him to join them for shots. At least she has *some* self-preservation instincts alive and kicking.

Beatrice, the lovely hotel receptionist, did her bit to match Nicolas in flamboyance this morning, clapping a hand to her heart and declaring to be devastated by her early departure. 'We will miss you, Jess. We hope we will see you again soon.'

'Me too, Beatrice. Thank you for everything – especially the ham,' Jess had replied, reluctantly handing over her key.

She gazes out of the window now as the train rattles further down the track, leaving Paris behind, along with her career dreams. Taking her home to her ordinary, chaotic life, where she'll have to turn her attention to bills, laundry, what to cook for dinner and the latest messy sagas that ebb and flow around her daughters like spring tides.

She can't wait to see them, though. They've chatted most evenings but it's not the same as being together in person, sharing day-to-day lives. She does her best to keep up with their ever-changing interests – Edie is currently obsessed with manga, while Polly name-drops a bewildering number of influencers that Jess has to covertly look up so that she can feel in touch. Mia's tastes run to obscure bands, gruesome true crime podcasts and make-up techniques, none of which Jess is able to get much of a handle on.

Having contacted David with her official excuse – *I've got all the material I need for the sample chapter, so thought I'd hop on an earlier train home* – they've agreed that she'll have the girls back this afternoon. She is delighted, and, reading between the lines, he is pretty relieved too. Everyone's a winner.

A new email has arrived from Lucas, she notices, clicking to open it. *Hope your train is on time and all well*, he has written. *I found a bunch of old photos in the archive this morning – wondering if they will inspire you for the sample chapter?*

There follow three attachments, captioned Poland Street, College Party and Little Bower Weekend, and Jess curses the laggy Eurostar Wi-Fi as she waits for them to download with painful slowness. Also – what, or where, is Little Bower? The first picture opens on-screen – a black and white shot of four women at a kitchen table laden with wine bottles and glasses, each with a cigarette in hand. Jess zooms in, picking out

Adelaide (the tallest, with long hair and a sharp fringe), Esme (owlish glasses, a shy smile), Margie (crop-haired, laughing with her mouth open) and Jeanette, whose face is obscured by a cloud of smoke, but who looks to be wearing a rather racy velvet top with cutaway sections, no doubt designed and made herself.

There they are, she thinks, gazing at their faces with a thrill. You can tell by their relaxed body language how close they are with one another; these incredible, young, not-yet-famous women, all of whom would go on to make their mark on the art world. And having a right laugh too, if this photo is anything to go by. Imagine being part of their gang. Imagine going through the ups and downs that the four of them did, collectively and individually, and none of them having the remotest idea, at this point, that they were bound for greatness.

She sighs, wishing that Adelaide had been even a tiny bit nicer to her. That she had extended towards Jess so much as a fraction of the warmth evident in this photo. It could have been the best job of Jess's life, writing the older woman's stupid book. Never mind.

The second photo reveals another black and white scene, this time featuring ten or more people at what looks like a fancy dress party. Hunting around, she finds Adelaide in a Marie Antoinette–style wig and gown talking to a handsome man dressed as a pirate. There's a Cleopatra (Esme, possibly?), someone's face poking out of a gigantic cardboard toothpaste tube, and a man who's come as Salvador Dalí, if the large upturned moustache is anything to go by.

Having only encountered Adelaide as serious and forbidding,

it's nice to see this younger, fun side of her amidst friends, Jess thinks. How often does she look back at these times, and how do they make her feel? Fond, melancholic, regretful?

Now for the third photo. Little Bower Weekend is the caption, which makes Jess think of a garden, maybe a leafy arbour, but when opened, the picture shows a pebbled beach. There's the famous foursome once more – Adelaide, Esme, Margie and Jeanette – this time dressed like bathing belles, in bikinis, lipstick and high heels (a nightmare on the pebbles, Jess imagines) as they strike provocative poses. Despite her hangover, despite everything, Jess laughs out loud at the scene, because she can't help but love their attitude. This photograph is in colour – thank goodness, because the bikinis are red, yellow, orange and teal, and really pop against the pebbles and summery blue sky. It's glorious!

Something is tugging at her subconscious, though. Little Bower ... she's heard that name before. Is it the name of the beach itself? Surely not, it doesn't sound remotely maritime, she thinks, turning to Google and typing in the words. The top result is from a property article in *The Times*, dated five years ago, and she reads the words '. . . Little Bower, former shared studio of the London Bohemian art collective, is back on the market as a family home after a painstaking redevelopment . . .' Ahh – that must be why she remembers it.

The second result in the list is slightly more sinister. 'Little Bower, the mysterious site where art met death,' she reads, and remembers with a shiver that yes, of course, this was the infamous scene where a young man's body was found outside years ago. Back in the eighties, maybe? She's hazy on the full story, but remembers from her research there being a broken upstairs window and a suicide note in a typewriter. She opens the article, feeling rather ghoulish, as she reminds herself of the salient details. Colin Copeland, the deceased, was an unemployed twenty-six-year-old so-called 'loner' from East London, whose death was recorded as suicide, despite his sister, one Eleanor Copeland, insisting that this verdict was wrong. *He was happy, he had plans!* she is described as having said. *A typed suicide note? Give over. He couldn't even spell 'suicide', let alone carry one out. And why would he jump through a closed window, rather than an open one? Answer me that!*

Questions still swirl around whether anyone else had been at the property at the time of Colin's death, the article states. The artists concerned were all questioned but had solid alibis, according to the police inquiry. Little Bower is up a lane without any direct neighbours, but on the day in question, a dog walker claimed to have seen a car parked outside the property, which is situated just over two miles outside Hythe.

Jess's eyes widen a fraction at this last detail. Was it Hythe Beach in the photograph, then? If so, Little Bower must be less than an hour's drive from her home in Canterbury. Forty-five minutes, probably, on a good run. She tries to remember what else she knows about the house – that one of the group, possibly Jeanette, bought it as a rundown hovel, after her first big show in the late sixties. Or did she inherit it? Whichever, she and various friends spent a summer patching it up and redecorating, and turning it into a home from home, a place to paint and sketch and think, away from the hustle of London life. But why did Colin Copeland end up there? she wonders, glancing back at the joyful beach photo on her screen. How does his death fit into the history of Little Bower?

Damn it, and now she's hooked in again when she knows she can't afford to be. She has already lost this job, she can't let herself become reattached emotionally. Nevertheless, there's nothing to stop her from taking a quick trip over to Hythe herself, is there? Tracking down the house and finding out more about the story, just out of interest. Forget the book, maybe there's a newspaper article in this, if she can dig around enough. Why not?

You might think you already know me, but I'm afraid you don't. You have no idea. And I'm not even sure yet how much I will tell you of my story, my life, because I'm not one who trusts easily. When you've finished reading this memoir, you'll understand why. One thing I can promise you is that everything you'll find on these pages is true. It's exactly what happened. And if you want to judge me for any of my behaviour, then go right ahead. I won't care.

Jess is at home, and all is right with the world, now that she's squeezed each of her girls, caught up with their latest news, put a wash on, and had a well-earned gin and tonic on the sofa with a sulky tail-flicking Albertine. It's the following morning now, Friday, and she's decided to strike while the iron is hot – or at least while Adelaide's voice is still fresh in her head. If she can rattle out the bones of a sample chapter today while the girls are at school, she can devote herself to them over the weekend. Maybe even suggest a day trip to Hythe tomorrow, with a detour to Little Bower on the way home?

106

She rereads the words she's just typed on-screen, her nose wrinkled. The tone she's captured certainly sounds to her mind like Adelaide, but will the woman in question disapprove of the unconventional, almost aggressive style she's establishing here? Will she think Jess is taking the mick if the sample chapter starts this way? Well, so be it. 'If you can't handle the truth, Adelaide,' she mutters, fingers hovering above the keyboard, 'feel free to stop reading.'

I was born in January 1945, in Rudge Street, East London, in the freezing back room of a cramped terraced house. It was night-time and my mother swears that I emerged into the world at the exact moment the house across the road was being bombed. Everyone in the room was screaming blue murder, so my first impression of the world was presumably one of utter pandemonium. Make of that what you will.

Jess can feel herself getting into her stride. She's rather enjoying taking on Adelaide's crisp, no-nonsense voice, although obviously this is helped by having pages and pages of her directly transcribed speech to copy from.

I was the third of four children, with two older brothers, Robert and Peter. William, my favourite brother, was born the following year. I won't tell you what happened to William because it's really none of your business, but I did love him.

She bites her lip. Too much? The publishers would baulk at such a wilfully combative line in a finished book, but the phrasing will hopefully highlight to Adelaide (and Lucas) the ridiculous position that she has adopted thus far, guarding the more painful moments of her life with overly zealous secrecy. Who knows, it might even force her to get over herself and be more forthcoming with whoever ends up writing the damn book. Miracles do occasionally happen.

The front door suddenly crashes open and Jess's fingers skid on the keyboard as she jerks in surprise. What the hell? It's only eleven-thirty; nobody should be home from school yet.

'Hello?' she cries, jumping to her feet and rushing into the hall. 'Who's— *Mia!* What's the matter?'

There's her eldest daughter weeping buckets, collapsing on the carpet, school bag still hanging on one arm. She topples to one side as if she's been shot, drawing her legs up into a foetal position. Jess runs over to her.

'Darling! What's wrong? Are you hurt?' Someone's stabbed her, she thinks immediately. She's been mugged, assaulted. 'Oh lovey,' she says, kneeling beside her and rubbing her back. There are no wounds she can see, nothing obvious. 'What *is* it?'

'It's Zach,' sobs Mia, the words gulping out of her. 'He ... he's going out with Georgia Greene. I thought he ...' Further sobs engulf her so that she can hardly speak. 'I thought he liked *me.*'

Oof. Invisible wounds, then – but ones almost as bad when you're seventeen. Jess reaches down to cradle her. Thank goodness she is here, and not Paris, able to scoop up her girl in this moment of need.

'Oh no,' she says sympathetically. So much for Mia's cool 'just friends!' claim from the other week, too – she was clearly holding out for something more, something deeper. Poor Mia. Jess remembers only too well the pain of teenage rejection. The agony of a crush looking elsewhere.

108

'I feel such an idiot, Mum,' Mia cries, still a storm of tears. 'I'm so stupid!'

'You are absolutely *not*,' Jess retorts. 'He's the stupid one for choosing anyone else over you. What a loser. He's going to be so embarrassed when he realises what a massive dumb mistake he's made.'

But her words seem to bounce right off her crying daughter, who appears inconsolable. This is where it begins, Jess thinks as they remain on the hall floor together, Mia's face sodden with tears. This awful toughening up we all have to do when it comes to love; the nasty surprises that can catch you out, right when you least expect them.

She frowns, remembering the smirk on Zach's face that morning when she'd caught him emerging from Mia's bedroom. If she sees that boy again, he's going to feel the fiery blast of Jess's wrath, that's for sure.

'But I know it hurts the first time it happens,' she adds, because Mia probably wants softness rather than lioness ferocity right now. Then she hesitates. 'Did you ... You were careful with him, right?'

Mia hiccups, wipes her arm across her eyes, then pulls a face. 'Mum. Please. Not now.'

'I'm taking that to mean you were, but ... okay. I won't pry. You don't have to tell me anything. Although obviously you *can*, any time; you know that, right?'

Mia rolls her eyes so melodramatically it's a miracle they stay in their sockets. At least she's stopped crying though. 'Like I'd take relationship advice from you, anyway.' She wriggles free of Jess's arms and gives an enormous sniff.

Stung, Jess passes her a tissue and Mia blows her nose with a honk. This is how it is with her – accepted one moment, pushed away the next. You have to take what closeness you can get when it's on offer, while simultaneously trying to absorb the bursts of blame. Still, Jess has feelings too. It's not the easiest balancing act.

'What would help now?' she asks evenly after counting to ten in her head. 'Cup of tea? A cuddle with the cat? Me giving you a lift back to school?' She folds her arms. 'Because we both know you're not meant to be home at this time of day, so ...'

Mia gives a 'so what?' shrug. 'I've signed out ill, they're not expecting me back,' she says. Then her face changes. 'By the way, Mum, what's going on with Dad? Is he seeing someone else?'

The about-turn is so swift and unexpected Jess almost experiences whiplash. 'What do you mean?' she asks, before adding, 'Not that I know about.' It's as if the ground has shuddered beneath the worn hall carpet. David and another woman again? How is she meant to feel about that?

'Dunno, I just ...' Mia shrugs again. 'He was being a bit weird. Cagey.'

Weird. Cagey. That doesn't sound like a man delirious with love, but what does Jess know? She missed every sign going last time around, after all.

'I ... hmm,' she says. 'Your guess is as good as mine.' She eyes her daughter more closely. 'Would that upset you, if he was?'

'Me? No. Not really. As long as it's not someone horrible. Why, would it upset you?'

110

Jess hesitates, trying to find the right words. 'I don't know if I'd be *upset*,' she says carefully. You never know with Mia, what is going to be repeated and to whom. The girls are unaware of the full details behind their parents' split; as far as they're concerned, Mum and Dad simply fell out of love with one another ('Like lots of people do. But we still love *you*, very much').

A grubby little affair was one thing, but for David to move on to a proper, full-blown relationship . . . ? It would certainly feel more final, she concludes. But that might be . . . good?

'I'd find it a bit odd to begin with, I guess,' she goes on. She's ruffled, no doubt about it, like a cat whose fur has been stroked the wrong way, but otherwise she can't quite pinpoint her feelings.

Mia leans against her, friendly again. 'Men, eh? Bloody men!' They laugh, somewhat wanly, and then Mia parrots, 'What would help now, Mum? Cup of tea? Cuddle with Albs? Or the two of us going wild and cracking open some cider together?'

Jess snorts. 'Definitely not,' she says. Then something occurs to her. Something that might take both their minds off disappointing matters of the heart. 'But I see your cider suggestion and raise you with one of mine: how do you fancy checking out a house where a mysterious death took place?'

Mia's eyes brighten. Of course they do. This kid regularly plays gory tales of serial killers into her ears for fun. 'Seriously? What happened?'

'Well,' says Jess, 'that is the question.' Sod it, she's dying to see the house herself, and if Mia's already signed out of school, then ... She gets to her feet and grabs a jacket and her car keys, holding them up in the air. 'I can fill you in on the story along the way. Coming?'

'Hell, yeah,' is her answer. 'Let's do it, Mum. Road trip!'

Chapter Twelve

Adelaide knows all too well why she's been having such a turbulent week. She always dreads the run-up to Remy's birthday on the calendar, because he's ever-present in her mind beforehand and her emotions rise accordingly. Today's the day – and not only that, it would have been his eightieth. She can only imagine how he would have milked the celebrations: a huge party somewhere glamorous, with him at the centre, absolutely lapping up the attention. He would have become such a sprightly old man, she's often thought; white-haired, dapper as ever in a sharp suit and polished shoes. The man was so stylish he could have pulled off thick specs and a pair of hearing aids with aplomb. He'd have procured himself a silver-topped cane to pose with, whether he needed it for mobility purposes or not.

Instead, thinks Adelaide, pushing open the heavy wooden gate at the entrance of Père Lachaise, he was laid to rest here in this cemetery over twenty years ago now, as rain drizzled down the collars of the mourners, as tears splashed on to the winding cobbled pathways. His sons, slight and delicately boned, flanked Coco beneath black umbrellas, all three of them ignoring Adelaide just as she did not acknowledge them. *What a tragedy*, people murmured as the rain pattered down. *What a waste.*

Today there is no rain, just the scent of parched earth, the faint stirring of a breeze through the leaves of the trees. Does anything of Remy still remain here, she wonders, or is he merely a memory in the air? If there's such a thing as a soul, she thinks that his has perhaps drifted back towards Roquefort-les-Pins by now, the village where he grew up. He'll be whistling around the sun-baked stone cottages and through the pine forests, she imagines. He always did love the south.

'Come on, Jean-Paul,' she says, as her dog hangs back, sniffing the gatepost. It's eight o'clock on Saturday morning and they've come to pay their respects early because the French TV channel Canal+ are rerunning a documentary about Remy this evening, to mark the day, and it's been heavily trailed. There will almost certainly be hordes of people tramping through the cemetery to visit his grave later, and she doesn't want to be noticed. The early start is also because the day is forecast to be another hot one, even by Paris standards. The news is full of wildfires rampaging across Europe, skies filled with smoke, and she has started dreaming about frozen landscapes, with gales so bitter they take your breath away. Most Parisians with any sense have left the city by now, but here she is, still slogging on like a fool. She dabs at her forehead where it's already moistening.

'Come *on*, darling, before we both melt,' she pleads.

Her love story with Remy began in Nice, when her first French exhibition opened at a gallery there. She was twenty-eight and it was summer, the long hot day just starting to cool at last as the private view began, the night before the official launch. The other women there seemed either to be wearing cute minidresses or cool trouser suits, with sunglasses pushed up on their chic bobbed hair. Adelaide, meanwhile, was wearing a white kaftan she had made herself, with huge draping sleeves and a plunging neckline. *COURAGE*, she had stitched inside the hem, for old times' sake, and in a strange way, it helped. Her nose was sunburned from an afternoon spent on the beach, and her feet were bare; she worried for a moment she looked more Victorian orphan in a nightdress than artist of the moment, until she had two quick glasses of champagne, squared her shoulders and resolved to stop caring so much. Situated as they were, just off the Promenade des Anglais, you could hear the seagulls through the large open windows as the sky slowly turned pink beyond.

She was in a strange mood that evening; everything felt a little dreamlike, highly coloured. Amidst the dizzying winds of fortune buffeting her career, she was also coming to terms with the fact that her father had recently died – liver failure, after decades of alcoholism. One day she'd been at his funeral, standing alongside her hatchet-faced mother and brothers for the first time in years, the next she'd been on the plane to Nice. It felt as if she'd left something behind in England, something of herself. She didn't even like her dad at the end, hadn't done for a long time, but she couldn't yet square the fact that she'd never see him again. It left her feeling off balance, as if she'd lost her magnetic north. But then there was Remy walking towards her, and she recognised it, even then, as a moment of profound significance.

The air feels a degree cooler in this part of the tranquil cemetery and Adelaide raises her face to it gratefully. This is the best time of day to visit, before the tourists arrive in rucksack-toting packs, ticking off the treasure hunt of grave-stones they have set themselves: Piaf, Chopin, Wilde, Morrison, Proust, and all the others. Remy too, now, of course. He would have been thrilled to secure a spot here, she thinks to herself, pausing to nod respectfully at the tomb of Georges Seurat as she passes (rest in peace, Georges). The cemetery is huge but even so, they don't just allow any Tom, Dick or Harry to be buried within its grounds these days – there's a waiting list, and leases to be kept up for the privilege. Following Remy's death, Adelaide had made the application herself, with the backing of Coco, his other ex-wife, but over the years, she has wondered if it was selfish of them to keep him in Paris, however grand his final resting place. He had a complicated relationship with the city, put it that way.

Remy had been invited to her private view in Nice, along with a number of other emerging local artists, and Adelaide can picture him now: slight and sinewy in a mustard paisley shirt and tight trousers, sexy in the way he held himself proud and upright. Five foot seven herself, she was taller than him if she wore high heels, and his modest stature never failed to startle her because he had such a huge personality, the sort that could captivate a room within seconds. Her heart thudded as he introduced himself, telling her he thought she was very

116

talented, his grey eyes flickering over her as they spoke. Since Simon Dunster, she had avoided any involvements with men – 'I'm too busy,' she'd say dismissively – but found herself drawn to Remy nevertheless. Attracted.

It was still a rarity at that point to have a man respond to her art with compliments and thoughtful questions, rather than simply telling her what they thought she was trying to do (or, more usually, what they thought she *should* do). Her career was taking off – a painting of hers had been bought by the Museum of Modern Art in New York (such a thrill and honour), and there was talk of her representing the UK at the Venice Biennale – and she was having a wonderful time experimenting with more graphic styles in her work. And yet some men – many men – still seemed determined to explain her own pieces back to her, as if she was too stupid to decode them herself. ('So the gold sections of the piece represent capitalism, I'm assuming? Do you understand the concept of capitalism, Miss Fox?') She loved confounding their expectations, needless to say; she would always argue back, even if they were right, making up false responses on the spot if need be. ('I'm afraid you're quite wrong, the use of gold is a reference to Byzantine art, where it symbolised divine, transcendent light, embodying the invisible spiritual world. Do you understand what I mean when I say "Byzantine art"?')

Her critics were at a loss how to handle her, often resorting to snide put-downs. *Naïve. Simplistic. But is this* art? they would ask, making clear their own views. By contrast, Remy was so sure of himself, he didn't find it demeaning to praise her as a great artist, equal to her male counterparts. 'Yes, darling, but also I was trying to get into your knickers, don't forget,' he told her when she said this to him once.

Whatever, in the giddy unreal space that somehow straddled the darkness of death back home and the joie de vivre of this beautiful, sunlit city, she fell for him, hard and fast, pretty much from the first moment their paths crossed. For the rest of the evening, she remained aware of him wherever he was in the room, her body responding to him like a chemical reaction, her heart quickening each time he glanced back at her. And so, when the private view came to an end and the gallerist suggested an aperitif in a nearby bar, it seemed the most natural thing in the world to invite him along too.

This was their beginning, sweet and true − a single shot arrow meeting its target − but the relationship was never so smooth again afterwards. Theirs was a passion that ran like a furnace; sometimes it burned, sometimes it destroyed. They split up, they flung themselves back together; they screamed, shouted and loved with equal intensity. Their careers took them around the world − New York, Venice, Melbourne, Tokyo − but they both did their best work at the house they eventually bought in a small Provençal village just outside Avignon. It was their wedding present to one another, a space where creativity reigned supreme, where the rest of the world melted into the distance behind them.

She has reached his grave now, a grey marble stone, and thankfully it appears she is the first person there today.

'Hello again, old friend,' she says, her voice cracking on the words, because even now, when it's been more than twenty years, it hurts to remember that he's no longer around. That he won't ever look her way again; he won't inspire her, make her laugh, whisper something outrageous in her ear. She holds on to the top of the grave as she carefully bends to place the ribbon-wrapped white roses at its base, hoping her knees won't give out halfway down. 'You old sod,' she goes on ruefully. 'Always did have to disappear on me, didn't you? Always needed to have the last word. Oh, Jean-Paul – no!' Too late. Her dog has just cocked his leg unceremoniously on the marble stone, his stream of pee splashing the stems of the roses. 'Oh Lord.' A bubble of laughter rises in her throat. Remy was a dog-lover too, at least. He wouldn't mind a bit of pee on his grave, Adelaide is sure of it. Heaven knows, the two of them went through far worse together.

Her fingers tighten on the gravestone as she remembers his passing, which has always been such a weight on her. What else could she have done, though? Like her father, Remy was hell-bent on sliding face-first into a bottle, and nobody, it seemed, was able to haul him back up again. Then, of course, after his death, that bitch Monica had only compounded the misery.

She straightens up, trying to pull herself together, but it's no good, her heart is full to the brim with emotions and she has to dab her eyes and blow her nose, then take a few deep breaths in the hope of controlling her feelings. Lost in her own world, she doesn't hear the footsteps approaching behind her until there's a soft throat-clearing, a tentative voice. 'Adelaide? I thought you might be here.'

Chapter Thirteen

'Mum, I think I've found something,' calls Mia, rushing into the kitchen. It's Saturday lunchtime, and Jess is scrambling eggs in a pan. Here we go, she thinks. Although she doesn't regret driving them both out to Hythe yesterday in order to look at Little Bower, she hadn't banked on quite how enthusiastically Mia would throw herself into subsequent investigations. At this rate, she'll have the first episode of her own true crime podcast recorded and launched by the end of the day.

'More detective work?' Jess asks, grinding salt and pepper into the saucepan just as four slices of toast pop up. 'You couldn't butter those for me, love, could you?'

'More detective work,' Mia confirms, obligingly getting a knife. 'Headline news – I've found Colin Copeland's sister.'

'Wow!' Jess swings round to see a look of triumph on her daughter's face. 'Good going, Scoop. And? What have you discovered about her?'

'Well, she's pretty ancient now' – this could well mean that she's Jess's age, knowing her daughters' views on what qualifies as 'ancient' – 'but she's still not over what happened.

She's got a whole website about the injustice of Colin dying, and guess what?'

'What? How's that toast coming along?' Jess asks, turning the heat down under the pan.

'Your friend Adelaide is mentioned in her ramblings – more than once. And Eleanor – Colin's sister – found someone in the nearest village who saw Adelaide there at the time of Colin's death!'

Colin's death, indeed. Mia is talking about him as if he's a character in one of her podcasts, rather than a real person who died tragically young.

'At the *actual* time of death?' she pushes. Mia hasn't expressed any wish to be a journalist, but Jess is keen to instil in all of her daughters a healthy respect for facts.

'Well, no, not the *actual* time – like she didn't see Adelaide pushing him out the window or anything – but she was there *around* the time. Like, the day before.'

Jess doesn't reply immediately. Mia has become completely sold on the idea of Adelaide being a secret murderer, and Jess, although still nursing complicated feelings about the artist, should probably try harder to discourage her. If Mia starts repeating her theories online, she can imagine Lucas coming down pretty heavily with lawsuits and muzzling orders. 'She does have an alibi, remember,' she says, before sticking her head out of the door and yelling 'LUNCH!' to the other two.

'Yeah, one that Eleanor Copeland thinks was totally cooked up after the event,' Mia replies, eyes gleaming. 'He was in love with her, did you know that? Colin. He was mad about her.'

'Mad about Adelaide?'

'Yep. Eleanor reckons his room was practically a shrine to her. Loads of pictures of her stuck on his walls. He cut out newspaper clippings about her too, and kept them in a book.'

'Right. Like a superfan?' Jess dollops egg on to the buttered pieces of toast.

'More like a stalker. An obsessive. So, what I'm thinking happened is this: he followed her to the house one weekend, and she was like, "Do you know what? Fuck this—"'

'Er, less of that language, please.'

'—And kills him. Maybe accidentally, but still – she does it. I mean . . . it could have happened like that, right?'

Edie and Polly clatter into the kitchen, arguing hotly about a bottle of nail varnish they are both claiming as their own.

'Let's talk about it later,' Jess says to Mia, knowing her refereeing skills are about to be called into play. Even she, multitasker extraordinaire, can't manage two demanding conversations concurrently.

Nonetheless, as lunch gets underway, Jess can't help but admit to being intrigued by the mystery surrounding the place. Having pulled up in the lane yesterday, parking a short distance from Little Bower, she felt properly shivery to be there, at the former artists' studio. The house was set back from the road, a building that didn't want to be found easily, and was immediately striking, with its red bricks and tiled roof. The brick gave way to half-timbered sections beneath the eaves, and the windows at the front and side were huge, easily double the height of ordinary windows, with timber frames.

'That's where he must have fallen,' Mia said in hushed tones, pointing to the window on the eastern side of the building.

She'd spent the entire car journey digging through old news stories on her phone, so she was by now an expert authority regarding details of the body's discovery. 'Thank God for dog walkers, right? They seem to sniff out all the corpses. Maybe we should get a dog?'

'What, so you can take it to sniff out corpses? That's not going to happen. We've got a cat for one thing, remember.'

'Anyway, it's lucky this dog *did* sniff him out, otherwise poor old Colin could have lain there dead for days,' Mia had continued, unperturbed. 'He broke his neck, died instantly, they reckoned. So that's something, at least.'

The house was quiet as they approached, with only the sound of the wind in the trees. Beyond the house was a field of sheep, heads bent as they cropped the grass, but otherwise Jess and Mia were quite alone. Jess knows from her earlier online searches that the house has been redeveloped within, but the view of it from the lane must have been the exact same one that Adelaide and her friends would have had when coming here for some downtime from London. She imagined them all tumbling out of a car in the driveway, with suitcases and easels, or lounging around in the garden drinking gin martinis and gossiping. The picture Lucas sent her, of them clad in bikinis posing and laughing on the beach, came back to her mind and she felt a pang for the fun they must have had.

So immersed was she in her imaginings that it took her a moment to notice a face peering out of an upper window. For a wild split second, she felt as if she'd slipped back in time, and that it was Adelaide or Margie about to heave up the sash and call down to her, invite them in for a cocktail, and goosebumps immediately sprang up all over her arms. Back in the real world though, the middle-aged woman frowning there was presumably the current owner of the house, wondering why Jess and Mia were snooping about.

'We'd better go,' she muttered, not wanting to have to explain themselves.

Forking scrambled egg into her mouth now, while trying to negotiate a nail varnish peace treaty, she thinks back to Mia's breathless discoveries, of Eleanor Copeland's website and its claims. One thing's for sure: there's definitely more to the story than first meets the eye. But is it her place to investigate any further?

Chapter Fourteen

It's Coco, of course, beside her at the grave, with her own bouquet – far more lavish than Adelaide's affair, with foliage and cellophane. About twice the size, and with no added dog pee splashes either. This, in a nutshell, is how it has always been with her and her rival, she thinks, trying not to roll her eyes.

Coco must be in her late sixties by now but could pass as much younger, dressed in black, her hair an immaculate blonde bob. Beside her, Adelaide feels like an ageing, sweating elephant.

'Hello,' she says, hoping Coco didn't witness Jean-Paul's small controversial act moments earlier. 'How are you, and the boys?'

Coco was Remy's other wife, the one he abandoned her for at the end of the eighties. Furious and wounded like never before, Adelaide had reacted by leaving France for a perfectly timed commission in Tokyo, painting knot gardens for a gallery by day (strangely soothing) then overdoing it on the sake by night. Once that came to an end, she picked the job offer that was furthest away from Remy and Coco (pregnant already), accepting a place lecturing at the fantastic art school in Ottawa, which she surprised herself by loving. While Remy and Coco had one son, then another, Adelaide worked hard, nurtured her students, and was inspired by the majesty of the landscapes around her. She also found herself in a relationship with a sturdy good-natured Canadian photographer called Brad ('Bradelaide' the press nicknamed them for a while, which he loved and she hated) but deep down, she knew her heart was still in Paris.

'We're very well,' Coco replies, laying her bouquet on the grave so that it all but covers Adelaide's. 'Maxime is a journalist for *Le Figaro* these days, while Romain works at Opera Bastille.' She gives a small one-shouldered shrug, as if to say, naturally, her amazing sons have found their deserved high-status positions within French culture. 'And me, I am busy with my charity work.'

'Marvellous,' says Adelaide tightly. *Like a pretty little fairy,* Remy had described her that first time in his infamous diary, but his adoration wasn't to last. *Alas, she is but a doll, a doll with an empty brain. Nothing that interests or amuses me,* he was writing by the end. Not that Adelaide can afford to be smug, when he said far worse about her, the old bastard. In fact, the hotly contested publication of his diaries two years after his death was the one and only time she'd felt any kind of alliance with Coco. He had treated them both abysmally over the years. And his brutally honest diaries, sold to the highest bidder by that Judas Monica, humiliated them equally once copies hit the shelves. (She still hasn't forgiven Monica for that. Adelaide never should have introduced her to Remy in the first place, let alone encouraged him to take her on as his manager too. It goes without saying that Monica will come out of Adelaide's memoir very badly.)

She stares unseeingly at the grave, feeling a dull throb of rage at her former husband's multiple betrayals, the bruising to her heart still an ache. He let her down so badly, only compounding his infidelities by dying on her without so much as trying to recover. But he *did* love her, she reminds herself, thinking of him arriving in Berlin to pick her up once she'd finally been deemed well enough to leave the hospital. He had rescued her, taking her to Provence for a quiet recovery, just the two of them; exactly what she had needed.

'By the way,' says Coco, 'I was clearing out some of his belongings the other day, and I found a couple of things you should have. There's a small watercolour with your name written on the back – "For Adelaide", just that – and a letter for you, too, still sealed in its envelope, attached to the painting with a piece of tape.'

'A letter?' Adelaide repeats, startled. 'From Remy? What does it say?'

'I haven't *opened* it,' Coco says, folding her drapey black cardigan crossly around herself. 'I just said, it's sealed in an envelope. You might not think very much of me, Adelaide, but I do at least respect other people's privacy.'

Shame you didn't respect another woman's marriage, Adelaide feels like saying but doesn't. 'Well … thank you,' she replies, rather grudgingly. Even now, years on, she resents having to thank her for anything. 'Should I drop round to pick them up, or … ?'

'Perhaps we could meet for a drink. Catch up,' Coco says, much to Adelaide's surprise. What on earth do the two of them have to say to each other, after so long? *He loved me most! But I gave him two precious sons!* 'You look suspicious,' Coco comments, 'but this is not a trick.' She sighs, gesturing at the grave before them. 'Life is short, right? Too short to have enemies, to feel bitter. We could have a drink together, no? Moan about the terrible husband we had. Talk about how we loved him, also, perhaps.'

Adelaide swallows, uncertain how to respond. Her pride is saying *I'd rather die!* And yet she feels a twist of curiosity too, for what the two of them, Remy's pair of wives, might find to discuss. *Aren't you lonely?* Jessica asks earnestly in her head (shut up, Jessica) but it's true that she has deliberately made herself an island in the last decade, repelling social contact when the world has proved too much. She might disagree with Coco that life is too short for enemies (never) but it can become tiresome on an island, she has found of late.

'Very well,' she says eventually. 'Yes. Let's do that.'

A short while later, she makes an excuse to leave so that Coco can have Remy to herself. Despite everything, she's intrigued. A small watercolour, with 'For Adelaide' written on its back, one last letter . . . What will they say to her? Does she even want to know?

Chapter Fifteen

By the time the weekend is drawing to its close, Jess feels very much as if she'd like a second weekend to recover from the first. She's done three loads of laundry – David's washing machine apparently saw zero action while the girls were staying – she's restocked the food cupboards, she's been her usual taxi service, dropping the girls into town and to friends' houses as requested. She's bought Polly some new PE shorts and Mia a replacement phone charger (somewhere on this earth there is a vast pile of mislaid items that belong to the Bright girls, she is convinced). If that's not enough for one woman, she's also finished and sent off her sample chapter to Adelaide and Lucas, along with an invoice for the outstanding amount. Sometimes, very occasionally, Jess feels as if she is bossing life. It's bloody exhausting though, doing so much bossing single-handedly, she thinks, emptying the dishwasher that evening. However satisfying the achievements, it's not the same as having someone with whom to share them.

In the next moment, Mia's cryptic comment about David comes back to her. Is *he* still going through life single-handedly?

she wonders. Or has a new person appeared in his world, a person who means something to him, like Mia seemed to be suggesting? Then she's back to that awful evening from two years ago – *Jess . . . I need to tell you something* – with him awkward and defensive, pacing around the room, and her so stunned she could hardly take in the words.

Maybe his friends have been busily pairing him up at dinner parties and evenings out, like hers have tried. Maybe he's met a gorgeous colleague, the female version of him, who lives for sports and will happily discuss fast bowler stats and batting averages until the stars spangle the sky. No, wait, that was Bella, the twenty-five-year-old publicist in Brisbane. *I've been unfaithful*, David says again, pacing wretchedly, unable to meet her in the eye. *She's how old?* Jess remembers stuttering, revulsion curdling in her guts amidst the pounding shock. Not once had her eye even strayed towards another man during their married years. The idea of him peeling another woman's clothes off, his hands all over her body, their secret phone calls and text messages, covert arrangements in hotel rooms . . . It was as if he'd swung a wrecking ball at her world, and it was collapsing around her in rubble. *Jesus, David!* she had cried, hardly able to take it in. *How could you do this to us?*

There are some questions to which there are no answers though, she thinks grimly, sorting cutlery into the drawer. And there are some revelations from which there's no coming back, like it or not. Her thoughts turn to Adelaide and how hard it must have been for her when that twat Remy ditched her for the much younger Coco. From what she remembers of his explosive diaries, Remy had already slept his way around Parisian society by then, but for him to take up with pretty, vacuous Coco, after the fierce, passionate intelligence of Adelaide, must have been the ultimate kick in the guts. Still, Adelaide eventually forgave him, didn't she? She loved him again. Jess can't imagine such a volte face herself, but experiences a twist of regret that she won't get to hear the story recounted by Adelaide personally, for that part of the memoir. Never mind.

The dishwasher emptied, she shuts the door, feeling tired. If David's got a new partner, then good luck to him – and to this mysterious woman, too, for that matter. Jess, on the other hand, is far too busy to entertain such notions.

A week goes by, and a hefty payment from Adelaide lands in Jess's account, but there is no word, even of acknowledgement, regarding her chapter. Oh well. Perhaps it's for the best, seeing as Edie has been caught truanting again, Mia is still nursing a broken heart and Polly cracked a bone in her wrist in a cricket match which meant an A&E dash. Jess is glad she can be here, dependable home-based Mum, as they collectively limp on towards the end of the school year. Sometimes, however much you'd like a job to be the idealised version of your dreams, you have to recognise it for what it is, then take the money and move on. Which is exactly what she's been trying to do over the last few days: writing and submitting her agony column and pitching various features ideas – including ones about travelling alone in your forties, rediscovering a favourite city twenty plus years on, and a humorous piece about ghostwriting experiences. In desperation, she even pitched a piece about cat people and dog people to *Our Pet* magazine.

She's had a few interested sniffs – one broadsheet features editor was quite keen on the ghostwriting piece, until Jess made it clear that no, she couldn't actually divulge any personal details for risk of litigation, at which point they went cold on her. The pet magazine didn't even reply. Now she's wondering about proposing a feature about the London Bohemians and their lasting influence on contemporary art. A quick reread of the contract drawn up by Lucas reminds her that she is not permitted to reveal elsewhere any information learned in conversation with Adelaide – i.e. no hatchet jobs allowed – but there's nothing to stop her from researching this particular period of art history in retrospect.

Unfortunately a number of the members are no longer alive: Esme suffered a stroke several years ago and died in a nursing home on the south coast, Rita had a heart attack at her Galway home back in her sixties, and Jeanette had throat cancer and recovered from that, only to catch Covid in the first wave and die alone in a London hospital. Margie is still around at least, although lives in Pasadena these days, having retired from artist life with a couple of rescue dogs and armfuls of grandchildren, from what Jess can glean online.

Her fingers close reflexively around the snow globe on her desk as she takes stock. She's loved snow globes ever since she was a little girl and her Essex nanna gave her one for Christmas, featuring Father Christmas striding out across a snowy landscape, sack of presents on his back, a tiny robin perched on one shoulder. It was in her bedroom the whole time she was growing up, a calm little oasis on her chest of drawers, until the day – she must have been thirteen or so – she managed to drop a French dictionary on it, crumpling the globe to tiny irreparable shards. Farewell, Santa. Godspeed, tiny robin.

She upends the snow globe in her hand, letting the tiny white flakes flurry and settle. This one was given to her for her birthday a few years ago by Polly, and has the London Eye, Big Ben and Tower Bridge all crammed together (impossibly), along with a London bus and a black cab for good measure. 'Because you love London and you love snow!' Polly had cried triumphantly when Jess opened it, while David mouthed 'sorry' in the background, presumably thinking he'd aided the purchase of a particularly shit present. But – 'Clever you, I love it!' Jess had cried, hugging her daughter just as she'd hugged her Essex nanna that Christmas. 'Now I can have snow whenever I want to.'

Just as she's wondering, rather despairingly, if any features editors out there would be interested in a piece about snow globes (in July? Probably not), her phone rings. Her heart gives a nervous skip when she sees Lucas's number on the screen, because she can't lie, the chapter she sent off the other week was pretty unflattering in its depiction of Adelaide. You would not read it and think, *She sounds nice.* Is he going to have a pop at her for it? she wonders uneasily. What if her barbed words have caused Adelaide to suffer heart failure, or plunge into a demise? Mind you, she has been paid for the work, and promptly too, so it would be odd for him to be calling to complain now, wouldn't it?

Only one way to find out. She puts a hand on her heart and takes a breath. Then she slides her finger across the screen to answer the call. 'Hello?'

Chapter Sixteen

Adelaide stares down from the kitchen window to the square below, lost in memories. Remy's birthday is now over but he's still on her mind, not least because, irony of irony, an apartment in Place des Vosges was something he'd always dreamed about. She'd put in an offer on this place at the end of the nineties in a rush of anxiety and desperation, hoping it would give him a reason to live, but he'd died before she'd even signed the paperwork. Typical Remy. One last kick on his way out.

Down below, a tour guide is leading a sun-hatted group around the square, a Czechia flag tied on to his backpack, and Adelaide finds herself back in Prague, reliving a night she'd rather forget. She and Remy were at an after-show party in the city, where his exhibition, Le Temps du Monde, had been launched – to mixed acclaim as it would turn out, with some critics even mockingly calling him 'Monsieur Adelaide'. (This, needless to say, was about as welcome as an escaped convict knocking at the door.) But that was yet to come – the launch itself had been stuffed with Prague's great thinkers and cultural heavyweights, the buzz was positive, and although Remy had

135

become white-faced with temper earlier in the week over the placement of the paintings (reducing at least one poor gallery staff member to tears), he had relaxed into the role of star for the evening, visibly puffing up as the praise kept rolling his way.

It was a November evening, and Prague was cold and dark, with snow thick on the ground, blanketing the rooftops. Solitary lamp posts punctuated the old stone bridges like lit sentries, while the bars and restaurants were steamy-windowed, the comforts of warmth and merriment within. The gallery had thrown an after-party in the restaurant of an Old Town hotel, all white-clothed tables and silver service, a jazz trio noodling away in one corner. The mood was jubilant, until soon after the main courses had been cleared away, when Remy vanished without a word.

'Mister Lavigne, he is ill?' the Prague gallerist asked as the waitresses began bringing out the desserts – gargantuan slices of chocolate-and-cream-layered cakes, with coffee being served in thin scalding streams from tall silver pots.

'Is everything all right, Madame? Some problem with the food, you think?' the maître d' fretted in a low voice, hands behind his back as he leaned in towards Adelaide.

'What happened to Remy?' a journalist from the *Prague Post* asked, eyes gleaming with interest. 'Where is he? Something we should know?'

She couldn't answer their questions. She was as confused as they all were. Her eyes flicked continually to the restaurant exit, the doors of the toilets, hoping he would reappear with an apologetic smile, a story, some explanation. She even left the room and wandered around the hotel reception area searching for him – had he gone to make a call? Did he need a moment alone? – but he was nowhere to be seen.

Did he humiliate Coco so publicly too? she wonders now. Of course Coco has long been a star fixture in Adelaide's Art of Revenge shitlist so she's not about to start feeling *sorry* for the woman, but she can't help some idle speculation. From reading Remy's diaries, she knows he slept with a Moulin Rouge dancer the day after his son Maxime was born (could infidelity *get* any tackier?) but she imagines Coco was cocooned in a maternity wing with her baby at the time, blissfully unaware of her husband's atrocious behaviour. Having seen the other wife so recently, she has found herself unexpectedly interested in having that drink with her. The prospect of exchanging war stories with one who also fought on the same front is becoming more desirable by the day. And, of course, she is captivated by the thought of the final painting, final letter, with her name on. Irritatingly, she and Coco have been unable to find a convenient time in which to meet, and now the other woman has left town for Île de Ré, where Maxime has organised a fortnight-long break for the whole family.

The coffee machine hisses like a furious cat and Adelaide switches it off, trying not to think about Coco cycling girlishly around the island with her sons and their partners. She probably still has great legs, without a varicose vein in sight, and looks sensational in a huge floppy sun hat and Jackie O sunglasses. Is it too unkind to hold out hope for a veering bus, a distracted motorcyclist, a driver drunk at the wheel after a second lunchtime glass of wine? She supposes it is.

Back in Prague, she had gulped down a brandy at the bar before returning to the table, a nervous energy knotting up inside her. Yes, it was strange, she said to the woman next to her, trying to maintain her composure. No, he'd never done anything like this before. The chic wool dress she was wearing stuck to her back where she was sweating; her pressed powder useless when she attempted to tone down her flushed cheeks in the ladies. Dinner thankfully over, she marched back to the reception, a fixed smile making her jaw ache, and asked if someone could discreetly check the gents' loos and the various other bars around the hotel. Still nothing.

He would be back at the hotel across town where they were staying, wouldn't he? She would walk into the room and hear his excuses, his apologies. But as she pushed open the bedroom door a while later, she'd found it dark and silent, the bed neatly made, taunting her with its emptiness. Hovering in the doorway, snow melting on the shoulders of her coat, she suddenly remembered the way he and a waitress had been smiling at one another earlier that evening, and felt something crumple inside her. He wouldn't have, would he?

Oh, Adelaide. She could go back and shake herself for being so trusting. Of course he would. And of course he had. And he'd go on, moreover, to pull similar stunts again and again and again.

The doorbell sounds and she jumps out of her memories. It'll be Lucas, who rang first thing, suggesting he join her for her morning walk 'so that we can chat'. Heaven knows what *that* means. Has he stumbled upon something damning in the archive? Or is he about to ditch her too?

'On my way,' she calls, as she and Jean-Paul make their way down the stairwell.

It's another scorching day. Not yet nine o'clock and the air already feels sticky. The city will be clammy and slow-moving today, the streets crammed with sweaty tourists. For the first time in years, she finds herself thinking rather wistfully of drizzly English summers where everyone complains about the terrible weather. She'll be lying on the cool tiles of the kitchen floor panting like Jean-Paul if the temperature rises any higher here.

'So – good news. The publishers love Jess's sample chapter,' Lucas tells her as they cross the square. The trees are in full leaf and provide moments of blessed shade when dawdled beneath, but here they are in the centre without so much as a branch separating their bare heads from the sky. Lucas has a stern expression on his face, she notices, her heart sinking. Past experience tells her this means he's made up his mind and will not entertain any argument. 'And I have to say, I love it too!' he goes on. 'The writing is vibrant and entertaining, and I think she's really caught you, down to a tee – there's a spikiness that's very engaging.'

'Hmm,' Adelaide says. In truth, the chapter had taken her by surprise. Who knew apple-cheeked Jessica had such a mean streak in her? There's no cosiness, no romanticising, only Adelaide's pithy words, faithfully reproduced and ordered into crisp, articulate sentences. The other sample chapters that came back from earlier writers were revoltingly gushy in comparison. 'I'm not sure,' she goes on. Transcribing a few childhood stories is one thing, she figures, but wielding the knife against Simon, Remy, Coco, Monica, and all her other almighty grudges – that's quite another. Can Jessica really attain the levels of viciousness Adelaide would like to inflict?

'I think we should go ahead with her,' Lucas says, 'although please, for the love of God, you'll have to be nicer to her. No more hissy fits. No more holding back.'

'Hissy fits?' Adelaide repeats, drawing herself up to her full height with such indignation, she all but puts her back out. Be nicer, indeed, she thinks crossly. The day Adelaide adopts 'Be nicer' as a mantra to live by is the day she might as well shoot herself in the head. 'It's no wonder your wife left you, if this is the way you speak to women,' she retaliates, unable to stop herself.

A moment passes where he says nothing, but the set of his mouth lets her know that her rebuke is a low blow. Yes, all right. He has a point. 'Sorry,' she mumbles, but he's already speaking again.

'She's been to Little Bower, you know,' he says. 'There are photos on her Instagram. So I'm hoping that's a sign she's still interested in you, and the book.'

A prickle of unease skitters down Adelaide's back despite the muggy July morning. Jessica's been poking around Little Bower? She doesn't like the sound of that. What's she hoping to find?

'Hmm,' is all she says again. To give Jessica her credit, the small traps that Adelaide had set for her – the falsehoods, the deliberate omissions – were clearly spotted and sidestepped each time. The woman is not as gullible as she looks.

'You don't agree the chapter was well-written?' Lucas asks.

140

They're still in the middle of the square, waiting while Jean-Paul sniffs around the legs of a bench, and the next thing they know, a young man with floppy brown hair is rushing towards them, looking intent. Oh Lord. This'll be a starstruck fan, no doubt. She can spot them a mile off.

'Miss Fox? It *is* you, right?' he asks, an excited quiver in his voice. English, posh, the type who expects to be given everything he wants; she's met enough men like him to last her a lifetime. 'Can I get a selfie?'

'No, you certainly cannot,' she tells him. How she dislikes this fad of cameras in one's face, strangers encroaching on her personal space, expecting her to smile performatively into an outstretched lens. They can bloody well bugger off, the lot of them.

He looks crestfallen but backs away nonetheless. At least he's not muttering that she's a bitch like some of them do. 'Fair enough,' he says, then salutes her. 'Sorry to bother you. I find your work astonishing. It's a real honour to meet you.'

'Thank you,' she says graciously, then promptly dismisses him by turning to the dog. 'Come on, Jean-Paul, it's the same bench you sniff every single day.' The young man takes the hint and walks away, no doubt to try and take surreptitious photos from a distance. Whatever. She doesn't have the energy to care.

'Back to the memoir ...' Lucas prompts and she groans. She's tired of thinking about Jessica, the memoir, the whole stupid idea. She would like to travel back in time and return to Provence; paint apples like Cézanne, dive into an aquamarine pool, let the water close above her head. Switch off from the world. She remembers the pool she and Remy had at their Provençal house, how he would dive in so neatly, his lithe body drawing a perfect arc from land to water, leaving barely a ripple. She wants to spool all the way back, and make different choices. Try again.

'The publishers are keen,' Lucas says again, as if she cares what a bunch of people she's never met in London think. 'They're really behind this pairing. Think what it could mean for you – huge renewed interest in your work. Your story reaching thousands of people – millions, even – around the world. That'll be one in the eye for anyone who's ever wronged you, won't it?' he adds goadingly. 'The idiots who didn't believe in you.'

She eyes him suspiciously. She hasn't told him – or anyone, for that matter – that she means for her memoir to be the ultimate act of revenge. Has he guessed at her intentions?

'Perhaps I should talk to her,' she concedes after a moment as Jean-Paul finally concludes his bench explorations and they set off once more. 'See if we can bear the thought of working together for a little longer.'

'Or maybe I could speak to her?' Lucas suggests. 'Test the waters.'

'Oh, all right,' she says. 'And you can take that smirk off your face, too,' she adds without even having to look at him. 'Don't go thinking I've become a pushover in my dotage.'

'That'll be the day,' he replies.

PART TWO

Chapter Seventeen

A few weeks have passed and Jess is back on the Eurostar, headed for Paris once more, but everything feels different this time. *She* feels different. What a thrill to have some power for a change, to be able to say to Lucas that no, she *couldn't* immediately hotfoot it back to France actually, even if his spiky old aunt *was* clicking her fingers – she had some other very important work lined up first. She supposed she'd be able to return to the memoir by August. (Truth be told, the so-called important work didn't exist: she was taking the girls for a week's holiday in Norfolk, but he and Adelaide didn't have to know that. Let them think she's in high demand and doing them a favour by saying yes at all.)

The timing is fortuitous too, as David is having the girls for the next fortnight of school holidays. For the rest of the summer he'll be covering test cricket matches around the country, and then jetting off to India come the autumn for the Men's Cricket World Cup, so this is pretty much the only fortnight Jess can commit to Adelaide in Paris. Will that be enough for her to gather all the information she needs from her subject? It's going to have to be, she thinks. Plus there are always video calls, even if Adelaide apparently detests them.

Jess still isn't used to carving up school holidays with her ex-husband this way; it's only the second summer they've had to do such a thing. The prospect of David taking the girls away without her feels very strange. They left yesterday morning for Italy, where he's apparently rented them a fancy-sounding Tuscan villa with its own pool, according to Polly. It's not a competition, obviously, but this will certainly outdo Jess's own recent holiday arrangements, with them staying in a slightly damp-smelling (but otherwise delightful!) cottage a mile's trek from the nearest beach. 'Seriously? I've got to share with Edie *and* Mia?' Polly had exclaimed in dismay on arrival. 'God, Mum, this is a punishment, not a holiday!' (Jess sometimes thinks that Polly must have been a princess in another life; she definitely has the air of someone who feels permanently short-changed in this one.) 'We're getting a bedroom *each* in Italy, you know. All with our own bathrooms and everything. Not like . . .'

'Shut up, Polly,' Edie had told her, and for a moment, Jess had thought she was in for some daughterly loyalty, until her middle-born added, 'Like we want to share with you either!'

As for Mia, who spent the week in Norfolk exhibiting the world-weariness of a seventeen-year-old who was there entirely under duress, she has sprung a small surprise on Jess and David. By the way, she won't be getting on the plane back from Italy with her dad and sisters at the end of that holiday, she's going to get a train to Nice the day before, where she's arranged to meet a group of friends for a girls' holiday. 'Don't worry, I've saved up and I'm paying for it all myself!' she said when this bombshell was dropped.

'That wasn't the bit I was most worried about,' Jess replied. Still, after some discussion, she and David have consented to the plan. Mia will be eighteen in September, after all, and has promised to a) be sensible, b) look after herself, and c) answer her bloody phone when her mum needs to check in every now and then. Times are changing, thinks Jess, gazing out of the train window as the English countryside speeds by.

In the meantime, she has her own adventures to think about, with a full two weeks in Paris now on the horizon, plus a further four months of writing afterwards, with the aim to deliver a first draft of the book by Christmas. Guaranteed income! A fantastic publishing team! Solid work for the rest of the year! What's more, following a pep talk from Becky, she's laid down a few ground rules of her own. 'Don't you dare let her shout at you or treat you like shit again,' her friend had said. 'You're a human being with feelings, even if she isn't.'

Jess hasn't been quite as blunt as all that, but she has spelled it out to Lucas – or Luc as he always signs off in his emails – that if she's going to write a good memoir, she needs to have all the facts available to her. 'I know full well Adelaide was holding back on me half the time before,' she said when they spoke on the phone. 'I can't do my job if she's keeping important details to herself.'

Let's see if things are different the second time around anyway. She's booked into the same hotel as previously, and is already looking forward to catching up with Beatrice, not to mention seeing Valentin at the brasserie. More excitingly, she's wasted no time in arranging a new date with gorgeous Georges, which makes her feel hot and bothered (in a good way) whenever she thinks about it. You bet she's packed her favourite black jumpsuit for the occasion, the one that always makes her feel glamorous and sexy. It's summer! It's Paris! He's a very handsome old flame! How many more reasons does a woman need to dress up?

She touches the golden charm around her neck, her fingers closing about the tarnished half-heart shape. Following some major ransacking of all the boxes stowed in the attic, containing ancient diaries, school magazines, photo albums, university essays and the like, she had found it: the necklace that mirror-matches Pascale's, bought over two decades ago, that fateful summer in Paris. She'll probably never know the truth of what happened to her friend back then, but maybe she can revisit some of their old haunts as a means of honouring her memory.

That's for Future Jess, though. Right now, she has a juicy novel to read, plus a cup of tea and a large flaky *pain au chocolat* from the buffet car. As the train plunges into the channel tunnel, she finds herself looking forward to the next fortnight on the other side.

Chapter Eighteen

To say that Adelaide is jittery about Jessica returning to her apartment on Monday morning sounds ludicrous but . . . well, the fact is, she *does* feel rather churned up inside at the prospect of starting over, knowing that this time, she's in it for the long haul. No more weaselling out of questions she doesn't like the sound of. No more avoiding difficult truths.

There's the doorbell ringing, right on time, and there's Jean-Paul leaping up from his cool refuge on the kitchen floor to emit a shrill volley of barks, and there goes Marie-Thérèse, tromp tromp tromp, to answer the door. And so they begin again.

'Morning, Adelaide, morning, Jean-Paul!' says Jessica, walking in, looking rather chic in a short-sleeved white satin shirt and cropped navy trousers. She's carrying a large bag, and goes on to produce not only a packet of doggy treats – 'We're friends now, aren't we, Jean-Paul?' – but also a box of PG Tips teabags, some crumpets, a jar of Marmite and a block of Cadbury's Dairy Milk chocolate. 'Just a few treats from home for you,' she says, setting them out on the coffee table.

It's so thoughtful of her that Adelaide is momentarily lost for words. Back in her day, she became used to grand gestures – armfuls of flowers, awards, champagne receptions – but it's been a long time since anyone thought to offer her small everyday gifts like these. Ridiculous, really, that a packet of supermarket-brand crumpets and some teabags could cause tears to prick her eyes, but there you are.

'That's very kind of you,' she says. 'Gosh, I haven't had Marmite for years.' She reaches out to touch the yellow lid of the Marmite jar with a little smile. 'Decades. Thank you. I always knew you were the right person for this job.'

It's a joke, of course, a little joke at both of their expenses, and not especially funny, but it serves as an icebreaker because Jessica smiles in response, and says, 'Oh, absolutely, me too!' Then they look at each other, rather apprehensively at first, but it's as if whatever happened before is now over and they can move on. Here's hoping, anyway.

Marie-Thérèse is ordered to make them a pot of tea with Adelaide's new gift and then they get down to business. Jessica begins by suggesting they spend some time up front discussing the memoir as a whole, so that they're on the same page, so to speak, from the outset. They need to think about structure, she says, establish what Adelaide wants the book to *do*, and if there are particular areas she wants to focus on more than others. She has an idea about calling each chapter by the name of one of Adelaide's paintings, and has already drawn up a provisional list.

'Just a thought,' she says, retrieving a typed piece of paper from her bag. 'Also, have a think about what's off limits to readers. I know there are certain areas you weren't keen to get into last time around – which was fair enough – and of course the final say on everything will be yours. But—'

'Nothing's off limits,' Adelaide interrupts. 'I'll tell you whatever you want to know. Everything. In fact, I'm looking forward to getting a few things off my chest, setting the record straight once and for all.'

Jessica's eyes widen. 'Even ... what happened to your brother?' she checks. 'And – well, I apologise for sounding indelicate – but you mentioned a rape ...'

'Yes, I'll tell you about that. And I'll tell you how I burned his flat down afterwards. And ruined his face for ever,' Adelaide says briskly, which causes Jess to look even more startled. Appalled, possibly. Buckle up, kiddo, she thinks. That's just the start of it. Then she takes a deep breath because, despite her bravado, the next words will be harder. 'I'll tell you about William too.'

Jessica meets her gaze. 'Are you sure?'

Adelaide takes a moment, reconsiders. *Is* she sure? It's the part of her life where the retelling will feel most like self-flagellation, rather than hitting out at someone else. She's carried William's story around with her for so many years; she is used to bearing its weight alone by now, like a burden on her back. What if she releases it aloud into the air, on to a printed page, and the load feels reduced as a result? Would that be a good thing, or would it be nobler to continue bearing the punishment? She shuts her eyes briefly, takes in a breath. Squares her shoulders. Then she gestures towards Jessica's phone.

'Is that thing recording?' she asks.

★

William was the nicest boy that ever lived. Fourteen months her junior, the two of them had been the best of friends from day one. 'Peas in a pod,' their mum used to say, eyes fond, when she was in a good mood. 'Thick as thieves,' she would mutter disapprovingly whenever they were naughty. William had a shock of brown hair, blue eyes, freckles and, in Adelaide's memory, always a missing tooth. He had a loud laugh and could be exuberant, although he was given to shyness too, hiding behind their mum's legs whenever the garrulous, cheek-pinching aunts were visiting. He and Adelaide loved nothing more than mucking about in the old bomb sites around Stepney with the other boys and girls from the neighbouring streets, even though this activity was strictly forbidden by everyone's parents.

'We would play down by St Katharine Docks, which had been heavily bombed in the Blitz and was pretty derelict,' she tells Jessica, conjuring up the place in her mind: the empty warehouses with their broken windows so that you always felt as if you were being watched, the murky water slopping against the dock walls, the stark holes on the horizon where buildings had once stood.

'In the summer we sometimes went to Yorkshire to see my grandparents, or we'd stay with one of our aunts who had a house in Surrey – she had a proper garden, which we thought was ever so posh,' she says. She's back there again as she speaks, racing up and down the lawn with her brothers, trying to climb the apple tree, her hands turning green with the lichen on its trunk and branches. They must have looked such ragged little urchins, the four of them, she thinks, as Jessica punctuates the conversation with detailed questions: where in Yorkshire, and how would they get there? Can she remember the name of the street where her aunt lived? Anything else about the house – smells? Pets? How Adelaide felt – happy, homesick, free? – whenever she was there?

Adelaide spins this out for as long as possible, recounting everything she can think of, which is plenty. But there comes a point where she finally has to look the end of William's story in the eye and say the words aloud.

'And then one summer, when I was ten and William nine, my mum and dad said they had a big surprise for us,' she goes on. 'They'd been saving all year, and we were going to have a seaside holiday, our very first one, in Margate, for a whole week. Well! You can imagine the excitement. We were beside ourselves. We'd never had so much as a glimpse of the sea before; it was something you only heard about in stories.' A wistful feeling steals in as she conjures up their collective giddiness once more, how she and William had clutched one another in glee as their mum broke the news. 'And then we arrived, and it was such a thrill, seeing that huge stretch of blue for the first time. How vast the sky seemed above it. A proper Turner sky,' she adds, although of course that phrase meant nothing to her at the time. She thinks of herself as a little girl, gazing up at the screeching seagulls, her hair in plaits, freckles all over her nose.

'The train was packed, and delayed too, I think,' she goes on, 'and so we were all rather hot and bothered when we arrived in Margate, but almost immediately, as we headed down to the seafront, our spirits lifted with the newness of the place, the adventure it felt just to be there. My brother Robert said, "Even the air smells different here!" and we all put our noses up like dogs, sniffing away until my mum told us to pack it in, polite children didn't *sniff*, and if we didn't stop making such a show of ourselves, we'd be straight back to London on the next train.' The scene has unspooled in her head as clearly as if it took place just yesterday. Astonishing the way that can happen, when she often couldn't tell you what she was doing last Tuesday. 'I haven't thought about that for decades,' she confesses.

'It's a great image,' Jessica says, smiling encouragingly.

'We were staying in a boarding house a street or two back from the main beach,' Adelaide goes on. 'And for the first few days, we were in heaven. The weather was perfect – we spent hours on the beach every day, building castles on the beautiful pale golden sand, running in and out of the water. Peter and Robert could swim but William and I couldn't, so—' She falters for the first time, gulps a breath. 'Sorry,' she mumbles, knotting her fingers in her lap as the rest of the sentence sticks in her throat. It's harder than she imagined to find the words.

'Take your time,' says Jessica. 'Say as much or as little as you want to right now. We can come back to this later if you prefer.'

Adelaide nods, pleating the folds of her skirt between her fingers, remembering the warm sunshine on her bare limbs, the dazzle in her eyes. She can almost feel the wet sand squidging between her toes again as she crouched at the water's edge digging moats and channels with her hands. The taste of egg and cress sandwiches and salted crisps, packed up in greaseproof paper for them by the boarding house landlady each morning. How one day they had unpacked the picnic to discover soft iced buns with glacé cherries on top there too, and they'd all cheered with delight.

'And then, one afternoon, we were playing beach cricket with some other children,' she says. She can feel it now, the weight of the damp tennis ball in the curve of her palm. Her sport-mad brother Peter had patiently shown her how to bowl, moving her right arm back and around in a circle, and she took to it as if she'd been playing all her life. 'Nice work!' an older boy in the group cried when she bowled out William with her first try, and Adelaide felt the heady glow of an older child's praise rush around her body as she tried to look nonchalant.

'William didn't want to play any more,' she tells Jessica. He was small for his age and one of the youngest there, and a couple of the older girls had taken to tittering whenever he flailed the bat around or fumbled a catch. She hesitates, remembering his flushed face, the brightness of his eyes that told her he was close to tears. 'This is boring, let's play castles again,' he'd said to Adelaide, tugging at her arm.

'And I felt conflicted,' she tells Jessica quietly. 'Because I loved playing castles with my little brother but I loved being with the big kids too. Feeling that I'd moved up a notch to their gang. Been accepted.'

Jessica has stopped chipping in with her endless questions, Adelaide notices in the charged silence that follows. She's being sensitive, no doubt, but it only serves to make Adelaide feel utterly alone. She shuts her eyes briefly but there's Will's small disappointed face in her mind, the downturn of his mouth as if her rejection is the final straw. She opens them again immediately because it still hurts to picture that skinny little boy pleading with her.

'I said no,' she goes on, the words an effort to drag from her mouth. 'I turned my back on him.' She's trembling all over and Jean-Paul, sensing her distress, comes to her side, pressing his body against her leg. She could cry for his kindness as she reaches down, comforted by the sheer solid goodness of him. What did humans ever do to deserve the love of dogs?

'William went into the sea on his own, even though he knew he wasn't allowed to,' she says, the room hushed as if the very walls are listening. 'None of us were watching him.' She swallows, imagining his slight frame as he would have waded into the treacherous water, his bare shoulders pink from the sun and rigid with defiance. Was he crying? she has always wondered. He must have felt so rejected in that moment. 'Later on a man said a wave had just knocked him right over. He must have been pulled under before he knew what was happening.' She presses her lips together. 'It can take seconds for a child to drown, you know. They can be there one minute and gone the next. And that . . . that's what happened with Will.'

She can't help herself: a sob comes out with his name and she puts a hand to her face because it still feels so raw, so painful to think about him struggling for breath under the water as his small lungs filled. She remembers the shout that went up along the beach behind her, the chill that travelled the length of her as if she knew, on a cellular level, that her life was about to change for ever. The game stopped. They turned. Someone

156

was screaming and then Adelaide's mum was racing across the sand towards a man in red shorts who was staggering out of the sea holding the limp, pale body in his arms. 'My baby!' Adelaide's mum was screaming. 'My baby boy!'

'Oh Adelaide,' Jessica is saying somewhere nearby. 'How awful. I'm so sorry.'

Adelaide can no longer speak. She feels overwhelmed by the emotional storm raging inside her, the memories she has locked away for so long assaulting her like bolts of lightning.

'I have always blamed myself,' she says, choking on the words. 'If I hadn't pushed him away ...'

'Oh no! You mustn't blame yourself,' Jessica cries passionately, and she must have got up from her chair because in the next moment, she's pressing a tissue into Adelaide's palm, putting a gentle hand on her back. 'You were only a child yourself. A *child*, Adelaide, you mustn't take any blame. Every sibling that ever lived will have chosen someone else to play with at some point. Of course what happened wasn't your fault.'

Adelaide tries valiantly to recover herself but it takes a few moments. 'Thank you,' she manages to say eventually, wiping her eyes and blowing her nose. Jessica slides back to her own seat where she waits in respectful silence, her expression one of concern when Adelaide finally dares chance a look. 'Sorry,' she mumbles, patting Jean-Paul if only to give herself something to do. 'Goodness. I feel as if I'm in therapy.' She blinks a couple of times, pushing away the later memories of that holiday: the desperate – and hopeless – attempts to revive William on the sand. The numb trek back to the boarding house, her head ringing with shock and guilt. It didn't seem real for ages and ages. How could it be real? Her aunts arrived in a twittering cluster, helping them pack up, supporting Adelaide's mum bodily into the train carriage. And then they were home, to the terrible emptiness that was their house without Will there, and an ache began in Adelaide that has lasted throughout all the years since.

'It's hard to lose someone,' Jessica says quietly. 'It must have been devastating for you. But we can pay tribute to his lovely nature in the book, can't we? We can chart his place in the world, immortalise him in print. I know it's not the same . . .' She breaks off as Adelaide dabs her eyes again. 'Should I make you a cup of tea? Or would you rather have a break, get some fresh air?'

Limp after telling her story – one that she never even told in full to Remy – Adelaide isn't sure *what* she wants. She feels like one enormous tender bruise. But Jessica is kind, she acknowledges. Kind in a way that means Adelaide has not been left feeling embarrassed or vulnerable about her emotions.

'Fresh air sounds good,' she agrees eventually.

Ten minutes or so later, and Jessica has shepherded them to Chez Louis, a small pavement café which has a bowl of water outside for thirsty dogs, and comfortable wicker chairs. This *was* a good idea, Adelaide thinks, already revived for being outdoors, instead of trapped inside with her worst memories.

'According to Beatrice at the hotel, the pastries here are sensational,' Jessica says, as they take seats at a free table. She adjusts the parasol above them so that Adelaide is bathed in cooling shade.

'Well, we *are* in Paris,' Adelaide can't resist reminding her. 'Excellent pastries are not difficult to find.' Nevertheless, as she ties Jean-Paul's lead to her chair handle, she finds herself tempted by the sight of a fat sticky *pain aux raisins* being delivered to a nearby table, while Jessica, having gone inside to inspect the full range on offer, returns having decided to try a *chouquette*, a small golden choux bun studded with sugar crystals.

'*Deux, peut-être?*' the waitress suggests when she comes to take their order. 'They are *very* little, Madame.'

'*Absolument,*' replies Jessica, dimpling. '*Merci.*'

'And for you, Madame?' the waitress goes on, turning to Adelaide. Then she clutches at her chest, eyes wide. 'Oh, Madame Fox! This is such an honour! I love your work!'

'Thank you very much,' Adelaide says, dreading the inevitable selfie request. But the waitress merely gushes a breathless 'I am *so* happy to meet you, Madame' before remembering her place and blushingly taking the order.

It's enough of a distraction to lessen the tension that previously gripped Adelaide's body although she's not looking forward to the moment when Jessica will say in that bright way of hers, 'So! Where were we?' as a means to nudge them back into the aftermath of Will's death. But instead, she looks rather dazzled herself.

'Wow,' she says. 'Does that happen often?'

'Most days,' Adelaide tells her, and starts describing some of the more outlandish encounters she's had: complete strangers asking her to sign parts of their bodies (with one woman even getting a tattoo of the resulting signature), others who presented her with drawings, flowers, declarations of love . . . But then something terrible happens. She hears a bark and realises that Jean-Paul has shot out from under the table towards a West Highland terrier, his lead dragging behind him.

'Jean-Paul!' she shouts in alarm. The road is pedestrianised so there are no cars but all the same, you get bicycles speeding down these streets, and idiots on electric scooters, fast enough to smack straight into a small dog who isn't looking where he's going. 'Jean-*Paul*!' In frantically hauling herself up from her chair, she bashes against the table, which will see her garlanded with a bruise the size of a saucer tomorrow. Jessica is nimbler and faster, thankfully, and leaps up in an instant, rushing over to grab the end of the Staffie's lead.

'Jean-Paul, you chump!' Adelaide cries, stumping towards them, her heart pounding with the exertion. She is to blame though, not tying his lead to the chair securely enough. Too caught up in her own woes, her guilty memories! But he's okay, she realises in the next moment, stooping a little and putting a hand to her heart. In fact, he's having a marvellous time, prancing about with the Westie, mock-fighting as the two dogs take it in turns to rush at one another and spin about. It's all Jessica – and the Westie's owner – can do to remain on two feet as the dogs chase around.

'I'm sorry,' Adelaide says in French – to Jean-Paul, mostly, but also to the Westie's owner, a very chic-looking older woman with neatly shingled white hair and huge sunglasses, wearing a long dusky pink dress and Birkenstock sandals. 'I thought I had tied him to my chair but – Jean-Paul!' She finds herself lapsing into English in her agitation as he leaps up at the woman with great exuberance. 'That's enough.'

The other woman smiles and bends down to make a fuss of the excited Staffie. 'That's quite all right,' she replies, her accent transatlantic. 'Aren't you the sweet one, hey? Lovely boy!'

Jean-Paul is usually rather stand-offish with other dogs, likewise with humans that aren't Adelaide, but in the next moment, he's rolled on to his back right there on the pavement so that this white-haired woman can give him a belly rub, an honour he normally reserves for Adelaide alone. Since when did he get so fickle? Jessica hands over his lead and Adelaide gives it a small tug.

'Come on, now,' she tells him. 'Sorry,' she says again to the woman.

The other woman takes the hint and stands up. 'Nice to meet you both,' she says.

'You too!' echoes Jessica, giving the Westie a friendly pat. Then they head back to the table, where the waitress, still looking starstruck, is setting down their drinks and pastries. 'Flipping Nora, are you okay?' Jessica asks Adelaide. 'This morning is turning into a rollercoaster for you, all in all.'

Adelaide smiles faintly at the 'Flipping Nora' – something her own mother used to say. She hasn't heard it for years. Sinking into her seat, still holding tightly to the lead, her heart finally slows from the shock. Jean-Paul, the little wretch, is lying down again as if he wouldn't dream of dashing off anywhere.

'I'm fine,' she says, breaking off a piece of the *pain aux raisins* and posting it into her mouth. The buttery pastry is crisp and flaky, dissolving on her tongue, and for a moment, William is back in her head, there on the beach, exclaiming rapturously over his iced bun as if it was the finest delicacy in the land. How her sweet-toothed younger brother would have loved the cakes and desserts here in Paris, she thinks with sudden fondness. And what she would give to have him across the table from her now, eyes alight as he recounted his latest doings! She has often wondered about the man he would have grown up to become, how their lives might have overlapped in all the years after that Margate day. Everything could have been so different with him there at her side. Her dad might not have drunk so much. Her mum would have been happier. As for Adelaide herself, would she have even left home at sixteen, as she did? Would she have become the person she is now?

Jessica is right though, she decides – she owes it to him to bear witness to his life as well as hers, to record everything for posterity.

She manages a small smile at the younger woman, indicates her head towards Jessica's phone. Deep breath, Adelaide. You can do this. 'Shall we?' she says. 'I'm ready to go on whenever you are.'

Chapter Nineteen

Dare Jess say it? She's tentatively enjoying this new working relationship with Adelaide so far. No sarcastic remarks. No being made to feel gauche or like some kind of village idiot. They are polite to one another. Respectful, even. She's pretty sure Adelaide is finally being honest with her too. The version of her childhood that has emerged today has been far fuller, far richer than the slim pickings offered up previously.

Admittedly, they are a mere day into the fortnight. There's plenty of time for things to go wrong – for shouts and sulks, for Jess to be ordered home once more on a petulant whim. She mustn't get ahead of herself. But as she leaves Adelaide's apartment at two o'clock that first Monday afternoon after several long sessions of talking, there is a spring in her step; the particular bounce that comes from knowing you are on to something. That there's a good story with your name on it, and still plenty more to come. If Jess gets this right – if the two of them can stay the course – then the memoir could be the making of her. The source material is

163

already incredible – inspiring, unexpected and deeply moving. Unbearably moving at times, in fact.

Her eyes cloud, remembering Adelaide's grief that morning. The pain on her face, the tears sliding down her cheeks for a precious lost brother. Jess had urged her to let go of her feelings of guilt but she could see that the artist has castigated herself over his loss in all the years since. The journalist in Jess might have been thrilled to have the story unravel with such raw honesty, but the woman in her could only empathise and feel sorrow at her subject's distress. (The sister in her intends to call her brother for a proper chat soon. Maybe sort out a time they can catch up in person later this summer.)

She hopes Adelaide will be okay following the tumult of their session. 'You know, I live pretty near Margate myself,' she'd found herself blurting out as they were saying goodbye. 'If you ever wanted to . . .' Then she'd faltered, because why on earth would a person want to revisit a place associated with such trauma? It's not as if Adelaide's going to have a jolly day out there and go home with a stash of souvenirs. 'Sorry, I don't know why I said that,' she was forced to conclude. 'Ignore me.' Adelaide's expression told her that was exactly what she planned to do, as they agreed on a time for tomorrow. It's hard, picking through difficult memories. As she of all people knows.

'Heading back now, are you, to write everything up?' Adelaide asked as she was about to depart. 'Or are you going to enjoy some sightseeing first?'

Wow, check out Adelaide and her small talk, Jess marvelled, trying to hide her surprise. But it felt significant too, that the other woman was making an effort to get to know her for the first time.

'I'll probably go back and jot a few things down, yes,' she replies, 'although ...' She hesitated. 'Well, at some point, I want to revisit the place where I worked for a while, after university. Hotel d'Or, do you know it? I had a good friend there back in the day.'

'In Faubourg Saint-Germain? Yes, I used to do a lot of pavement-café sketching around there, years ago now. There were always fascinating characters to draw.'

'Oh God, I can imagine!' Jess replied, picturing some of the wealthy guests she'd encountered, the men in tailored suits, the women dripping with jewels and furs. It's funny to think about Adelaide sitting nearby observing the comings and goings of the beautiful people, with the likes of Jess and Pascale sneaking out for cigarettes and coffee in their black and white uniforms. 'I wonder if our paths ever crossed back then?' she added with a shy smile. 'Anyway. I'll leave you to it. See you tomorrow.'

She picks up her pace now as a memory returns to her, of walking into the tiny basement staff bedroom she and Pascale shared, to see her friend standing before the mirror, applying mascara.

'Jess, if I were to ask you to help me with something a bit dangerous ...' Pascale had begun, voice cagey.

Pascale, she noticed, was wearing Jess's new dress, the tight, black off-the-shoulder one she hadn't even worn herself yet.

'Hey! Cheeky cow,' she'd interrupted. 'Who said you could borrow that?'

'Ahh.' Pascale paused, one set of eyelashes thick and spiky, the other soft and fuzzy. 'You don't mind, do you? Please! But I look so beautiful in it, *non?*'

Hotel d'Or might have been a glamorous sanctuary for its guests, but for the staff cleaning up after them, it was sheer hard work. On this occasion, Jess was knackered after a long shift that had involved scrubbing umpteen skid marks from toilets, removing used condoms from bed linen, and fending off not one, but two over-amorous male guests who viewed the chambermaids as fair game. In short, she wasn't in the mood to admire her friend's beauty, especially as Pascale had the annoying knack of looking better in anything than Jess did. It was particularly aggravating when the dress in question was her own, meaning that now she would always be reminded of how much sexier Pascale looked in it.

'Suit yourself,' she growled, slamming into the bathroom.

It was only later, shampooing her hair as the steaming water fell around her, that she replayed Pascale's opening remark. *If I were to ask you to help me with something a bit dangerous . . .* What the hell was that about? But by the time she emerged, clean and fragrant, wrapped in towels, Pascale had gone, leaving only a faint breath of sandalwood perfume behind her.

Well, where was she going? the head of housekeeping, Sylvie, asked the next morning when Pascale wasn't there for her shift.

What did she tell you? the neatly bearded police officer asked a few days later, when Pascale's parents had raised the alarm. *People don't just disappear, mademoiselle. Who was she going to meet?*

Jess didn't know. She couldn't answer. All she could hear

in her head was Pascale's strange unfinished question. Help with what? she fretted. What, exactly, had her friend got herself into?

People don't just disappear, the police officer had said, but they did, apparently. They could vanish into thin air, new black dress and all. Walking along the street now, Jess's fingers close around the gold charm on the necklace, the trinket that has remained half a heart ever since that day, never to be reunited with its pair. Oh, Pascale. Whatever happened to you? Where did you go?

She's been wandering blindly all this time, steeped in old memories, but realises in the next moment that she's about to pass Brasserie Les Amours. She'll put her head in to see if Valentin is working, she decides, because she could do with a friendly face right now. And if he *is* working and chooses to upsell her a cold glass of wine and a late lunch, then who is she to say no?

Alas – for her, anyway – he must have a day off because another apron-clad waiter is attending to the outdoor tables today. Never mind. Lunchtime wine is probably a bad idea anyway, when she has some poignant material to transcribe this afternoon. Then she notices that the elderly man she previously spotted at the nearby *crêperie* is there once more, sipping a tiny espresso at one of the pavement tables. Today he's wearing a white linen shirt and tan trousers, his feet in stylish loafers that are conker-coloured and every bit as shiny. His white hair is neatly cropped and he has on black-framed glasses as he studies the newspaper on the table before him, carefully licking a finger before he turns a page. He's always there, alone, she registers with a small frown, wondering what his story might be.

As if he can detect her gaze, the man glances her way and raises one hand in a wave. '*Bonjour, Madame*,' he calls and she blushes to be caught staring, before waving back.

'*Bonjour*,' she replies and then, on impulse, veers towards him. '*Ça va?*' she asks politely, trying to make up for the staring.

'*Ça va bien, merci*,' he replies. He has amused-looking brown eyes and rises in his seat as she approaches. '*Et vous?*'

What is she doing? She has work to be getting on with – that Margate memory won't write itself up – but when he gestures to the seat opposite his with a friendly smile, she finds herself smiling right back and sitting down.

'*Merci!*' she says, then adds in answer to his question, '*Bien, merci*.' She pulls a face at her rather basic answer. '*Pardon. Je suis Anglaise et . . .*'

'Ahh! I did wonder,' he says in English when she falters again, and she blinks in surprise at the American-sounding twang in his voice. She'd had him down as a local through and through. 'My name is Alain, I'm French-Canadian. I grew up in Quebec but then met the most beautiful woman from Paris forty years ago and so . . .' He shrugs. 'Life took me here.'

'How romantic!' Jess sighs, delighted. Okay, and he *does* count as a local, then, if he's been here forty years. 'There are so many love stories in this city.'

'Ahh!' He smiles and leans a little closer. 'Does that mean that there is a love story for you here also?'

She should be so lucky. 'No,' she says, but in the next moment finds herself thinking of Georges, and the killer jumpsuit hanging in her hotel bedroom, ready for their date in two days' time. 'Although . . . well, maybe.' Now she's blushing like crazy. 'I mean . . . probably not. But you never know, right?'

His eyes seem twinklier than ever. 'In this city, anything is possible,' he says conspiratorially. 'And love is always the answer, I think.'

'Love is a good answer,' she agrees, although she feels something of a hypocrite for saying this when the ruins of her marriage are still smouldering behind her. Just then she hears the ringtone she has set for her daughters' calls. 'Ahh – my phone,' she says, delving into her bag. 'I'm sorry – I'm going to have to—' Her fingers close around it and she rises from her seat again. 'Nice to meet you, Alain,' she says, swiping the screen to answer the call. It's Edie, she sees. 'Take care.' Then she turns and leaves him to it. 'Hi darling,' she says. 'Everything all right?'

Edie is Jess's most sensitive child, always has been, able to tune into people's moods with the accuracy of a seismometer detecting earth tremors. At the age of three she unnerved Jess with a couple of spooky utterances that made it sound as if she was aware of a past life – 'My name before was Gwendoline and I had two brothers' was one of them, 'I miss having horses' another – and perhaps because of this, Jess places a lot of stock on her middle daughter's intuitions.

'There's something up with Dad,' was her verdict on the phone this time, and Jess felt her skin tingle at such portentous words, remembering how Mia too had commented on David's strange behaviour. Walking back from the market later with a few provisions – some crusty bread, a gooey wedge of Brie, scarlet tomatoes almost bursting with ripeness and a bag of rosy nectarines – she ponders on what, if anything, she should do. Unlike her older sister, Edie didn't think David was necessarily in love, but she's convinced there's something he's not telling them. 'He's very quiet,' she said. 'Not really listening to us when we're all chatting. Like he's in his own world.'

Should Jess worry? Say something to him? She's only got her daughters' word that anything is wrong; it's not as if she's seen evidence of any altered behaviour herself. Maybe he's undergoing a long dark night of the post-separation soul – God knows she's had those times since their split where she's felt unmoored, uncertain. Times when she isn't quite sure who she is, without David there reminding her. She wonders who he's talked to about their break-up, if he's managed to get beyond all the shouty football-based chat with his mates and open up.

Lost in thought, it takes her a moment, on entering the hotel, to realise that Beatrice is on reception this afternoon and looking pleased to see her. 'It *is* you! I saw your name on the room list this morning and thought – can it be that there is *another* Jessica Bright staying with us so soon? No! And I am glad!'

'Oh, I'm glad too, Beatrice!' Jess cries, momentarily forgetting her quandary. 'How are you? That blouse is gorgeous, by the way, it really suits you. Oh, and how was your daughter's piano exam, did it go okay?'

Beatrice flutters her eyelashes self-deprecatingly. 'Thank you,' she says. 'And yes, Mathilde passed the exam, she was very happy.' She pretends to wipe sweat from her forehead, although, in true Beatrice style, she looks immaculately made-up and groomed, as if she has her own microclimate that is fresher and cooler than the heatwave everyone else is slogging through. 'It is good to see you again, Jess.'

'You too. I'm looking forward to a proper catch-up,' she says, before remembering, too late, that she's a guest here, rather than Beatrice's actual friend. Which is rather a shame, when she likes the other woman so much. 'I don't suppose ...' she says before she can stop herself. 'No. I'm being silly.'

'What is it? You want to ask me something? Tell me there is not another dog you have to feed,' Beatrice says, pulling a funny face. 'A lion this time, maybe?'

'No, no dogs or lions.' Jess can feel herself turning pink. 'I was just going to ... Well, you can say no, obviously, but I wondered if you might want to go for a drink some time, that's all. But I know you're busy,' she adds, giving Beatrice an easy excuse so that she can decline.

'You want to go for a drink? With me?'

Oh God, has she crossed the line? Jess thinks, embarrassed. It's a bit unconventional, admittedly, what she's asking the other woman. 'Well ... yes, but only if you—'

'I would love to! We must do this,' Beatrice interrupts, beaming. 'And I will take you to a very cool bar. The coolest. Let me see ...' She checks her phone. 'Thursday evening?'

'Perfect!' replies Jess. Georges on Wednesday, Beatrice on Thursday ... catch a load of her and her Paris social life. 'Let's hope your cool bar has enough wine for us.'

'Watch out, Paris!' Beatrice cries theatrically, just as two large tourists laden with suitcases arrive through the front door and look startled by her declaration. Stifling her giggles, Jess leaves her to deal with them. Oh, but that was nice, wasn't it? she thinks, heading upstairs to her room. She might have a memoir to write but she's definitely going to have fun in her free time too.

Chapter Twenty

When Adelaide enrolled as a student at Goldsmiths, it wasn't only the drawing and painting lessons that lit up her synapses like the Oxford Street Christmas decorations. She quickly discovered how much she loved learning about other artists' work too, getting to know who had gone before her and the historical context in which they had worked.

Until then, she had never set foot inside a gallery, but Ursula, her mentor, soon set about changing that, ordering her to visit the National Gallery, the Courtauld Institute, the Tate, and a whole host of smaller institutions around the capital. Whitechapel Gallery too, situated minutes away from where she'd grown up. It might as well have been in a different country.

Now that these doors were opening before her, her eyes were opening too. All those Renaissance portraits she'd dismissed as a bit stiff or boring took on a whole new perspective when she learned that the artists of the time had enjoyed incredible sway as the only people able to create a flattering (or not) image of royalty, the Pope, the wealthy. What power there must have been behind their paintbrushes! She loved seeing artists' unfinished work too – what the underpainting of a Gainsborough revealed, what Schiele's sketches told her.

Her brain thrummed with styles and eras, modes and geniuses, as she lapped them up. She changed her favourite contemporary artist from one week to the next, as she wandered around exhibitions featuring works by Miró, Freud, Dalí. Before long though, she gravitated towards female artists old and new – Morisot, Kahlo, Boty – for the wisdom they could impart. She fell in love with the photography of Diane Arbus. She became obsessed with the abstract art of Hilma af Klint; she experimented with botanicals during a Georgia O'Keeffe phase. It seemed as good a way as any to learn her craft, emulating the works of her best-loved artists, and she devoted hours to the study of their techniques, peering at the mark-making, trying to figure out how exactly they had achieved their greatest pieces.

Then, that first summer abroad with her friends, wandering through the Uffizi, she came across one of Gentileschi's masterpieces for the first time: *Judith Beheading Holofernes*. Reading in her guidebook how it had been painted after the rape of Gentileschi by the Italian painter Agostino Tassi, she felt immediate shivers down her spine. Yes, she could see the cold, righteous anger that had been painted in Judith's face, the strength in her arms, the tightness of her knuckles as she held down Holofernes' head. The solidarity of the maid by her side too, the urgency of the pair. You could almost hear the blood gurgling from the man's throat, smell the tang of iron in the air. All of this contained violence and passion from a woman in the seventeenth century! It blew Adelaide's mind.

The following December, when she herself had been raped, she felt numb for days afterwards, as if something had doused her inner flame. She wondered if art school had been a mistake, if she really belonged there after all. She skipped classes. She stayed in bed for days on end, feeling as if her spirit had shrunk to a tiny dead speck, floating lost within the shell of her body. Eventually Margie persuaded her to come in for the last day of the winter term and she dragged herself out of the house, feeling as if she was having an out-of-body experience as she walked along the street, unable to quite remember how to be Adelaide Fox any more. And then who should she see, swaggering through the college entrance ahead of her, but Dunster himself, cock of the walk, without a care in the world. What had changed for him? Nothing. How was it possible that he could blithely carry on with life when he'd left her broken and diminished, without a second thought?

That was when she felt it – the same rage that had burned through Gentileschi all those centuries earlier. The rage experienced by multitudes of wronged and abused women over the years in between. It fuelled her as she torched Dunster's flat a short time later; a satisfying act, but one that didn't completely quench the vengeance roaring within her. She found herself drawn back to Gentileschi's artistry; to Judith's courage, to Artemisia's revenge. She probably shouldn't go ahead and actually behead Simon Dunster herself, much as she would have enjoyed taking an axe to his pink neck, but maybe she could update Gentileschi's famous painting?

'That's how I came to paint myself as Judith in a new version of Artemisia's work,' she says now to Jessica, who has gone uncharacteristically silent. 'And Simon as Holofernes. There is real blood in the painting – my blood – from where I cut myself and mixed it into the vermilion. And do you know, it turns out to be incredibly satisfying creating a painting of your enemy's painful, gruesome death. Very pleasing indeed. I recommend it to anyone – make sure you put that in the book,' she adds, jabbing a finger.

Jessica's eyes gleam with sympathy. 'Did it help?' she asks quietly. 'You went through a horrific experience. Do you want to talk about your feelings around—'

'What's more,' Adelaide goes on, unstoppable. No, she absolutely doesn't want to talk about her 'feelings'. 'I entered the piece for the college's show that summer, with an exploratory note. Let the world see the face of my rapist and what I wished upon him, I decided. Let my feelings be known to all!'

Jessica swallows. 'And ... the college showed the piece?' she asks faintly. 'What were the repercussions? Did everyone recognise Simon?'

Adelaide sighs, revisiting her frustration all these years later. 'The college was too weak to go anywhere near it,' she replies, voice ringing with contempt. 'Too cowardly. Scared of legal issues, not least because of who Simon's dad was. They gave me some guff, of course – said they felt that it wasn't technically good enough to include in the show because ... I can't remember now, some cooked-up excuse. The painting *was* good enough, though, and we all knew it.'

Jessica shifts on her seat. 'Listen, talking of legal issues, we really ought to consider—'

'Still, I wasn't about to let them stop me,' Adelaide continues before Jessica can burst her bubble. 'And although the painting is yet to be shown in public – as it turns out, *everyone* is terrified of the merest *hint* of litigation – it became the first in a collection that I like to call Revenge.'

She bestows a hard bright smile on Jessica who looks more than a little unnerved. (Good. It has taken Adelaide years to perfect that smile.)

'And this collection . . .' Jessica says, sufficiently absorbed to let herself drift off topic. 'You still have the paintings?' Her face changes as something else occurs to her. 'And should I take it that other significant people feature within them?'

'Correct,' Adelaide says. 'I still have them. And yes, all my enemies are there on canvas, being murdered or tortured in one way or another by my own fair hand.' She steeples her fingers together, maintaining eye contact. 'Believe me, it's a proper rogues' gallery. As will be detailed in our book.'

'Wow. How incredible,' Jessica says. 'So where are the paintings now? Was the plan originally to exhibit them together?' She has become animated, leaning forward with eagerness. Look at her with the bit between her teeth, ready to run.

'I'm hoping we could do something like that, once the memoir is published,' Adelaide replies. 'The paintings alongside the corresponding sections of the book, perhaps. Although for the time being, they are mostly within my archive. In my old studio, across town.'

'Wow,' says Jessica again. 'Might I . . . I mean, it would be amazing to see them, if that's possible? We could reproduce them in the book, maybe? Although ...' She grimaces before she can proceed any further with the idea. 'The thing is, I can imagine the publishers' lawyers getting very twitchy about that, just like Goldsmiths did. In fact, this whole episode with Simon Dunster has legal problems written all over it, unfortunately. Earlier, when you spoke about, um, burning down his flat ... I should warn you that the publishers almost certainly won't want his name in print, or anything that could get you – or them – into trouble.'

Naturally Adelaide has already thought about this. 'No,' she replies. 'They won't want any trouble, I agree. But I am willing to take full responsibility for my words. That's the point – I *want* to name names. I want to punish everyone who has ever hurt me. And if they decide to sue me – let them. I'm happy to have my day in court and get the truth put on record. I'm too old and angry to let anybody intimidate me.'

Jessica bites her lip, apparently unconvinced. 'Right,' she says cautiously. 'Well ...'

'You don't need to worry about legal issues,' Adelaide assures her. 'You're here to write down my story. And that's what I'm trying to give you, if you'll let me get on with it. Okay?'

'Okay,' Jessica replies, but she's still wary. What's happened to that bolshy streak of hers? 'This is all pretty big stuff, Adelaide,' she goes on after a moment. 'And I was so caught up in what you were saying, it seemed wrong to interrupt you for details. But can we rewind to you painting your first Revenge piece for a minute, please? It would be great to include a few lines about what was going through your head. Does it feel different, painting something like that when your emotions are running so high? Are you able to detach yourself from the subject at all during the process – to think about the brushstrokes, say, rather than the story behind them?' The questions are falling out of her in a rush now, so thick and fast that Adelaide is in danger of forgetting the first ones. 'Also, were you able to work from memory, when you were painting Simon's face? Or photographs? Surely you didn't have him pose for you?'

'I felt . . .' Adelaide pauses to consider, to place herself back there at the time. There in her tiny workspace in college, dressed in the brown workman's overalls she favoured during this period, her hair piled up on top of her head, the ancient two-bar heater the only thing preventing her from freezing in the icebox of a studio. You could always hear someone's radio playing – Radio Caroline had just launched; the Beatles and the Merseybeat sound all the rage. The canvas she worked on was large, by previous standards – almost two metres in height – and by the end of a session, the muscles in her arms would be aching from the sheer bodily effort it took to get so much paint on the vast-seeming space. People don't think about the physicality involved with a big canvas – going up and down ladders, the exertion of working with a lot of paint; you could finish the day with your body and mind equally exhausted. And yet the hours would vanish without her really noticing anything else other than the image that was coming together before her.

'I felt rage, yes,' she goes on, 'but by giving myself something to do with that rage, it transformed into a white-hot kinetic

179

energy. A force, like I'd never had before. It actually became exhilarating, like I was riding a wave so powerful I just had to hang on and go with it.' She experiences a sudden pang for her old drive, the stamina she once had.

'Passion can only get you so far though,' she adds. 'It's the concentration of the detail – the brushstrokes, as you say, the light falling across the scene, getting the texture of the fabric right, making the blood look convincing, delineating the tendrils of hair ... all of that sends you into a sort of ... well, trance. A different place, where your brain is working hard to get everything down, exactly as you see it in your mind's eye. I find it very calming actually, when I am deep in this process. Nothing else seems to matter – not Simon, not Remy, not C—' She breaks off. 'Nothing crowds into my mind. My hand becomes my brain; the paint and what I do with it is all that counts.' She stares at her hands, mercifully free of tremors today, and curses the ageing process that has slowly been taking art away from her. How she misses those days when she could devote herself to a canvas and forget the rest of the world.

'Wow.' That's the third wow from Jessica in the space of ten minutes, Adelaide notes, as the younger woman stares at her, shaking her head a little. 'That was ... Gosh, it's wonderful to hear you talk about this. So interesting. This is in no way meant to sound rude or disingenuous, but sometimes I sort of forget that you're this ... this genius, Adelaide. And then to sit here and have you describe the process of your creativity ...' Her eyes are wide. 'I actually feel quite awestruck to be ... well, in the presence of greatness. *Your* greatness.'

Adelaide doesn't know what to make of this. Having been

180

immersed in the art world so long, her bullshit detector is permanently on alert and she knows better than to take gushing compliments at face value. Yet there's something about Jessica that is so earnest, you could believe she genuinely means all this stuff.

'Thanks,' she replies after a moment, albeit suspiciously. 'Anyway. Perhaps we should ...'

But Jessica, rifling through a notepad, is not ready to continue just yet, it seems. 'Before we go any further,' she says sweetly, 'I was setting up a timeline yesterday and realised that there was a fairly significant omission from the narrative so far: namely that you haven't told me much about how your friendship with Margie Flint came into being. Now I know this is also a touchy subject,' she gabbles, putting a hand up as if warding off any forthcoming argument – you bet it's forthcoming, thinks Adelaide – 'but could you at least talk about your first impressions of her, how your friendship developed, all the good stuff of the early days?' There's a momentary pause where Adelaide struggles for an answer, until Jessica picks up once more. 'In the spirit of giving me the truth, the whole truth and nothing but the truth?'

Adelaide sighs. Talk about boxing a person into a corner. And although there was, obviously, a lot of 'good stuff', as Jessica puts it, it's not something she often allows herself to think about. She reaches down to pet Jean-Paul while she stalls.

'Maybe we should take a break?' she says. 'Marie-Thérèse?' she yells in the next moment. 'Are you around? We're dying of thirst in here. Any chance of a cold drink?'

Jessica gets to her feet. 'I can get those,' she offers, bending over to put the used cups back on the tray.

'No, you won't,' Adelaide tells her. 'I pay that woman good money to— Marie-*Thérèse*! Where the hell is she?'

Jessica sits down, pulling a face and not very discreetly.

'What? Why are you looking like that?' Adelaide hears herself bark.

'Because ... Well, whoever you are, genius or not, there are ways of speaking to people, aren't there?' The words burst out of Jessica as if she has been trying to dam them for some time. 'Nice ways. Polite ways. And ... not to beat around the bush, quite aggressive ways too. Which can be horrible for the person on the receiving end.'

Adelaide bristles. Hang on, she feels like retaliating, I thought I was a presence of greatness two minutes ago. Now you're lecturing me on *manners*? Then she turns her glare on Marie-Thérèse as the woman herself finally tramps in, her expression as sullen as ever.

'Ahh, there you are. We'd like a jug of iced water, Marie-Thérèse. Please,' she adds stiffly, feeling Jessica's eyes upon her. *Quite aggressive ways too.* Oh, shut up. 'And some biscuits as well, if there are any.' There's that look again. '*Please.*'

'Not so hard really, is it?' Jessica murmurs − or rather, Adelaide thinks that's what she says, but when she fixes her gaze upon the younger woman and asks in her most freezing voice, 'What was that?' Jessica merely blinks, as if surprised, and says, 'What, me? Nothing.'

Just when Adelaide was starting to warm up to her, as well. She should have known it was too good to last.

★

182

Margie had caught Adelaide's eye the first day they met, both new to college, waiting at the front desk to collect their student passes. Margie was wearing a black and orange geometric-print shift dress with a clashing mustard-yellow cardigan that was almost as long as the dress itself. Her white-blonde, shoulder-length hair was held off her face with a paisley fabric band, and she had gold hoop earrings, daringly large. For some reason there was a black skull drawn on the back of one hand. Amidst a sea of young women in pastel-coloured, full-skirted dresses and neat little bags, she stood out a mile as someone different, someone interesting. Adelaide, who was feeling increasingly out of place with the titters of these well-spoken girls who'd spent their summers painting watercolours in Cornwall and Norfolk, immediately pegged Margie as a kindred spirit and possible friend. And so it turned out.

A working-class girl from Southend, Margie was tall and outspoken, creating bold impressionistic pieces with great sweeps of colour. There was always a cigarette hanging from the side of her mouth – the number of times she'd forget, caught up in her work, and let one smoulder down until it burned her lip – and she jangled with cheap jewellery, to the extent that some of the boys in their year nicknamed her Jingle Bells.

'We became as close as sisters,' Adelaide tells Jessica now, a wistful note in her voice. 'We'd have done anything for one another – and frequently did.'

'Tell me about some of those occasions,' Jessica urges. 'What scrapes did the two of you get into?'

'How long have you got?' Adelaide replies, and laughs, only

for the sound to snag in her throat as she remembers her dearest friend's face once more, the glint in her eye, her wide smiling mouth. How the two of them would spend hours making themselves new outfits together for nights out – tiny little dresses with belts and large buttons, their hair teased into enormous beehives, liberal amounts of kohl and lipstick.

'Oh my God, please tell me there are photos of the pair of you,' Jessica begs as Adelaide describes them.

'I definitely have a couple but she probably has m—' Adelaide breaks off, unwilling to finish the sentence. She knew she'd have to talk about Margie for the book, but recounting 'the good stuff' for Jessica keeps blindsiding her. Because it *was* good. It was so good that suddenly it seems unbearable that they're no longer close, that she can't call her up and reminisce about the old days. Can't ask, *Hey, have you got any photos of us in our finery?* She swallows down her feelings. 'Yes, I'm sure I have some,' she says, clenching and unclenching her fingers in her lap. 'Will that do for now?' she asks, aware of the pleading note in her voice. 'Perhaps we could come back to her some other time, when I feel less . . . ?'

Less . . . ? She isn't sure what word to use. Fragile? Precarious? For the world-weary cynic she professes to be, the last two days have shaken her up like a margarita.

Jessica takes pity on her. 'Of course,' she says. 'Absolutely. Let's shelve that for now, then. Perhaps we could talk instead about your last year of college, your favourite memories and significant moments from that time?'

Safer ground – yes. Adelaide accepts with gratitude the easier route she's been offered, and begins parcelling up a few anecdotes accordingly. Seeing the Beatles at the Astoria in Finsbury Park; Margie getting thrown out when she tried to rush the stage during 'I Wanna Hold Your Hand'. The terrible flat they moved into with mould and rats, plus the biggest rat of all, their sex-pest landlord. Gatecrashing a party in the Kings Road and meeting Julie Christie and Peter Blake. Getting high for the first time and falling in love with a Scottish model called Alastair, who had the best cheekbones in London. Putting on her final show and being approached by Jonty, an up-and-coming agent who wore turtlenecks and thick-lensed Michael Caine–style glasses. Moving out of the terrible flat but not before they'd painted obscene, unflattering pictures of the sex-pest landlord on every wall, plus warnings about his behaviour in foot-high lettering.

'No way,' Jessica keeps chuckling (rather unprofessionally, Adelaide can't help feeling). 'Amazing. What a life you've lived, Adelaide. What an extraordinary life!'

Adelaide is smiling herself, having enjoyed recounting so many stories of naughtiness and exuberance. When did she last lose herself in laughter as she has done today? You can become so absorbed in bad times and grievances that you forget to glance back at the glorious, golden days of one's youth. But here they are again, newly excavated and fun to remember. Yes, fun!

Still, this is only the prelude in many ways, she supposes, saying goodbye to Jessica a short while later. She's fully aware that the trickier stories still loom ahead; creaking icebergs in the ocean. Embarking on this memoir, she'd always planned to dig everything out of herself and on to the page, like a surgeon dispassionately cutting away a tumour. Her belief remains that an artist should be able to confront the truth unflinchingly, however monstrous it may be. But now that she's here, with less than a fortnight left to tell her tale, and time ticking ... does she still have the bold staring eye that is required, or will she break at the last, and look away before her story is completed?

Chapter Twenty-One

Jess leaves Tuesday's session reeling with all that she's heard, her head full of Swinging London, Carnaby Street and the terrible vengeance wreaked upon one Simon Dunster. Sure, it's all great copy, but some of it feels like a live bomb in her hands that she doesn't know what to do with. Barely has she left Place des Vosges than she retrieves her phone and dials Luc's number. This is too big to handle alone.

'Hi, this is Jess Bright, the writer for Adelaide's—'

'I know who you are,' he interrupts, sounding amused. 'Is everything okay?'

'Not really,' she tells him. 'To be honest, I'm kind of worried about some of the things Adelaide has said in the last couple of days.'

'Ahh. Right,' he says. 'Where are you? Not still in the apartment, I take it?'

'I just left. The thing is, she got up to some pretty wild stuff, according to her stories. And I've flagged to her that the publishers are sure to have conniptions at some details, but she wants to tell me everything anyway, she says. Seriously though, I'm a bit concerned she might get into trouble by speaking so freely.' A new and terrible thought strikes her. 'And actually – so could I, if I'm party to this knowledge, and don't do anything about it. I mean ... she burned down a man's flat, Luc. She could have killed him. As it was, it sounds as if she maimed him, possibly for life. What am I supposed to do with that? Will the editor feel obliged to speak to the police? Then there's the Colin Copeland case too ...'

She breaks off, remembering how Adelaide had almost said his name when speaking about her Revenge series of paintings. She backtracked quick as anything when she realised her error, but you bet your life that Jess spotted it, after the lurid allegations Mia's been making. 'I mean, I'm only guessing here, but from what she's already let slip, she knows more about his death than she's said previously. So if she confesses anything to me ...' Jess pictures grainy footage of herself, pale and anxious in a Kent police interview room, her conscience forcing her to divulge what she knows. In fairness, she did *ask* Adelaide to give her the truth, but never realised her truth would be quite so ... well, incriminating.

'Hmm,' Luc says. 'Are you finished for the day? Have you had lunch yet? I was about to go out and get some food if you want to join me – my flat isn't far from Adelaide's. We can talk more then.'

Two young women walk by just then holding open polystyrene cartons of delicious-smelling falafel and chips, and Jess's stomach gives an instant growl of longing.

'That would be great,' she says, because her stupid brain is, by now, imagining her behind bars for withholding information

188

about a historic case of arson and possibly the attempted murder of Simon Dunster. Not to mention whatever happened with Colin Copeland. Jess has watched *Orange Is the New Black*, she'd be absolutely pathetic in prison, bullied to within an inch of her life.

She gets a grip. Hopefully it won't come to that. 'Oh, and also I wanted to ask you about the archive – if I can look through it at some point. Adelaide said it would be okay.' Her arms goosepimple as she visualises herself discovering the Revenge paintings. It'll be pretty chilling to look at the image of Adelaide beheading Simon, knowing what she does now.

'Sure, any time. Maybe tomorrow?' he suggests. 'I'm free all afternoon then, if that works for you. In the meantime, do you know Monsieur Pélican? Look it up, it's a restaurant on a barge not far from Adelaide's. It's kind of touristy but their pizza's decent. I could be there in ten minutes if you fancy that?'

'Sounds good,' says Jess. 'See you soon.'

Monsieur Pélican, a riverside barge, is moored near Pont Marie and has a parasol-shaded terrace adjacent, Jess discovers a short while later. The picnic benches on its sun deck are full of holidaying families tucking into burgers, while twenty-somethings take photos of their brightly coloured cocktails, angled to include the river as backdrop. For a moment, noticing a woman with three daughters all heatedly talking at once, Jess has a pang for her own girls, on holiday without her, but then spots Luc and puts them resolutely to one side. Business first.

The restaurant is busy, but by some miracle, Luc has found

a spot in the shade, halfway down the deck. Here the benches give way to smaller tables with comfortable-looking rattan seats, and Jess feels the knot in her stomach begin to loosen as he spots her approaching and waves. A waiter whisks past with a couple of incredible-smelling pizzas, good enough to make her nose twitch, and she touches the charm around her neck, remembering how she and Pascale would sometimes get slices of doughy margherita pizza for lunch from their favourite Italian café near Hotel d'Or. But Jess shouldn't think about her now either.

'This is great,' she says, sitting down. It's as if Luc has managed to conjure up exactly what she needs on this summer's day: to sit in a pretty place, far removed from the darkness of the Simon Dunster story. The air smells of sun cream and chips, and pleasure boats packed with photo-taking tourists cruise by at stately speeds. Give her two minutes and she'll be unable to resist a cocktail herself.

They order food and drinks, and then Jess takes a deep breath and goes on to detail her worries. *Snitches get stitches*, she hears Edie warn in her head, and experiences a slight queasiness, until she remembers that her job here is supposedly to tell the whole *world* Adelaide's secrets. If the world can handle them, that is.

'I know all publicity is supposedly good publicity and yeah, she'd sell a shedload of books on the back of so much drama, but I can't see this having any kind of happy outcome for Adelaide, can you? And this is just what she's told me so far. She's hinted enough times that there are plenty of other meaty stories to come.'

He drums his fingers, thinking. He's wearing a white short-sleeved shirt and she finds herself admiring how tanned his arms are as she waits for him to speak.

'I guess I should read everything before we submit the first draft,' he says after a moment, and Jess has to snap back to attention, realising that she's still staring at his arms. Embarrassing. 'I can flag to her any risky areas,' he goes on. 'But in the meantime, maybe it's good for her to get this stuff off her chest.'

'Yes, but . . .' Jess doesn't want to make this all about her, but he doesn't seem to have grasped the possible wider repercussions. 'Well, not to put too fine a point on it, *I* don't want to go to prison either,' she says. Her voice must have risen, because in the next moment, the woman at the table nearest theirs turns round and eyes her with interest. Jess responds with her best Adelaide scowl and then, thank goodness, the waitress arrives with their drinks, a Pelican beer for Luc and a *jus de pamplemousse* for herself.

'Who said anything about prison? And how come *you're* suddenly going there? I don't follow,' he says when they are alone once more.

Jess sips her juice – sour-sweet and icy-cold; perfect. 'As an accessory to her misdemeanours!' she hisses. 'Doesn't that make me liable, or something? Shouldn't I have performed a citizen's arrest the minute she told me she set fire to Simon the Shitbag's flat, carted her off down the nearest nick?'

'Not at all,' he replies. 'I'm starting to think you didn't actually read that contract I spent ages drawing up. It specifically exonerates you of any form of complicity because I had

191

a feeling this might happen. Look, you definitely won't end up in prison. You can stand down with the Free Jess Bright banners and petitions to Parliament.'

'Oh.' A weight lifts from her shoulders, the very air against her face suddenly a degree more refreshing. 'Seriously? All right. Thanks. And Adelaide's going to be okay too? I mean, I won't shop her if you're worried about that, but ...' She trails off, feeling as if she's playing a part in a bad movie. I won't shop her, indeed, she thinks, cringing at her own melodramatic language.

'I'll make sure she's not incarcerated either,' he assures her. 'I can't exactly see her going for the grey prison joggers and hoodie in any case.'

'God, no,' Jess says. 'Although ... well, I did look into it, and—'

'You looked into it? Because you seriously thought it might be a possibility?'

Jess can tell he's holding back a laugh, and feels the back of her neck grow hot. 'Well ...' she says again, but can't think of any explanation other than the truth. 'Yes, all right, I did. Yes,' she goes on defensively. 'And in the UK at least, women don't have to wear uniform in prison, so ...' She blushes because she can tell he's struggling to keep a straight face. 'What can I say, I have a vivid imagination.'

'So I'm learning,' he replies, but his smile is one of amusement at least, rather than as if he thinks she's a complete idiot. She hopes. 'Well, I'm grateful for your concern around Adelaide's prison wear – good to know.'

'Oh, shut up,' she says, squirming at his teasing.

'How are you finding her this time around, anyway?' he goes on. 'Is she behaving herself?'

'Um ...' She pauses, caught between diplomacy and honesty. 'Well, she hasn't asked me if I'm deaf or merely stupid again, at least ...'

'What? She didn't!'

'And she's certainly telling me everything, and I'm pretty sure none of it's fictitious now either,' Jess goes on, rather enjoying the appalled look on Luc's face. Then she relents. 'Today we actually had a real laugh together about some stories from her youth. She can be very funny.'

'Adelaide was laughing?'

'Yeah! Tears in her eyes at one point – good tears – at a story about her and her friends getting one over on their old landlord.' Jess smiles to remember the moment, Adelaide with a hand on her chest, positively wheezing as she tried to finish her sentence. 'Although that's rare,' she admits. 'Most of the time ... well, she's quite dark, isn't she? Not one of life's natural optimists. And she seems very keen to get one over on anyone who's ever pissed her off. She went on for a solid fifteen minutes at least about her first agent, Jonty, and why he turned out to be a dickhead.'

Luc nods. 'She has her reasons to be on the dour side,' he says. 'She was depressed for a long time after Remy died, and lockdown was awful for her, I know. She really went into herself – hardly painted, barely saw anyone for days. Thank goodness she had Jean-Paul, because she must have been lonely.'

Jess feels a guilty twist inside for having called Adelaide

'lonely' the last time she was here. No wonder the other woman blew up at her.

'Catherine and I – my sister, that is – we were hoping that having a new exhibition and the memoir to think about might cheer her up a bit, but maybe that was too simplistic,' Luc goes on. 'Although I'm glad to hear that she was laughing today. That sounds more positive.'

'Agreed,' Jess says. There's a beat, and then curiosity gets the better of her. 'Where do you fit into this whole set-up, if you don't mind me asking? You're here for the summer too, is that right? What have you left behind in the UK?'

He seems taken aback to have the spotlight switched in his direction. 'Wow ... okay,' he replies eventually. 'Um ... well, I guess I've left behind a divorce? A redundancy. Some slowly desiccating pot plants. All the impressive stuff.'

'Ahh. Sorry,' she says, regretting her nosiness. 'Me too,' she adds. 'Although mine is a separation, but it's a mess all the same.'

'I didn't know that,' he replies, and she's wondering why he thinks he *would* know when he adds, 'I've been reading your parenting column. And your agony aunt page. I thought everything was peachy on the domestic front.'

He's been reading her work? Cringe. 'Oh God, you haven't,' she says, suddenly embarrassed. All those personal, intimate snapshots of her life, her family; it's like finding out someone has been through your knicker drawer.

'Yeah, when Adelaide first suggested you for the job – or rather, I thought she did – I checked out your interview of her and some of your other work, before approaching you,' he says, then hurries on before they can dwell on the dismal Wrong-Jessica saga. 'But that's why I thought you'd be good in the first place, because your writing is so sharp and perceptive,' he says. 'You write with your heart on your sleeve, and bring everything to life so well. What? Why are you looking at me like that? I loved that column you wrote about the nit plague – it was brilliant! Really made me laugh.'

'Oh, stop,' she says, unsure if he's taking the piss out of her. Probably. David always treated her magazine work like it was the lowest of the lowbrow, compared to the deeply important world of sports journalism. Get enough chimps in a room and they'd write one of Jess's columns; that was his subtext enough times. Despite his kind words, Luc probably thinks the same underneath too.

'You're good!' he tells her now though. 'You must know that?' Still suspicious, she has to check his expression, but he seems sincere.

'Er … thank you?' she replies cautiously, just as their pizzas arrive, plus the tomato and mozzarella salad he ordered for them to share. The pizzas are a tiny bit scorched around the edges, just the way Jess likes them, and as the waitress wishes them a cheery '*Bon appetit*' and turns to leave, Jess begins cutting slices with gusto.

'Good shout,' she says as the smell of hot cheese and basil drifts up to her nose. 'I needed this.' Then, to change the subject from her writing, she asks, 'So have you got any work on while you're over here, other than what you're doing for Adelaide?'

'Some consultancy stuff,' he says. 'Although this summer, I

can't help feeling . . . Well, I'm wondering if I need to change things up a bit. If being here isn't the catalyst for some big decisions.'

'Like what?'

'Like . . .' He pauses to chew thoughtfully. 'I've been working in the legal profession since I graduated,' he says. 'And it's been great – interesting, important work. Decent colleagues and pay. Respectable, you know. I probably would have stayed in the firm for ever if there hadn't been this wave of redundancies. But now that I'm out of that way of life – the long hours in the office or in court, the procedures, the routine, the same old commute – I don't feel in any great hurry to pick it up again.'

'Midlife crisis?' she teases.

'Oh God, it probably is, isn't it? It's strange though. With that and my marriage ending last year, it's like someone's pressed pause on life as I knew it. The treadmill has stopped and here I am in Paris, wondering where I'll go next.'

'And . . . ? Have you come up with anything? What would be your dream, if there was nothing standing in your way?'

He wrinkles his nose. 'Asked like a true agony aunt,' he teases, which makes her squirm. Please let him not have read any of the columns where she's dished out sex advice, she would actually rather die. 'Oh, I dunno. I haven't got that far yet,' he says, but he's looking away and she wonders if that's true. 'How about you?'

She spears a piece of tomato from the salad and pops it into her mouth while she thinks. It's ripe and juicy, dressed with olive oil and black pepper; the taste of pure summer. 'My career treadmill had a similar malfunction this year too,' she says. 'Although I must say, I've always hated treadmills. Running and running and never getting anywhere.'

'Plus there's always that terror of getting one of your trainer laces stuck in the mechanism somehow and being pulled over,' he agrees.

'No *way*! That's one of my recurring nightmares!'

He laughs, somewhat shamefacedly. 'I know, I read it one of your columns. Sorry!' he says as she throws back her head with a groan. 'I couldn't resist. Go on, you were about to tell me about your dream life.'

She's still embarrassed to be caught out by someone quoting her own words back at her, but on the flipside, it's also kind of flattering. He really *has* read her work, enough to remember whole chunks of it. 'Well, any dream life of mine needs to factor in three teenagers, which rules out anything *too* thrilling or outlandish,' she replies, 'but work-wise, I'd love to achieve something . . .' She pulls a face. 'I was about to say "impressive", which sounds tragically needy. But you know, something that makes other people say "Wow!" – that would make me feel like I've made it, I'm a success.'

'I'd say writing two columns for years on end, and all your other journalism, is pretty impressive,' he points out.

'Yeah, you might *think* that, but believe me, there's this whole hierarchy in the print world, and some people really do love to put you in your place,' she tells him, feeling herself flush again. 'Judgey snobs, who look down on anyone writing populist content like me, rather than the highbrow, prize-winning stuff.' Right on cue, her old boss Lucinda's face flashes back into her head. *The thing about Jess . . .* It still pisses her off, all those years later. Why can't she let it go? 'That's why I was chuffed to get the gig with Adelaide, even if it was an accident. Because at last, it's something profound on my CV again. Nobody will be calling the memoir "fluff" or "lightweight" or any of those other patronising words that only seem to get bandied around with female writers.' Her voice wobbles with sudden indignation and she tries to row back to a place where she feels less emotionally on show. 'Well, let's hope not, anyway, for Adelaide's sake.'

'I didn't realise,' he tells her. 'God. That must be annoying. He says, stating the bleeding obvious,' he adds. He raises his glass. 'Well, here's to you and your clever, funny writing, Jess. And fuck everyone else.'

This last is so unexpected – and so *not* what she thought he would say – that she bursts out laughing. 'I'll drink to that,' she splutters, raising her glass and clinking it against his. 'Fuck the lot of them. Especially Lucinda.'

'Yeah, definitely her. I've no idea who you're talking about but she sounds a terrible person,' he says. 'The worst.'

They smile at each other and then something disconcerting happens. That's not ... that wasn't a *frisson* she just detected, was it? For a wild moment it felt as if her nerve endings had jangled to attention. As if her heart was expanding inside her ribcage, and ...

Well, it couldn't have done, she decides hurriedly, looking away. For one thing, an expanding heart would be biologically impossible. And for another, she's not fourteen, getting crushes on boys again. She's here to work, to be professional. She's out of practice with frissons, that's all – it's probably indigestion because she's eating too quickly. Also – hello! – she's got a date with *Georges* tomorrow evening. So if there are to be frissons and strange heart sensations, she should definitely save them up for *him*.

'Anyway,' she says, aware that an odd sort of silence has unfolded between them. She's not used to the company of men, that's the thing, she tells herself. No wonder something in her body has gone nuts at being opposite a good-looking man in Paris. 'So ... about the archive. How should I get there tomorrow?'

He explains where the archive is located, in a former studio rented by Adelaide, and they agree a time to meet. Then he begins telling her about some of the photos he's come across within its contents, and the creased old letters in spidery handwriting, and the exhibition brochures thrown carelessly into a carrier bag. He's been trying to sort everything out chronologically, he says, but it's all a terrific muddle. 'As for the paintings ...' he goes on, pantomiming horror. It sounds as if there are just stacks and stacks of old canvases, some dating back to her student days even; ancient paintings laced with cobwebs that have never been looked after properly. He's been cataloguing them the best he can by cross-referencing them with the list of exhibitions he has, but there are some that have never been shown – Jess gulps in a breath here, thinking of the Revenge collection – and others that have been painted over or need professional restoration.

They're having such an interesting chat that it comes as a shock when the waitress reappears to take away their empty plates and glasses, and Jess realises they've somehow been there for an hour and a half. How did that happen?

'Gosh, I'd better go,' she says, conscious of her laptop silently awaiting her, the chats she'd hoped to arrange with the girls. His afternoon too, that he probably wants to get back to. 'But thank you for your time – for all of this.' She waves a hand around, encompassing the barge, the lunch, the two of them. Not 'the two of them' like *that*, she amends mentally, feeling flustered again. (Oh God, what's wrong with her?)

They have a small argument over who's going to pay, which he eventually wins but only after she's promised to pay next time, whenever that may be. Then they make their way off the barge and down to the riverbank.

'Thanks again,' she says, wondering if they're going to hug or maybe kiss each other's cheek or …

No. He's unlocking a bike padlocked nearby and looking preoccupied; he doesn't seem about to do either. 'Good to chat, Jess,' he says, stashing the bike lock into a rucksack. 'Oh,' he adds with a certain gruffness. 'And a farm, by the way.'

'A farm?' she repeats, not following.

'My dream. If there was nothing standing in my way.'

Even then it takes her a moment to spool back through their conversation. 'Oh! Wow, that's a pretty big leap. You really want to be a farmer?'

He shrugs, looking a bit shy. 'Well, I'd have a smallholding, yeah. Maybe an orchard. A lovely hairy pig, perhaps. I'd grow loads of vegetables. Definitely have a tractor. Rewild a few acres …' He spreads his hands rather bashfully. 'That would do me. That's the dream.'

She smiles at him, feeling delighted – flattered, even – that he's shared this with her. 'I like your dream. I can totally see you on a tractor,' she says. Then she has to wrench herself away because now he's looking pleased and there's this strange sort of moment between them – another! – where it feels as if they've bonded. Over a hairy pig and some vegetables, of all things. She's not imagining it, is she? 'Anyway. I'll see you tomorrow,' she says, to snap them out of whatever weirdness is taking place. 'Bye!'

Chapter Twenty-Two

'He sounds dodgy to me,' Margie tells her, puffing out a long stream of cigarette smoke. 'What are you going to do about it?'

'What *can* I do? I can't exactly confront him, can I? I'm hoping he'll get bored and give up. Move on to someone else,' Adelaide says. The year is 1980 and the two of them have come to Little Bower for the weekend, along with various other friends, but it's early morning and only Adelaide and Margie are up so far. They're in the kitchen where Margie's made them a black coffee each (they're out of milk) and Adelaide's just confessed to her about her strange hanger-on, how it's a relief to get out of London, where she's not expecting to see him peering around every corner at her. Last night was the deepest sleep she's had in ages. There's a lot on her mind.

'Maybe you should confront him. I would. Just ask him, what do you think you're doing?' Margie stabs the air with her cigarette for punctuation. 'What is your fucking problem, mate?'

Adelaide smiles faintly because she could have guessed,

almost to the word, that this would be her fearless friend's suggestion. The two of them are in their mid-thirties now and college already seems a long time ago, what with them both having enjoyed success with their careers. Following the exhibition in Nice, Adelaide's work has also travelled to galleries in Berlin and Amsterdam, whereas Margie is making a name for herself in the sculpture world, with a piece recently appearing in a show at the Guggenheim Museum in New York. They continue to be best friends but see less of one another these days, not least because Margie is married, with a three-year-old, and has settled in the suburbs, while Adelaide and Remy live in a Primrose Hill townhouse, fully immersed in London life. They still have Little Bower for get-togethers though, and Adelaide feels increasingly appreciative of the chance to leave everything else behind and reconnect with her truest friends. This is the first time she's ever spoken about the man who keeps following her; the first time she's acknowledged out loud how it's been troubling her.

'The thing is . . .' she says, then breaks off. 'You're going to think I'm an idiot.'

'Of course I'm not. Well, no more of an idiot than I already think you are. Tell me.'

Adelaide looks at her friend's face – the face she knows so well, with her white-blonde hair cropped short, the bluish circles beneath her eyes that are now due to her son's atrocious sleeping habits, rather than late nights in the studio. 'The other day I saw him and . . . there's just something about his face. For a moment, I thought he was Will.'

'Oh, Ad.' Margie gets it immediately without any need for

further explanation. Sometimes it's as if their thoughts are in sync, connected on a plane where words are unnecessary.

'Yeah. I mean, he's not, obviously. But I thought, very clearly, *There's William.* Which totally muddied the waters for me. My face must have shown my feelings – I probably even looked at him in a certain way; longingly, hopefully. Now I'm wondering if he's completely misinterpreted that, and ...' She rubs her eyes, wishing for the millionth time that the man really could have been her brother. Her lost love. *There you are!* he might have cried with that mischievous grin of his, hurrying over to clasp her in an embrace. He's often floated into her dreams over the years, and she's always been thrilled to see him, but now he's there every night. It's almost as if he's trying to tell her something.

'I don't know,' she goes on. 'It's complicated. I don't believe in reincarnation or any of that rubbish but ... Well, what do *you* think happens to a person's soul when they die?'

Margie grinds her cigarette into a large scallop shell they use as an ashtray. 'Nothing. It ceases to exist,' she says with a shrug. She's wearing her nightgown still, an oversized pink and white striped shirt, and it slides off one shoulder with the movement. 'Come on, Ad. He's not your brother. He's some weirdo, and you shouldn't let him off the hook like that. I hope you're not blaming *yourself* for this either, because however you looked at him, I'm pretty sure your face didn't actually say *Feel free to follow me around like a creep.*' Her eyes narrow. 'What about that French boyfriend of yours, can't he scare the weirdo back into his cave?'

Adelaide looks down because Margie and Remy dislike one

another and she's never been sure why. 'I'll figure something out,' she says. 'Don't worry about me.'

Jessica arrives, as usual, on the dot of ten o'clock and is shown in, as usual, by the lugubrious Marie-Thérèse. 'A tray of tea things, Marie-Thérèse,' Adelaide requests in French before feeling Jessica's gaze upon her and adding, '*Please*. If it's not too much trouble. If you can bring yourself to make the effort.'

Later that evening, when thinking about this scene, she realises that she was only being sarcastic for Jessica's benefit; it's because she can't stand being told what to do, how to behave. But for Marie-Thérèse, the sarcasm appears to be the last straw.

'Make the *effort*?' she repeats with a look of fury. 'Madame Fox, I always make the effort! I make an effort every single day in this house for you, and you treat me like the dirt I am always cleaning. You cannot even be polite for one second without being nasty in the next. So no! I will not make your tea for you.' At this point, she rips off her apron and throws it to the ground, that red nose of hers in the air. 'I will not clean and cook and wash and iron, I will not buy food for your smelly dog. I will not make your disgusting bed. I am leaving now and you will have to do all that work for yourself. I am *done*!'

With a stamp of her foot marking the end of this tirade, she whirls around and flounces away.

'Oh dear,' says Adelaide, taken aback.

'Do you want me to go after her?' asks Jessica, looking concerned. 'Or will you?'

'Go *after* her? After that little performance? I jolly well will not,' Adelaide replies, coming over all English in her indignation. How dare she call Jean-Paul smelly? Her bed is *not* disgusting!

'But don't you think ... Maybe if you tried apologising ...' It's a moot point though as, in the next second, they hear the slam of the door, so loud that Jean-Paul's ears fly up in alarm. 'Maybe not,' Jessica says, deflating. 'Um ... Shall I make us some tea instead? Or would you rather go out again?' She peers at Adelaide. 'Are you all right? That was fairly horrible. Although ...'

'I am absolutely fine,' Adelaide says before Jessica dares to start blaming her.

The atmosphere eventually settles, and they continue working, with Adelaide recounting tales from her early twenties. Where to begin? Perhaps by resuming her enjoyable attack on Jonty, the suave agent who told her he would change her life, only for her to discover within a matter of weeks that he devoted all of his time to the male artists on his books.

'We might have enough on Jonty now,' Jessica puts in, interrupting one especially vitriolic anecdote. 'Maybe you could talk about ... um, what was making you happy at this time?'

'Making me *happy*?' Adelaide repeats, trying not to roll her eyes. But then she remembers the chance meeting with David Hockney, who was generous about one of her pieces, leaving her so thrilled she could hardly speak. 'I was pretty happy about that,' she concedes. Then she describes the various pittance-paying jobs she took on to make ends meet around her painting: as an assistant in a Kings Road gallery for a while, a stint as an usherette in a West End theatre, a short-lived period working as an early morning cleaner at the Royal Academy. Mentioning the latter post only makes her think about Marie-Thérèse, and her furious exit though, and her voice falters. Annoyingly, Adelaide will now have to endure the tiresome process of finding someone else to come in. She's already dreading the call to the agency, after they were so sniffy to her last time. *Madame, there have been many complaints about you*, the jumped-up manager chided. *And we have already sent you over half of our staff by now!*

'Adelaide . . . ?' Jessica prompts, jolting her back to the room.

'Yes, yes, sorry. Where was I? Yes, the Royal Academy. Here's a story for you. I only picked up the cleaning job in the first place because a pal of mine from Goldsmiths was working there, and got me on the books. And, as it turned out, pushing a hoover around those grand halls, dusting and mopping beneath some of the greatest paintings in the world . . . it was simply too tempting an opportunity for someone like me, longing to have my work seen and admired, when Jonty didn't seem in any hurry to make that happen. So . . .' She smiles, feeling a rush of fondness for the impulsive, bold young woman she once had been. 'So I sneaked a painting of mine into their summer exhibition. Switched it for some dreary landscape – goodness knows why such a boring piece was picked in the first place – and printed up a little card with my painting's details and price, to match all the others there.'

Jessica is sitting forward, eyes bright. Adelaide hasn't told this particular story for a long time; clearly Jessica hasn't come across it before.

'No!' she exclaims in delight. 'That's hilarious! How

much did you price it for? Did anyone buy it? How long before someone noticed your work shouldn't have been there at all?'

'Five hundred quid,' Adelaide says airily. 'More like ten grand in today's money. It was very bold of me, I admit. Extremely naughty. My heart was thumping so wildly as I switched them over, I swear there was a moment I thought I might be having a heart attack. But I got away with it.'

'Oh my God, I *love* this. This is fantastic. Tell me more about the painting. Was it one you were particularly proud of? Were you making some kind of statement with it?'

Adelaide snorts. 'Not really,' she admits. 'A statement that they should have had better security measures in place, perhaps. As for the painting . . . Well, back then, there was some very twee stuff around – *Still Life With Flowers*, *Spring Meadow*, that sort of claptrap. Mine was a portrait of Margie, full-face, with a cigarette to her lips, and this wicked look in her eye. *Woman Having a Cig*, I called it.' She can picture it now, painted in oils one quiet afternoon when they were bored. Margie didn't like it, said her nose looked too bulbous, but Adelaide was rather pleased with the tonality, the direct gaze she'd caught on canvas.

'And it hung there for – gosh, several days, at least, before someone tried to buy it. Rather flatteringly for me. Of course, when the mysterious buyer inquired about how to go about it, down came my little house of cards. The management were absolutely livid, sacked me on the spot, told me I was lucky they didn't take the matter to the police for – I can't remember, deception, maybe – oh, and stealing the dreary landscape. As if I'd want that on my wall! No, I'd stuffed it down the back of a filing cabinet in a carrier bag.'

Jessica splutters. 'Oh, that's all right then.'

'The Academy wanted the whole matter hushed up, but unfortunately for them, I had a friend working on the *Evening Standard* at the time. I passed it on as a snippet of gossip, and the next thing I knew, a journalist was in touch, wanting all the details. A photo of me and my painting was on page seven the following day, then a couple of other papers picked it up as an amusing "And finally ..." kind of story. It was discussed on some Radio 4 arts programme, too. Best of all, someone from Buckingham Palace got in touch with the *Standard* to say that Princess Margaret herself was interested in seeing the painting!'

'No *way*,' Jessica says, mouth open. 'Seriously? This is the story that keeps on giving. So you sold the painting to Princess Margaret? Oh my God! Did you meet her?'

'No, no, neither of those things. My mother never forgave me for that, I have to say.' She can picture her now, poor old Geraldine standing there with her hands in the sink as Adelaide recounted the story. *And you said no? To Princess Margaret? You never did. Please tell me you're joking. Oh, I give up, Adelaide. I really do!* 'It wasn't anything negative about Princess Margaret – in fact I loved the thought of her, of all people, owning a painting called *Woman Having a Cig* – but by then, Jonty had actually pulled his sweaty finger out and had been on the phone to his contacts. We had an offer from an extremely wealthy collector, I don't remember his name, who offered to pay a thousand pounds for it. How could I say no?'

'Wow. Adelaide. *Wow*,' Jessica says. 'That must have been incredible. Can you remember what you spent the money on? Did you celebrate in a particular way? And what did Margie say about a portrait of her receiving such attention?'

'She was furious, actually, because she didn't even like it,' Adelaide replies. 'Said I'd disfigured her in public. Then Margie's mum Edna got wind of the whole story, out in Southend, and *she* was raging too, because she didn't know Margie smoked.' Her lips twitch in a smile; she still remembers the phone call that came, how everyone else in the house could hear Edna Flint's fury from the receiver. 'As for celebrating, we all went to Ronnie Scott's, as I recall.' She's back there in the dimly lit Soho club in an instant. 'Of course, back then, Ronnie was playing most nights himself – on saxophone,' she adds when Jess looks blank. 'I seem to remember a few of us clambering up on stage to dance with the band after one too many whiskies.'

'Always a sign of a good night,' Jessica says, with the air of one who has done so herself.

'I do remember Margie retaliating though,' Adelaide goes on. 'With a portrait of her own, no less – a horrible one of me, in charcoal, that made me look positively witchlike. *Woman Counting Her Thirty Pieces of Silver*, she called it,' she says, chuckling at the memory. 'Absolutely hideous picture. She actually went to the Royal Academy with it, asked the president at the time if he'd like it for his office. "A tenner to you," she told him, but he turned her down, funnily enough.' She snorts with amusement, remembering her friend's feigned indignation. 'Dear me, we had some fun back in those days, we really did.'

'Sounds like it,' Jessica says. Then she hesitates. 'Maybe I could ...' She breaks off. Opens her mouth then shuts it again. 'How about if I got in touch with her?' she suggests tentatively. 'To see if she still has the picture. Wouldn't it be brilliant if we could feature both of them in the book? I think readers would love—'

'Oh no,' Adelaide says at once, before Jess even finishes the sentence. 'Definitely not. Please don't.'

'Perhaps I could just ...'

'No,' Adelaide repeats. 'And don't ask me again.' She brushes an imaginary crumb from her skirt, her previously buoyant mood vanishing. 'I think that will do for today, don't you? You probably need to do some writing while I ...' She deflates even further, remembering that she no longer has Marie-Thérèse to make her lunch, to clean and tidy, organise dinner, empty the dustbin. 'I also have much to be getting on with,' she says heavily.

'Of course,' says Jessica, rising from her seat with some reluctance as if hoping for a last-minute change of mind. None comes. 'I'll see you tomorrow.'

Chapter Twenty-Three

Hotel d'Or hasn't changed all that much in the last twenty or so years, Jess thinks, standing on the pavement before the white-stone former mansion house, with its smart black-and-gold-painted doors flanked by manicured shrubbery in elegant stone pots. Everything about its grand frontage says elegance. Through the doors, she can just glimpse a slice of the hushed marble-pillared lobby area with its thick pale carpets and grand piano. The restaurant will be full for lunch right now, she guesses; the waiting staff shouldering platters with silver domed lids, amidst the pop of corks, the genteel clinking of heavy cutlery. Welcome to your sanctuary from the rest of the world. Try not to think about the underpaid workers clearing up after your every move.

After Adelaide ended today's session so abruptly, Jess came here on impulse, jumping on the metro out to Faubourg Saint-Germain before she could change her mind. As she stands there, wondering whether she should sidle in, for old times' sake, or if the uniformed doormen have already clocked her as Not Rich Enough, a jet-black Bugatti pulls up in front of the doors and the staff spring to attention. One rushes over to assist the new arrivals with their luggage while another takes the car key with a small bow, and prepares to park the vehicle. Jess eyes the new arrivals – both in sunglasses, him in tech-bro gear: a crumpled white T-shirt, dark jeans and trainers, all of which probably cost more than Jess's monthly mortgage payment. The woman is wearing a black halterneck dress and wedge sandals; her toned arms and tiny waist no doubt the hard-won assets of daily personal trainer sessions.

It's hard not to stare at the glamorous people and their air of entitlement, walking arm in arm through the hotel doors without a word of thanks for the hard-working staff who make all of this possible. She can't help remembering Pascale's disdain for the rich, and often very rude, guests for whom they were the chambermaids here back in the day. 'They think, because they can afford to stay in this place, we are a species below them,' she would sniff, rolling her eyes. 'The way their eyes glide over us – like we are not really people, not worthy of a single *look*.' Around this point in the outburst, she would bang her chest. 'Are we not humans too, with our beating hearts, and our minds capable of joy and love and pain? *Mon Dieu!* They know nothing of what it is to exist in the real world. Nothing, I tell you!'

Jess agreed. It's why she still goes out of her way to be nice to service staff everywhere – in bars, restaurants, hotels – having been in that role herself. It's probably also why Adelaide's high-handed manner towards Marie-Thérèse rankled with her from day one. 'They know nothing,' Jess would reply, 'and yet have everything. How is that fair?'

'And they are as messy as pigs! So careless with their everything! And the worst taste! Pfft. Give me their money, I will spend it far better. Believe me!'

Jess couldn't argue. It never ceased to shock her quite how cavalier the hotel's guests were with their possessions. They'd check out, leaving brand-new clothes unworn in the wardrobe, and never, as far as she knew, call the hotel afterwards, asking for them to be sent on. Jewellery was frequently discarded, glass bottles of scent abandoned on dressing tables, still half-full. The hotel had strict rules about staff handing in such items, but Jess and Pascale's boss, Sylvie, had been a chambermaid herself and often turned a blind eye to the occasional bracelet or perfume bottle that ended up stashed in a pocket.

For Jess, it was merely part of the job, but Pascale frequently let it get to her. Worse, she started to look for ways in which she could strike back. 'I'm telling you, I will seduce a rich man one day,' she liked to say after a shift, as they changed out of their uniforms in their shared quarters down in the hotel's mould-smelling basement. 'I will seduce him, take all his money, then break his heart. Maybe kill him. Then we will see who has the best life.' This would all be accompanied by a confident smile. 'You can come too. We'd be Thelma and Louise,' Jess remembers her announcing one time.

'Yeah, because look how well that ended,' she'd snorted in reply.

Pascale had put her nose in the air. 'Not *this* Thelma,' she said grandly, poking a finger into her cheek and pouting.

Jess thinks of these bold words, years after her friend said them, and a shiver runs down her back, even though the day is warm. Pascale had been twenty-two then, barely older than Mia is now. Full of bravado and sass but slender enough that she could easily have been overpowered by an angry man. Hurt. Killed and dumped in the river ... Oh, Pascale. You didn't go and try something stupid, did you? She hears her making that last cryptic request once more – *Jess, if I were to ask you to help me with something a bit dangerous* – and bile rushes into her mouth at the memory.

Then she hears a voice. *'Madame? Puis-je vous aider, Madame?'*

One of the uniformed doormen is suddenly by her side and she straightens up. He is tall and broad-shouldered with a rugby player's body. In his mid-twenties, she guesses, and handsome; his skin golden, his dark hair neatly cropped beneath the red cap that is part of his uniform. His mum must be proud of her smart son, Jess thinks, imagining a photograph of him in his finery up on a mantelpiece.

'Non, merci,' she replies but finds herself stalling nonetheless. She is a journalist, after all, and there's nothing worse than an unfinished story. 'Although ... well, I used to work here myself, back in 1998,' she continues in French. 'And I'm trying to track down a friend I worked with then. Pascale Bernard – have you ever heard that name?'

He blinks. 'Pascale Bernard? No, sorry,' he replies.

'How about Sylvie, does she still work here?' she persists. 'In housekeeping? Small, Black, loud laugh ...'

She's lost him. He's bewildered. 'Sylvie?' he repeats.

'Yes – in housekeeping? I was just wondering ...'

He shakes his head, his eyes already moving away towards an elderly lady with white bouffant hair who's approaching the hotel laden with LaCroix and Dior shopping bags. 'Sorry, Madame. I am new here. Excuse me.' And then he's hurrying towards his elegant new target to assist her with her purchases.

Jess exhales, realising only then that she'd been holding her breath. Of course he can't give her any answers. What was she expecting? There *are* no answers, that's the whole rotten point. She walks away, her skin prickling all over. Leave it, she tells herself. Pascale has never shown up on any internet searches; in Jess's heart of hearts, she knows her friend is probably dead. Why rake up the past now? Besides, she has an archive and Luc to get to, she remembers, picking up the pace.

Adelaide's archive is contained within her former studio, out in Belleville, on the north-east side of the city. Rue Sainte-Marthe is shaded and narrow, the shopfronts almost all brightly painted. The sound of a jazz clarinet drifts from an open upstairs window, a couple of lads on mopeds buzz past, and an elderly man smokes a roll-up from a doorway, watching as Jess walks by. She reaches out to stroke the warm fur of a black cat draped along a window ledge, wondering how Albertine is faring back home alone. Becky has sent her a few photos so far, plus a breathless story about Albertine seeing off a fox the other day; it sounds as if the cat couldn't care less that her family are away again, to be fair.

She almost misses the anonymous-looking brown door because it's so drab; she expected something far grander, more impressive. But a few moments after her knock, there's Luc letting her in, telling her to watch the steps because the carpet is pretty threadbare, and she's following him up to the second floor of what was once an old house. The rooms have all been converted into studios, he tells her, and Jess finds it tantalising to walk past the other closed doors, wondering what is being created behind them.

In her heyday, Adelaide had a much larger studio in Montparnasse, Luc tells her as they reach the second floor and he slots a key into the door. She and Remy shared it, but then, when they split up, she moved everything here, before jetting off for a job in Japan. 'And here we are,' he says, pushing open the door.

Jess takes a breath, imagining a younger Adelaide coming up these very steps, with armfuls of work and a broken heart. As she follows Luc into the studio, she anticipates the scene: a light, airy space with clean white walls, perhaps a mini fridge full of champagne for the good days. Shelves of paints and brushes. A huge skylight to let the sunshine pour in. But instead ...

'Oh gosh,' she gulps, because the large room is complete chaos. There are boxes piled upon boxes. Stacks of paintings propped messily against one another. A dusty bottle-green filing cabinet with teetering heaps of paperwork dumped on top. Carrier bags stuffed with – what? Drawings, notepads, correspondence? She stares around, dumbfounded. Everything she has gleaned about Luc is that he is organised and competent, someone with a fine attention to detail. How can he bear to work within such a mess?

'It's a tip, I know,' he says cheerfully. 'Come through, to where it starts to look a bit less like a major crime scene.' He gestures ahead and Jess realises that there is a second room through an open doorway that's partially hidden by a stack of blue storage crates.

'Ahh,' she says in relief moments later, because this second room is a welcome change from the melee of the first. It's much lighter, for one thing, with a huge sash window, through which the yellowy afternoon light floods in. There's a desk and office chair against one wall, with a laptop and a pair of speakers, and a printed timeline stuck up at eye-level above. There's a kettle and small coffee machine on a new-looking red filing cabinet. A large fan on the floor. A couple of framed sketches on the wall, as well as a few photos of Luc with some boy or other. His boy? She'll get to that later. 'This is better,' she says. 'Thank God for that. I had visions of you having to work in that hellhole back there all summer, and ...'

'Yeah, I could tell from your face,' he says with a grin. He goes over to the sash window and heaves it up. 'So she dumped everything here, went to Tokyo, then took the job in Ottawa after that. This place was abandoned for years, effectively. Not even *insured*, can you believe? She went back to London in the mid-nineties, nursed her mum while she was dying and stopped painting altogether for a while. Remy had left Coco by then, so he was sniffing around her again – not that she was interested at first. Eventually she came back to Paris, to this very studio, where she returned to her art.'

He gestures around and it's only then that Jess notices that the bare floorboards below her feet are spattered with flecks of paint in every shade. 'She worked on the entire Bird series here,' he goes on. 'Pretty cool, eh? You're standing in a genuine place of art history.'

'Very cool,' Jess agrees. She's seen the iconic pictures of Adelaide from that time, wearing overalls with her hair twisted up on her head, barefoot and smoking a pipe. The Bird series, as Lucas calls it, is a collection of paintings featuring imagery around flight and freedom, with shadowy female figures. You can tell that the set was painted in a time of personal upheaval because, even to the eye of an amateur such as Jess, there's real passion apparent in the brushstrokes, a fuck-it attitude that comes through every piece. And something in that passion clearly resonated strongly with its audience because the series proved to be a great comeback moment, the paintings exhibited all around the world over the following decade. Feminist art critics in particular embraced the works. Proof that a weak man can never crush a strong woman, they said. Rejoice that another great woman is free of her ball and chain! Well – until Adelaide got back together with Remy as he was dying, anyway.

'So,' says Lucas, 'let me show you how far I've got.'

He sits at the desk and starts taking her through his system – the dating of works, the cataloguing of correspondence. 'As well as archiving, she's asked me to compile a list of significant works, in the hope that we can approach galleries about a great, and possibly final, exhibition to be shown when the book is published.' He pushes the hair out of his eyes; it's warm in the room despite the breeze through the window. 'So a pretty massive job, all in all. But wonderful, too. Extraordinary. A dream for someone who likes organising stuff.' He points both thumbs into his chest with a self-deprecating smile.

'I can imagine,' Jess says. 'Exciting too, with so much material to work through. Have you come across any hidden gems? Oh, and have you found a painting called *Woman Having a Cig?*'

'The one she snuck into the Royal Academy? No, that's privately owned,' he says, 'but I can show you a photograph of it, and the press clippings from that time too, if you'd like.'

'Oh, I'd love that, yes, please,' Jess says at once. 'She told me about it this morning – I hadn't heard that story before.'

'It's a good one, isn't it? Imagine having the balls to do that,' he says with a laugh, sitting down at the laptop. He flexes his fingers theatrically above the keyboard. 'Now then. Give me a minute to work through my incredibly complicated system . . . Do have a look around while you wait.'

She doesn't need any further urging and heads back into the other room. She won't mess up anything he's already sorted, she tells herself, but nonetheless, the thought of being the first to stumble upon something that's been buried for years is properly thrilling. It's like rummaging through a jumble sale, she thinks as she stands before a pile of boxes and opens the top one at random. Inside are ten or more notepads, and she plucks one at random and begins to leaf through. There's no date to be seen on any of the pages, but she guesses this is an early notepad – perhaps from Adelaide's college days? – because the style is naïve and immature, the pencil marks often tentative. The sketches are largely still lifes – arrangements of flowers in vases. Fruit in a bowl. A collection of kitchen utensils in a jar – interspersed with the occasional portrait that she peers at with more interest. A handsome boy with his collar turned up, pouting out of the page. A young woman blowing a dandelion clock, eyes closed. An older woman with thick glasses

220

and a stern expression. (Adelaide's mother, perhaps?) Turning the pages only prompts more questions. Was this street scene a view Adelaide knew well? Was the hastily sketched pub a regular hangout of hers?

She picks up a different notebook and flicks through it. This must be from a later period because you can tell immediately that the hand at work is more confident in the mark-making, that thought has gone into the compositions. There is sometimes humour evident in the drawing now, storytelling even, Jess thinks, pausing to smile at a picture of an old man licking an ice cream with an expression of bliss. She takes a photo of the sketch, musing that it would be lovely to choose a couple of early pieces to go into the book. If these early drawings are fascinating to her as a know-nothing, they will no doubt be of even greater interest to Adelaide's fans, or indeed anyone who has ever studied art themselves.

Then she notices a stray piece of paper with a loose, black-ink sketch of a man sitting at a table with a glass of wine. Is this Remy as a young man, perhaps? Jess takes in the watchful stare of the sitter, the slight lift of the head as if in challenge. The body language is languid, unafraid, and she feels intuitively that there's an intimacy between subject and artist. If this isn't Remy, she'll be interested to know who it is, she thinks, taking another quick photo.

'Got it,' calls Luc at that moment, and she replaces the notepad with some reluctance and returns to the main room, where he has laid out a number of newspaper clippings across the desk. 'The system works!'

'Amazing,' she replies, leaning over to look at the yellowing clippings, now encased in plastic folders. 'Why This Plucky Student's Painting is the Summer Exhibition's Most Talked-About Piece' is the headline in one of them. 'Outrage of Cleaner's Deception' thunders a less approving editorial. 'Who IS *Woman Having a Cig?*' asks another and Jess stifles a laugh, wondering if this is the article that Margie's mum came across, imagining the woman's disbelief at seeing her own daughter's face staring back from the newspaper. She peers closer at this last article, where the painting has been reproduced, loving the expression captured in Margie's eyes. Even in black and white, you can almost smell the smoke that curls around to frame the top of the head.

'Here, I've got it in colour if you want to see it,' Luc says, swinging the laptop round.

Of course she wants to see it. 'Oh wow,' she says, drinking in the image there on the screen, imagining that lazy afternoon on which it was created. The burnt orange background makes Margie's bleached hair and red lips sing out of the picture; the skin tones are fabulous, the smoke gorgeously wispy against the clean lines elsewhere in the portrait. From listening to Adelaide talking about her tuition and studies, Jess has learned to look closer at paintings for their shapes and contrasts, and notices that the whorls of smoke are subtly mirrored by the waves of Margie's hair and the creases in the white top she's wearing. The nose is a little on the chunky side, admittedly, but somehow that only adds to the appeal.

'I love it,' she says. 'It's so vibrant. I feel like I know Margie, just looking at her. I'm there with them, in on the moment.'

'I love it too,' he says. 'And when you see how bright it is, how it catches the eye, I can't believe it wasn't spotted in the summer exhibition sooner.'

'Same! It must have totally popped off the wall. Do you think you could email me the image, please? The publishers are going to include some photos and artworks in the book, right? We should start drawing up a list between us.' Then she pauses, eyeing the painting again. *Help a sister out*, Margie seems to be saying to her. In the name of female solidarity, shouldn't Jess at least try to intervene in the two friends' estrangement? 'By the way,' she goes on, treading carefully. 'I was wondering about contacting Margie to see if she still has the companion portrait she drew of Adelaide in retaliation. What do you think? It would be good to feature both, wouldn't it? It's such a brilliant coda to the story.'

He looks at her. 'I'm not sure Adelaide would be happy about that.'

'She wasn't when I suggested it earlier,' Jess confesses with a sigh. She doesn't get it. Here's Jess, who would give anything to see *her* old friend again – and all Adelaide has to do is pick up the phone, fire off an email, and they could be back in touch. 'Don't you think it's sad, the two of them still not speaking after all these years? It would be great to get them back together again, when they were such good mates.'

He screws up his face. 'Yes, but—'

'And sometimes, if people are too stubborn or proud to reach out to one another, wouldn't you agree that it's only right that someone else should step in?'

'You're the someone else in this scenario, I take it?' he asks dubiously.

'Absolutely! A good friendship is one of the most precious things in the world. Especially between women. I don't see what the harm would be in trying to fix their relationship, pull a few strings behind the scenes in order to help them find a way back into one another's lives.'

He shakes his head. 'Honestly? I wouldn't get involved. If Adelaide wanted them to be friends again, she'd have sorted that out for herself by now. She must have a good reason for the radio silence. And she won't thank you for interfering.'

Jess says nothing but she isn't convinced. What if the so-called 'good reason' is merely that Adelaide is too pig-headed to extend an olive branch – or receive one, for that matter? She's certain that if she can bring the two of them back together, once they've got over whatever ruck caused the rift in the first place, their main feelings will be mutual gladness. If being an agony aunt has taught her anything, it's that everyone needs a helping hand now and then. Maybe she could do a spot of secret digging around, see if she can find some contact details for Margie. Adelaide never needs to know, does she?

'So, what sort of thing would be helpful for you to see while you're here?' Luc asks, as if the subject's closed. 'Shall I find what I've got from the early years, if you're working chronologically? There's a bunch of photos from when she was a student, and a couple of hilarious school reports, for starters.'

'That would be brilliant,' Jess replies. Then, because curiosity has got the better of her – 'Oh, and talking of photos, who's the kid in these pictures with you?' She gestures to them, seizing the opportunity to take a closer look herself. Luc and the boy on a beach, dripping wet and clutching bodyboards, both laughing. Luc and the boy in some diner or other, both drinking out of a gigantic chocolate milkshake with a straw each, wearing matching baseball caps. Her eyes slide back to the beach picture with a hasty glance at Luc's bod: it's pretty ripped. 'Is he your son?' she asks, dragging her gaze away again.

'No, that's Hen, my nephew Henry,' he says. 'Catherine's boy. He's eighteen now, just done his A levels.' He's fiddling around on the laptop as he speaks. 'I don't have any kids,' he adds, before opening a new document and leaning towards the screen. 'Right, let's see what we've got.'

The afternoon slides by very pleasantly. Luc is working his way through a new crate, cataloguing and cross-referencing everything he comes across, occasionally holding up something of particular interest – a photograph, a sketch – to show her. Jess, meanwhile, begins sifting through the documents he's provided her with, all of them adding colour and context to the recordings she's made with Adelaide. A brochure of the Work exhibition is especially thrilling; its pages contain details of all the pieces included in the show and somebody (Adelaide herself?) has annotated it with jaunty little comments. *SOLD, hooray!* is written beside the listing of an apron titled *What a Load of Rubbish*. Jess comes across a photograph of Adelaide with her parents – and yes, the sketch of the older woman definitely *is* her mother, she decides, comparing the two with the satisfaction of a case-cracking detective.

'Blimey, look at this bloke,' Luc says, holding up a portrait of a man who's so beefy he's virtually bursting out of his suit. He has a thick neck, heavy eyebrows over squinty eyes, and has been painted with his elbows perpendicular to his body, holding his right fist with his left hand in a threatening manner.

Luc's wiping a cobweb from the man's face, and it's only when the dust clears that Jess gets a proper look at him and feels something inside her vibrate in response.

'Wait, I think . . .' she murmurs, coming closer. She stares at the man's domed forehead, his prominent nose, leering mouth. 'I've seen him before,' she says. 'Is there a date on this? Any other details?' A bad feeling comes over her, one she can't explain. 'It's weird, but I think I've met him,' she says.

'How could you have met him? This is a really old painting. He might not even be alive any more,' Luc points out, turning the canvas over.

'When I lived in Paris before. I was a chambermaid years ago,' she explains, just as he says, '1998, this is dated.'

'That's when I was here,' Jess says. Her skin is prickling as if her body knows something she doesn't. 'I think maybe he used to drink in the bar of the hotel where I worked.' Yes, that sounds right. She can picture him with a brandy and a cigar, leaning on the bar, booming with laughter to a group of men around him. She and Pascale would sometimes have a drink there after work, even though management weren't keen on staff mingling with guests. Their friend Delphine worked behind the bar and would always pour them massive glasses of wine and charge them a fraction of the ordinary price when her boss Thierry was looking the other way. Jess takes a photo of the painting, planning to ask Adelaide about the man. It's probably nothing, she tells herself, returning to her pile of papers. Her imagination running away with her.

'Oh wow, Valentin would *love* this,' she says a few minutes later, discovering a photo of Adelaide literally being sewn into a ballgown by two other women – fellow students, perhaps? Jeanette? 'Valentin works at the brasserie near where I'm staying. He studied fashion at the College of Art here,' she explains, seeing Luc's mystified expression.

'You've made a friend already?' he asks, bemused. 'Jess, you've only just arrived!'

'Mate, I've made *loads* of friends,' she replies with a laugh, ticking them off on her fingers. 'Beatrice, the hotel receptionist – we're going out tomorrow night, actually; Valentin and his lovely boyfriend Nicolas; Alain, this sweet older guy, who's been struggling since his wife developed dementia ...' She feels her eyes mist as she recalls their last conversation at the *crêperie*. 'They took the decision to move her into a care home a month ago,' she goes on, 'and Luc, I thought for a minute he was going to cry as he told me. Reading between the lines, he's pretty lost without her. He's always at the *crêperie* on his own, when before they would ... What? Are you *laughing* at me?'

'No!' he says, which is patently untrue. 'Well, all right, yes, but only out of surprise. I mean, I've been here nearly two months and haven't really met anyone, let alone befriended them and heard their life stories. How do you even do that?'

'What do you mean, how do I do that – I want to know how you can be here two months and *not* get to know anyone!

Not even your neighbour, or someone in your favourite café, or … ?' He's shaking his head. 'Oh Luc,' she teases. 'This is pitiful! And it's called being friendly, anyway. Taking an interest in other people.'

'What, going up and talking to complete strangers? I'm a Londoner, I'm not about to do that,' he protests. 'Anyway, it's not at all pitiful. I like my own company, thanks. I've got friends coming over from England every few weeks … Catherine and Hen are staying next week too. So you can get that look off your face, I'm absolutely fine. Having a very nice time, in fact!'

'Hmm,' she says. 'Well, if you get bored, let me know, because I'm sure Alain would appreciate the company. He's ever so nice and has had such an interesting life, but you can tell he's lonely.'

'Thanks, but I'll pass,' he says, his dark eyes amused. There's a beat, and then he adds, 'You know, for a minute, I thought *you* were about to ask me out, not try and fob me off with Lonely Alain.' He glances at the clock on the wall – which is lucky because it saves him from seeing the startled expression on her face. (He's joking, right, about her asking him out?) 'Talking of which, it's nearly six, can you believe. Are you hungry? There's a good Italian restaurant up the road – or Dixième Degré on the corner is great.'

'Six, is it really?' Jess can't believe time has skidded past so quickly. She hasn't even mentioned the Revenge paintings, her whole reason for coming here. 'How did that happen? I swear it was half past three, like, ten minutes ago.'

'Time always seems to vanish here,' he says, getting up and

stretching from where he's been kneeling over a crate. His shirt rides up with the motion and Jess tries not to look at the golden slice of belly on display, remembering how good the rest of his body looked in the beach photo. 'So – shall we get something to eat?'

'Oh. Shit, no, I can't,' she says in a fluster. 'I'm going out on a d—' She doesn't quite finish the word 'date' because her phone suddenly pings with a message and she sees it's from Sexy Georges himself. 'Or am I?' she mutters, tapping the screen.

Her heart sinks because it appears he's letting her down at the last minute. *Jess! Désolé!* the message begins, followed by a convoluted explanation in French text shorthand that her brain can't immediately translate. 'Damn it,' she says to herself. She's been looking forward to a flirty dinner out ever since she first made contact with him again; she's even changed her mind about what to wear, having now settled on a floaty pale blue Grecian-style maxi dress that's drapey enough to disguise all the *frites* and *vin blanc* she's had lately. Is it terrible to admit that she's also planned what underwear to wear, and which perfume? It *is* Paris, after all, and if you can't wear sexy underwear in Paris, then where can you?

'Everything all right?' Luc asks. 'Is this Alain texting you, or Valentin, or some other Parisian hunk?'

His words are flippant but then she glances up from her phone to see that there's a strange expression on his face, one she can't quite read.

'Hang on, I just …' She peers back at the message – something about drinks with colleagues, she works out. It's only then that she realises that Sexy Georges is not in fact cancelling, but apologising because he won't be able to meet her until nine, rather than eight. 'Oh! Okay. Sorry about this,' she says, firing off a reply. *No problem. Nine works for me. See you later.* Her heart gives a rapid skip. 'Cool. Yeah, I'm meeting someone for dinner at nine but . . .' She screws up her face. 'Christ, *nine*, there's no way I can last that long without eating *something*,' she confesses, thinking aloud. If they meet at nine, it's going to be ages – half past at least – before any actual food arrives in front of her. She'll be weak with hunger by then. Unattractively hangry, possibly. If she has something snacky with Luc now, she can keep the starvation wolf at bay, she figures. 'Sod it, yes. Let's go and eat. Good call!'

They carefully pack up and refile all of the documents they've been looking at, and, as they set off back down into the street below, Jess feels full of cheer. It's busier now, with a pleasant summery buzz in the air. Couples and groups of friends are sitting at the pavement tables with beers and cocktails, music plays from the bars and restaurants; it feels as if everyone is leaving work in the mood to have fun.

'This place is meant to be good,' says Luc, pointing down a side street, at the end of which they find a sweet outdoor bar with brightly coloured parasols, jungly vines rampaging up the white-painted walls and Dua Lipa's 'Love Again' blasting from a speaker.

'Perfect,' says Jess, not least because she and her girls love this song – and in the next moment, she's transported to her car with them all singing along at the tops of their voices.

There's such a joyful holiday vibe, in fact, that she can't resist ordering an Aperol spritz when their hipster waiter appears at the table. Yes, and some olives and cheese, while they're at it. Ooh, and why not a portion of fries to share as well?

'So,' Luc says, once they are tucking in. 'Who are you having dinner with later? Is this another new friend, or ... ?'

'Not exactly,' she replies, popping an olive into her mouth. God, it's delicious. 'Georges and I used to see each other when I was working here and ... well, that's it, really. We've arranged to catch up.' She detects a sudden awkwardness between them in the next moment. Or is the Aperol spritz blurring everything? 'It's not like a date-date,' she confirms, feeling defensive. 'Just two old friends.'

Busy spearing an olive, he doesn't respond immediately. Then he asks, 'Have you been on any date-dates since you and your ex split up? Or are you not at that stage yet?'

'I haven't. It's not really been ... No,' she says, thinking of the occasions her friends have tried to set her up, how utterly disinterested she has been each time. How busy she has been with the girls moreover, how determined she is to put them first while they all adjust to the new post-separation way of life. 'Not that I'm in a mad hurry. How about you?'

They chat for a while – about how awful it is to go through a marriage breaking down but also the relief of starting to come through the other side; the unexpected pleasure in realising that the world is still turning, that life continues to offer everyday joys: sunsets, laughter, purring cats. Conversation turns to her daughters, then childhood experiences; she asks him more about his smallholding dreams and only teases him a little bit when he confesses to drawing up a spreadsheet with links to his favourite farm machinery and equipment. Perhaps she's emboldened by the second drink because then she finds herself admitting that she's been looking up agricultural courses on his behalf.

'Only because I remembered that one of my friends has a neighbour who works at the university near me,' she says, stumbling over her words a little at his startled expression. 'Agriculture and science, or something, at Canterbury. University of Kent. But I investigated a bit further, and there are loads of brilliant places where you could study. Hadlow College – that's near Tonbridge – looks amazing, and—' She breaks off. 'What? Why are you looking at me like that?'

'I'm just . . .' He shakes his head. 'Surprised. I mean – you don't have to take me on as an agony aunt case, Jess, if that's what this is about. I can sort my own life out.'

'I know you can! Absolutely!' She feels embarrassed now. 'Sorry, I was just trying to . . .' Another sentence goes unfinished and she shrugs, unsure how to get out of this hole she's managed to dig.

'What do you think that's all about?' he asks, his eyes swivelling briefly to the waiter who's bringing a huge plate of nachos loaded with salsa, guacamole and cheese to the neighbouring table. 'If you don't mind me saying so, you seem quite keen to get involved with other people's lives.'

'Only in a helpful way!' she protests, because the criticism feels a bit too near the knuckle. 'There's nothing wrong with that, is there? I wish I had been able to help *more* people, frankly!' The words burst out of her, and there are tears in her eyes as she thinks of Pascale; she grips her hands under the table, trying to pull herself together.

He looks – understandably – a little unnerved by the outburst but doesn't pry. 'Okay,' he says after a moment. 'Well, thanks. Hadlow College, did you say? I'll have a look.' He glances again at the nachos nearby as if magnetically drawn. 'Are you still hungry, by the way? I might order some of those if you fancy sharing?'

The thud of her heart is receding and she nods. 'The night is still young,' she says. 'Definitely.'

The night *is* still young, she tells herself in the loos, splashing water on her face to try and tone down the hectic colour in her cheeks. There's plenty of time before she has to leave. Except all of a sudden, after really good nachos and a hilarious detour into embarrassing university stories, it's eight o'clock and she's still in the clothes she's been wearing all day, her make-up's completely worn off, and her feet probably stink in her sandals. She'll never have time for the shower and blow-dry she'd been planning, nor the careful application of sexy eye make-up that always takes longer than she thinks.

'Fuck!' she yelps, jumping up. 'Oh God, sorry, Luc, I've got to go.'

'Are you sure?' he asks, sounding disappointed. 'You could . . . stay?'

She's in such a flap though, trying to flag down a waiter so that she can pay the bill – *no, it's my turn, you got the pizzas, remember* – that she doesn't answer. She's already checking on her map app the quickest route back to the hotel and cursing her own poor time-management. It's only a few minutes later, once he's insisted that he'll pay – *no, really, it's fine* – and she's quickly hugged him goodbye and rushed off down the road, that his words come back to her. *You could . . . stay?*

She stops dead in the street, his handsome face flashing into her mind. The question in his dark eyes. 'Shit,' she says aloud, because this is all getting a bit too complicated, suddenly. Far too confusing. Is she reading too much into that moment? He was probably only being friendly, wasn't he? Enjoying their chat. Yes, it's almost certainly that, and nothing more.

She carries on walking, pushing Luc to the back of her mind. Don't be so silly, she tells herself. Besides, in a short space of time, she's going to be reunited with gorgeous Georges. There's no point overcomplicating things.

Chapter Twenty-Four

'What do you mean, you don't have anyone suitable?' Adelaide asks crossly, drumming her fingers on the kitchen table. It's Thursday morning, and this is the third cleaning agency she's called so far. As predicted, the company she's always used in the past flatly refused to send her a new housekeeper, or even a cleaner. Marie-Thérèse must have trotted out a good old sob story to them, she thinks, jaw clenched.

'It is the summer, Madame,' the woman replies, rather acidly, to Adelaide's ear. 'Our staff are allowed to take holidays, too.'

'I'm not saying they're *not*, I'm just saying I'm—'

'Goodbye, Madame,' says Frosty-Knickers and hangs up on her. Actually hangs *up*, on *her*, Adelaide Fox. When all she's trying to do is pay someone good money to clean her apartment and take care of her needs! Don't these idiots *want* her business? You'd think she'd been put on some kind of cleaners' blacklist!

A momentary flicker of paranoia takes hold in her head. She's not really on a blacklist, is she? 'I'd better bloody not be,' she mutters to Jean-Paul.

For now, she'll have to abandon the cleaner hunt and get on top of the business end of the morning herself. She needs to walk Jean-Paul, shop for provisions, wash up all the dinner things from last night, make her bed, give the bathroom a once-over ... Heavens. How do people manage? She messages Jessica asking her to arrive an hour later than usual, and calls for the dog. Fresh air and a constitutional; let's hope it's enough to reduce her fiery mood to a simmer.

Down by the river, the breeze feels a little fresher, the city bustle at a remove. Few of the tourist boats are out on the water yet and the scene is one of serenity. She and Jean-Paul stick to the shade wherever they can because otherwise the pavement becomes too hot for his small feet. It's during the summer especially that she finds herself missing the great green spaces of London, imagining how Jean-Paul would love the chance to get off the lead and romp across the grassy vistas of Parliament Fields. How enraptured he'd be, coming across so many picnickers with portable barbecues – so many delicious smells to pursue, so many tempting sausages and sandwiches to attempt to steal!

The thought makes her smile before a wave of melancholy follows. Will she ever return to London now, or even to England? Possibly not. A memory unfolds, of lying in Fordham Park, the nearest green space to Goldsmiths, with a bunch of friends one summer's evening where the low sun had become liquid bronze in the sky. Five or six of them lounging around smoking roll-ups and drinking cheap wine from the bottle (Christ, they were so unsophisticated) while they put the world to rights. All those big existential questions they answered so passionately, seen through a lens of loyalty and justice; how they were prepared to lay down their lives for a cause. Oh, to be young and idealistic again! she thinks, glancing down at Jean-Paul, who has paused to sniff around a particularly pungent bin.

Except, she remembers, when it came to the crunch, one of her friends *had* actually put her future on the line for Adelaide's sake, and without a second thought. Had come to the rescue in the nick of time, even if the consequences were more dreadful than either of them could have expected. Had she even heard the car engine that day? She can't recall now. All she could think about was Colin Copeland coming towards her with a look of terrifying determination in his eye, and her own self screaming in sudden fear because she knew for certain it would not end well. Then came the merciful sound of footsteps running up the stairs. An angry shout. And the next thing she knew ...

Adelaide blinks out of her old memory, only to realise that, down by the bin, Jean-Paul has discovered an abandoned takeaway box he is keen to investigate further. The box once contained fried chicken but now is merely the coffin for its bones. 'Oh no, you don't,' she says, hauling at him, because every dog owner knows the horror stories of splintering chicken bones and she'd never forgive herself if that was to be Jean-Paul's fate. He, on the other hand, seems insistent that he's willing to take the risk and plants his feet firmly on the ground, resisting removal.

'Oh dear,' says a voice behind her, sounding amused. 'They

just smell too good, don't they, darling? Will none of the litter louts *think* about the dogs? Hello again, by the way.'

Adelaide turns, somewhat flustered, to see a white-haired woman in a flowing orange and pink dress, a Westie on a lead at her side. It takes a moment to contextualise her – ahh, yes, the woman whose dog Jean-Paul had rushed over to greet the other day – but at least Jean-Paul's attention is diverted by the Westie and she can drag him away from temptation.

'Hello,' says Adelaide as the dogs greet one another by some mutual bottom-sniffing that sees their two leads quickly entwined.

'Guys, guys!' the woman cries. 'Jeez Louise, imagine being so excited by the smell of someone else's butt . . . You'll have us over in a minute, you two!' Laughing, she unwinds her lead around Adelaide's and gently pulls the Westie to one side. 'Are you going this way? Lovely! We'll join you, if we may.'

Adelaide might have said a polite no on another day – or even an impolite one, let's be realistic – but on this occasion she's still frazzled from all of the tasks yet ahead of her and ends up acquiescing.

'Of course,' she says, rather stiffly, even though the woman's already in step with her and it didn't actually seem to be a question.

'Have you been in Paris long? We're only here for the summer but I said to Jim – that's my husband – we can't be away from Meg – that's the dog – for so long, she would get very confused by our disappearance. Although, I should caveat that by saying I was adopted as a baby; I'm always projecting my abandonment issues on to everyone else, even my dog.

She probably would have been fine but how can I take such a chance? Anyway, here we are, all the way from Montreal, and isn't it marvellous? The buildings, the history, the *food*! I'm having the best time!'

A Montreal highlights reel immediately flickers through Adelaide's head – the autumn colours of St Helen's Island reflected in the wide blue Lawrence river, the Gothic splendour of the Notre-Dame Basilica, Brad insisting she try poutine, laughing as he promised on his mother's life that it would taste better than it looked (he was right, thank goodness). Only a couple of hours from Ottawa, it had become a fun place for them to hang out at weekends. It takes her a second to travel back into her body again, into the conversation, and she isn't sure which part of the woman's monologue to respond to first.

'Well, I initially lived here in the eighties,' she says in the end. 'But I've moved around a fair bit.'

'The *eighties*! Now I feel like a jerk. So of course you know how marvellous it is. We took Meg along the linear park yesterday, isn't it fabulous? Like a secret garden up there above the buildings. And the catacombs are quite something, aren't they? We went last week and I'm still having nightmares. Apparently my husband's found an amazing taxidermy museum that he wants us to investigate this afternoon ... I'm already feeling like the summer won't be long enough for us.' She elbows Adelaide in a friendly way. 'Sorry, listen to me rattling on. I'm Frieda. Are we the same sort of age, do you think? I'm seventy but being here makes me feel like a teenager again. The romance!'

Adelaide is just thinking that Frieda is a bit full-on for her liking, particularly this early in the morning, when a couple of youths on rollerblades roar past them at top speed, almost close enough to knock Frieda over.

'Hey! Assholes!' bellows Frieda after them without missing a beat, and sticks up her middle finger for good measure. Maybe she isn't so bad after all.

'I'm Adelaide,' Adelaide says as they continue along. 'Adelaide Fox.' Frieda is clearly no art lover because the name seems to have absolutely no bearing on her. Not so much as a twitch. 'Sounds like you're having a great time. Have you been to any . . . ?' She hesitates, but no, it's impossible to stop herself. 'Any galleries while you're here?'

'Me? Oh no, I'm not one for that sort of thing. Jim and I, we both worked in the construction trade; I don't know one end of a paintbrush from another. Give me a great building any day.'

'But a building is a kind of art, no?' Adelaide feels compelled to say. She has never been to the linear park or the catacombs herself, and hasn't actually heard of this taxidermy museum, but given the choice, she'd always rather be in the Louvre or Musée d'Orsay or the Pompidou – or any of the city's world-class galleries, for that matter.

'Is it? Or is it instead a feat of physics and skilled labour? Okay, probably a bit of both,' Frieda concedes. She smiles at Adelaide, and Adelaide, surprised by the friendliness in Frieda's eyes, finds herself smiling back. 'So tell me – do you feel continual bliss, living in a city like this? Apart from imbeciles on rollerblades, that is. Is life one magnificence after another?'

'Heavens, no,' Adelaide snorts. 'I battle through a hundred annoyances every day just like every other human being.'

'Like what? Your breakfast croissants are just too perfect?'

'I wish! More like the half hour I've spent on the phone this morning trying to sort out a cleaner with no luck. Having to fight my way through the mobs of tourists every time I leave my apartment. The busker on the square who only seems to know "La Vie en Rose" or "Non, Je Ne Regrette Rien". I can't tell you the number of times that I've felt like giving him something to regret, but it must be in the high thousands.'

Frieda laughs. 'He'll be playing "Oui, Je Regrette Tout", by the time you've finished with him.'

'Damn right, he will be,' Adelaide says, laughing herself. Despite her earlier crotchetiness, she can feel herself warming to this woman as they proceed along the river path, chatting. There's something refreshingly young and energetic about her that makes Adelaide in turn feel a little more alive. Perhaps she's become jaded about living in the most beautiful city in the world, because seeing it through Frieda's eyes is surprisingly uplifting.

It's with some disappointment, then, that she realises they've walked much further along the river than she usually goes. 'I'm afraid I need to head home,' she says, conscious of all she must do before Jessica arrives. 'But it was nice to talk to you.'

'You too! I hope our paths cross again, if not our dogs' leads,' Frieda replies. 'Oh, and by the way, do you want the number of our cleaner? She's very good, if kind of fearsome and monosyllabic.'

'I can live with fearsome and monosyllabic if there's also a "good" in there,' Adelaide says thankfully. 'Yes, please.'

They come to a standstill, phones out, because Frieda, like Adelaide, cannot walk at the same time as doing anything technical. Frieda has to find a pair of glasses at the bottom of her vast black handbag first, then laboriously types in Adelaide's number to forward the details.

'There we are,' she says and Adelaide's phone pings in confirmation a second later. 'And if you ever want to go for a cocktail or a glass of that delicious French rosé, you just say the word, because I will be *in*. Good to meet you, Adelaide. And you too, darling Jean-Paul.'

'Bye, Frieda,' says Adelaide, smiling faintly as she turns and heads back in the opposite direction. It's rare to meet someone who has no idea who she is, but it's oddly refreshing to speak on an ordinary level for once, without any of the usual silly fawning or obsequiousness. *And* she now has the number of a taciturn cleaner to boot. The day has definitely taken a turn for the better.

Chapter Twenty-Five

TO: Rook Associates Talent Agency Inc.

FAO: Margie Claremont née Flint — please forward

Dear Mrs Claremont,

I am currently in Paris, in the process of writing Adelaide Fox's memoir. Unsurprisingly, your name has come up a lot so far (in a good way, I hasten to add). I have loved listening to her stories about your exploits, triumphs and fun together. Which is why I'm now getting in touch, because . . .

This is where Jess stalls, every time she tries to compose an email to Margie. She keeps being put off by the memory of Luc's warning look — his disapproval, even — when she suggested getting in touch with Adelaide's old friend. But then she'll remember Adelaide breaking down in tears previously when talking about her, and it seems the most obvious thing in the world that of course Jess should smooth the way to reconciliation. Simply asking if Margie still has an old drawing she made of Adelaide is legit, right? Nobody can argue with that. And yet she can't quite find the words.

Jess sighs and pushes the laptop away. Maybe she's not in

the right frame of mind today. Last night was ... well, the word 'rollercoaster' springs to mind, if that isn't too much of a cliché. Having wrenched herself reluctantly from the Belleville bar and Luc, she had hotfooted it back to the hotel, all set for the fastest makeover ever ... only to discover on her return that a new text had arrived, this time saying that Georges wouldn't be able to meet her at all now. He was very, very sorry. He was broken-hearted. He hoped he could make it up to her with the dinner of her dreams the following week, maybe Monday?

'Oh fuck you, Georges,' she had all but howled, throwing the phone across the room. After a five-minute slump on her bed, she had then proceeded with the fastest makeover ever, before heading straight back out again to Brasserie Les Amours, her nearest happy place. There she had ordered a large glass of wine and steak frites, followed by another large glass of wine with Valentin once he had finished his shift.

'This Georges, he is no good,' was Valentin's pronounce-ment, 'whereas Monsieur Luc, now he sounds nice ...'

'Maybe it's me,' Jess had said dolefully, ignoring the second half of Valentin's sentence. 'Not special enough. Not good enough.'

This has long been one of her secret worries: that she's just not that deserving of anyone's love and attention. No doubt a therapist would home in on her dad walking out on the family when she was a little girl, but it was actually something that really got to her about being married to David – that she seemed to love him more than he loved her. Not only was she the engine of the household, powering the family along, she was also the one – the only one – who kept charging up the battery of their relationship. It would be Jess organising dinner dates for the two of them, or booking tickets to see the comedian they both liked, or resignedly texting him links to a pair of nice boots when he said, shamefacedly, on Christmas Eve each year that he couldn't think of what to buy her. It turned out he was too busy thinking about himself – or rather, his dick, and how he wanted to stick it in the nearest pretty Australian publicist.

Now here's Georges, blowing her off at the last minute. She's starting to think there's a common denominator: her.

'What? No!' Valentin protested passionately, banging a fist on the table. 'I completely disagree!'

'Why don't people fall in love with me though, Val? Like, properly? Enough to buy me a nice Christmas present? Is it that I'm just not that ... that great?'

He looked perplexed – probably at the Christmas present reference because she hadn't said any of that stuff out loud. But he rallied quickly enough at her closing question. 'You *are* great, my darling. I know you are! And Nicolas knows you are! We will adopt you and shower you with Christmas gifts, even though, Jess, here is the news: it is August, not December. But we will do that for you, okay?'

She laughed because he was being so thoroughly charming, and it was extremely nice to have someone say such things. 'Thank you,' she mumbled, leaning against him with an affectionate nudge.

He nudged her right back. 'And next time – if you decide to *give* this Georges-piece-of-shit a next-time chance, that

245

is – maybe just stay with Luc? I think that will be a good idea. Team Luc!'

'Not Team Luc,' she felt obliged to argue. 'Anyway, that's enough about my dismal love life. Tell me your news.'

That's enough about my dismal love life will end up on her gravestone at this rate, she thinks now, abandoning her email to Margie for the time being. She turns to an audience who are at least bound to her by blood. *Morning, girlies, how are we doing today?* she writes into the family group chat, with a slight pang as she sees their bright faces in photo-form on her screen. *Hope you're having loads of fun, can't wait to hear everything when we're back home again. Don't forget to send me pics! Love you all xxxx*

A message comes in immediately from Mia. *Ask Adelaide about the red car that was spotted outside Little Bower around the time Colin died!!* is all it says, and Jess rolls her eyes, knowing already that she will be asking no such thing. *Adelaide can't drive!* she fires back, exasperated. They are yet to reach Colin's death in the narrative but Jess is already apprehensive about how Adelaide will tell this particular chapter.

Edie's response is to send a selfie of her still in bed, pulling a face. Polly, meanwhile, sends a beret emoji, reminding Jess that she has promised to buy her one. At least nobody has mentioned David behaving oddly again, she tells herself, sending a final *Have a great day! Maybe chat later?* Then she grabs her bag and heads out to Adelaide's apartment for today's session. Time to immerse herself in someone else's far more exciting life once more.

★

Trust a woman – that's Jess's new motto. Don't bother with unreliable men. Because after work that day, of course Beatrice from the hotel is still up for a drink, exactly as arranged. Absolutely no breakneck changes of plan or cancellations from *her*.

Beatrice looks immaculate as ever when Jess meets her in the hotel lobby – not a hair out of place, her eye make-up perfect. She has changed into wide-leg black palazzo pants, teamed with a dove-grey halterneck top that ties in a huge bow at the back of her neck, and she has switched her demure at-work diamante stud earrings for large golden hoops. Never in a million years could Jess – in her rather faded pink maxi dress and gladiator sandals – look so chic, but it's kind of a thrill to be seen out and about with someone this beautiful. As they start walking towards Le Mélange, Beatrice's favourite bar, Jess notices that all the men – and a lot of the women – turn and stare as they pass. At Beatrice, obviously, not her, but all the same, she finds herself preening a little from the reflected attention.

Le Mélange is a cellar bar, with no huge sign advertising its whereabouts; definitely the sort of place you have to be in the know about. Jess must have walked past it every day since she's been in Paris, and never once imagined there would be such a vibrant space tucked away there out of sight. Inside, the bar is strung with pink fairy lights, the walls are covered in cool graphic prints – a gallery in itself – and there is intimate booth seating, as well as some larger central tables. The clientele, much to Jess's delight, is *not* exclusively made up of hip young Parisiennes – this place has almost the feel of a local back home, with a couple of older men perched at the bar with fat glasses of cognac, a whole cluster of excellent-looking middle-aged women (her tribe) clinking cocktails at one of the big communal tables, plus people in their twenties and thirties, fresh from the office, at a guess, drinking wine. There's also a fifty-something couple and a younger blonde woman (their daughter?) all laughing about something the daughter is showing them on her phone, and their unselfconscious hilarity makes Jess smile. There's a good vibe here.

Beatrice leads them through the bar and out into a courtyard area with huge jungly plants in terracotta pots between the tables. Benches line the perimeter, scattered with brightly coloured cushions. There are mismatched lanterns hanging from a raised canopy, and the joyful thump of a hip-hop track in the background.

'*Yes*, Beatrice,' Jess cries rapturously as they take a seat outside beneath a scarlet parasol. 'I knew you'd know the best bar in Paris. This is great!'

'But of course I know the best bar in Paris,' she replies, spreading her hands and batting her eyelashes. 'And now I will recommend the best cocktail – a Soixante Quinze. I think in English you call it a "French 75"? It is a classic! Champagne, gin and lemon syrup – okay?'

'Delicious – perfect,' says Jess happily. She's starting to think she would like Beatrice to take on the role of being her permanent guide through life, if this is the standard so far.

Once the waitress has brought their cocktails, Beatrice raises hers in a little toast. 'To friendship,' she says. 'It is good to know you, Jess. Many of our guests, they arrive and then they leave, and we never learn anything about them other than they thought the bed was too hard, or that we should invest in air conditioning.' She pulls a face. 'But you are different. You are interesting! I like that you are here, a woman the same age as me, and you are having fun in Paris.' She elbows Jess. 'Maybe I will go to London and work for a while, no? And talk to everyone in my hotel, like you, I think.'

Jess laughs. 'Good luck with that! One, if you're going to work in London, you're staying with me. And two, no one talks to anyone in London.'

'In Paris, the same. Apart from you. That is why I like you!'

Jess smiles at her, feeling touched, and raises her own glass. 'To friendship,' she says, and takes a sip. The French 75 is, of course, utterly delicious. Two out of two for Beatrice. 'Talking of friendship,' she goes on, 'can I ask your advice?'

'But of course! What is it?'

It is a relief to talk to Beatrice about Adelaide and Margie – a relief to have a different kind of response from the ones she has so far received from Adelaide (tears, clamming up) and Luc (frowning and dissuading). Empathetic Beatrice gets it at once.

'This is terrible!' she cries. 'And they have still not spoken? Why did they even argue?'

'I don't actually know,' Jess confesses. 'We haven't got that far yet.'

The highlights from today's session with Adelaide included gems such as appearing on the very cool *Late Night Line-Up* where she was interviewed by Joan Bakewell ('an absolute darling'), having two paintings selected as part of a British Council exhibition called New British Creatives that toured Europe for eighteen months in the late sixties ('even my mother was impressed') and her first solo exhibition in Nice one summer, where she met Remy for the first time. So far in the narrative, Margie is still very much Friend Number One.

'What would you do, if you were me?' Jess goes on. 'I keep nearly emailing her – Margie, I mean – to try and get the ball rolling, but something stops me every time. I do want to help, though.'

'Then I think *yes*. Helping is good. Absolutely!'

Helping is good. Exactly; Jess's personal mantra. Helping *is* good. How can anyone argue with that? 'Then I will,' she says. 'I'm going to get those two magnificent women back together and that's that!'

Beatrice pumps a fist in the air. 'Yes, Jess! You will. I know it!' She points at Jess's phone, sticking out at the top of her bag. 'Go on, do it now. I will find us a menu for food – did I tell you the food here is divine, too? – and you write your message to her before you change your mind. Don't let me down!'

She gets up without another word and sashays off, greeting a couple of people she knows along the way. Meanwhile, Jess, emboldened by Beatrice's surety, obediently searches for one of her half-finished draft emails. What's the worst that can happen? One – Adelaide gets a bit cross with her (again). Two – Margie doesn't reply. Neither outcome is exactly the end of the world.

Her fingers stab away at the screen as she finishes composing the email. *It would be great to have the chance of including your drawing of Adelaide in the memoir, if you still happen to have it,* she writes, then hesitates. Anything else? In for a penny ... she tells herself, and adds, *Let me know if you want me to pass on any message to Adelaide, too.*

She bites her lip, reading back the whole thing. It's short, polite and businesslike, apart from that rogue last line. Chances are it will be read by an assistant of Margie's anyway, who won't care. There's no real harm there, she tells herself, taking a deep, nerve-holding breath and pressing 'Send'.

'Done?' replies Beatrice, reappearing with menus and two new cocktails for them. 'Bravo. You know, you make me think of my dad.' She laughs, possibly at Jess's confused expression. 'I don't mean you are a tall sixty-five-year-old man from Senegal—'

'I *was* wondering,' Jess puts in.

'But he too likes to get people together. It makes him so happy.' She goes on to describe the charity her dad – Moussa – set up, back in the eighties, when he was newly arrived in France and didn't know anyone. It's an organisation for men who are possibly a bit socially adrift – divorced, or new in town, or out of work, perhaps – where they can mend things together in a big garage, over in the 18th arrondissement.

'I love this!' Jess cries. 'Your dad sounds amazing. What a great idea.' Then inspiration strikes. 'Oh! Can I tell Alain about it? The guy I mentioned the other day, whose wife has dementia, and has had to move into a home. He used to be an engineer, this would be right up his street.'

'But of course,' Beatrice replies. 'There is an open day on Saturday, in fact. Perhaps he could come along? And you too, if you would like to find out more.' She smiles. 'Look at us, pairing everybody up. Trying to make everyone happier. We are the best people, I think, no?'

Jess laughs. 'We are absolutely the best,' she agrees, crossing her fingers beneath the table. Let's hope Adelaide agrees when she discovers what her memoirist has done now.

The hours pass in a pleasant blur of good cocktails, great food – 'the most delicious African food in this district', according to Beatrice – and a lot of chat about their families and lives. Luc is missing out on so much, Jess thinks, as she and her new friend swap stories, painting pictures of their individual worlds for one another. It's only towards the end of the evening, when she is quite tipsy and queuing for the ladies, that she notices a familiar face emerging from one of the cubicles.

'Marie-Thérèse! How are you?'

Marie-Thérèse is almost unrecognisable without the apron, tied-back hair and red eyes. No downtrodden air of misery about her now – here she stands looking ten years younger in jeans and a pretty pink peasant top with a drawstring neck, her brown hair loose around her shoulders. She does a double take upon seeing Jess, then smiles a little warily.

'Jessica. Hello,' she says, washing her hands at the sink.

'Are you okay? I've been thinking of you. Do you have another job yet?' Jess asks in French. 'I'm sorry you felt you had to go.' It's fair to say that Adelaide already seems to be regretting losing her housekeeper, judging by all the huffing and complaining that went on when she made them both drinks that morning. Jess couldn't help noticing that there were some dinner things left unwashed in the kitchen, plus

252

an ironing board abandoned there. It hasn't taken long for standards to slip, put it that way.

Marie-Thérèse shrugs. 'Not yet. But me, I am not sorry about leaving.' Her pointy little chin rises defensively as she turns her hands under the feeble drier, shaking them impatiently in the lukewarm air. 'Because she is a nasty woman. A rude woman! And bad too, I think. Evil. That disgusting painting in her wardrobe . . . I nearly screamed the first day I saw it.'

'The painting?' Jess repeats, none the wiser. 'In the *wardrobe*? What painting is this?'

'Ahh – you have not seen it, then. You are lucky. I still have nightmares – about it, and about her!' She gives up on the drier with a last flick of her wrists. 'Be careful,' she adds, making steps for the door. 'You don't know what she's capable of – but I do.'

'Wait, tell me more!' Jess is dying to hear the full story, but has reached the front of the queue for the loo, and the urgency of her bladder ultimately wins the battle. 'I'll catch up with you!' she cries, as they part ways, wondering what on earth this painting might show (and why is it in the *wardrobe*?). Alas, when she re-emerges from the toilets, Marie-Thérèse seems to have left Le Mélange, despite Jess making two careful circuits of the place. Damn it!

She heads back towards the courtyard, eager to tell Beatrice this curious nugget of information, only for her phone to buzz with a message from David. *Do you have a minute to chat?* is all it says. Oh shit. Why does he have to be so infuriatingly vague? *Are the girls okay?* she fires back instantly, adrenalin spiking. Standing there, waiting for him to reply, she glimpses the middle-aged couple and their daughter opening a champagne bottle, and the woman hugging her daughter looking proud and tearful. She's not sure she can bear other people's happiness right now if her own is at stake, she thinks, swinging her gaze away. *David??* she types impatiently when he doesn't reply immediately. For heaven's sake! It's so unfair to send a message like that and *not* expect her to flip into sheer panic one second later.

Finally he replies. *Girls are fine. Sorry, didn't mean to scare you,* which is something at least. She puts a hand to her heart, feeling it shift down from fifth gear to third, then glances outside to where Beatrice has fallen into animated conversation with the people on the next table. David's request must be important, she figures, or he wouldn't be asking. And then her daughters' previous musings about his odd behaviour come back to her. Is this all connected, maybe? What's going on?

I'm out with a friend but can have a quick chat if you want? she replies, only for her phone to ring in the next second. He's keen, then.

'Hi,' she says. 'What's up?'

'Jess,' he says, and in that one word she can tell he is stressed. 'Thanks. I didn't know who else to talk to.'

'About what? Are you all right?'

'I'm not sure. I've ...' She hears him sigh, even with the deep bass of the music and the many conversations taking place nearby. 'I've made a doctor's appointment for next week, because ... Well, because I found a lump. And it's not going away. In fact, I think it's got bigger, if anything.'

'A lump? Where?' Oh no. David has always been something of a hypochondriac – nobody in the world suffers as badly from a cold as David – but a lump is different. A lump is a *lump*.

'Well ... in my testicles, actually. So ... yeah. Obviously feeling a bit on edge.' The sudden gruffness in his voice is pitched between defensiveness and fear. She pictures him hunched over, tension in his shoulders, a flicker of vulnerability in his eyes. David does not like being vulnerable. To be fair, who does, but he, of all people, likes to put on a good display of competence. Of being invincible.

'I can imagine.'

'And I'm here with the girls, and I can't ... I can't enjoy the holiday because I keep thinking ...' Was that a *sob*? 'I keep worrying that ... that this might be my last summer with them, and what if I die, and leave them without a dad, and ...'

'I'm sure it won't come to that,' Jess says, just as Beatrice glances around, looking for her. Jess pulls a face and points to her phone, then holds up two fingers, mouthing *deux minutes*. 'And of course you're having these thoughts – anyone would.' She's having them now herself, naturally, picturing the girls dressed in black at their father's funeral, and the complex emotions this image provokes. 'But the doctor will give you a clearer picture next week,' she goes on bracingly, as much to herself as to him. 'I bet it's something harmless like a cyst or, I don't know ...' She scours her brain for possible medical information. 'Or ... an infected hair follicle, maybe, or ...'

'Yeah, sure. Almost certainly,' he says. 'Yeah. Sorry, I shouldn't have bothered you. It's just ... It's been on my mind and I've had a drink, and ...'

'That's okay,' Jess tells him. He sounds so different from his usual bombastic self: the David who leaps on a plane across the world for work, who talks confidently and fluently about sport, politics, the latest piece of tech. The David who knowingly caught the eye of a twenty-five-year-old red-headed Australian publicist across a crowded room and thought to himself, *Yeah, why not?* Now he seems crestfallen, defeated. Or maybe he's just shattered after five days' solo parenting abroad. Their daughters can do that to a person.

'The girls have noticed something's up though,' she goes on. 'Mia and Edie have both confided in me that they think you're seeing someone.'

'Oh shit, really? Well, I'm not,' he replies. 'Obviously I'm not.' She hears his hesitation, senses his doubt. 'Have you ever told them—?'

'No,' she replies before he has to say that woman's name.

'Okay. Thanks.' He's relieved now – and so, in a funny sort of way, is she; relieved that she can answer him honestly, that she has kept her promise not to reveal the dirty laundry of their marriage. God knows there have been enough times when she's been tempted, when the girls have taken his side, blamed her for the separation, and she's wanted to howl, *You don't know the half of it!*

'That's for you to tell them if ever you decide to,' she says, because sometimes it's hard work being the saintly one. 'Let me know how you get on next week, won't you?' she adds. 'Or if—' She's about to lapse into her old bad habit of subjugating her own needs to his. *Or if you need me to come back early* – it was there on the tip of her tongue. She folds the words back, unsaid, into her throat. She doesn't have to do that any more. 'Or if you need to chat again,' she says instead, the most she's willing to offer.

'Thanks,' he says. 'I will.' He hesitates. 'You having a good time there? Work going well?'

'Yeah, great, actually,' she replies. 'Talking of which, I should get back to my friend. I've left her all alone at the table, so . . .'

'Yes,' he says. 'Okay, take care then. Bye, Jess.'

She frowns as she rejoins Beatrice, replaying the conversation in her head. He *will* be all right, won't he? She might not want to be married to him any more, but it's not like she can erase the bank of feelings for him that built up, layer upon layer, over the years they spent together. Plus, it's the last thing she wants for the girls, for them to experience the worry and upset of having a very ill parent, or worse.

'There you are! Everything all right?' Beatrice asks.

Jess forces a smile. She will think about David later. 'Fine,' she lies, before reminding her friend that she'd promised to tell a juicy-sounding story about some badly behaved guests who'd been staying at the hotel the week before.

'My God! Yes, the Janviers . . . now, this will shock you, Jess. Prepare to be shocked!'

Regaled by tales of the Janviers and other notable guests of years gone by, as well as still weighing David's news at the back of her mind, Jess completely forgets her tantalising conversation with Marie-Thérèse until they've left the bar. It is dark now, with the moon a pearly glimmer through the clouds. A breeze sends an empty Coke can rattling along in a nearby gutter and the sudden noise makes the two women

257

clutch at one another giggling. Conveniently, Beatrice's husband has promised to pick her up outside the hotel, so they are both walking there together, arm in arm, a little unsteady after their cocktails.

'Oh! I didn't tell you who I bumped into in the loos!' Jess cries, before launching into the whole exchange. 'And you can bet your last euro I will sneak a look at this wardrobe painting, just as soon as I get the chance,' she finishes.

'Wow! Well, you can bet *your* last euro that I am going to be asking you about it every single day until you *do*,' Beatrice responds, wide-eyed. 'Now I am imagining the worst, the very worst of your Adelaide. But how bad can it be, do you think?'

'Bad enough to give Marie-Thérèse nightmares,' Jess replies, suddenly remembering Adelaide talking about the Revenge paintings. *They are mostly within my archive*, she said. Mostly – does that mean one of them has been stashed in her apartment? 'It's a mystery for now. Yet another Paris mystery for me,' she adds, thinking of Pascale, as she so often does. In the next moment though, cogs turn and a new thought comes to her. 'Beatrice! Can I show you a picture of someone?'

'*Chérie*, you can show me anything,' Beatrice declares, squeezing her arm affectionately.

'It's probably nothing,' Jess says, searching on her phone for the portrait of the beefy man that had startled her in the archive the day before. 'But I don't suppose you recognise this man, do you?'

It's the second time she's asked that question today, having shown the same photo to Adelaide during their earlier session together. 'Oh! Gosh. Yes, him,' Adelaide had said. 'He commissioned the portrait then refused to pay for it, complaining I'd made him look too ugly and fat. Idiot. I made sure to put it in the next public exhibition of mine after that, just to annoy him.'

'Can you remember his name? Anything else about him?'

Adelaide had peered over the top of her glasses at Jess. 'Why? What's it to you?'

'I'm not sure.' How can she articulate the neck-prickling instinct she has when she looks at the picture, the conviction that he is in some way linked to the Hotel d'Or, and possibly even to Pascale's disappearance? It sounds melodramatic, but she sees his gigantic hands, his broad shoulders, the mean expression on his face, and the thought that rises each time is, *Did you kill my friend?* She had a flash of memory of him in the bar there, boasting to the group he was with. Did he perhaps send a drink over to their table? Flirt with beautiful Pascale and maybe arrange to go out with her, just the two of them? She was certainly dressing up for *someone* that last night Jess saw her. But who?

Standing beneath a lamp post, showing the picture to Beatrice, Jess feels as if she may have known his name once, that it's on the tip of her tongue. Didier? Laurent? Victor? *Victor*, that could be it, she thinks, a bell jangling distantly in her mind.

'He might have been called Victor,' she says, trying it out aloud, although she can hear the doubt in her own voice. Besides, even if her instincts turn out to be correct, and the man has some connection with Pascale's disappearance, what can she do – take matters into her own hands and avenge her? Maybe she's been spending too much time with Adelaide, she thinks as Beatrice peers at the photo. At this rate she'll be adding a dagger into that painting herself, stabbed into the man's thick neck.

Beatrice shakes her head. 'Sorry, no,' she says. 'But if you forward it to me, I can ask around. Why, what's the story?'

Jess leans against her, the long day and night catching up with her. 'He's familiar,' she says, 'but I can't think why. I've just got a hunch I need to find out whatever I can about him.' She squirms, suddenly self-conscious. Usually she makes a point of working only with facts, not hunches, but for Pascale's sake, she has to try every avenue left open to her. Hasn't she been making toasts to friendship this very evening? Enough talking the talk on this one. It's time for her to walk the walk, once and for all, and see if she can get any closer to uncovering the truth. Whatever it takes, she vows.

Chapter Twenty-Six

Afterwards, Adelaide remembers, it was as if the air rang with the crash for a long time. A dog barked somewhere in the distance and they both flinched. 'Do you think he's dead?' she asked in a hoarse voice.

That terrible, terrible day, she thinks, trying to turn her attention back to the cryptic crossword on her iPad. It's her early evening ritual: the mixing of a gin and tonic (always with lemon, always with ice; one of the few things she enjoys doing for herself), the grateful descent into her most comfortable armchair with a view out on to the square, and then a satisfying workout for the brain. Afterwards she might allow herself an episode of *Fake or Fortune* or a gruesome detective drama, depending on her mood. Now then. What does the setter have for her today? *Miserable attempt on a motorway results in disaster* (12), she reads, but the words dance around without connecting in her brain. It's hard to concentrate when you have just been reliving a moment of extreme trauma; when memories relentlessly bombard you, however hard you try to hold them at bay.

She glances down at Jean-Paul, who's lying, as ever, by her feet, paws flexing in his sleep; maybe he's dreaming about running away from her and snatching any old chicken bones he feels like. But running away, as she knows herself, is not always the right thing to do.

'Of course he's bloody dead,' Margie had said, standing beside what had been a window seconds earlier, but was now a ragged hole, man-shaped, with triangles of glass standing in jagged sentry around the frame. 'Look at the way his neck is twisted. There's no way he's about to get up again. Thank God.'

'Fuck,' said Adelaide. She was shaking all over from head to foot; her heart seemed on the verge of pounding right through her ribcage. 'What are we going to do?'

This is no good. This is not getting the crossword started. She's got to snap out of this terrible loop of reminiscing. It's not like she can change anything now, is it?

She sips her gin then turns to the next clue, forces herself to focus. *Sounds like an asthmatic bird* (6). Ahh – that's more like it. PUFFIN, she types in, remembering how she and Remy spent one June tootling around Scotland. They'd planned it as a trip of inspirational landscape painting, although if her memory serves her, there was also a lot of arguing about map-reading during long car journeys, as well as copious amounts of cheap whisky and energetic sex in drab boarding houses. Occasionally sex on a tartan blanket out on the heathland to break up the long argumentative car journeys, too, if they were in a particularly remote spot. On the day she's thinking of, they'd taken a boat trip out from someplace on the head-land, east of Edinburgh, and spotted puffins nesting on their burrows up on the cliffs, their dear little comical faces so cartoon-like. Remy's pronunciation of the word 'puffin' had made her laugh every time.

He had loved Scotland, she remembers. *Better than England*, he liked to tease her, much to the glee of any passing Scots, who'd congratulate him on his good taste. The weeks the two of them spent there seem like a dream now. They'd found an abandoned country and western cassette in their rental car, but once they put it into the player, it jammed and refused to be switched off, so that no matter how glorious or dramatic the scenery around them – the majestic heather-covered peaks, the forests, the remote white-sand islands – the soundtrack accompanying each vista was one of plangent betrayal and heartbreak. The painting had been great at least, the two of them setting up easels *en plein air*, defying everything the land threw at them – gusts of wind, sudden showers, those interminable midges – in the name of art. There must still be a whole sketchpad of her watercolours in the archive, she thinks to herself, wondering if Lucas has come across it yet.

Then she remembers the photos Jessica showed her the other day following her visit to Belleville: the aggressive, beefy man (what *was* his name?), a pencil sketch of an old man with an ice cream, a line drawing of Remy. She's all but stopped drawing these days – partly because of the tremors that grip her hands (please let it not be Parkinson's, she keeps thinking, too scared to ask a doctor), but also because she can't see the point any more. She hasn't really seen the point of anything much, other than her dog, for some years, to be fair. She imagines a small sketch of herself now, hunched wistfully over an iPad, her gnarled bare feet up on the chaise longue. Those feet would be good to draw, she thinks dispassionately. Her hands and face, too. The body in decline: an ongoing study.

But anyway. She's digressing again. Where was she? *At the end of time, create soup – that's the way out* (6, 5). It must be an anagram, she thinks, grabbing her notepad and jotting down the letters. ESCAPE ROUTE, that's it. How apt, when the escape she and Margie made all those years ago has been on her mind.

'What are we going to *do*?' Margie had repeated, already marching back across the room. 'I'll tell you what we're going to do. We're going to get in my car and hotfoot it back to my place, that's what we're going to do. Nobody knows I'm here. Did you tell anyone other than me you were staying?'

A mute shake of the head from Adelaide, who was struggling to comprehend what had just happened. *The man is dead. He crashed through the window right there and now he's dead.* A horrible humming sound inside her head rose in pitch. She felt hysterical. How the hell was Margie managing to stay so calm?

'Good, so we'll head to mine, and we'll tell anyone who asks that we've been there the whole weekend. We've seen nothing, we've done nothing, understand? Right – come on.'

If Adelaide could wind back time and change anything, it would be that day in Little Bower. If things had been different, she and Margie would still be friends, she was sure of it. Weird Colin Copeland would have lived another day. But instead . . .

'Ugh, stop it,' she scolds herself aloud, knocking back a large gulp of the gin. It's not as good as usual, unfortunately; she must have forgotten to fill the ice tray yesterday so there was only one cube left for tonight's drink, when ordinarily she likes at least three clinking around. That's the problem when you lose your domestic help – it's such a faff trying to keep on top of everything. She's messaged and called Frieda's cleaner Clothilde several times but still hasn't had a reply. Must she beg for help? Is this what she has been reduced to?

In the meanwhile, she wonders if it would be outrageous to go downstairs and ask at the nearest brasserie for some ice to take away. They're practically neighbours, after all. Her thoughts circle back to her earlier conversation with Frieda. *Lucky you, living here*, she had enthused. *So much beauty on your doorstep! All these wonderful bars and restaurants to try!* Frieda wouldn't think twice about going down and asking for ice, she tells herself. In fact, Frieda would order an actual gin and tonic from them, and enjoy watching the world go by while she drank it.

The trouble with living anywhere, though, is that you stop noticing the beauty, you stop trying the wonderful bars and restaurants. You do if you're Adelaide, anyway. You spend your evenings arguing with *Fake or Fortune* on the TV instead; you while away the hours silently wrangling with puzzles on a screen, with the occasional one-sided conversation with your dog. What's Frieda doing, right now? she wonders. What's Jessica doing? No doubt both of them are out in the city, soaking up the sights, enjoying a summer evening with a splendid view and a glass of very good wine. And here she is, frowning again at that first crossword clue – *Miserable attempt on a motorway results in disaster* (12) – while life passes her by. 'You're never too old for some fun, are you?' Frieda had proclaimed, when talking Adelaide through their reasons for coming to France (Jim's retirement; her 'heart event' that snapped them out of their comfortable drift). 'Never too old for an adventure!'

Ha. MISADVENTURE, that's the answer, Adelaide realises, typing the word with satisfaction. Then she snorts. Is that the universe giving her a prod, maybe? She's not a superstitious woman, but can't help feeling that both the crossword setter and Frieda have conspired to make a point to her this evening.

She heaves herself to her feet, closes the door on the mess inside the kitchen (tomorrow, she vows) and goes to inspect her reflection in the bathroom mirror. Oh, to hell with it, she thinks, uncapping her favourite red lipstick and applying two coats. She pats her hair into shape then bustles up to the bedroom to find a nice necklace, to spritz on some perfume. Much as she dislikes being in the wrong, she has to admit that Frieda has a better attitude than her, more gung-ho gumption. Since when did Adelaide become so old-headed that she gave up on her own sense of adventure? Somewhere along the line she's allowed herself to coast into the calmer waters of life, to putter along like an old barge.

Well, not tonight. Jean-Paul will be fine on his own for an hour if she leaves the radio on for him (he seems to like the polite, clipped tones of the World Service). Meanwhile, she'll channel her new friend, and head out for a drink with plenty of ice, and a side order of people-watching. Maybe she'll even take a notebook with her, and a nice sharp 2B pencil, and sketch some passers-by, like she always used to enjoy doing. Why not? Her hands haven't completely given up on her yet.

'Fun, Jean-Paul!' she comments as she picks up her bag a few minutes later. 'I wonder if I can still remember how that's done?'

Chapter Twenty-Seven

By the time it's Saturday, Jess is more than ready for a break from working on Adelaide's memoir – and a break from the woman herself, for that matter. Wonderful as it is to plunge into another person's fascinating life and all the surprising stories therein, the experience is markedly less wonderful when the person in question keeps issuing unexpected demands that are not part of your job description. Like picking up fresh fish, meat and fruit from the market ('It is so hot and I am very tired today'). Like ironing a pile of tea towels ('I don't know how to iron!'). Like running the hoover around the living room ('Jean-Paul sheds so much at this time of year and my eyes aren't good enough to spot all the hairs. You don't mind, do you?').

To be fair, Jess doesn't mind that much – for one thing, it *is* very hot, and Adelaide's ankles *are* very swollen, and if she says she's tired, then Jess believes her. She doesn't even mind the ironing and hoovering because God knows she's already an expert at these tasks. It's just ... Well, she has other things to do, frankly. Like writing Adelaide's book, the job she's actually being paid for. But how can she say no?

Maybe her annoyance is partly because she hasn't managed to sneak a look inside Adelaide's wardrobe yet, and can't see a way how, either, without some serious subterfuge. Adelaide's bedroom is on the top floor of the apartment, and there's absolutely no reason for Jess to go up there. Besides, she doesn't see herself as a natural spy – she's loud on her feet, clumsy, she'll give the game away in two seconds if she attempts any snooping around.

She also feels out of sorts following David's phone call from the other night, echoes of which are still resounding through her head. He will be all right, won't he? He plays football with his mates every week, he runs and cycles. He eats healthily. She can't help worrying though. Having spent so many months trying to detach herself from him, trying to reinvent herself outside of their old marriage, it's discombobulating having him lean on her again, as if they are still husband and wife. Or is that selfish of her? Probably.

Still. He'll be home later today, with Edie and Polly – in fact, they'll be in the air right now, she realises, possibly flying overhead this minute. He'll have his doctor's appointment and get some answers. Meanwhile, the remaining member of the family has successfully managed to get herself to Nice yesterday (well done, Mia), where she's now with her three best friends, hopefully about to have a really fun week and not get herself into too much trouble. Or any trouble, in fact.

Now Jess has the weekend to herself, and she's bloody well going to make the most of it. She spent an enjoyable morning in the air-conditioned bliss of the Pompidou Centre, strolling through the contemporary art section, trying to educate herself, particularly around Adelaide's peers, and now she's on her way to meet Alain. The plan is for them to travel together to 'Little Africa', as the area is known, where the workshop run by Beatrice's dad is holding its open day.

The Rue de Rivoli is heaving with shoppers at this time on a Saturday, and she weaves nimbly through the side streets to avoid the crush, until she's back in the Marais. She finds herself wondering what Luc's been up to, remembering their Belleville evening on Wednesday, how enjoyable she'd found his company. He's been in touch a couple of times, with pieces of information she's asked for, but hasn't asked about her date. Perhaps it's just as well. Nobody likes to admit they've been stood up.

Talking of dates with Frenchmen, she just has time to grab a bakery lunch before she meets Alain, she decides. But in the next moment, she realises that her phone is ringing at the depths of her bag, and is surprised to see her eldest daughter's name on the screen.

'Hi love! Everything okay? How's Nice this morning?' She's heading towards the bakery on Rue des Rosiers – Beatrice's recommendation – only to prick up her ears when she hears what sounds like a sniffle down the line. 'Mimi? Are you all right, darling?'

'Oh Mum,' her daughter gulps. 'Everything's gone wrong. I'm—'

Whatever she is trying to say gets lost in a wail, and Jess comes to a halt in the street in alarm. 'What is it? Are you hurt? Where are you?'

Terrifying images streak through her mind – a moped accident, she thinks, her heart pounding. A mugging. A terrible tattoo decision.

'I ... I'm coming to Paris,' Mia hiccups instead. 'I'm on the train.'

Jess blinks several times, trying to process this. 'But ... your holiday,' she says dumbly. 'With Clara and Erin and—'

'Don't say their names! I *hate* them!' Mia cries, the words jerking out of her in distress. 'You won't *believe* what they've done!'

'But lovey ...' What won't she believe? What on earth has happened? Jess has a million questions but opts for the most pressing one. 'Did you say you're coming to *Paris*?'

There is the muffled sound of a weeping teenager blowing her nose. 'Yeah, Gare de Lyon,' Mia says, pronouncing it 'lion' like the animal. 'Mum, can I stay with you for a bit? I just feel so ...' A gigantic sniff ends that particular sentence. 'I can't believe he could *do* this ... I'm so *embarrassed*, Mum, and *humiliated* and ...'

'Oh darling.' It's something about that boy, then. That bloody boy Zach, last seen scurrying from Mia's bedroom; the boy whose pretty neck she will wring the first chance she gets. And now her little girl is sobbing on a train, somewhere between Nice and Paris, and all alone. 'Of course you can stay with me,' she says, her mind racing as she tries to jigsaw together her two worlds. 'I mean, I'm going to be working most of the time' – and going out with Georges on Monday, if this date of theirs ever actually happens – and she'd been hoping to meet Luc's sister Catherine, and Henry, who are apparently arriving in the city today. All the things she's most been enjoying about her glorious trip of independence are floating away before her eyes, a dream breaking into shards and evaporating. But Mia takes priority. 'Don't worry,' she says, raking a hand through her hair. 'We'll figure it out. Now, what time does your train get in? I'll meet you at the station. Everything's going to be okay, do you hear me?'

Thankfully Alain is sympathetic when Jess apologises for no longer being able to accompany him to the open day, explaining the phone call from Mia, the tears, the impending arrival. 'My children are grown up now,' he tells her, 'but I remember the turmoil of those teenage years. Everything is a drama, right? Of course you must meet your daughter, Jess. Family comes first.'

He heads off and the nervous energy whistles out of her in a long exhalation. Now then. She has just under two hours before she goes to meet Mia. Two hours left of being Jess, before she has to slip on the somewhat heavier overcoat of 'Mum' again. Her mind turns to her laptop and the piles of notes back at the hotel. She should really use this chance to get ahead of herself, seeing as her work time is about to be seriously impacted from here on in.

On the other hand, she reflects, this could be her last opportunity to indulge in some proper me-time for a while . . . To idle in the sunshine with a book and possibly a very nice sorbet. Decision made. She will enjoy her last free afternoon in Paris, and that's final. Then she will head over to Gare de Lyon to scoop up her tearful daughter, and ascertain just how slowly and painfully she will have to exact her retribution on those who have wronged her.

Later, she's waiting in Gare de Lyon for the Nice train to arrive when a message comes in from Beatrice. *I think your friend is having a good time*, she has written, followed by a string of photos: Alain peering over an open car bonnet with a couple of other men his age. Alain having coffee in an outdoor space, deep in conversation with a different man. A tall Black man with a grizzled beard, wearing a Senegal Calling T-shirt (Beatrice's dad, Moussa, surely) addressing twenty or thirty attendees, his face animated, his arms outstretched as if he's giving a barnstormer. Alain's face is visible in profile at the bottom right of the picture, listening intently.

Jess is so used to seeing him alone that it takes her a moment to recontextualise him in this new setting. And sure, a picture sometimes only tells half the story – for all she knows, the rest of the time he was bored out of his skull – but it fills her heart with gladness to see him apparently enjoying himself in these captured glimpses. From what Beatrice has said, the workshop isn't only about mending things on site. Teams of volunteers from the group partake in community work together – painting schools and retirement homes, for instance. Tree planting at a new 'edible forest' in the 20th arrondissement. There are cookery lessons for the men who never learned how, who have found themselves alone and ill-equipped to look after themselves. There's a running group and a cycling club for those who like such things. Even if Alain doesn't make the best friends of his life there, hopefully he will at least find a few people he can talk to about what he's going through, and engage in interesting activities. There. Good work, Jess. She's helped someone.

'Hi Mum,' comes a voice just then, and here's her girl in front of her, tanned from the Italian holiday, her hair pushed back with a turquoise bandana Jess doesn't recognise, a massive red backpack almost engulfing her slender frame. *'Bonjour,'* she adds sheepishly.

'Hey!' Jess envelops her in a hug, or as best as she can with that gigantic backpack muscling in on the embrace. 'Hello, gorgeous. Are you okay?' She kisses the top of her daughter's head, feeling the strong animal connection between them as surely as she did in the moment when her baby girl was first placed against her bare breast. Back then, bleary-eyed and blood-spattered in the maternity unit, if you'd shown her a photo of the moment now – her embracing this leggy young woman with her auburn hair and piercings, her strong young arms, bare golden calves and the no doubt reeking baseball boots – if you'd said, *Look, there's the two of you meeting up in Paris in years to come. You're writing a famous artist's memoir; she's just travelled alone for six hours on the train* – she'd never have believed it. And yet here they are.

'Oh love,' she says as she feels her daughter's body convulse in a sob. Because you can tough it out for so long when you're seventeen – in a showdown with friends, on a tearful backpack-shouldering walk to the station, through a long solo journey across a foreign land – but there's something about receiving the kindness of one who loves you that can break

274

you in an instant. 'It's okay. It's going to be okay. Whatever's happened, we can fix it.'

Mia pulls herself away after a moment and sniffs, her eyes damp. She looks knackered, Jess observes sympathetically. Whatever fight has propelled her this far, she's running on empty now.

'Have you eaten anything?' Jess asks. 'Do you want something to drink? Let's walk along the river for a bit, towards Notre-Dame; there'll be a million places to sit and chat. Want me to carry that backpack for a while?'

Mia knuckles her tears away. 'It's fine,' she says. 'Thanks, Mum.'

It's mid-afternoon by now, and the air is humid, the sky overcast. It feels as if a storm is gathering force, Jess thinks, shepherding them out of the station and down towards the river. There are hordes of holidaymakers at every turn – clustering outside shops, pausing to take smile-flashing photos of each other, seated in sun-hatted rows onboard the tourist boats. 'God,' mutters Mia, 'it's like the whole world has come here on holiday.'

Eventually they find a riverside bar that has everything for their middle-aged mum/emotional teenage daughter needs: a free outdoor table, some great-looking cakes on display, and a grungy guitar-band soundtrack playing. Boxes ticked, Mia wrestles her arms free of the backpack and lets it drop to the ground with a weighty thud.

'So,' says Jess, once they've ordered drinks and something to eat, 'do you want to tell me what happened? Who should I be putting on my hit list?' She mimes aiming a rifle, squinting through its sight; joking, but only just. She remembers when Edie was being bullied in year seven and she had full-scale fantasies about taking down the bitches involved, poking her thumbs into their eyes, kicking them in the kidneys, you name it – until she remembered that said bitches were eleven-year-old girls, and she was supposedly a responsible adult. All the same – don't get between this lioness and her cub, or you'll regret it.

Mia purses her lips. 'It's not a game, Mum,' she snaps, staring down at the table.

'Sorry. I wasn't being facetious.' No, she absolutely meant it. 'Go on, tell me. What happened?'

There's a deep and heavy-hearted sigh. 'Well, the thing is . . .' Mia props her chin in her palm, her gaze flicking briefly to Jess before returning to the painted metal table. There's such a naked look of woe on her face that Jess's insides turn over. Oh God, what *is* this? She's not pregnant, is she?

'What, sweetheart?' she asks in trepidation.

'The thing is, when we were together . . .' Mia's cheeks have turned red, her voice drops to a mumble. 'Zach took some photos of me.'

Oh no. So not pregnant but digitised, presumably. On a hard drive, out there in pixelated nudity for evermore. Who would be a teenager in this day and age, honestly?

'What sort of photos?' she asks, although she can already tell they are not your average fully dressed selfie. Shit.

'Some . . .' Mia swallows, and Jess has tears in her eyes suddenly, looking at her face and seeing all the other Mias there – the gurgling, sunny baby with the single pearly tooth. The three-year-old with the red fleece hat she loved so much that Jess would come in to check on her at night and find her asleep wearing it. Aged seven, with long plaits and a gap in her teeth. And now look at her – beautiful and gangly with her tawny limbs and glinting purple nose piercing, stumbling over the words she's trying to say. 'Some nudes,' she manages eventually.

'Right,' Jess says, determined to sound neutral, even though she really wants to groan her daughter's name aloud, to howl at her for being so reckless. 'Let me guess – and he promised he wouldn't show anyone. That they were just for the two of you.'

Mia's lowered gaze is enough of a reply. 'I know it was stupid, please don't patronise me by saying anything I haven't already said to myself,' she replies, clenching her fists. 'It's not my fault I haven't had a great relationship model, after all.'

'Hey!' Jess says, wounded. 'I'm doing my best, all right?'

The waitress appears by the table just then, like a referee calling half-time by dishing out their orders: a Diet Coke, *croque-monsieur* and fries for Mia, an apple pastry and a coffee for Jess. Mia falls ravenously upon her *croque*, moaning 'CHEESE' as if she's half-starved, and it's left to Jess to pick up the conversation once more. Deep breath.

'So I take it other people have seen the pictures,' she says, wincing on her daughter's behalf.

'No, but ...' Tears glimmer in Mia's eyes. 'He keeps dropping hints on his socials that he's got them and everyone in our year is egging him on to post them. When I met Erin and the others, even they were giggling and taking the piss, asking if I could give them sneak previews.' She puts down the *croque* abruptly and grabs a serviette in order to wipe her leaking eyes, her voice low and trembling. 'Everyone knows, Mum. They're all laughing at me. What if he posts them and everyone sees? I won't be able to go back to school again. I don't even want to go back to Canterbury. I just . . .' She puts her head in her hands. 'I want to *die*.'

'Oh lovey,' Jess says, putting a hand on her arm. Christ, she doesn't envy today's teenagers with their online lives, unable to switch off after school each day, when the rest of the world is ever-present on a smartphone. 'That Zach, honestly, what a total piece of shit he turned out to be.'

'I know.' Another massive sniff. 'And my friends too. Not friends any more.' A new tear spills from one eye and rolls down her cheek.

'Him threatening you like that . . . is that even legal? I'm sure his parents would take a very dim view of his behaviour,' Jess goes on. 'Let alone the police. I bet school wouldn't be happy either.'

'Mum! Don't you dare call the police!' Mia squawks, looking horrified. '*Or* school. Oh God, I knew I shouldn't have told you. That's the last thing I want.'

'Yes, but . . .' Jess thinks helplessly of Edie and her 'snitches get stitches' catchphrase, but surely sometimes it's the only option? 'Okay, well . . . is there a way to steal his phone?' she suggests, thinking on the fly. 'Then smash it up, throw the SIM on the fire, hack into his cloud, or whatever it's called? Or stand over him with a gun to his head until he deletes everything?'

Mia glares at her. 'It's all a big joke to you, this, isn't it? For fuck's sake, Mum!'

'No! Why would you say that? I'm trying to help!'

'What, with stupid suggestions about guns and fires?' Mia shoves her *croque* back into her mouth and chews furiously. 'Don't bother.'

They're back in familiar 'you know nothing' territory and Jess exhales, feeling as if she's totally misplayed her hand. It's a lot easier answering Dear Jess problems on her agony aunt page, that's for sure.

'I'm sorry,' she says, with a pang for the days when she could fix everything for her girls with a consoling hug. 'We could ask your dad to go round and have a word, maybe?'

'*No,*' Mia groans. 'Look, just forget I said anything, all right? I don't want to talk about it any more.'

'Okay.' Jess gets the message – back off – although her mind continues to turn over possibilities. There must be something she can do. In the meantime, she opts for upbeat and practical as her best immediate option. 'Well, we can't change what's happened, but you're here now, with me – and do you know what the best revenge is? Having fun. Living a great life,' she says. 'We've got the whole of Paris here at our feet, and I'm off until Monday. We can do whatever you want.'

'Will I get to meet Adelaide?' Mia asks, perking up. 'Only I've been doing some more digging on that guy's death, and I have questions for her. For the podcast I'm going to make.'

Oh Lord. 'Well . . . if you do meet her, you have to promise me you won't start grilling her. And I'm not sure I want you to make an actual podcast about this either. She has a very litigious nephew who'd probably drag us into court.' He wouldn't, obviously, but Mia doesn't need to know that. 'Promise me you won't?'

There's a flicker in Mia's eyes for a moment, then she replies, 'I promise.' They smile at each other. 'By the way, can we go on the big wheel while I'm here?' she asks. 'Oh, and to Boulangerie Moderne?'

'What's that?'

'It's where Emily from *Emily in Paris* always goes for breakfast — and it's a real, actual bakery,' comes the excited reply. 'On my way here, I found a website where you can visit all the iconic places in the show. Like the café where Emily and Mindy eat, and the park where she goes jogging, and where her office building is ...'

Jess shakes her head. She's never seen the show herself, none of this means anything to her, but if it makes her daughter happy ... 'Absolutely,' she says. 'We can do all of those things. Now eat up! We'll drop your bag off at the hotel and then we've got a city to explore.' As for Zach, he'd better watch his back, she thinks to herself. Because one way or another, she's going to put a stop to his nastiness, just see if she doesn't.

Chapter Twenty-Eight

'The art world,' says Fiona Bruce. 'A place of outrageous fortune. But beneath the surface lurks danger ...'

It's early Saturday evening, and Adelaide's on her chaise longue again, feet up, with her hand in a bowl of grapes, watching another episode of *Fake or Fortune*. Anything to avoid the housework, she thinks. The kitchen sink is still piled up with dishes, and the laundry basket is now full, while clumps of Jean-Paul's fur drift around like small hairy tumbleweeds on the kitchen floor whenever there's a breeze. She's finally heard back from Frieda's cleaner, Clothilde, at least, but the other woman has said, somewhat gruffly, that she's unavailable until Friday, take it or leave it. Friday is better than nothing, but that's still nearly a whole week away. Adelaide will have to figure out how to use the hoover and washing machine in the meantime, worse luck. Maybe after this programme, she tells herself, unconvincingly.

This episode features three paintings claimed to be by Turner; Adelaide doesn't remember ever having seen it before. As the show gets underway she realises why: it's because the three pieces were apparently painted in Margate, where Turner had his mistress, Mrs Booth. Two of the paintings are even called *Off Margate* and *Margate Jetty*, and Adelaide has to shut her eyes briefly on hearing this. She's never been back to Margate herself since the dreadful holiday when William died and has always tried to avoid seeing pictures of the town or even reading about it.

It's only a *place* though, she tells herself now, her hand hovering above the remote control momentarily before she returns it to her lap. A place on her TV screen, at that; it can't hurt her at this distance, when the worst already happened, nearly seventy years ago.

Brave words, but it's not long before the cameras arrive in Margate, and there's the beach once more on her screen, with Turner's beloved Kentish sky a vast stretch of light above the seafront. She realises she's holding her breath. There it is. That's where it happened.

It's strange, but after opening up to Jessica about that dreadful day, she's been able to feel a little more compassion for her younger self, as if a scar has begun healing over the wound. *You were only a child!* Jessica had exclaimed, and the funny thing is, she's never really acknowledged that element before. But it's relevant. She *was* only a child. A little girl, who wanted to carry on playing cricket. She didn't do anything wrong.

Her breath leaks out of her, and it's as if a chunk of the ice that's been lodged in her heart, for all the decades since, cracks and breaks away. Melts. There's something about reliving old times for her memoir that is changing her, she thinks. It's as if she's pulling back the curtains in a dark room, reminding herself that there's a world outside. That, amidst the bad times, life can still be – indeed, has been – incredible. In some ways it's a shame she's avoided ever revisiting Margate, when there's the wonderful-sounding Turner Contemporary gallery there now, as well as Tracey Emin's exciting new art school. (Adelaide has a soft spot for Tracey Emin, whose work she admires very much.) She has become entrenched in her own space, as if everywhere else is closed off to her. But talking to Jessica about her travels – to the Uffizi, to Nice, to Margate, even – has woken something inside her, stirring up questions around whether she will ever travel to these places again. She's long assumed not, but why does that have to be the case? What's stopping her?

The phone rings and she pauses the programme to answer. It's Lucas, who perhaps can detect her strange mood from her voice, because he asks, 'Are you okay?' in a worried sort of way.

'Oh ...' She casts around for some excuse, not wanting to tell him the truth. 'Actually, I'm a bit fed up about the cleaning situation, to be honest,' she tells him, her eye falling on the dust along the hearth. 'Marie-Thérèse walked out on me a few days ago, and I've found it difficult to get a replacement for her. Someone's coming by the end of the week, but ...'

'Hmm,' he says. He does like a problem to solve, her nephew, and it's a great relief in the next moment when he says, 'Leave it with me, I'll see what I can do. But before then, I've actually got Catherine and Hen staying; we were about to go out for dinner and I wondered if you wanted to join us.'

'Oh,' she says again. Once upon a time her instinct was

to say yes to anything: another drink, a party, a commission abroad – but these days the word 'no' is always on the tip of her tongue. No, I'm too tired. No, I'm too old. When did that happen? When did she stop saying yes?

'I've got a reservation at Chez Janou, I'm sure we could add another chair to the table,' he coaxes, and Adelaide glances at the TV screen where the presenters have just arrived at Tate Britain, still on a mission to determine the provenance of these so-called Turners. She enjoyed going out the night before, didn't she, for her gin and tonic and impromptu sketching session, she reminds herself. It had felt good to re-engage with her city on a summer's evening. She can still say yes to life, can't she?

'Yes, all right,' she replies, on impulse. Chez Janou always used to serve a very good plate of duck breast with rosemary, she remembers. Not to mention their collection of pastis. And she hasn't seen Catherine for – gosh, five years or so. Fingers crossed her son Henry isn't as annoying as her ex-husband was. The Brockes clan don't seem very good at long-standing relationships, all in all.

She reaches for the remote and turns off the TV. That's quite enough of Margate for one day. She and Luc make arrangements, then she heaves herself to her feet, suddenly invigorated at the thought of going out once more. 'It's the World Service for you again, old friend,' she tells Jean-Paul, who gets up too, hoping for an unscheduled walk. 'But if you're very good, I'll sneak back some duck for you in my napkin. *And* a few of my chips.'

Chapter Twenty-Nine

'Mia, how do you fancy a job while you're here?' Jess asks on Sunday evening. They're about to go out for food, and the room they are now sharing – the hotel has been extremely accommodating – is currently strewn with various items of Mia's clothing that have been tried and rejected. Waiting for her daughter to complete what appears to be an exhausting make-up application session, Jess perches on her side of the bed, reading a message that's just arrived. 'Earning a few euros for a bit of work every day?'

Mia pouts at her reflection. 'Doing what?'

The two of them have had a lovely time so far, even if it has been largely visiting *Emily in Paris* sites for Mia to post all over her Instagram ('Everyone is *so jealous* you wouldn't *believe* it'). She's had the occasional wobbly moment, but it appears there have been apologies made by the girls she was meant to be holidaying with, and one of them even says she's threatened to report Zach to the police if he doesn't delete the pictures and leave Mia alone. (Apparently it's all right for friends to do this sort of thing, just not mothers.) Whatever, amends are being made, bridges rebuilt. Give it a few days and Jess hopes it will all be *eau* under the *pont*, as they say. If not, unknown to Mia, Jess has managed to get hold of Zach's mum's number, via Becky, and is on standby to put in a call. Her intel from Becky is that Zach's mum, Rose, is a fully paid-up feminist who would absolutely rip her son a new one if she heard what he's been up to. Either way, the sisterhood are pulling together.

'Good question,' she replies now. 'Well, originally – and I hope this is okay – I asked Luc, Adelaide's nephew, if he might need a hand in the archive next week, with you in mind. Just so that you're not hanging around bored all the time while I'm working with Adelaide,' she adds, as Mia swings round looking displeased.

'In a dusty old *archive*? Ugh, no thanks,' she says, returning to the important business of eyelash curling. 'And isn't he the one who's going to sue my ass when my podcast drops? Maybe I should keep my distance.'

'Nobody is going to sue your ass because this podcast isn't going to happen, remember?' Jess says. 'And it's lucky you don't want to work in the archive because he doesn't have anything for you to do there anyway.' Which is fair enough, she acknowledges. She's not sure she'd welcome with open arms an unknown seventeen-year-old to 'help' with her work, either. 'But I'll tell you who *does* need a hand, who he's just suggested instead: Adelaide.'

That gets her interest. 'Doing what? Helping her with her painting and stuff?'

'No, it's …' Jess hesitates because she's already sure Mia

286

will say no. 'It would be cleaning. She's lost her housekeeper recently so—'

'*Cleaning?*'

'Just some hoovering and washing up. Maybe some ironing . . .' Jess's voice peters out because she's not even sure her daughter knows how to iron, let alone if she should be allowed free rein on Adelaide's (presumably expensive) clothes. But then something occurs to her. *Clothes.* In Adelaide's *wardrobe.* Ever since that intriguing conversation with Marie-Thérèse in the Mélange loos, Jess has been longing for an excuse to peer in there. If Mia is hoovering Adelaide's bedroom, then . . . 'Oh go on, say yes,' she puts in quickly. 'She'll pay you, obviously. And maybe you could help me too. Do some of your ace detective work.'

'What, for my podcast? I'm *kidding*, don't get your knickers in a twist.' Mia turns her head from side to side, inspecting her eyelashes in the mirror. 'How much will she pay me?'

'I'll find out,' Jess replies, although in the next moment, decides to keep quiet about the wardrobe mystery. If the painting inside is that bad, she probably shouldn't encourage Mia to go snooping. Not unless she wants to give her nightmares for the rest of her life. 'So you're interested, then? Theoretically?'

'If she's not going to fleece me or shout at me, and if I don't have to do anything, like, really gross then . . . sure. I suppose so.'

'Great,' says Jess, returning to her phone. 'Oh, and also, Luc's nephew Henry is here in Paris this week, if you want to hang out with someone your age. He's eighteen apparently.'

'Henry, nephew of the nephew . . . sounds wild,' Mia replies sarcastically. 'No thanks.'

'Suit yourself.' Jess is about to reply to Luc when she notices that a new email has arrived in her inbox. It's from someone called Raph Claremont, and, not knowing anyone of that name, she's about to ignore it as spam when she notices the subject line: Re Margie Claremont. Oh God. A reply at last. She opens it at once.

Dear Jessica,

Thank you for your email to my mother, Margie, regarding a drawing she once did of Adelaide Fox. My name is Raphael and I'm Margie's eldest son. Before I get any further, I'm afraid I have some bad news . . .

'Oh no,' says Jess, reading on.

'Now what? She's given the job to someone else?' guesses Mia.

'What? No,' Jess replies distractedly, glued to the message.

Mom is pretty ill right now and although she remembers the drawing you mentioned (very fondly, I might add), she is staying with me and my wife while she recuperates, and so is unable to look through her files in search of it. Sorry not to be more helpful at this moment. Best wishes, Raph and Margie.

Margie's ill . . . this is indeed bad news. How ill? Jess wonders, biting her lip. Ill enough that she needs to be looked after while she recovers. But the word 'recuperates' gives her hope that it's nothing terminal at least. As for the phrase 'very fondly' . . . this too is grounds for Jess to feel optimistic. If Margie isn't consumed by hatred and resentment towards her former friend, then surely there's a way back for them? Surely it's not all over just yet?

The following morning, Jess hasn't decided what, if anything, she should do with her new information about Margie. She wants to tell Adelaide the situation in the hope it might prompt her to take action and let bygones be bygones – if a bunch of raging teenage girls can sort out their differences, then why can't two women in their late seventies, after all? – but she knows already that Adelaide will not be happy about her getting involved in the first place.

She's still mulling this over as she and Mia head out of the hotel. Beatrice is on reception following a weekend off and, on seeing them, gives a squeal of excitement. 'Ahh! Your girl – Mia, yes? Wow, you are gorgeous, *ma chérie*! And your *maman*, she is so proud of you. She has talked and talked about how fantastic you are!'

It's an exaggeration, admittedly, but one Jess is glad for as her daughter glows bashfully. 'Hi,' Mia says. 'I'm guessing you're Beatrice. She's talked about you, too.'

'Your mother, she likes to talk, *hein*? But we like that about her, right?' Beatrice laughs. 'By the way, Jess – your man in the painting,' she goes on. 'My uncle Babacar thinks he looks like a man called Doof.'

'*Doof?*' Disappointment washes through Jess. She's never heard this name, she's sure of it. 'That doesn't mean anything to me.'

Beatrice shrugs. 'That's his nickname – or *was*; my uncle thinks he is dead now. And Jess, I am glad you didn't know him because he was not a good person.' Her eyes flick to Mia as if she is guarding her next words. 'Violent, I think. Something of a . . . how do you say – gangster?'

'Gangster, yeah. *Doof*,' Jess repeats to herself, in case the name prompts any resonance, but nothing comes. Has she been clutching at straws all along? 'Okay. Thanks anyway,' she says.

'What was that about? What painting?' Mia asks as they leave the hotel and head along the street. She's wearing a T-shirt and shorts, her long hair twisted up into little coils either side of her head, with green sparkly eyeshadow and gold hoop earrings.

'It's . . .' Jess doesn't want to get into it now. She should have known better than to trust a hunch. 'Just one of Adelaide's paintings. I thought I recognised someone from a long time ago, when I worked in Paris before. Talking of which,' she goes on, because she'll have to break this news at some point, 'I'm going out tonight. With someone I used to know from then.'

Mia shoots her a look. 'What, a *man*? Does Dad know about this?'

Mia can be positively Victorian at times, when it comes to the morals of her parents. And honestly, Jess is pretty sick of the girls all treating David like some kind of martyr, with her cast as Villain Number One.

'No, he doesn't, because there's nothing *to* know,' she replies through gritted teeth. She remembers their phone conversation from the week before and wonders when his doctor's appointment is. 'The person I'm meeting – Georges – is an old friend, nothing more. Stop doing that!' she laughs because

Mia is pouting and mouthing 'Georges' in a supposedly sexy way. 'Anyway, here we are, this is Place des Vosges where Adelaide lives,' she says, glad to change the subject. She has mixed feelings about the date tonight as it is – will it be a case of just friends? More than just friends? 'Fancy, isn't it?' she goes on, gesturing round, taking in the grandeur and symmetry of its red-brick houses, the arches bordering the square, the trees and neatly clipped central lawns.

Mia pulls a face. 'It's all right,' she says. 'I thought it would be posher though. Isn't she, like, really rich?'

Mia's been watching too many *Real Housewives* shows; she thinks 'posh' equals smoked glass and chrome, an azure pool in the back garden and a Range Rover in the drive.

'This whole square was built by a French king back in the early 1600s, I'll have you know,' Jess tells her. 'Well – okay, not built by his own hands, but built *for* him. You can't get much posher than that, mate.'

They walk along to Adelaide's door and Jess is about to press the bell when she hesitates. 'So – just to recap: she might be grumpy but please don't retaliate. Be polite even if she gets your back up. She's an old lady and set in her ways. And, for the love of God, don't start asking any questions about Colin Copeland or Little Bower, okay? This is not a podcast recce situation, understand?'

Mia's eyes roll up to the heavens. 'Yes, Motherrrrrr,' she says sarcastically. 'Any other orders? Should I leave the room bowing each time like they do with the royal family? Clean her shoes by licking them?'

'Just act like you do with your grandmas, that's all I'm

asking. Or your strictest teacher at school. Yes? Right. We're going in.' She presses the bell then bursts out laughing at Mia's exaggerated nice-girl face, all wide-eyed and simpering, a butter-wouldn't-melt smile. 'Perfect,' she gurgles, trying to tamp down her rising hysteria.

Once inside, they're greeted by Jean-Paul, which has Mia immediately falling to her knees and making the most enormous fuss of him. All of Jess's girls are animal-lovers; it's been their lifelong quest to have a dog. Even when Jess was pregnant with Polly, four-year-old Mia was asking if they couldn't just get a puppy instead of a baby. *And I stand by my judgement,* she'll say whenever the story is recounted.

'Oh my God! You're so gorgeous!' she croons now, scratching behind Jean-Paul's triangular floppy ears. 'You're such a handsome boy! Can I have a paw? Oh Mum, look at him!' Not content with giving her a paw, Jean-Paul leans in to lick her face and she giggles, suddenly seeming about twelve again. 'Hey, you, you're licking off my blusher, ' she cries, twisting away with a laugh.

'And Mia, this is Adelaide,' Jess cuts in, rather drily. 'Adelaide, my daughter Mia, who's going to do *all* your cleaning while we're working; whatever you need doing. Not just play with the dog. Right, Mia?'

Mia scrambles to her feet. 'Oh. Sorry,' she says. 'Hello.'

'Hello,' says Adelaide with the glimmer of a smile. 'Actually, if you don't mind taking the old boy for a W-A-L-K later on, that would be very helpful.' She spells the word out but Jean-Paul looks up eagerly nonetheless, as if he can spell as well as shake a paw on demand. Mia looks equally eager, Jess notes. 'But first, perhaps you could give the kitchen a good going-over. Let me show you where everything is ...'

Jess takes a seat while Mia trots off to receive instructions, hoping that this will work out. Minutes later, they hear the dim sound of music from the kitchen – 'Will that be a problem for you? I can ask her to turn it down,' Jess frets but Adelaide waves a hand, unbothered – then the two of them resume their own work. Chronologically, they're up to the late seventies now, with Adelaide in her early thirties. Her career is building, as are those of her friends, and the press have started to call them the London Bohemians – 'lumping us together, as if a woman couldn't possibly be successful on her own,' Adelaide comments waspishly.

Not that any of them seemed to mind the 'lumping together', as they were still very much a force to be reckoned with. They exhibited together, socialised often and continued to spend communal periods at Little Bower when possible, although as several of the women, including Esme and Margie, began to start families, these occasions became less frequent, with what sounded like a chasm beginning to split the group. *The breeders and the artists*, as Rita apparently put it – which can't have helped matters.

Adelaide has spoken more about Remy by now – the tempestuous nature of their relationship, how he dragged his heels about moving to London to be with her ('France will never forgive you for stealing me away,' she quotes him as saying). What comes across most is his growing lack of respect for Adelaide's work, despite – or perhaps because of – it being far higher regarded than his own art.

'It was difficult for him,' Adelaide concedes. 'Back then, men wanted to feel in charge of women; they were seen as weak, or unmanly, if they didn't dominate their wives or partners.'

'He couldn't handle your success,' Jess puts in. 'He undermined you.' She thinks about David, how he too could never praise Jess for the work she did, as if by doing so it might leech something away from his own career glory.

'Yes, he undermined me,' Adelaide echoes. 'And I let him, more fool me.' She's wearing a slate-grey tunic top today, and crimps the lower hem of it between her fingers. 'Why do we women do this?' she wonders aloud. 'Why do we put up with bad behaviour in the name of love? I held his hand when he was dying, I was there for him until the bitter end but ...' She shakes her head. 'He wasn't always there for me.' Then she turns her eagle eye on Jess. 'Are you happily married, Jessica? And if so, what's your secret?'

'Don't look to me for insider knowledge,' Jess replies, holding up her hands, bare of any wedding ring. 'We split up just over a year ago. He was unfaithful to me and ...' She shrugs, aware of Mia in the next room; aware too of the need to be professional. That said, she's always been a sucker for a woman-to-woman chat. 'It kind of broke me, really. We tried to stay together but in doing so, I lost all my self-respect. It reached the point where I couldn't pretend any more, and I told him as much.'

'Good for you,' said Adelaide. A moment of understanding passes between them. 'You'd think an artist, of all people, would be able to draw a line under things, but that has never been the case for me. When I found out back in 1980 that Remy had been unfaithful yet again, I felt broken too. And being in the public eye, everyone knows your business, everyone whispers about your humiliation, your downfall. It is *awful.*' Her hands are trembling, Jess notices with sympathy. 'Worse, though: not only did he have the affair, but he went on to paint this incredible nude of the woman in question, and included it in an exhibition of his in Berlin ...' She shakes her head, eyes flinty at the decades-old hurt. 'Well, you might already have read about this in your research, but I took it upon myself to destroy the painting at the private view, and threw a whole can of silver car paint over it.'

Jess *has* heard the story, and she's seen the photos, besides. It's a moment in Adelaide's life that is often cited in features about her, partly because it was the start of a huge breakdown, which saw her sequestered in a psychiatric hospital for some time afterwards. 1980 was a traumatic year for Adelaide in other ways: Jess has heard rumours that she gave birth to a child while in hospital, a child that was spirited away out of her life. It was also the year of Colin Copeland's so-called suicide.

'I bet it felt pretty great, chucking the paint like that, ruining his big moment,' she says.

Adelaide's expression has been stormy until now but then her lips quirk in an unexpected smile. 'Absolutely,' she says. 'Nobody has ever put it to me quite like that before but yes, it was wonderful. I felt so exhilarated. As if power was running through every vein.'

'You were too good for him,' Jess tells her.

'And you, clearly, were too good for your cheating ex-husband,' Adelaide replies. 'So if you ever need some paint ...'

Jess laughs and there's a genuine feeling of camaraderie in the air, possibly the first true one Jess has experienced here. Is this how it used to be with Adelaide and Margie? she wonders, last night's email on her mind. She really must try to work the conversation around to Adelaide's old friend, so that she can pass on the news about Margie's illness, see if it inspires any thoughts of reconciliation. If she dares, that is.

'Funnily enough, I bumped into Coco the other week – Remy's other wife,' Adelaide goes on, the smile fading from her face. 'Not my favourite person in the world but we do at least have our survival from him in common. She told me that she's found an old letter from Remy with my name on it, plus some canvas or other.'

'Oh wow,' Jess says, intrigued. 'When will you be able to get them, do you think? Have you arranged to pick them up?' She hesitates as an idea occurs to her, then plunges in. 'I could get them for you, if it's awkward.'

'Thank you, Jessica, but she's out of town at the moment. Typical Coco – she knows how to wind me up. Maybe she'll regret it, when she hears about the memoir, eh?' That glint is back in her eye. 'Because there's a woman who'll get it with both barrels, you wait.'

They've gone off track, however interesting this diversion has been, and Jess tries to steer them back to 1978 – before Berlin and the breakdown, and a full decade before Coco's arrival on the scene. She's not in any hurry to hear the savaging of Coco ahead of time. 'So, to return to what we were saying earlier: you and Remy were living in Chalcot Road, sharing a studio nearby in Fitzroy Road ... Who were you spending your free time with then? What did you do in the evenings? I know that Little Bower was still part of your life, but what about weekdays, your usual sort of routine?' She takes a breath. 'Were you seeing much of Margie?'

'Let me think . . . Well, we went out to dinner a lot – there was a good crowd in the area, lots of socialising. Rita and Fred in Camden, Jeanette and Archie over Chalk Farm way. We'd go to the cinema, and the pub on the corner – what was it called? The Prince of Wales, maybe? – and we were invited to all the shows and launches, of course. It was quite rare that we were in, just the two of us, during the evening – which was as well, really, when we'd spent the day in the studio together, I suppose.'

Jess presses her on a few details – the food they might have eaten at dinner parties (a lot of fondue and moussaka, apparently; masses of Black Forest gateau), anecdotes about famous or interesting people she encountered, any of the art shows that were especially meaningful or memorable. She doesn't manage to engineer the conversation around to Margie but it's all interesting and upbeat stuff. That is, until Adelaide returns to one of the axes she likes to grind, in this case, lambasting a critic. Today's target is Walter Burroughs, a critic who apparently savaged her in print around this period. By now, Jess has come to heartily dislike these rants of hers, the potshots at fellow artists, critics, establishment figures. Maybe Adelaide thinks it will make for salacious reading but Jess finds it all grindingly negative and depressing.

'And another thing about Walter Burroughs,' she's saying, getting into her stride, but perhaps Jess's growing frustration is apparent on her face because Adelaide stops mid-sentence. 'What? Why are you looking like that? Are you even *listening* to me?'

It's so long since Adelaide used that tone of voice on her that Jess flinches. 'I'm listening, but ... Well, I can't see how Walter Burroughs' onion breath – or the fact that you hated the way his Adam's apple moved in his throat, or the gossip you heard about him having an affair with his secretary – I don't think that's relevant to your narrative, to be honest.'

'It's relevant because he was vile about me in print!' Adelaide retorts, her cheeks becoming flushed. 'This is my chance to answer back, Jessica. This is the point of the whole book!'

'Is it? I thought the point was to tell your life story,' Jess replies. 'Not to go off on vindictive tangents about petty grievances, or—' Adelaide draws in such a sharp breath that she suddenly loses her nerve. 'I mean ...'

'Petty grievances?' Adelaide thunders. 'You wouldn't be saying that if you knew how damningly he wrote about my work. How insultingly!'

The music has gone off in the kitchen; Jess has the horrible feeling that Mia is listening. And perhaps a month ago she would have crumbled in the face of Adelaide's temper, but instead she stands her ground. 'What I mean,' she says, hoping to sound conciliatory, 'is that life goes on, right? Sometimes you have to let stuff go.'

'Oh, *do* you,' Adelaide says sarcastically, and Jess immediately feels like a hypocrite because she's hardly 'let go' of what David did with Bella, has she? Nor the bitterness about her old boss Lucinda. She definitely hasn't ever let go of the conviction

298

that she failed Pascale, on what was almost certainly the last night of her life.

'Look, I'm sorry if—' she's saying when the door creaks open to reveal Mia standing there, her eyes darting from Jess to Adelaide and back again, like a spectator at Wimbledon.

'Um ...' she says warily. 'I've finished the kitchen.' Jean-Paul barrels over to her at once, breaking the tension. 'Hey, darling,' she croons, leaning over to make a fuss of him. Then she straightens up and meets Jess's eye, her expression pitched somewhere between nosiness and solidarity. 'Everything all right, Mum?'

'Yes. Thank you.' Jess's face flames. It's disconcerting to have her daughter overhear her get such a dressing-down. Embarrassing, too. Why couldn't Mia have been on the other side of the door when she and Adelaide were laughing earlier, getting on so well? *Wow, Mum's really good at this*, she might have thought then. Now she must be under the impression that Jess is making an absolute pig's ear of the job. Great.

Adelaide gets to her feet, her face unreadable. 'Perhaps this would be a good moment for you to take this lolloping idiot out for his constitutional,' she suggests to Mia, as Jean–Paul gallivants between the two of them. 'Let me find you his lead and dog treats.'

Jess sinks back into her chair as the two of them leave the room. There's no way she can bring up the subject of Margie now, she realises, disconsolate. How can she tell Adelaide what she knows without all hell breaking loose?

Chapter Thirty

Adelaide is still fuming as she issues the girl a set of strict instructions about watching out for cyclists, and steering clear of an over-friendly black poodle to whom Jean-Paul has taken an irrational dislike. *Honestly!* She understands that it's a journalist's job to write a good story, but she has hired Jessica precisely to tell a specific *version* of her story, and nothing more. How dare she start throwing her opinion around, criticising Adelaide for her feelings? Petty grievances, indeed. If Jessica doesn't watch herself, there will be a whole chapter devoted to *her* failings, and what an interminable headache it has been working with her.

As Adelaide returns to the room, Jessica rises to her feet. 'Adelaide, I am so—' she begins humbly, that pink lipstick of hers almost bitten away with agitation.

Adelaide puts up a hand to silence her, in no mood to discuss the matter further. 'Let's not,' she says. 'Okay? I'll "let that go" as you seem so insistent on, and talk about my work in 1978. Let me see ...'

She goes on to describe the Flame series of self-portraits

she painted during this time, which show her holding lit matches in various settings, various poses. Although she'd rather die than admit aloud any regrets around what she did to Simon Dunster, her act of vengeance still smoulders on her conscience, nevertheless. The sound of the timbers catching, the sudden roar as the nylon carpet went up – the memories feel like blackened pieces of her soul. Painting herself holding a flame over and over again – clothed, nude, indoors, outdoors – was a confession of sorts. Repentance.

'Aunty Adelaide's having a book written about her because she's been so successful,' Catherine had explained to her son Henry as they had dinner together the other evening in Chez Janou. 'Are we going to be very shocked by what you reveal, Adelaide?' She was smiling, her long dark hair falling prettily around her face, clearly assuming – wrongly – that her decrepit old relative couldn't possibly have too many outrageous skeletons in her closet.

Buckle up, dear, Adelaide had thought privately. 'You're going to be absolutely horrified,' she'd said with devil-may-care insouciance. Now she's wondering if she should have been quite so blithe. Because they probably *will* be horrified, let's face it, when everything comes to light. Disgusted, even. Wishing they weren't related at all. She remembers the publication of Remy's diaries, how devastating it was for those left behind, her and Coco like collateral damage, bloodied at the side of the road as the juggernaut of his book thundered through their lives. She has the capacity to shock a lot of people with her revelations. She will hurt some of them too. Annoyingly, Jessica's comments on that continue to ring around her head. *Is* it petty of her to dig up old fights for the sake of getting the last word? Will anyone other than her care that she's spent years thinking up how to humiliate her enemies?

The narrative has reached the lowest part of her life, and Adelaide feels her stamina – and courage – deserting her. Sighing, she pushes a hand through her hair. 'Do you know, I might save the events of 1980 for another time,' she says. Chronology be damned. 'I promise I'll tell you everything, but not today. Can we skip on to 1982, when I left Berlin for Provence? That was a good period. I would like to talk about that. I won't even need to slag anyone off,' she adds tartly.

Perhaps Jessica still feels bad about piping up earlier because she doesn't protest. 'Of course,' she says, turning to a fresh page in her notebook. '1982 it is. What was happening then?'

After the tumultuous events of 1980 and its seemingly end-less repercussions, 1982 ended up being one of the best years in Adelaide's life. Sprung from the psychiatric ward, Remy had whisked her away to Provence to convalesce. It was a time of deep contentment for her. They bought a house together high up in the hills, with views over the forest, where the nightly darkness was so deep and black, it made Adelaide feel as if she was a primitive being at the dawn of time, far removed from the rest of the world. They immersed themselves in new artworks – close botanical studies for Remy, whereas Adelaide turned her hand to rolling, luscious landscapes, devoid of all troublesome humanity, merely nature in its ripe, plentiful beauty. They swam, they cycled into the village on market days for food and wine, and existed mostly in their own blissful bubble, with all of their old arguments and betrayals coming to seem as if they had happened to two other people. They forgave each other and got married. It was as if the bad things had never happened.

After a year or so, they spread their wings a little, taking on a flat in Paris too – 'Maybe one day, we will be able to afford an apartment in Place des Vosges,' Remy had sighed hopefully – and both showed their new work to great acclaim. It was Adelaide's first time living in the city and she fell in love with it. She remembers thinking of Cézanne's famous line – 'With an apple I will astonish Paris' – and worked hard to find her own 'apple' which she could offer the city. She began painting portraits of interesting Parisians she met, trying to capture their lives, tell their stories with her brush. She also put together a series of miniature self-portraits that she called An Artist Comes to Town, depicting joyful images of herself around the city, as a visual love letter to her new home.

'Oh!' And then it hits her, her creaking memory still functioning, albeit on a lag. 'Victor Dufresne, that was it,' she says. 'The man in the painting you were asking me about.' His portrait came much later, obviously, and of course he had commissioned it, but she kept up the practice of having a variety of sitters for many years.

Jessica goes quite pale. 'Are you sure? I was told this morning that he was called "Doof".'

'Yes, short for Dufresne,' Adelaide replies, remembering him swaggering into her studio, all thick neck and heft, eyeing the place up as if casing it for a robbery. 'Not a pleasant person, anyway.'

'Do you know what happened to him?'

'No, and I don't want to,' Adelaide says. He had stood there in the studio like a macho man, slotting one fist into his other hand, like he could barely contain his own violence. 'Hopefully he came to a horrible end – or is that too petty for you?'

There's a strange expression on Jessica's face as she shakes her head. 'No,' she says. 'Not at all.'

By now Mia has long since returned with Jean-Paul, having picked up some lunch items from the boulangerie as requested, and they've all had a break. Then the bathroom was cleaned, and the laundry taken care of, while Adelaide went on with her narrative. She's so immersed that it startles her to have Jessica ask, 'Should we call it a day now, do you think?' and then realise that, somehow or other, it is three in the afternoon, well beyond their usual finishing time. 'Goodness, yes, we must,' she replies. She has become quite hoarse from talking so much.

Jessica and Mia leave soon afterwards, and an odd mood descends on the quiet apartment, the stories Adelaide has told that day still lingering as she eases herself into her chaise longue. *Life goes on!* she hears Jessica saying once more in that exasperated way, and she frowns to herself. The intervention had taken her by surprise. On balance, she preferred it when Jessica was calling her a genius or laughing at her stories, rather than today's impatient-sounding criticism. *Let it go!* But it's not that easy. Is it?

She munches an apple, suddenly uncertain of herself. She had embarked on the memoir utterly steadfast in her quest for vengeance. The waters have muddied since then though. Now she feels ... Well, that's the thing. She's not quite sure how she feels about the book any more, what she wants it to do. The whole experience reminds her of all the times she would begin a new painting, only for it to turn out looking completely different from what she originally intended.

Her phone bleeps, interrupting her doubtful feelings. Probably some company or other sending her an advert, she thinks; a scammer attempting to dupe her out of her savings. But it's not.

Hey Adelaide, Frieda here, she reads instead. *Jim and I are going to try a Lebanese restaurant for dinner tonight and I wondered if you were free to join us? Would love to chat some more if so. Let me know!*

Dinner with a garrulous holidaymaker she has barely met, plus her no doubt boring-as-hell husband ... Two weeks ago, Adelaide would have replied with a curt *No, thank you*, or ignored the message altogether. And yet something has definitely shifted inside her, because, to her great surprise, she is tempted to accept. Well, why not? Maybe it will give her something else to think about other than her own uncertainty.

That would be lovely – thank you, she replies before she can change her mind. There. Not vindictive or petty, but perfectly pleasant. Life going on. Happy now, Jessica?

Chapter Thirty-One

Adelaide's not the only person in a contemplative mood. As soon as they get back to the hotel that afternoon, Jess sits down with her laptop, trying to find out what she can about Victor Dufresne. There's very little about him online at first glance, but she vows to keep on digging. Maybe he has absolutely nothing to do with Pascale but Jess will follow her nose in the meantime. It's not like she has many other avenues to explore right now.

Mia lets out a groan when her mum shows no sign of coming off-screen. 'This is boring,' she says. 'Can't we go out and do something?'

'Well ...' Jess feels pulled in two directions. 'The whole reason for me being here is to work, remember. I need to type up some notes after today's session with Adelaide.' She hopes that the older woman isn't too annoyed with her for sticking her oar in today – as a ghostwriter, it's hardly Jess's place to start ordering her subject around, but there's only so much bad-mouthing a person can listen to, or read, for that matter.

'Yeah, but I'm bored,' Mia complains, flopping back on the bed.

'Right,' says Jess, her patience already fraying. 'Well, like I said, I could see what Lucas's nephew is up to, if you want ...'

'Ugh, stop *offering* him to me like that. *No!* Why would I want to hang out with a boy I don't even *know*?' Mia presses a pillow against her face with so much drama, it's a shame that no one from the board of Oscar voters is passing to witness the performance. 'I wish I was with *Dad*,' she adds in a muffled voice.

Jess knows her buttons are being pressed but it's hard not to rise to the bait. 'Well, maybe you should have gone back home instead of coming here, then,' she replies heartlessly. 'Now, if you don't mind, I need to—'

'God, Mum! Thanks for making me feel unwanted!' Mia cries, hurling the pillow to the floor.

'I'm not trying to make you feel unwanted, but I wish you'd stop trying to play me off against your dad all the time,' Jess blurts out and then it's as if the dam gives way. 'It's not fair, Mia. I know the break-up has been difficult for all of you girls but I'm doing my best, okay? I'm trying!'

It's the sharpest she's been with her for a long time. Part of Jess's own self-punishment for the separation has included letting her daughters lash out at her with words, to take it, take it, take it all this time. There are limits though.

'Sorry,' she says, when Mia doesn't immediately reply. 'Look, I didn't want us to break up either, you know. I would have stayed with him for ever, probably, if—' She breaks off in the nick of time, aware of her promise to David.

'If what? What happened?'

Jess presses her lips together. 'It's not for me to say,' she replies. 'And that's not really the issue.' She sighs. 'I'm trying as hard as I can to make it work for everyone, I swear. So cut me some slack now and then, all right?'

Mia sits up, not quite meeting her eye, but nods. Jess'll take that. And given that she's going out with Georges tonight, she supposes it's only fair that she spends some time with Mia now. Resignedly she closes the laptop then gets up. 'Go on, then. Let's find ourselves another iconic *Emily in Paris* landmark and get an ice cream or something,' she suggests, softening. 'And you can help me choose a beret for Poll, and hunt for souvenirs. Sound good?'

Mia nods again, this time with a small smile. 'Thanks, Mum,' she says.

That evening, Jess gets ready feeling distinctly giddy. Third time lucky: neither she nor Georges has cancelled, and dinner at his place is set to happen. She'll have a starter of *oh là là*, and a side order of *va va voom*, please, she thinks, applying sparkly brown eyeliner to one eye then the other. No, she won't, she amends in the next moment as Mia exclaims at something on her phone from the bed. How can she entertain ideas of *va va voom* when she'll have to return to this room, this daughter, who will surely be caustic in her disapproval if there's any just-been-ravaged dishevelment to be seen?

'Oh my God, guess what?' Mia says, sitting bolt upright. 'He's done it, Mum. Zach.'

'He's ... ?' Jess's blood runs cold. Why didn't she get on

the phone to that boy's mother while she had the chance? 'What, posted the photos?'

'No, deleted them. Erin sent her brother Dougie round to his house – he's like six foot eight or something and a proper meathead – and he basically forced Zach to get rid of them all.' Mia snorts as another message comes in. 'Ha! Even better. His mum came back from work and walked in on them arguing and Dougie told Zach's mum *everything*. She went absolutely ballistic and now he's, like, grounded for *ever*. And apparently he's going to apologise to me in front of everyone. His mum insists!'

'Oh love!' The tension leaves Jess's body at once. 'That's brilliant news. Fantastic. I'm glad your friends turned it around.'

'Yeah,' Mia says happily, speed-typing replies. 'Me too.'

'I'd better give that hitman a ring, hadn't I?' Jess jokes. 'Tell him he can stand down now. No need, mate – the sisterhood have got this.'

Mia smiles but then her eyes narrow a fraction as she notices Jess rootling through her make-up bag. 'Talking of men,' she says. 'This guy whose house you're going to tonight. What do you know about him? Because ... no offence, but he might have turned into an axe murderer since you last saw him. There are some bad people out there. You might have been out of the dating game for a few decades, Mum, but I haven't.' She puts her phone down in order to peer more beadily at her. 'Also: *is* this a date? Genuine question.'

Oh help. Now Jess will have to give a genuine answer. 'It's probably not a *date*,' she replies carefully, rolling on some lipstick then peering at her reflection. Too red? Too red. 'More of a catch-up. Like when you saw Josie again, after she'd moved schools.'

Mia's expression is so withering, it's lucky there aren't any plants in the vicinity. 'Mum – not really. For one thing, I didn't feel the need to put on my favourite dress and loads of make-up, and spend ages fannying about with my hair before I saw *Josie*.'

The girl's got a point. Jess removes the too-red lipstick and tries a different shade. Better. 'Okay, honest answer – I don't know,' she says. 'Will that do? I was madly in love with him when I was twenty-two but I'm a different person now to who I was then. He will be too. We'll probably reminisce about being young – if we can both remember so far back, that is.' She could show him the portrait of Victor Dufresne in case he recognises him, she realises, skin prickling. Or see if he ever heard anything about Pascale following her disappearance.

Capping the lipstick, she drops it into her bag, then stands back from the mirror and smooths down her dress. After having a massive dither in front of the wardrobe, she's changed her mind yet again and is wearing her pale pink maxi dress, which enhances her tan, plus her gold paper-clip necklace and gold gladiator sandals. Not bad, she decides, turning to face her daughter. 'Now – are you sure that you're all right with me going out? I won't be too late or—'

'I'm sure,' Mia replies. 'I'll probably just get some falafel and wander round for a bit. See if I can find any crack dens or armed criminals to while away the hours with.'

'Ha ha. Please don't.' They smile at each other. 'Okay, well, I'll see you later. Don't do anything silly, and ring me if you need me, yeah? Otherwise ...' She hesitates, suddenly doubtful. Is there not something kind of seedy about leaving her seventeen-year-old daughter alone in Paris while she goes off for dinner with an old lover?

'Bye, Mum,' Mia says when she doesn't finish her sentence. 'Why are you still even here? Just go, already! And don't *you* do anything silly.'

Her daughter's sarcastic words ring in Jess's ears as she leaves the hotel and sets out for Georges' place. Despite their ups and downs, she's enjoying having her around on the whole. Not only is Mia good company, it's also been fun to have her installed as a spy in Adelaide's flat while she does the cleaning, although, as usual, her daughter's morbid imagination has got the better of her, more than once. *Evidence of other murders?!* she messaged Jess this morning, along with a photo of a dozen or so gleaming kitchen knives. *Poison!!* came another message, with a photo of a bottle of turps in a cupboard. At least she hasn't shoved a microphone under Adelaide's nose and started interrogating her about Colin Copeland's death, but Jess has been somewhat on edge the whole time, half expecting it.

Georges' flat is in the 11th arrondissement, twenty minutes' or so walk from the hotel, and Jess picks up a bottle of Sancerre along the way. It's a balmy evening and by the time she arrives, her sandal straps are chafing the tender skin on her feet and beads of sweat have gathered along her hairline. Great. Sweaty and blistered, just the look she was aiming for. Having blotted her face with a tissue, she raps the metal knocker on his front door, her heart mimicking the sound with a sudden frenzied gallop. Okay. Here we go.

The door swings open and he's there in the doorway, backlit by the warm lighting of his apartment. Tall and still handsome with grey streaks in his chin-length light brown hair, he's dressed in a white shirt and jeans, a gold chain gleaming at his throat. Barefoot, like he's wandered in from a hippy ranch. Sexy as all hell.

'Jessica! *Mon Dieu!* Is it really you?'

'Hi!' she says – squeaks, rather, as he sweeps her into his arms and crushes the air out of her. He smells delicious, of soap and wine, and, squeezed within his embrace, the years momentarily drop away from her so that she's a young woman again, intoxicated by this handsome, charismatic man. Her body feels loose and liquid at the memory; a thrill sweeps through her. How she had worshipped him back then. And here she is again, his heartbeat ticking against hers. *Hello.*

Hands moving to her shoulders, he steps back. 'Let me look at you,' he commands, then whistles. 'Jessica, we are time travellers together, non? Suddenly I feel young again. Time has been good to you, my darling.'

'Blimey, Georges, it's been pretty good to you too,' she hears herself say faintly as he takes one of her hands and kisses it. The skin tingles where his lips touch it and her heart pounds again, remembering the two of them entwined on his futon, back in his old flat; how teasingly he liked to remove her clothes, piece by piece. He looks *incredible*, she marvels as he leads her into the kitchen, where a couple of steaks await bloodily on a plate and some jazzy music is playing in the background.

312

His body is still lean and taut – if only she could say the same about her own – and the skin on his face is smooth, and pretty unlined, even though he must be, what, early fifties by now?

His kitchen is like something from a magazine – uncluttered, minimalist, everything in white and cream; the sort of kitchen Jess could probably have an orgasm over, given a few minutes' intense contemplation. Stop thinking about orgasms, she chides herself, as her eye skates over the marble worktops, the old-fashioned range cooker, the scrubbed pine table set for two. Even his potted herbs along the windowsill are bushy and verdant – a far cry from the leggy supermarket basil and miserable-looking coriander that sit parched in her own kitchen.

'Wine?' he asks, holding a bottle of red in one hand. He's already made a start, she can see, with a half-full long-stemmed glass beside a bowl of salad. She imagines him preparing food there, jazz playing, wine at hand, evening light streaming through the window, and there's such a wide crevasse between this image and her own dinner-making reality back home that her jealousy is like a kick in the stomach.

It's not a competition! as she would say to her girls, though.

'Yes, please,' she replies. 'So . . . gosh. This is a bit weird, isn't it? Oh, I brought you something,' she remembers, passing over the Sancerre, which is no longer quite as chilled as when she plucked it from the *supermarché* fridge fifteen minutes ago. It's possibly redundant too, if he's already cracked open the red, but never mind.

He gestures for her to take a seat on one of the stools at the kitchen island, then pours her wine. They clink glasses, smiling at one another. Has he had Botox, she wonders distractedly, or is that smooth face down to sheer good luck in the gene pool and possibly some decent retinols? She probably shouldn't ask him outright, but if she gets the chance to snoop around his bathroom, you bet she's going to take note of any skincare products she comes across.

'Here's to old friends,' he says, eyes soft. 'So! How did life turn out for you, then? You're a journalist, you said – writing a memoir?' He whistles under his breath. 'Impressive, Jess.'

How satisfying, how ego-boosting it is to go in with that as her intro, rather than the usual agony aunt and mum columnist line! 'Yes,' she says, drawing herself up a little on the stool. *Yes, I am impressive, Georges. Yes, I can be highbrow, actually.* 'Of Adelaide Fox, the artist, do you know her work?'

'Hmm – married to Remy Lavigne, is that the one?' he asks, putting a griddle pan on the stove and lighting the gas ring.

Jess winces on Adelaide's behalf at this reply – her subject would detest being described merely in association with her ex, rather than in terms of her work and career. 'Yes, probably most famous for her Bird series of paintings,' she feels obliged to say. 'Her last big show was called Darkness, about eighteen years ago,' she goes on, adding 'after Remy died' for his benefit. 'I interviewed her when the exhibition came to London and we hit it off, so when it came to finding a memoir writer, she got in touch again.' Okay, so this is not *strictly* how events played out, but he doesn't need to know any of that. 'And here I am,' she says with a modest shrug.

'And here you are,' he echoes, meeting her eye as he puts one bloody slab of steak after another into the pan. (She tries

314

not to think about the presumption he's made about her eating meat. For all he knows, she's been vegan for the last twenty years, but never mind. Perhaps he's a bit old school about these things.) As if reading her mind, he glances from the sizzling meat over to her face, then asks, 'This is okay, yes? You still like steak?'

And there she was thinking he was presumptuous, she scolds herself, when, if anything, he's been thoughtful, remembering what a steak-frites girl she was back when they were together.

'Absolutely, yes,' she replies. 'Thank you.' She sips her wine. 'So – tell me about yourself. Do you have any kids? Has there been a *Madame Georges* at any point?'

'Me? No. Definitely not.' He gazes performatively around him, gestures with the spatula. 'You can imagine kids here? No, thank you. Friends of mine who have taken that route – their lives have shrunk overnight. Their tiny lives, concerned with their tiny offspring – no, it's not for me. I am a free spirit, I prefer the good life – to travel, to explore, to go out when I want to. I can go to the theatre, eat at the best restaurants, stay out all night dancing if I like. With children, that is not possible.'

He's making it sound very noble, the child-free life – travelling and exploring and fine dining, but come on, thinks Jess, does he *really* still stay out dancing all night at his age? Isn't that kind of naff now? To her ears, it sounds like a well-used line that he's been trotting out for the last few decades, a line that's past its own use-by date nowadays. Although maybe she's too tiny-minded, after having concerned herself with her three tiny lives for so long?

315

'It's just different, I suppose,' she says evenly. 'I have three children and yes, when they were little, life did get pretty domestic, but they're all teenagers now, so I feel as if I'm coming through the other side of that. I mean – look, I'm here in Paris on my own, for instance! Having a great time.' Here in Paris on my own, if you don't count my seventeen-year-old daughter, anyway, she amends in her head. She won't be telling him that either though.

'I bet you're a good mother,' he says.

'Well . . .'

'You're definitely a sexy wife,' he goes on, flipping the steaks. He raises an eyebrow, and to her embarrassment, she feels heat flow into her face.

'Um . . . maybe once,' she says, trying to laugh off the fluttering feeling in her tummy. When did anyone last call her sexy? Does he really think she's sexy? 'Although I'm not married any more,' she adds quickly.

That eyebrow is at work again. 'You're not married any more,' he repeats. 'Ahh. Now that interests me.'

Oh Lord. Does he mean that, or is he just saying what he thinks she wants to hear? *Is* that what she wants to hear? She feels muddled, unsure whether to flirt right back or to hold off until they know one another better again. Does he think she's just come round for dinner and sex? (*Has* she just come round for dinner and sex?)

'I guess a lot has changed after so many years,' she says, rather primly. Her blood seems to be racing around her body, along with a gallon of adrenalin, and she puts her palms flat

316

on the kitchen island, trying to anchor herself. 'I see you're an architect these days, that must be interesting.'

He roars with laughter. 'Ahh Jess, I have made you shy, yes? Calling you sexy – you are flustered, I see. Changing the subject.' He takes the steak pan off the heat, leaving the meat to rest, then hoists himself up on to the worktop, legs dangling, smiling over at her. He wags a finger. 'Don't think I haven't noticed.'

'Georges, I—' Then she laughs too because he's right, and it's as if nothing has changed, and he can still see through her. But a few minutes later as she tries to take the conversation into deeper waters – their careers, hopes, regrets, politics, even, only for him to keep twisting it back into charm and innuendo – she corrects herself. Because things *have* changed, haven't they? *She* has changed, for one – she's a grown-up now, no longer the admiring little acolyte she was back then, content to remain in his shadow. She's a match for him these days, in terms of outcomes and experience – so why is he still treating her like a blushing student? Worse, why is she still blushing?

He serves dinner – steak and some miniature roast potatoes and a pungently herby green salad – and gestures for her to take a seat at the small table while he fetches grainy mustard, salad dressing and a jug of iced water. The whole set-up is straight from an Instagram post – simple, classy, perfect. She almost wants to take a covert photo to send to Becky who, like Jess, lives in a house of clutter and noise, where dinners are burned or just a bit shit half the time. 'Thank you, this is really lovely of you,' she says as he sits down opposite her at last.

He raises his glass. 'What can I say, I am a really lovely man,' he replies. 'And you, I think, are a really lovely woman.'

She raises her glass back at him. 'Well, I'm not arguing with any of that. But thank you. It's nice to see you again. Obviously life is very good.' From where she's sitting, she can see a guitar propped up in the corner of the room and it reminds her how he used to serenade her back in the day – Neil Young, U2, Crowded House. Nice that he still plays, she thinks, and is about to mention it when she jumps. A young blonde woman has suddenly appeared at the back door, trying the handle then peering through the glass and rapping at it.

'Oh!' Jess says in surprise. 'You have a visitor.'

If she didn't know better, she might have assumed the young woman was his daughter, she thinks, as he turns to look, then gets up from the table. With her hair loose and wavy, halfway down her back, and wearing a strappy white dress, the woman – girl, really, she can't be much older than Mia – has large, expressive eyes and make-up that has clearly taken considerable effort. She squeals happily as Georges opens the door and tries to throw her arms around his neck but he seems less thrilled about her arrival, gently disentangling himself and shaking his head.

Left at the table, Jess can't quite follow their rapid French exchanges, but the gist she's getting, from tone and body language, is that the woman is very familiar with Georges. She touches him constantly, cajoling him, head cocked, batting her eyelashes provocatively, while he is apparently less keen to reciprocate. Or, at least, he's less keen to reciprocate while Jess is in the background, she thinks, cutting into her steak with a small frown. Who is the woman? She clearly knows her way around his apartment, judging by the way she appeared at the back, as if expecting to walk straight in. A neighbour? A friend's daughter?

The blonde girl hooks a finger into the belt loop of his jeans, tugging him towards her with a little pout and Georges looks annoyed, glancing back in Jess's direction and shaking his head again. Then he goes out of the door, putting his hand on the girl's shoulder to steer her away around the side of the building. No way, Jess thinks, open-mouthed, as they vanish from sight. What the hell . . . ? She keeps replaying that intimate little belt-loop tug in her mind, a gesture so personal, so knowing, it's surely one made by a lover. But the girl must be half his age, if that. Jess puts her cutlery down, feeling as if her appetite has deserted her. Maybe it's a niece? But no – there was definitely something sexual about the way she kept touching him. Oh Georges. What on earth is he doing?

He reappears just then, his mouth quirking, eyes hooded as if he's rattled. Only for a moment though because then he slides back into his seat, smooth as ever. 'Sorry about that,' he says. 'A colleague – she wanted some information about a client.'

Jess does not believe this for a second. Pull the other one, love, she thinks. She's not the same gullible, wet-behind-the-ears girl he used to know. 'A colleague, eh?' she says, her gaze direct. 'Looked a bit more than that, from where I was sitting.'

Now it's his turn to be flustered. 'Well – we have dated a couple of times, but it was only a bit of fun, you know.'

Not really, Jess thinks. Can't say I do know. And maybe

the girl didn't know that either, judging by the way her face fell when he didn't invite her in. 'Right,' she says neutrally, staring down at her plate of food. God. It's a bit gross, isn't it, a man in his fifties still messing around with women so much younger? She bites her lip, picturing the girl in her swingy white sundress, ruched at the top over her small chest, falling to a zigzag hem above her knees. She's pretty sure Mia and her friends have similar dresses, probably from Zara or H&M, cheap and cheerful, bought for the summer. Is the girl also only here for the summer, like Jess was?

'You are not happy, I see,' Georges says teasingly, nudging her foot under the table with his. 'Have I shocked you, Jess?'

'No, I—' Yes. She's shocked. And she definitely doesn't want to have sex with him now, if his preference is for nubile girls without so much as a stretch mark or crow's foot to call their own. Mind you, if that's the case, then he probably doesn't want to have sex with her either. 'Well, a little bit,' she concedes.

'But I am not married, I am not cheating,' he retaliates. 'I am not hurting anybody.'

'True,' she says. He seems to think her shock has been caused solely by the fact of another woman turning up at his back door while he's having dinner with her; as if she's put out because he's shown her disrespect. What, does he think she's set her heart on this dinner as the big romantic event of her summer or something? Well, all right, she *was* feeling that way earlier, she acknowledges, but not any more. You're not that big a deal, babe, she feels like telling him. 'Great steak,' she says instead, weakly changing the subject. She's wishing she hadn't come here now. To think that she'd hovered in the hotel doorway, wondering if her going out was a bit seedy, when his entire lifestyle looks to be way seedier. 'Tell me what you're working on at the moment,' she says, starting to feel desperate.

'Jess, it is only fun. It is only sex and fun,' he says, rolling his eyes at her. 'Your face – you're looking at me as if I'm a bad person. I am not a bad person!'

'Of course you're not,' she says, like the faithful people-pleaser she is. She remembers this about him now, that he couldn't bear any form of criticism, couldn't bear to be mocked or not taken seriously. There is a fragile, insecure man beneath the handsome trappings, within the stylish home. She's his guest here, she shouldn't start having a go. But then again, do you know what, she's got three daughters, and she's not a big fan of predatory men in general, who chew up and spit out young girls for so-called 'sex and fun'. Is she projecting here? Making wild assumptions? Yes. But her gut tells her that this is how it is. 'Although she seemed pretty young, your "colleague",' she finds herself saying. 'Wouldn't you rather date someone ... you know – with a bit more life experience? Someone your age? Our age,' she adds, and then cringes, hoping it doesn't sound as if she's coming on to him. *Don't worry, Georges, you're quite safe from my advances,* she adds drily in her head.

He shrugs. 'Age is not important to me,' he says, forking salad into his mouth. 'It's the person that interests me. Their energy. Their vibe.' He narrows his eyes slightly as if he's suddenly finding her lacking in those things, as if she has failed his test. Yeah, whatever. He's already been marked down to a zero on hers.

'Mm, and a good connection too,' she says breezily, not wanting this to turn into an argument. 'That's what they say on the reality dating shows, isn't it? Do you get that sort of thing over here, or is French TV too sophisticated?' Before he can even answer, she launches into a description of a programme she and her daughters watched earlier in the year, expounding at length about how they're always glued to the dramas between couples. She's talking too much, but it's all safe, neutral content, and at least it helps the tension between them dissolve at last.

The perils of nostalgia, she thinks to herself, as conversation turns to films they both love, and then his tips for what she should see and do while in Paris again. Her memories of him have always been precious to her but while he's remained sexy and charming in the intervening years, there's been no accompanying emotional growth. Sometimes a memory should be left alone, rather than held up and re-examined in the cold light of a new day. Although ... An earlier intention returns to her. 'By the way, do you remember my friend from the hotel back then, Pascale?' she asks. 'I don't suppose you've heard anything about her since then, have you?'

'Pascale ...' He frowns, apparently unable to place her. 'Remind me.'

'Dark hair in a ponytail, gorgeous brown eyes, big boobs, loud laugh,' Jess says, listing attributes that might have registered with him. 'She vanished.'

He nods, a flash of sympathy crossing his face. She had been so worried afterwards, sobbing into his chest for days on end before eventually deciding to go home a few weeks later. 'I remember. Your friend, yes. No, I don't think I heard anything, sorry.'

'Never mind. How about this man?' She fumbles with her phone. 'Victor Dufresne. Do you know anything about him?'

'Jess, what is this? No,' he says. 'I have never heard of him.'

'It doesn't matter,' she says flatly. Another dead end. He moves to top up her glass but she covers it with her hand. They've finished dinner by now and she's thinking about the walk back to the hotel, wanting to keep her wits about her.

'Coffee? Brandy?'

'Thank you, but I'll pass. I should probably go, Georges, I've got work in the morning.'

It's a bit feeble but he doesn't push her, as if he knows there's no point. Nor does he offer to walk her back, or call her a cab. He's probably already wondering how soon he can ask Blondie back round, Jess thinks as they say goodbye.

'Good to see you, Jess,' he says, kissing her once, twice on her cheeks.

'Good to see you too, Georges,' she replies. 'Thanks for a lovely dinner.' And then she's away, her sandals slapping against the pavement as she walks quickly down the road, unsure whether to laugh or cry.

She laughs. Then she groans aloud. Then she laughs. It's been a funny old evening, all in all.

Chapter Thirty-Two

As Jess passes the Mezze Saida restaurant a few minutes later, she's lost in thought, but if she'd happened to look through the window, past the colourful lanterns hanging there, she'd have seen Adelaide sitting at a table inside, with Frieda and Jim. Frieda looks fabulous in a long, saffron-coloured trapeze dress with huge wooden beads around her neck, whereas Jim, far from being the bore that Adelaide was dreading, wears a flamboyant paisley shirt and quickly proves himself to be the teller of all sorts of extraordinary (and hilarious) tales.

Admittedly, there was some awkwardness at the start of the evening, when Adelaide arrived and found Jim and Frieda seated at the back of the restaurant, near the gents' loos, only for the waiter – immediately recognising Adelaide – to apologise profusely and move them to far better seats by the window. 'What in God's name ... ?' murmurs Frieda when the waiter reappears with shot glasses of arak for them each, saying, 'Our gift to you and your friends, Madame.'

'What's going on?' she hisses once the waiter has gone. Her eyes widen. 'Are you, like, a *celebrity* around here or something?'

'Well ...'

Jim is quicker than his wife, though. His jaw swings open. 'Oh my God. You're the artist lady, aren't you? The really famous ... Do you know, I *thought* there was something familiar about you, soon as you walked in. Frieda, what the hell? Did you not ask Adelaide *anything* about her life?' He recovers himself and laughs, smiling delightedly at Adelaide and holding his hand out. 'Well, I never. I apologise for my philistine wife. It's a real pleasure to meet you. And a privilege too. Your painting – *Dawn in Provence*, is it? That's one of my all-time favourites.'

Adelaide feels a lump in her throat because it's one of her favourites too. And wasn't she only thinking about Provence the other day? Jim's words fling her back there immediately, to her spot up in the mountains with her easel, the smell of pine trees in the air, a blanket around her shoulders as the dawn crept above the horizon in a glimmering golden band.

'Thank you,' she says. 'That's really nice to hear.'

Frieda, meanwhile, still has a hand clapped to her mouth, her eyes huge and startled. 'Adelaide! You're famous! And you've let me make such a jackass of myself, too.' Then she giggles, suddenly girlish. 'That is *very* cool, though. You are one modest lady. Jeez Louise, if I was famous, it would be the first thing I'd let people know about myself, whether they wanted to hear it or not.'

'Agreed,' Jim puts in, pulling a funny face across the table. 'By the way, can I ask you something as an artist, Adelaide: what do you think of my shirt? Because I love it but my beloved wife has strong thoughts on the matter, and never lets me wear it without *hearing* those strong thoughts.'

'It's a very nice shirt,' Adelaide says diplomatically, laughing at the smug expression that appears instantly on his face. 'Very tasteful.'

'Oh, *Adelaide*,' Frieda cries, mock-exasperated. 'Just when I thought we were going to be friends. She's being polite, damn it, Jim, can't you see that?' she adds as he preens himself, pretending to brush an imaginary crumb off one arm. 'Be honest, now. We all know that shirt is an abomination. An absolute vomit of colours!'

Jim could hardly be more triumphant. 'If it's good enough for a famous artist—'

'I mean, some of my best work was created on hallucinogenic drugs,' Adelaide goes on with a wink at Frieda, 'and I'm not saying that the designer of that fabric was *also* smashed out of their head, Jim, but—'

'Ha! *Yes*, Adelaide!' cries Frieda, victorious.

'But as an artist I'm all for experimentation – and I'm grateful moreover that there are people like you, bold enough to make a stand for the' – Jim clutches his own face as if in extreme pain, and it's hard to speak for laughing all of a sudden – 'a stand for those experimental art school students ...'

'Crushed,' Jim moans, hands still covering his face. 'So crushed.'

'I'm joking,' Adelaide tells him, patting his arm. 'I'm winding you up. Who wants to live in a world where everyone dresses like a catalogue model? Not me.' She picks up her glass of arak. 'Cheers, anyway. Thank you both for asking me to dinner with you.'

'Thank you for coming, Famous Artist, especially as you've already got us free shots,' Frieda says, holding up her own glass. 'I've no idea what the hell this stuff is, but I'm willing to toss it down my throat in the name of a good night out, if you are?'

There's something so warm and likeable about Frieda and Jim, Adelaide already feels as if she's known them and their affectionate bickering for years. 'Hell, yeah,' she says (and when did she last hear herself say 'Hell yeah'? she marvels. Ten or more years ago?). 'To a good night out!'

And so it is proving to be. Once Frieda has got over the famous artist business, they chat away – about Montreal and Ottawa ('You taught at the *art school*, of course, you did say something about that. Wow, that's fabulous. Did you love Canada? Will you come visit us sometime, do you think?') and then on to Frieda's love of ice hockey ('Don't get her started, Adelaide,' Jim warns) and then the various places they have lived and worked.

On her way here this evening, Adelaide had felt a little trepidatious, wondering if her small talk was up to scratch. But Frieda and Jim are both good, engaging talkers, and draw her out of herself so skilfully, it's soon hard to remember why on earth she was ever worried. In some ways, Frieda reminds her of Margie, she realises – they have the same feistiness, the same quickness to laugh. A certain naughtiness of spirit that sees Frieda ordering a round of tequila shots for them all, just because it's a Monday and what the heck, as she puts it.

Although it hasn't all been plain sailing for Frieda, Adelaide learns, as the evening unfolds. It turns out that her first husband was a helicopter pilot who died in a tragic accident after they'd been together twenty years. She'd lost a daughter too, to meningitis when she was five, although still has a son. Throughout these seismic life shocks, she's somehow kept going: toughing it out in the man's world of the construction industry, raising her son, riding her horses, and cheering on the Habs, the hockey team she supports. 'Then life got *really* good when she met me,' Jim says, eyes soft. 'Or should I say, *my* life got really good when she met me? Yeah, I think that's what I mean.'

Adelaide really likes her. She likes them both. Is it possible to have a friend crush? If so, she's having one. Life can be *fun*, she marvels as they tuck into delicious mezze, and Frieda decides that they're all going to try a bottle of Lebanese wine. Life can surprise you. Frieda and Jim ask interested questions about her career, and she finds herself blossoming as she skims through the highlights.

'Wow,' Frieda exclaims. 'Can we arrange for an exhibition in Montreal so you can come over to Canada, do you think? You could stay with us, and I'll take you horse riding. Hey, and you could give Brad a call, for old times' sake . . .' she adds, winking, because of course by then, they've heard about that chapter in Adelaide's life too.

'Gosh, I . . .' Adelaide doesn't know what to say. Travel again, and this time even further than Margate or the Uffizi. 'I haven't left France for years,' she says apologetically. 'The last time . . . heavens, it must have been back in 2019, when I saw the Hilma af Klint show at the Guggenheim.'

'The whatty what now?' Frieda asks before saying, 'Okay, some art thing, I'm guessing. But – look, we're all trying to travel less with climate change, I get it. Good for you. But you reach our sort of age and – well, sometimes, you have to just go to the places you want to go. While you still can. Don't you think? The jet lag's a business, I'll give you that, but my God, I'm so glad I got to see Paris. I'm so happy that I'm here for the summer, living in the present, meeting folks like you, giddy on tequila, eating like a total fucking mezze queen, excuse my language.'

'Don't badger Adelaide,' Jim tells his wife, perhaps because he can see from Adelaide's eyes that there's more to the travel decision than mere distance. 'Now – how are we all feeling about dessert?'

They busy themselves with the dessert menu and thoughts about whether a coffee would keep them up all night if they chanced one now. Beneath the chatter though, Adelaide is experiencing what feels like a small but significant tectonic shift inside her. It's odd, but all she can think about is horse riding with Frieda. Even though she hasn't been on the back of a horse since she was a young woman, when the farmer along the road from Little Bower would allow Adelaide and her friends to take his horses for a gallop over the Kent Downs. Even though she'd probably struggle to actually heave herself on to a horse's back these days.

Life goes on! Jess exclaimed earlier that day. But it's only really in the last few weeks that Adelaide has entertained the possibility of life in the future, rather than harking back to the past. Suddenly it's there in her mind though, the paths that she could take unfolding before her. If she dares, that is. Dare she?

Chapter Thirty-Three

On Tuesday morning, Jess and Mia set off towards Place des Vosges for another day's work. It had slightly broken Jess's heart the evening before, returning to the hotel and seeing the look of relief on her daughter's face when she heard the date with Georges had been awful. 'Love ... you know that me and your dad, we're not getting back together, right?' Jess had said, as gently as possible, later on as they got ready for bed. 'Me not falling in love with Georges again doesn't change anything on that front.'

Mia, pulling on a soft cotton vest to sleep in, didn't reply immediately. 'Yeah,' she mumbled eventually. 'But I kind of wish you *would* get back with Dad. I'm not having a go,' she added quickly, perhaps remembering their earlier spat. 'That's just how I feel.'

'I know,' Jess told her, hunting through her washbag for a box of plasters so that she can tend to her blistered feet. 'And I'm sorry. Sometimes ... well, sometimes a story doesn't end the way you want it to, I guess. Life gets complicated.'

Padding over to the mirror, Mia sat cross-legged in front

of it. 'You know I said I thought he was seeing someone else?' she asked, closing one eye as she began taking off her make-up. 'I'm not sure about that any more. One night while we were in Italy, he was pretty drunk and said how much he was missing you. So ...' She shrugged, and there, in the movement of her shoulders, Jess could see the hope she'd been privately carrying inside her since then. Hope that scorched a hole through Jess's own heart, that weighed on her mind as she tossed and turned, trying to sleep later that night. Sure, she and David had loved each other once upon a time, they had been happy together. But by the end of their relationship, she was so deeply *un*happy, so chipped away by doubt, that she felt as if she had become half a person, no longer the woman she once was. This summer, she has felt herself coming back together; rediscovering the true Jess who finds joy in others, who loves life. Is it selfish of her that she's not willing to sacrifice that in order to try again with David, as her daughters so clearly want?

Once they arrive at Adelaide's and the day's session begins, Jess hears about Adelaide and Remy's second painful break-up, followed by his whirlwind romance and marriage to Coco. Braced for a lengthy segue into a full character assassination of them both, Jess is surprised when it's dealt with fairly briskly. Adelaide seems to have more energy today, going on to vividly describe her time in Japan and then the job she took in Ottawa, before the doorbell rings around one o'clock.

'Ahh. I'll have to tell you about the Bradelaide period tomorrow, I'm afraid,' she says, getting up to cross the room to the intercom. 'That'll be Lucas and Catherine, they're

332

coming to see if you want to have lunch with them. Sorry, I meant to mention it when you arrived, but with everything else on my mind ...'

'Oh,' says Jess, still caught up in descriptions of a snowy winter in Ottawa. Bradelaide? she wonders, bemused, before catching on to what Adelaide has just said. She hasn't seen Luc since the night in Belleville, where she has the feeling she pissed him off, banging on about Hadlow College and farming courses. *What's that all about?* he'd said, and she grimaces now to remember how she'd defended herself, possibly too zealously. She will try really hard to act like a normal person today, she decides as Adelaide buzzes the door mechanism to let them in. 'I'd better track down Mia, then,' she adds, getting to her feet. 'If that's all right, us leaving you a bit early ...'

'Of course it is,' Adelaide says. 'I think we've made good progress so far this week. I've got a few things I need to do anyway.'

There's *definitely* something different about her today, Jess realises as she locates Mia in the dining room where she's been cleaning glass and silverware. She'd go as far as to say that Adelaide seems ... well, *cheerful*, actually; an adjective Jess doesn't think she's ever paired with her before. She's wearing a rose-pink tunic, the prettiest item of clothing Jess has seen her in, and a glitzy gold necklace too, studded with twinkling peridot gems. What's going on?

'Hello again, sorry about all of these steps, Henry – do come in,' Adelaide greets the arrivals. 'Catherine, Henry – this is Jessica, who's writing my memoir. Jessica, my niece Catherine and her son, Henry. Oh, and here's Mia, Jessica's daughter,' she adds as Mia barrels around the corner, cleaning bucket in hand.

Mia's wearing a halterneck gingham playsuit and gigantic pink platform sandals today, her hair braided around her head, and she turns bright red as she walks into the introductions. Or has she gone that colour because eighteen-year-old Henry is tall and very good-looking, with his mop of black hair and Ramones T-shirt?

'Lovely to meet you,' Jess says, trying to smooth over the moment. 'And lunch with you guys would be great. Right, Mimi?'

Mia glares at the nickname – oh dear, has Jess embarrassed her? That didn't take long – and scuttles into the kitchen, muttering something about putting stuff away. Jess makes small talk with Catherine, who is friendly and pretty in cargo shorts and a faded blue T-shirt, and Henry, who sweetly takes the mick out of his mum's pronunciation when she says 'Montmartre'. ('What was that again, Mum? Got something in your throat there, have you?')

Mia's 'putting stuff away' apparently included a quick application of lipstick and mascara, and the deliberate unravelling of her plaits, because she emerges a moment later with her hair falling in waves around her shoulders like some kind of Renaissance angel. The effect is not lost on Henry, Jess observes, because he suddenly straightens up and stuffs his phone in his pocket. 'Mia, is it?' Jess hears him say as they set off down the stairs. 'I'm Henry. All right?'

Luc steers them to a brasserie that has seats in the shade and a good line in burgers and chips. He's the older of the siblings and Jess quickly gets a sense of their dynamic, with him taking the lead and Catherine falling in good-naturedly with his decisions. Having said that though, it only takes Jess asking what he was like as a teenager for Catherine, with a glint in her eye, to launch into stories of dreadful behaviour, in true younger sister form. Meanwhile, Mia and Henry have discovered that they are both going to Reading Festival later in the summer and are deep in discussion about which bands they're most looking forward to seeing.

The food arrives and they tuck in. 'So how are you finding Paris, Mia?' Luc asks, turning to her.

'It's cool, yeah, I'm having a good time,' comes the reply. 'I rented one of those trottinettes last night and went up to Sacré-Coeur and Pigalle—'

'Did you?' puts in Jess, because this is all news to her. 'What even is a trottinette?'

Mia pulls a face. 'Mum! Get with it. One of those electric scooters you see everywhere – like that one,' she says, pointing across the street to where a young man with massive headphones is zipping along, swerving around pedestrians with a certain amount of recklessness to Jess's mind.

'Can we get those?' Henry's already asking Catherine.

Luc meanwhile seems confused. 'How come you weren't together last night?' he asks Jess, glancing back to Mia. 'I mean – are you staying together, or ...?'

'Mum went on a *date*,' Mia is quick to say with full dramatic emphasis. Presumably this is revenge for Jess calling her Mimi earlier when she was trying to appear cool. 'With a creepy old pervert.'

335

'Mia!'

'What? Come on, you basically said those words yourself. He's even older than Mum and he still goes out with girls in their twenties,' Mia reports breathlessly. 'How grim is that?' Jess is still reeling from the 'even older than Mum' barb when her daughter puts a hand under her chin and bats her eyelashes. 'I'm going out with him tonight actually,' she goes on. 'As soon as he heard Mum had a hot young mini-me in town, he—'

'Er, no, you are *not* going out with him, don't even joke about that, lady,' Jess tells her, feeling hot herself, although not in a good way. Catherine must be getting a terrible first impression, she thinks wretchedly. 'I was just catching up with an old friend, that's all,' she explains, glaring at her daughter with shut-up-now eyes.

'Oh, this is the guy you were seeing the other night?' Luc puts in. He looks perturbed, as if wondering whether Jess's type is creepy old perverts. Of course – he doesn't know that she never actually *met* Georges last week, despite her hurried departure from the Belleville bar.

'Yes, except that by the time I'd got back to the hotel that night, he'd cancelled on me, so ...' This is all sounding worse by the minute. 'Anyway, that's enough about him. Moving on ... Are you having a nice time in Paris yourselves?' she asks, directing the question at Catherine and Henry. 'Luc proving to be a good tour guide?'

Catherine rescues her with a story about him taking them all the way across the city to his favourite restaurant on Sunday, only for them to arrive there and find it closed.

'*And* he got us lost in the Toiletries,' Henry sniggers.

ucy Diamond

'It's the *Tuileries*,' Catherine and Luc both say, while Luc adds, rather defensively, 'We weren't *lost*, I knew exactly where we were, it was—'

'Yeah, yeah, some gates were locked when they should have been open, we believe you,' Henry says cheekily.

'Classic adult move,' Mia says, joining in. 'Mum's really good at pretending she understands where we're going on the metro even though I can tell she hasn't got a clue.'

'Hey!' Jess puts in. 'I feel like there's some ganging up going on here.'

'Tell me about it,' Henry says to Mia. 'As for the souvenir shopping ...'

'Oh Jesus, the souvenir shopping!' Mia cries, throwing her hands in the air. 'Mum spent, like, twenty solid minutes thinking about whether or not to buy a snow globe in Montmartre yesterday.'

'It was *not* twenty minutes!'

'Twenty minutes, and she didn't even *buy* one after all that. I mean ...!' Mia has the expression of someone who has had to sit through the entire Ring Cycle on an uncomfortable chair rather than wait five minutes in a souvenir shop. 'I was like, just kill me now. Kill. Me. *Now*.'

'I will bloody kill you now, with my own bare hands, if you don't watch it,' Jess mutters. 'And it was chipped anyway, so ...'

'A *snow* globe?' Henry is saying over her, laughing, before catching Jess's eye and seeming to think better of it. 'Actually, I love snow globes,' he says, mouth twitching. 'Nothing wrong with snow globes.'

'Oh shut up, you two,' Catherine groans, laughing too. 'I'm

with you, Jess. I love snow globes too, *and* fridge magnets *and* I Heart Paris T-shirts, and you can't rush the buying of these important things. And if my ungrateful sod of a son doesn't watch himself, that'll be all he gets next Christmas. Take that as your official warning, kid.'

Once lunch has come to an end, Henry suggests, tongue in cheek, that he and Mia ditch the old people and go off on electric scooters together. Mia looks so thrilled by the idea that Jess doesn't have the heart to say no. Obviously she can't help throwing in a few pleas about being careful, when Henry's out of earshot. *Don't start showing off and doing anything stupid* is what she really wants to say but holds back. Once they've loped away, Catherine excuses herself and heads for the ladies, leaving Jess and Luc alone at the table. Without the bantering teenagers present, the atmosphere changes and they smile at one another a little self-consciously.

'How's it going? Everything all right? Sorry to hear your date was a bit crap in the end,' he says.

'Oh, don't be,' Jess replies. He's not mocking her, is he? she wonders, suddenly paranoid. 'It wasn't a big deal, just disappointing, really, to find out what a ... um ...'

'Creepy old pervert he was?'

'Pretty much, yeah. The shallow sort of guy I'd warn my daughters about. And for him to be carrying on exactly as he was twenty-five years ago ...' She pulls a face. 'I don't get it, but whatever. Horses for courses. Anyway—'

'I'm glad you didn't like him,' he says. 'I think ...' His gaze is very direct all of a sudden. 'I think I would have been a bit jealous.'

338

'Oh,' says Jess, taken aback. Is he saying . . . ? 'Um . . .' Before she can come up with a reply, they hear Catherine's voice.

'Je suis de retour, mes amis,' she calls, and in the next moment she's plonking a tray on the table before them, containing a full pitcher swimming with mint leaves and ice, plus three glasses. 'I took an executive decision when I was passing the bar,' she goes on cheerfully, taking her seat and looking very pleased with herself. 'Mojito, anyone?'

I think I would have been a bit jealous, Jess hears Luc say again, and her heart accelerates as she looks over at him. He smiles at her and she smiles back, suddenly giddy.

'Oh *yes*, good one,' she says to Catherine, adrenalin gushing through her bloodstream. It's hard to sound normal all of a sudden, when it feels as if Luc has just upped the ante between them. What is she supposed to do with that? She likes him, and thinks he's attractive, but the thought of getting into a new relationship is really daunting. Terrifying, actually. She doesn't have a clue what the rules are any more.

Thankfully she's distracted by Catherine pouring cocktails, and within minutes they are clinking full glasses together, toasting their good fortune to be sitting there in Paris on a sunny afternoon. It's almost as if that strange, charged moment between her and Luc never happened.

'Great mojitos,' Jess says, after her first cold sip, then has a sudden memory of drinking mojitos with Pascale in the Hotel d'Or bar. It hits her like a slap in the face: of course. That's where she should try next. If she remembers Victor Dufresne hanging around in the bar there, might someone else too? It's definitely worth investigating.

Chapter Thirty-Four

By Wednesday, Mia is feeling a lot less intimidated about being in Adelaide's grand apartment. Partly because she loves seeing Jean-Paul all day (he is so cuuuuute!), and partly because she hasn't broken anything or made any horrendous mistakes in her first two days of work there. Adelaide even said 'Well done' and 'Thank you' to her yesterday, which felt like a massive breakthrough.

She's also in a good mood because this will be her last day on the job, although her mum and Adelaide don't know that yet. Now that everything's been cleared up with her friends, Mia would sooner see out the rest of the week on a beach with them rather than hoovering an old lady's flat, so she's planning to head back to Nice tomorrow. Although typical, just as she was arranging this yesterday, she met Henry, who turned out to be the hottest – and nicest! – boy she has ever met, in her entire life. A million times cooler and more fun than the loser boys back in Canterbury, that's for sure. Yesterday, bombing around on scooters together, they kept putting on silly posh voices as they shouted things to each other, and her jaw actually ached from laughing that evening. 'Oh YAH, darling!' he kept booming, and it felt like the funniest thing ever each time. The only downside is that he lives in Devon, annoyingly far from home, but she's hoping she'll bump into him at Reading in August. If she's had enough cider when she sees him (likely), she's totally going to try and snog him, just watch her.

Today she's been asked to hoover the stairs and the top floor of the apartment, which is where Adelaide's bedroom is. 'No problem,' she said politely, hiding her excitement. She's never been allowed up there before. This is her chance to do some proper snooping.

Once at the top of the stairs, she gets out her phone and makes a quick recording. 'I'm standing outside Adelaide Fox's bedroom now,' she says in a low, dramatic voice, feeling a thrill to imagine thousands of people glued to her every word if (when!) she ends up making her own true crime podcast one day. 'I wonder if I'll find anything interesting inside?'

Heart thumping, she pushes the bedroom door open with a slight creak, then wheels in the hoover and shuts the door. Her eyes skim the room, taking in the large bed with a small dog-sized ramp leading up to it (now that is *adorable*), the ancient chest of drawers covered with jewellery boxes and perfume bottles, and a huge wardrobe that reminds her of the one in *Beauty and the Beast*, all curves and scrolls, with a big iron key in the door.

So where should she begin? What is she even looking for? She's not an idiot, she knows she's not about to find a signed letter of confession, but everyone has a few secrets in their bedroom, right? Switching on the hoover so that it sounds as if she's working, she crouches down to peer under the bed. There are some plum-coloured velvet slippers and a dog's water bowl, as well as some clear lidded boxes that appear to be full of jumpers. Nothing very exciting.

Next she opens the drawers of the bedside table for a swift beak around – a birthday card with French writing inside (no idea), an eye mask, half a packet of cough sweets – before doing the same with the chest of drawers, only to be repelled instantly by a load of old-lady pants (gross). Heaving a sigh, she's not feeling especially hopeful by the time she's reached the wardrobe, and nearly doesn't bother looking inside. But what the hell, she's here, she might as well, she decides, turning the key and opening the door.

At first glance, there's nothing interesting there either, just loads of clothes on hangers, and some lavender-scented pomanders. She's about to close the door again and abandon her sleuthing when the glint of something between two sections of clothing catches her eye. Pushing some of the dresses aside, she discovers a painting hidden right at the back of the wardrobe. She grabs her phone immediately. 'Guys, I've found a secret painting,' she whispers into the microphone, heart thumping as she scrabbles to pull it out and into the light. Then she gasps as she fully takes in the scene. 'Oh my God,' she says, her hands shaking so much she almost drops the thing. 'Oh my ... *Shit.*'

Her breath is jagged as she lays the painting on Adelaide's bed and quickly takes photos of it. 'Fucking Nora,' she says, whistling under her breath, forgetting about recording anything more coherent or descriptive because her brain is absolutely spinning. The painting is horrible but it's also amazing, because it's so real and so gruesome. Either side of a man are two women – sort of monster-women, really, dressed in black, with snakes in their hair and massive bat wings on their backs. Blood drips from their eyes and they're carrying huge whips. Mia's scant knowledge of Greek mythology comes solely from the Percy Jackson books, but she thinks the monster-women might be the Furies, all vengeance and threat. The face of one of them is distinctly recognisable as a much younger Adelaide, while the other is painted with short blonde hair and a wicked, grinning face. Between them, the man – Colin Copeland, she's sure of it – has bloodied scratch marks down his face and terror in his eyes, and looks as if he's falling backwards towards a huge window. You can tell that in the next second, he's about to plunge right through it. Just like the real Colin did, back in 1980. Oh my God. Is this painting saying what she thinks it's saying?

'Fuck,' gulps Mia, trembling all over. She can hardly believe that the stout, silver-haired lady downstairs, someone you'd pass in the street without a second glance, could paint something so violent and barbaric. That she's painted *herself* as a Fury, slashing a whip at poor old petrified Colin Copeland. She feels so freaked out – might she even throw up? – that she can't record anything for the podcast because she knows her voice will be wobbling all over the place. Fingers shaking, she texts her mum with a photo and message: *You won't believe what I've found. I think we should get out of here. I'm serious!!!*

But her mum, already a bit exasperated with Mia's texts and

photos about possible evidence, will have her phone on Do Not Disturb, she knows. What should she do? Well, put the painting back for a start, she decides. Because the last thing she wants is Adelaide bursting in unexpectedly, seeing what Mia has found and deciding she'll have to kill *her* as well as old Colin. The bedroom is up on the fourth floor; it's a long way down to the square below.

Jesus, this is *intense*, she thinks to herself, stuffing the painting back behind the dresses and locking the wardrobe door again. Dazedly she reaches for the hoover, when her phone pings. Oh, thank God. Is that her mum?

No, it's Henry. *Hey Meems*, he says and despite the horror of the past few minutes, she feels a fluttering sensation inside. As part of their posh Yah-ing imitations yesterday, they'd given each other stupid nicknames (his is Hen-Hen), and just reading the words is enough to conjure up his lovely face in her head. *What time do you finish work?*

Subtext: he wants to see her, she thinks, practically floating off the ground. He wants to *see her*! But the morning's events mean that she can't think about much else right now. *Soon as possible I hope*, she replies. *Your old aunty is actually mad you know. Like – I think she killed someone???*

She sends him a copy of the photo for good measure and quickly pushes the hoover back and forth before it can burn a hole in the carpet. He replies almost immediately. *Jesus. WTF?????*

I know right??!! And I'm trapped in her flat with her! She's sort of joking because it's all so wild, but at the same time, feels gripped by fear. Because how will this end? What is she meant to do with such disturbing information? She feels like a kid all of a sudden, and not a very brave one. Then she jumps at the sound of raised voices from downstairs. Adelaide seems to be really yelling at her mum about something. Whoa. What now? *Talk to you later*, she messages Henry, then switches off the hoover and shoves the phone in her pocket. Heart pounding, she scurries back downstairs where the shouting has only got louder, with some barking from Jean-Paul in the mix now as well.

She hovers outside the door, unsure whether or not to go in, but then it flies open, almost knocking her over, and her mum stalks out, red in the face.

'Don't *ever* come here again!' Adelaide screams after her.

Her mum looks like she wants to cry as she closes the door, her bag sliding off her arm in her haste. 'Get your things,' she says. 'We're out of here.'

Chapter Thirty-Five

Jess's heart is racing so wildly as they leave the apartment, she thinks she might have a panic attack. Oh my God. Everything has gone so wrong. Again! She's off the job. *Again!* And just when she thought they had turned a corner in their working relationship. That things were going really well.

'What happened?' Mia cries as they trudge down the stone steps for the last time. 'Why was she so mad with you?'

It's a relief to step out into the fresh air but a tragedy too because Jess knows she'll never go back to the flat now. 'I've blown it,' she says desolately.

'But how? What happened?'

They start walking towards the hotel, Jess still in a daze from how everything has unravelled so quickly.

'I tried to patch things up for Adelaide and her best friend,' she says, voice hoarse. 'But she was angry with me for going behind her back.' She shakes her head, imagining the self-righteous expression that would appear on David's face if he was there to hear this. *How many times?* he would say, rolling his eyes. *You just don't know when to butt out, Jess, that's your problem!*

What an idiot she feels, as she dully explains the rest of the saga. How she sat there this morning thinking that although she hadn't yet got to the bottom of Pascale's story – and perhaps never will – she owed it to Adelaide to at least put her in the picture about *her* old friend. And how, after Adelaide had recounted a few stories about her lecturing post at the Ottawa School of Art, Jess took it upon herself to make her move. 'And . . . Margie?' she prompted. 'How did she fit into your life at this time?'

It was a complete non sequitur and Adelaide shot her a suspicious look but replied nonetheless. 'We had lost touch by then,' she said stiffly. 'She had a little boy, Raphael, and was busy with him, then the family moved out to Pasadena. We no longer moved in the same circles.'

'But you were still friends at this point?' Jess pushed, even though she already knew the answer. It's such a shame that they fell out so badly! Of all people, she found herself thinking of her mum Samantha, who has always prized the company of other women. Bingo nights, knit and natter, her show-tunes choir, Pensioner Pilates (as she calls it) – Jess knows that these interactions with friends are the cement that holds her mum's world together. It's one of the few things Jess and Samantha have in common, the joy that comes from female friendships. Surely, despite her prickly nature, there's a part of Adelaide that misses that too?

Adelaide had gazed down at her lap, looking sad all of a sudden. 'No,' she said. 'We were no longer speaking.' She fell silent for a moment, before squaring her shoulders and picking up her thread. 'Now, moving on: in terms of the art

347

I was creating in Ottawa ...' she began, but Jess was unable to leave it there.

'She's ill, you know.' The words were out of her before she could stop them, cracking like bullets in the air. She regretted them immediately, a hand flying up to her mouth, because she'd fallen straight into the trap of sensationalism, shock tactics, and it wasn't fair. It was cruel, even. Adelaide turned her head, an unreadable expression on her face. 'I mean ...' Jess stuttered, mouth dry. She should have prepared better for this moment, she realised, but quickly reminded herself of what was at stake. All the good times the two of them had. Talk her round, Jess!

'How do you know this?'

'I ...' Confession time. 'So ... um ... I was hoping I could get hold of the drawing she did of you, following the *Woman Having a Cig* story,' Jess began, colouring beneath Adelaide's hard stare. 'And I contacted her in the hope that—'

'I asked you not to.' Adelaide's voice was devastating in its coldness. 'I distinctly remember asking you not to do that.'

'Yes, but—'

'Yes, but nothing!' Adelaide banged her fist down on the arm of her chair. 'Do you have so little respect for me that you would go against my wishes?'

Jess gulped a breath, trying to control the pounding of her heart. 'Adelaide, I have so *much* respect for you,' she said sincerely. 'Boundless respect. And it's kind of broken my heart, hearing about your friendship with Margie, knowing that—'

'It's none of your business! And it's absolutely not your place to start interfering. I can't believe you've betrayed my trust like this!'

348

Jess swallowed. 'It *is* sort of my business when I'm writing up your life story,' she countered. 'And I'm only mentioning it now because this could be your last chance to see her.' Was that too much? So be it, she decided. 'It feels like ... no offence, but it feels like you've given up on friendship. I mean ... there's being stubborn and there's being—'

'Given up on ... ?' Adelaide's mouth fell open, and something inside Jess withered and died at having spoken so bluntly. 'How *dare* you say such a thing? For your information, I haven't given up on anything. Although God knows I've been tempted enough times to give up on this damn memoir, especially with you writing it!'

'I didn't—' Jess tried but Adelaide's words kept coming, loud and passionate.

'I can't *believe* you've contacted her. I just can't believe you would do such a thing behind my back.' There were tears in her eyes suddenly; she looked utterly distraught. Jess was starting to feel sick inside. What had she done? 'Who do you think you are, to go interfering like that?' Adelaide shouted. 'To decide you know what's best for me? You know *nothing*!' She was crying by now, tears running down her face, and Jess felt wracked with guilt, knowing that she was the cause of this distress.

'I'm so sorry, I—'

'Don't come near me!' Adelaide cried, throwing her arms in the air. 'Just go. I don't want you to come again, either. Do you understand? You're sacked. Off the job. And this time there'll be no way back. Now get out!'

Mia is quiet once Jess has finished telling the story. 'God,

Mum,' she says. 'I really think she's a bit crazy. I don't know if this makes it better or worse,' she adds after a moment, 'but did you see my message? About what I found in the wardrobe?'

'In the ... ?' Jess doesn't follow immediately, consumed as she is by a wash of self-recrimination (how could she have been so *stupid*?), but then the words crash through into her consciousness. 'The wardrobe – no! What ... what was in there?' Oh shit. So much for protecting her daughter from whatever gruesome discovery she's made. Too late!

'This.' Mia puts her phone under Jess's nose, a painting on the screen. 'Look – I mean, she totally killed him, right?' she says, a note of triumph in her voice. 'Or rather they both did, Adelaide and that other woman, whoever she is.'

Jess comes to a standstill in the street. 'Shit, I think that's Margie,' she says, peering at the woman's face. Then her insides turn over as she takes in the picture as a whole. 'Bloody *hell*.' Even reduced to the size of a phone screen, the painting is so striking it makes her skin crawl. No wonder it gave Marie-Thérèse the heebie-jeebies, she thinks, pinching the screen and zooming into the faces: Adelaide, Colin, Margie. All there together in what looks like a painter's studio – an upstairs room at Little Bower, she guesses – with the dramatic tension of the huge window in the background, unbroken at that moment, but for how long? What happened in the next second, and the next?

Despite everything, it's a thrill to see the image, to get a glimpse at what might be the truth behind the story. So Adelaide *was* there, despite her alibi – and Margie too. Did they kill him together? She stiffens as another thought occurs to her. Does this have something to do with their falling-out and subsequent estrangement?

'Wow,' she breathes, looking at how Adelaide has painted the two women. They're the Furies, she thinks, goddesses of vengeance. Blood drips from Adelaide's eyes, her arm arched back ready to crack the whip, seemingly at the terrified Colin. She's painted him as the victim, which is interesting in itself, given that, from what Mia has dug up online, he was something of a stalker in her life, plaguing her with unwanted attention. Oh God, she has so many questions that will – infuriatingly – never be answered now. Not least the question of when Adelaide was planning to reveal this particular artwork. Presumably, like the Simon Dunster–beheading painting, it's part of the Revenge collection she talked about; a confession worked in paint.

She and Mia are both silent for a moment, taking in the commanding image. It's torture for Jess knowing that there's a complex, compelling story behind this painting that she will no longer be able to tell. How gutting to have come so tantalisingly close to the truth.

Mia nudges her. 'So ... what now?' she asks as they start walking again.

'Well, in a nutshell – we go home, I suppose. I look for a new job.' That's her summer falling in on itself in two short, dismal sentences, Jess thinks miserably. She'll have to change her train ticket for one leaving tomorrow instead, make arrangements for Mia too, and then, once back, there will have to be an immediate curtailment of spending until she can find some new work to pay the bills. The party's over for her in Paris, in other words. 'No point staying around here. Although . . .' She can't leave yet, she realises. Not when she is still no further towards the truth about Pascale. 'Well, there's somewhere I have to go to first,' she says. 'One last throw of the dice.'

'You mean with Adelaide? I don't understand, Mum.'

Jess sighs. It's boiling hot and she's still got the remains of a hangover after yesterday's afternoon of cocktails in the sunshine. She spots a bench in the shade ahead and gestures to it. 'Let's sit here a minute,' she says. 'Do you remember me talking about my friend Pascale, back then?'

'Yeah, the one you worked at the hotel with?'

'That's her. Anyway, she was really great. You would have liked her. Fun and naughty and . . . just great,' she says, when her words desert her. A sparrow is hopping about under a nearby tree and she gazes at its small brown body, its sticklike legs. 'Well. The thing is, I really let her down.'

'What do you mean?'

Jess presses her lips together, gearing up for the confession. She has never told anyone about this, she realises, not even David. 'She was going out one night and asked me if I'd help her – and . . . and I didn't.'

'Right.' Mia doesn't quite say the words 'Is that it?' aloud but she doesn't need to because they're written all over her face. 'Help with what?' she asks after a moment.

'I don't know,' Jess admits. 'She was kind of cagey about it – she said it might be something dangerous, even. I was in a bad mood that day, I'd had a long shift, and there she was, wearing one of my dresses without asking—'

352

'I hate it when Edie does that,' Mia puts in sympathetically.

'And I said no. Or rather, I went into the shower in a massive huff without answering her question, about helping her. And it's—' Her voice cracks as new tears rush into her eyes. 'It's haunted me ever since. That she asked for my help and I didn't give it. And then I never saw her again. The police were looking for her but we didn't hear any news. I stayed in the job for another few weeks but she never reappeared. She's almost certainly dead but I don't know what happened.' The sparrow pecks at a crumb and then a woman in rollerblades zooms past, and it flies away. 'Don't you see?' Jess goes on, remembering how that awful last month had weighed on her, the guilt unbearable. 'If I'd said yes, if I'd helped her in whatever thing she was planning, then ...'

'Yeah, but if it *was* dangerous, then you might have died too,' Mia points out. 'Sorry,' she adds, as Jess winces. 'But what if she was in trouble, and asking you to do something really bad? Things could have gone wrong for both of you. You might have ended up in prison. Or hurt. You might not have gone back to England and met Dad, you might not have had me ... I mean, *nightmare.*'

Jess sniffs and rummages for a tissue. 'I've always felt terrible about it,' she confesses in a low voice, blowing her nose.

'I can tell, but Mum, from where I'm sitting, it was totally unrealistic of her to say, *Can you help me, it might be dangerous,* in the first place, let alone expect you to say, *Ooh, sure, count me in!* I mean – that's not real, is it? *Nobody* would say yes, not knowing what they were agreeing to.'

Jess can't help feeling as if they're quibbling about semantics

353

rather than the actual guilt involved but she doesn't have the energy to disagree. 'I suppose,' she says. 'Anyway—'

Mia's still in full steam though. 'Look, you can't help everyone – that's just a fact. And you've helped loads of other people, haven't you, like me, and Edie and Polls, and all those losers who write to your agony aunt page,' she goes on, causing Jess to flinch on behalf of her 'losers'. 'Not wanting to get all psych-doctor on you, Mum,' she adds, 'but do you think that's *why* you're an agony aunt, maybe?'

'No, I—' Jess starts replying only to stop short, unnerved by her daughter's observation. Funny, but she's never put the two situations side by side before and wondered if there's a link between them. *Is* there a link? Can it really be as simplistic as that? It's true that she's always overcompensated in trying to help other people because of Pascale at the back of her mind, after all. 'Um,' she says after a moment. 'I don't know. Maybe?' She scrubs the tissue into her eyes, one after the other, only for Mia to gently stop her hand.

'You're getting mascara everywhere,' she scolds. 'So – what is this last place you need to go? And do you want me to go with you?' Her hand is still on Jess's and she gives it a squeeze. 'Maybe, whatever happens, we could have a little ceremony for Pascale afterwards? Like ... you could talk about all the wild things you two got up to and we could listen to her favourite songs, or eat some food that she really loved together? It could be a proper Paris goodbye to her. What do you think?'

Goodness, but Jess's heart is so full right now. Where did this grown-up, empathetic young woman come from, who has made such a perfect suggestion? A lump in her throat, she puts her arms around her daughter and kisses the top of her head. 'I think,' she replies, 'that's a great idea. Thank you. We'll toast Pascale and we'll say goodbye.'

Chapter Thirty-Six

It's not only Adelaide's hands that are trembling following Jessica's departure. Her entire body feels as if it's reverberating with distress. Once she has stopped crying and has pulled herself together, she rings Luc to update him on the news. 'Oh no,' he groans, and corresponding emotions cascade through her: guilt that her nephew sounds so fed up (with both her and Jessica, it seems) as well as anger, hurt, and frustration at Jessica's underhand tactics. How *could* she? When Adelaide specifically told her not to! What part of the word 'no' does the woman not understand? It takes her a little while to realise that there's sadness in her heart as well. Sadness that this whole episode has ended up in such a mess (again). Sadness too, despite everything, that her old friend could be very ill.

It's strange because Adelaide had always assumed that her feelings about Margie were set in stone by now. She figured she would remain completely cold towards her for the rest of her life. It has been years since their final argument, after all – decades. People have been born and died since then.

Wars have raged, leaders toppled. There has been a global pandemic, a climate collapse; the planet has been battered by fire and flood. And yet, perhaps because Adelaide has been re-examining so many memories from her long and eventful life – the glittering highs and bleak lows, exhilaration and despair – she has come to look back at the years with Margie from a different perspective. She has remembered how much she loved her, for one thing. How being with her was one of her greatest pleasures. How she has never laughed so much with anyone else, before or since, as she did with Margie. The splinter of ice that seemed to melt in Adelaide's frozen heart the other day? It has become a thaw without her noticing it, diluting the bitterness and resentment she has held on to for so long.

Her breath sighs out of her as she thinks about nursing her dying mother through the last weeks of her life, when the pneumonia took hold and never let go. Geraldine was so weak by then, her muscles stiff and inflexible from the Parkinson's, a stroke having robbed her of much of her communication skills. The indomitable, broad-shouldered Geraldine Brockes, mother of four, teenage swim champion, stew-maker, tea-slurper, deft with a sewing machine, owner of a temper that blazed like a furnace – to see this once mighty woman reduced to skin and bones in a hospice bed, it had broken Adelaide's heart clean in two. Is Margie suffering similarly? she wonders. Whatever happened between them in the past, it's horrible to imagine.

Death is so merciless, so undignified. Now she's remembering losing Remy four years after her mother, when his heavy drinking began to take its toll on his liver, when he kept suffering blackouts, losing whole days and nights and waking up with a split lip or black eye, having ended up in a fight somewhere along the way. He was unrecognisable by the end – sallow-skinned, gaunt, driven to destruction by his ceaseless thirst for one more drink. Try as she might to rescue him and show him that life with her was worth living – booking him into rehab clinics, promising him holidays, even buying his dream flat, for heaven's sake – he proved to be beyond saving. Uninterested in all her attempts.

Leaning back in her chair, Adelaide allows a space to open in her mind where she can properly inspect her feelings about Margie, following Jessica's blurted update. Silly, that it should be a shock, when the two of them are in their seventies now, but all the same, having been estranged for so long, there's a part of Margie that is always in her thirties for Adelaide: vibrant, opinionated, energetic. But of course she'll have the same wrinkles and creases as Adelaide, similar aches and pains when she heaves herself out of bed in the morning. The stiffening and slowing that happens to them all. What is Margie like, as an old woman? she wonders. Defiantly working and putting on a spangly dress now and then, or has she, like Adelaide, rather folded in on herself over the years? Whichever version, she doesn't want Margie to die, she realises – not yet, not with a haughty silence still stretching between them.

She reaches down to pet Jean-Paul, feeling numb. *This could be your last chance to see her,* Jessica had said. Is that true? Where would Adelaide even start, if they did see one another again though? They both hurt each other so badly. So irreparably, it seemed at the time. 'I trusted you!' she hears Margie screaming, back in their last dreadful row. 'How could you let me down like this?'

'Oh Jean-Paul,' she groans unhappily, stroking his lovely velvety neck. Where do they go from here? Not only in terms of her old friend, but in regards to Adelaide's life, her wretched memoir. She doesn't know if she can bear the thought of starting over with a new writer again. As for the rest of her life – it already seems an age ago that she was chortling away with Frieda and Jim in the Lebanese restaurant, looking at the future with a newly unfolding positivity in her heart. *You reach our sort of age and – well, sometimes, you have to just go to the places you want to go. While you still can*, Frieda had cried passionately. *Don't you think?*

'I just don't know, Frieda,' she says aloud now. 'I really don't know any more.' She glances down and realises that her phone is still faithfully recording the sounds of the apartment, even though Jessica is long gone, and reaches down to press 'Stop'. That's when it occurs to her. Maybe Adelaide doesn't need to work directly with a writer again – she's already got her own audio files of the sessions with Jessica, after all, and they can be transcribed in due course. She will finish the job alone, she vows. Then she will decide what, if anything, to do about the future and whether or not that includes Margie.

She takes a deep breath, settles herself in her chair and tries to put the unpleasantness of the morning behind her. Then she presses 'Record' again. Let's do this.

'1980 was a very difficult year,' she says. 'The worst year of my life. By the end of it, I was in a mental hospital in Germany, my relationship with Remy had come to a dramatic end, and my best friend was no longer speaking to me. Also, two people were dead ...'

Chapter Thirty-Seven

Jess insists they make a pit stop at the hotel in order to splash some water on her face, have a cold drink and then reapply her make-up. She changes her top for a lightweight pink blouse with puff sleeves and adds earrings and the half-heart necklace, as if putting on armour. It shouldn't matter what she wears but she wants to feel confident; the sort of woman who can get answers. Now that she's had her marching orders, this could be her last chance.

She and Mia exit the metro station to the sound of her phone ringing. *Luc*, she reads on-screen, and feels a lurch inside. Oh no. Presumably he's going to tear a strip off her for upsetting Adelaide and going behind her back. It will be no more than she deserves, she thinks, swiping to answer the call.

'Hi,' she says miserably, going to stand at the side of a tabac stall where she won't be in anyone's way. She puts a hand up to her other ear because they're right by the road and traffic is heavy. 'I'm guessing you've heard the news.'

'Jess, I ... I don't understand,' he says, sounding equally

doleful. 'You contacted Margie? I did warn you Adelaide wouldn't be happy about that.'

A bus roars by and she hunches over the phone. 'I know, but—'

'But what, you thought you'd do it anyway? Jess, I'm so gutted. I thought everything was going so well.'

Somehow him saying that he's gutted feels like the worst punishment of all. 'I thought so too,' she says helplessly, pulling a face at Mia. 'I just ...'

'You had to go and do the agony aunt thing,' he says. 'Get involved.' The lights have changed at the crossing nearby and a guy on a motorbike revs his engine, cutting out whatever Luc says next. Maybe that's as well.

'I'm sorry,' she says weakly. 'I was only trying to—'

'Yeah, help, I know,' he interrupts. 'But sometimes maybe the most helpful thing is to stay out of other people's business, have you ever considered that?'

'Luc, I only—' she says but then he interrupts with 'I've got to go' and the line goes dead. Did he really hang up on her? It seems so out of character for him that she has to look at her phone screen to believe it. Yes. He hung up on her. He's washing his hands of her, just like Adelaide did. She's let them both down.

'Mum, do *not* start crying again,' Mia instructs, grabbing her arm and pulling her along the pavement. 'Think of your mascara and forget him for now. Which way is the hotel?'

Jess sniffs, trying to get a grip of herself. Today is not turning out to be the greatest. Was it really only yesterday that she was drinking mojitos with Luc and Catherine, laughing in the

sunshine and feeling good about everything? Look how it's all
fallen apart with such gut-punching speed – and it's her own
fault. She has lost her job – and Luc's friendship – through
her own misguided interfering. Talk about self-sabotage!

'Come *on*,' says Mia. 'Stop feeling sorry for yourself. You've
got to be together when we go in the bar, for Pascale's sake
if nothing else.'

Jess nods, trying to put the phone call behind her. Mia's
right. She'll get to her hand-wringing and self-blame later.
Right now, she has questions to ask.

The Hotel d'Or bar is the same elegant haven it always was,
with panelled walls, stylish lamps that will provide soft yellow
pools of light come the evening, and comfortable leather arm-
chairs arranged around low tables. Piano music tinkles from
the speakers as Jess and Mia approach the bar, and Jess has to
ground herself for a moment because it's as if she's stepped
back in time. The bar is lit like a theatre set, and spotless, with
rows of spirits filling the ceiling-height shelves like books in
a well-stocked library. A young man polishes wine glasses at
the bar, and Jess feels pessimism take hold, seeing that he is
the only member of staff on duty. Like this whippersnapper
will know anything about a man who used to drink in here
twenty-five years ago! He probably wasn't even born then.

'Hi,' she says as they reach the bar, the words 'wild goose
chase' echoing around her head. This is the last time she does
anything on a hunch, she tells herself. '*Un Coca light, s'il vous
plaît*,' she says. '*Et* . . . Mia, what would you like?'

'Um . . . a beer?'

363

'Try again.'

'A vodka and Coke?'

'Nope. And again?'

Mia rolls her eyes but doesn't push it. *'Un Coca light aussi, s'il vous plaît,'* she says prettily.

The barman smiles at them both. 'No problem,' he says, getting down two glasses.

'Oh, and . . .' Jess retrieves her phone and shows him the photo of Victor Dufresne's painting. 'This man,' she says, switching back to French. 'Victor Dufresne. I don't suppose you know anything about him, do you?'

He stares at the photo blankly, shakes his head. Jess's heart sinks. She knew it. Of course it was too much to expect that she could come here and get any answers after so many years.

'Non,' he replies. But then – *'Mais mon oncle Thierry est ici. Un moment . . .'*

'What did he say?' Mia asks as the barman holds up a finger then vanishes into a back room.

'He said his uncle Thierry . . . Oh wow, surely it can't be the same one? There was a Thierry who ran the bar back when I worked here,' Jess says, her tummy turning over. She claps a hand to her face where the blood has rushed in. Please let it be him, she thinks. Please. She could really do with something good to come out of this whole trip, now that she's lost her job.

The barman returns with an older man in tow. His hair is salt and pepper these days, and he's put on a few pounds since Jess knew him, but it's definitely the same Thierry who worked here back when she did.

'Thierry!' she cries, startling him with her enthusiasm.

364

'Oh – *pardon*. I'm Jess. I was a chambermaid at the hotel a long time ago. 1998,' she explains in French.

His eyes narrow a little; he looks her up and down then gives a slow nod. 'Yes,' he says. 'You were here with your friend, weren't you? Patrice, was it?'

'Pascale,' Jess says, her voice barely a whisper. Her heart is really thumping now.

He nods again and is silent for a moment, seemingly lost in thought. 'You were asking about Victor Dufresne, yes?' he says eventually, his expression hard to read. 'Please – let us sit down. Eric will bring your drinks over. I have a story for you.'

Chapter Thirty-Eight

'For the record,' Adelaide says into her phone, 'we never wanted Colin to die. It was not deliberate. The whole thing was a terrible accident. A *tragic* accident? For his family, maybe. I think there was a sister who loved him. But for me? No, not really. I was glad to see the back of him, and you can judge me for those words however you see fit.'

She had been terrified that day at Little Bower when he appeared like that, saying such wild, unhinged things. Declaring that he loved her. That he wanted them to be together, and he knew she felt the same way. 'But I *don't*,' she had cried, increasingly unnerved as he advanced across the floor towards her, hands outstretched as if he wanted to take her in his arms. She was not a small, delicate woman by any means, but he was burly and determined with a manic glint in his eye; she didn't fancy her chances if it came to any kind of fight.

Thank God for Margie arriving out of the blue, claiming to have had a sixth sense, a prickle of alarm, following Adelaide's previous description of his behaviour. Adelaide had never been so thankful to see her friend – or anyone – as she was at that moment, with Margie appearing in the doorway, shouting 'Hey!' with such stridency it even stopped Colin in his tracks.

'What took place next is a bit of a blur,' she admits to the microphone. 'Everything happened at great speed and with enormous intensity. Colin had a hold of me while I tried to wrest myself away. Margie ran over and did her best to wrench him off me, but he was strong, he wasn't about to give in. Goodness only knows what was going through his head. The three of us were grappling there, pretty forcefully, all shouting at the tops of our voices. *Get off me!* And *Leave her alone!* And whatever mad stuff he was yelling, I can't remember now. And then ...' She swallows. Shuts her eyes. Pictures his red face, the veins on his head standing out, a pulse twitching in his throat. She inhales, giving herself a moment before she has to hear the smash of glass ringing down through the years in her memory once more.

'I remember thinking, very clearly, he's going to kill me. Because he was extremely angry by then – angry with me for not saying the things he wanted me to. Angry with Margie, too, for interrupting his big moment by coming to my rescue. And there was a bit of shoving, definitely some argy-bargy, but I promise you, neither of us pushed him out of that window.' Her fingers are knotted together in her lap and she stares down at them, the skin almost translucent with age. 'It's so long ago, it's all muddled in my head, but I think he must have lost his balance, because in the next moment he stumbled and ...' She swallows again, her mouth dry. 'And then he fell.'

SMASH. There he goes, for the hundredth, maybe

thousandth time in her mind's eye. That look of panic as he tripped backwards, toppling against the window. His feet went from under him with the impact, his arms windmilled frantically through the air, but he couldn't right himself, he was tipping and then he was falling. All the way down to his death.

You'd have thought Margie was used to people accidentally dying in front of her given the speed with which she recovered her composure and went on to draw up a plan. Putting on gloves to avoid fingerprinting anything further, they typed a suicide note and left it in the typewriter. Then, so quick it almost gave Adelaide whiplash, Margie was bundling them out of there, instructing her to get in her little red car, deciding aloud that she'd take them back to her place, give them an alibi. It was only once they were well on their way, Colin abandoned in a contorted position behind them, never to bother another woman again, that Adelaide came to her senses, and the argument started.

'We should tell the police,' she said, causing Margie to swerve in alarm.

'Are you crazy? We are not telling the police. We are not telling anyone about this, do you understand, Adelaide? We're taking it to our graves.'

'But we didn't *kill* him,' Adelaide cried. 'It's not our fault. He fell! And if we tell the police that, then—'

'You're not listening to me! What do you think the police are going to say if we drop into the nearest station and say, oh, there's a dead man at Little Bower, but it wasn't us, guv, definitely not. Yeah, we're two artists but don't hold that against

368

us, okay?' She snorted. 'It would be the end of us, Ads. They'd lock us up in two seconds flat. And then—' She gripped the steering wheel tighter, her knuckles whitening. 'Well, I'm trying to get my Green Card right now, aren't I? This is the last thing I want on my record. If we're going to move out to the States, I need to be squeaky clean.'

'Right, I get it. So this is about you being squeaky clean, is it?' Adelaide had been devastated at the news her friend was emigrating after her husband had been offered some big shot job in Pasadena. Now it felt as if Margie was doubling down on her decision, prioritising family over friendship once again. 'Well, guess what, you were just there while a man *died*. And if we don't go to the police, front up, tell the truth – that it was an accident, that he fell – then it's only going to be worse for us later. If they find out we're lying—'

'They won't find out we're lying! Jesus, Adelaide, when did you get so frigging holier-than-thou?'

'Oh, I don't know, since that weird guy just plunged to his death right in front of me, probably!' she shouted back. Her heart hammered in her chest as she pictured Colin with his neck twisted there on the ground, how his legs had been bent at terrible angles. His expression was one of shock, eyes open, mouth open. She found herself wondering how long it would be before a fox found him there, or a crow pecked with interest at a filmy eyeball. 'Oh God, stop the car, I'm going to be sick,' she cried, insides heaving in the next moment.

Adelaide can practically still taste the bile, decades later. How she had leaned over the roadside, shaking and retching, feeling as if she was trapped in a bad hallucination. 'This is all my fault,' she had said, getting back in the car moments later, wiping her mouth with an old tissue.

'Of course it's not your fault! You didn't ask him to follow you and pester you, did you? You never led him on.'

'But if I hadn't been there, he wouldn't have followed me, and . . .' She stared out of the window as the Kent countryside rushed by, still unable to believe he was dead. 'He would be alive now, if it wasn't for me.'

'That's bollocks. You can't blame yourself. That's like saying, if *I* hadn't turned up, he'd still be alive. Yes, sure, theoretically, but *you* might not have been. He might have killed you or raped you – he definitely looked as if he was going to hurt you, Ads. How could I let that happen after what Simon did?' It was starting to get to her now though, Adelaide could tell; the delayed shock catching up on her friend. 'Jesus, did that really just happen? This feels horrible.'

Safe in her apartment now, Adelaide forces herself to recount the details from the rest of that day – how they had returned to Margie's house, vowing to one another that they would never tell another soul about the incident. Margie's husband and son were away at the time but they made sure that a neighbour saw Adelaide there, and Margie trotted out a line about the two of them having a 'girls' weekend' together to cement the alibi. 'While the cat's away . . .' she'd said, twinkling at the neighbour, who laughed on cue.

The police came and spoke to Adelaide, having discovered pictures of her at Copeland's flat, and then interviewed the other Little Bower artists about their whereabouts, before concluding that there had been no foul play, and recording a verdict of suicide. 'The investigation was bungled, if you ask me,' she says into the recorder. 'Any detective with two brain cells would surely have queried a so-called suicide pitching themselves through a glass window, but none of us were asked any follow-up questions. I feel bad for his sister that we didn't tell the truth at the time, but it *was* an accident.' There's a lump in her throat, remembering the guilt she'd felt afterwards. It had been difficult to work, with Copeland's death weighing on her conscience, and she found herself sketching the scene over and over again in order to try and process what had happened, although she made sure to burn the sketches every time, fearful of the secret slipping out. She was drinking a lot, arguing with Remy and struggling to concentrate. And then, as if the universe was playing a dirty trick on her, she discovered she was pregnant.

'This is going to sound strange,' she says haltingly into her phone, 'and in hindsight, I don't think I was very well, but I became convinced that I was pregnant with the soul of Colin Copeland.' In some ways, saying this to the neutral shape of her phone rather than Jessica's expressive face is a blessing, because goodness knows how the writer would have reacted to *that* little nugget of information. Adelaide doesn't think she could have borne it if Jessica had laughed, when, at the time, it had felt very real and very frightening.

'I know there are rumours about me having had a baby,' she continues. 'I've heard the gossip with my own ears, from people who should know better. I told a few friends and my manager, Monica, in strict confidence, but someone must have blabbed. Monica, I bet.' She presses her lips together, still upset by the betrayal. 'But by then, I had already dealt with the pregnancy. The second death, that year.'

If Colin Copeland has haunted her nightmares in the years since, her unborn child has also remained a ghostly companion travelling reproachfully alongside her throughout her life. A child who would be in their forties by now, almost as old as Lucas and Catherine, making their way in the world, perhaps as an artist too – possibly a musician or storyteller or sculptor. She'll never know though. And she didn't want Remy to know either, that she'd had the foetus removed before it was any bigger than an apricot. She shouldn't have told him but, in a fit of frustration when he couldn't accept her not wanting to have sex one night, she found herself throwing the secret of the phantom baby at him, just to shut him up.

It shut him up all right. It sent him straight into the arms of Nadia Esposito, an Italian–American artist he hooked up with the very next night, and whom he ended up painting for his Berlin exhibition.

'And then,' Adelaide recalls aloud, 'if that wasn't enough, soon afterwards Margie and I had our biggest ever fight. One that there was no coming back from.'

A tear runs down her face and she clicks off the recorder. There's still so much left to tell about that awful year – the row with Margie and its repercussions, the fallout of the paint incident in Berlin and her enforced stay in the psychiatric hospital … She wipes her eyes, exhausted, and wonders who she's doing this for. Why she ever thought starting the memoir was a good idea. Maybe there are some stories that are better left buried after all.

Chapter Thirty-Nine

Thierry has quite a tale to tell Jess and Mia, in the Hotel d'Or bar. He doesn't know what happened to Pascale, but he *does* know what happened to Victor Dufresne the night that Pascale disappeared, because the bar could talk about nothing else for weeks afterwards once the story finally emerged. Dufresne was not a well-liked man, he recounts, with dry understatement. A violent, unpredictable type, he had made a lot of money through dodgy deals, and treated other people – particularly women – like dirt.

Jess nods, remembering Adelaide making similar observations. 'So what happened to him?' she asks, trying to hold down her impatience.

Thierry spreads his hands. 'Let me say now that this was a long time ago and it is hard to remember everything,' he begins. 'But Doof – Dufresne – was not seen for a while after your friend disappeared. Almost as if they had vanished together.'

'Oh no,' says Jess, fearing the worst. Surely nothing good is going to come out of that scenario.

Thierry goes on, describing how a story eventually emerged, 'but not for some weeks because he was embarrassed, you know? He did not want anyone to find out.' By the sound of it, Dufresne was fleeced by a woman he'd gone to dinner with. Perhaps he was unpleasant to her, Thierry conjectures, who knows, but Dufresne apparently woke up the next day with the worst headache of his life. 'And then he discovered that his wallet had gone, his car too, and yes, one of his bank accounts was all but empty,' he finishes.

Jess can hardly breathe. 'And Pascale ... Wait, what are you saying?'

Thierry shrugs. 'Like I said, we found this out weeks later. A month, even. The police had stopped asking questions about Pascale. But a barman sees a lot, you know? We are the eyes and ears of a place like this. I had noticed Pascale and Dufresne together in the bar before, and wondered to myself if the two things were connected. And if they *were* – if she was the one to trick him and escape in triumph, well ...' He mimes a salute. 'Then good luck to her. There were many women before her who did not have such a pleasant ending to their evenings, put it like that.'

Tears prick Jess's eyes because this – if it is true – is a wildly better outcome for her friend than any she has ever imagined before.

'She really might have done it,' she marvels. *I'm telling you, I will seduce a rich man one day*, she hears Pascale saying again. *I will seduce him, take all his money, then break his heart.* Dufresne's wallet, car, bank account ... if it *was* Pascale, she had gone all in. 'Oh, I hope that's why she disappeared.'

'I hope so too,' says Thierry with a gleam in his eye. 'And I choose to believe so.'

It's all Jess can do to stop herself from hugging him, but she holds back, not least because she doesn't want a mascara incident on his pristine white shirt. 'Thank you, Thierry,' she says, tears falling. 'I choose to believe it too.'

'Mum, what's happening? You're both talking too fast,' Mia complains, and then Thierry, smiling, squeezes Jess's arm and tells her it's good to see her again. 'Drinks are on the house, of course,' he adds, leaving them to it.

Jess doesn't know whether to laugh or keep crying as she recounts the story to her daughter, but by the end of it she is smiling. They both are.

'Oh my God, what a legend,' Mia says. 'Wow, Pascale. Did she drug him, do you think? I love the thought of her driving off in his car!'

'Me too,' Jess replies. 'She did always joke about us being . . .' Then she stops short. 'Thelma and Louise,' she says under her breath, as she remembers Pascale suggesting the two of them become outlaws like in the film. 'Yeah, because look how well that ended,' Jess had said in response, but Pascale had put her nose in the air. 'Not *this* Thelma,' she'd replied.

A thought slams into her. *Not this Thelma.* What if . . . ? She grabs her phone, opening Instagram on impulse. What was Pascale's surname? Bernard, that was it. *Thelma Bernard*, she types in, then holds her breath. It's probably too far-fetched, too crazy an idea, but . . .

'Mum, what are you . . . ?' Mia asks as the results pop up.

There she is. *ThelmaBernard1998*. It must be Pascale.

'I've found her,' Jess says, her voice little more than a whisper as she clicks on the name. 'I think I've found her.'

ThelmaBernard1998 set up the account twelve years ago, Jess sees. She has zero followers and has only ever posted one picture. But that picture is a close-up of a woman's throat and collarbones, with a gold half-heart necklace, like Jess's, gleaming there against her skin. Pascale left a digital calling card, just in case Jess ever came looking, she realises dazedly. Her friend didn't die that night, she lived to tell the tale; she really did get away. What's more, Jess thinks, crying all over again, it turns out she didn't even need Jess's help – or anyone else's – to do so.

The next morning Jess and Mia check out of the hotel, then hug goodbye. Mia's heading for Gare de Lyon, to be reunited later with her friends, and Henry's turned up to walk her there. (Somebody's keen, Jess notes with a smile as he heaves her rucksack on to his shoulder.) She, meanwhile, is bound for the Eurostar terminal in Gare du Nord. She's a grown woman and doesn't need anyone to hold her hand, but all the same, when she finds her seat on the train and gazes out of the window at the platform, she can't help a certain melancholy to be leaving so unceremoniously. Adelaide and Luc are probably glad to see the back of her, and fair enough. She knows she overstepped the mark. She was so caught up in her own narrative about Pascale, she projected her feelings on to Adelaide, someone she barely knows. She made all kinds of assumptions and ended up hurting the other woman's feelings, something she never intended. Meddling when she should have respected her wishes, her privacy. Lesson learned, she thinks with a sigh.

Once home, she will make a fulsome apology to them both, she vows as the train eases out of the station. She'll do her best to explain, and say sorry. It won't change anything but she does at least owe them that much.

The train picks up speed and she stares unseeingly out of the window, wondering if she'll ever return here. Last night she set up a matching Instagram account to Pascale's – *Louise-Stanton1998* – and then posted a similar photo of her wearing her heart necklace. She and Pascale liked one another's pictures and then had a brief exchange of messages – *Is it really you? Are you all right?* – and wished each other well. They have swapped numbers and are hoping to catch up in person again one day; Jess is already looking forward to their first riotous singalong of 'Hotel California' together. For the time being, though, she will enjoy letting go of that years-old guilt at last. She didn't let Pascale down, after all. She can move on.

And this is precisely what she does over the following days and weeks. She enjoys seeing the photos that come in from the South of France of Mia with her friends, glitter on their cheeks as they laugh into the camera together. She catches up with Edie and Polly, both tanned from Italy, and looking suddenly taller and more grown-up than before, if that can be possible. Polly's booked into a drama group with a bunch of friends for a week, while Edie has asked to do a couple of days at a manga club. In the meantime, Jess labours over a long email of apology to Adelaide, and a shorter one to Luc. *Working with you has been one of the highlights of my career,* she says to Adelaide, and it's not even an exaggeration. *I'm truly sorry that I betrayed your trust, getting carried away with my own ideas about what was the right thing to do. It wasn't my place to get involved, and I realise that now.*

Then she rolls up her sleeves and tries to put it all behind her as a lost opportunity. She grits her teeth and does a round of pitching, to anyone and everyone. She manages to sell a piece about Moussa's men's project in Paris to a men's health magazine, as well as, less glamorously, taking on some copywriting work for a company that manufactures worming tablets for pets. She doesn't have the luxury of fussiness any more, she's got to take what she can get – although to her relief, a sum of money does land in her bank account from Adelaide (severance pay, presumably) as well as a smaller amount, intended for Mia. So they won't be going under just yet, at least.

Before transferring the money to Mia, she asks her daughter to delete the photos of Adelaide's Furies painting from her phone. 'I know it's a scoop, I know it's amazing, but ... well, remember how much you hated Zach having private photos of you, knowing that he could show anyone any time? I think we have to apply the same justice to this situation too,' she says firmly. 'We don't know the story behind the painting, and Adelaide has never shown it publicly, as far as I can tell. We've got to respect that, I'm afraid.'

'But Mum ...'

'I'm sorry, but it's the right thing to do. Also, can I remind you, you *were* meant to be working, not poking around through her stuff.'

There's a fair amount of grumbling but eventually Mia deletes the images, having promised, hand on heart, she hasn't shown anyone else. So that's the end of that, at least.

During this time, Jess hears from David that he's had a reassuring doctor's appointment, although needs to wait for a set of test results to come back, just to be certain he's in the clear. She stops in for a coffee one Sunday when she's picking up the girls, and they have their most amicable chat yet, with him confessing how difficult he found the Italian holiday in terms of solo parenting. There was an issue with Polly 'accidentally' taking another girl's sandals from beside the pool that he had to deal with, as well as an evening where Edie confided in him about the ongoing toxic friendship situation at school and how unhappy it's been making her. By the sound of things, he handled both situations pretty well, though, on top of having to tackle Mia's abrupt departure and all the practicalities that ensued. Perhaps encouraged by him, Edie seems to have become a bit braver about seeking out new friendships, rather than getting sucked into the same old dramas, and has recently palled up with a girl from manga club who seems to be every bit as quirky and sweet as Edie herself. Maybe, just maybe, thinks Jess, she and David can make a decent fist of this separated-parenting lark between themselves, after all.

Elsewhere, Jess and Beatrice continue to exchange messages, with vague plans for Beatrice and her kids to visit, maybe in the autumn. Her new friend has also sent a selfie of her and Alain having coffee together at the *crêperie. He sends his best regards, Jess, and says he has made many friends at my dad's group,* Beatrice writes, and Jess positively glows to see his smiling face. She asks Beatrice to pass on her love, and also to ask for Valentin at the brasserie and hug him on Jess's behalf. *He says he will look you up when his designs make it to London Fashion Week*, comes the reply.

Then, towards the end of summer, Jess's brother Owen travels down to stay, along with Deanna and the children, for a week. With the house full, Paris seems further away than ever, as Jess organises day trips to Whitstable, London and Wingham Wildlife Park, as well as a traipse round some of the more local sights: the cathedral and St Augustine's for history fan Deanna, then the Beaney museum, which Jake and Ollie love.

It's good to spend some proper time with her brother and Deanna, who is not only thoughtful and funny, but seems to genuinely love Jess's girls ('the daughters I never had!') and makes a proper effort to get to know them all individually again – the best kind of sister-in-law. One night, while Deanna puts the boys to bed, Jess opens a bottle of wine and manages to tackle a tricky subject with her brother too: how she feels that their mum has always favoured him and his children over her and her family. To her surprise, he shakes his head, spluttering on his wine that this does not remotely match *his* lived experience. As far as he's concerned, Samantha is always sighing over *Jess* and Jess's wonderful daughters – especially when Jake and Ollie are playing up.

'What the hell . . . ?' Jess cries, baffled. 'But you're the golden boy! The paragon who has gifted her the best grandsons in the world.'

'Whereas you're a published writer who's spent the summer

in Paris!' he retaliates. 'She tells everyone about your work, you know. She's really proud.'

'With me, it's always been *my son the doctor*,' Jess says. 'Oh, did I mention my son? The doctor?' They both laugh but Jess thinks that there's some shared solace too. 'She obviously daren't say these things to our faces in case we get too big-headed,' she concludes eventually.

He snorts. 'No chance of that, when she's stirred up such inferiority complexes in us both. God! And there I've been, sulkily resenting you all this time.'

'Same! Sick to death of hearing about you, frankly!'

All in all, it's been great to have them stay, and they're already talking about a pre-Christmas get-together, and vowing to see more of each other from now on. They also make a pact to report back any compliments Samantha dishes out about the other sibling. 'Prepare to become immensely big-headed, against all her hopes,' Owen laughs, at which Jess guffaws. 'Well, *you'd* better prepare to have your phone melt down with all the hot praise that'll be pouring through it from now on,' she replies.

The last full day of their stay dawns, and everyone is so tired they sleep in late. Jess suggests they have a lazy brunch at home before they head into town and maybe take one of the punt tours out along the river. She's just whipping up pancake batter when the door goes.

'I'll get it!' calls Polly, who has been buying and selling lots of old clothes – hopefully all hers, and not anyone else's – on Depop all summer, making a small fortune apparently. It's probably the postman, weighed down with new packages for her, Jess thinks – so is surprised a moment later, when her youngest daughter rushes back into the kitchen, saying, 'It's for you, Mum – some old lady and a man and the cutest little Staffie wearing this amazing sparkly collar!'

'Uh-oh,' says Mia, who's still in her pyjamas, reading Ollie a Julia Donaldson story. 'That sounds like . . .'

Jess has already had the same thought. But it can't be, can it? Adelaide hasn't left Paris for years. Surely she hasn't come all the way to Canterbury. Has she?

Chapter Forty

Adelaide's final and fiercest row with Margie had come a few weeks after the abortion, misery heaped upon misery. She had been in a dark place, a hole of her own digging, and then Margie turned up at her door one morning, white-faced with fury, and the hole suddenly felt as if it had dropped another fathom in depth.

'I can't *believe* you told him,' Margie said, striding in without so much as a hello when Adelaide opened the door. 'I just can't believe it!'

'Told who?' Adelaide had been in discomfort from a pelvic infection for the last fortnight, bleeding and aching, and everything felt tender as she showed her friend into the kitchen and wearily set about making a pot of tea. Only Remy knew about the abortion so far and his reaction had been so violent, she was yet to open up to anyone else. Judging by Margie's angry expression, this wasn't the moment to mention her ordeal.

'Told *Remy*, of course. About Colin. Are you insane? Why did you do that? We promised each other!'

'I haven't told him anything,' Adelaide replied, wounded by the accusation in her friend's voice.

'That's not what he said last night,' Margie snapped, lighting a cigarette at the table and blowing a fast puff of smoke up to the ceiling. 'Announcing he knew all my secrets, with this nasty look in his eye. *I could call the police right now on you*, he said, the fucking weasely little ponce. What the hell, Adelaide? I'm meant to be emigrating in two weeks, so you'd better tell him from me, I'm not letting him sabotage the move, all right? That is not going to happen!'

'But I didn't say anything!' Adelaide cried – only to remember in the next moment the sketches she'd made so obsessively in recent weeks. All those incriminating drawings of her and Margie, there at Little Bower with Colin. She *had* burned them all, hadn't she? 'I mean—' Panic spiralled through her, nausea took hold. What if she had missed one, and Remy had found it? What if he was planning to blackmail her or punish her with it? She swallowed hard, thinking about the many drunken nights of late, nights she could barely remember. Had she opened her loose mouth at some point, let the alcohol do the talking for her? 'Don't call him names,' was all she could say, voice shaking, no longer able to meet her friend in the eye.

'I'll call him what I want, he's a shit. Threatening me like that. He could ruin everything for me, Adelaide! Don't you get that? I'm a mother! I have responsibilities! God! I'm so . . .' She banged on the table with a fist. 'You *promised*!'

Guilt and shame that she had inadvertently let down her best friend had been mounting inside Adelaide. But for Margie to then throw that in – *I'm a mother!* – so soon after Adelaide's abortion was too much to bear. 'So fucking what if you're a mother?' she shouted, fury burning up in her. 'Do you really think that makes you superior, that you must be special, just because your body squeezed out another body, like a fucking *animal*? Big deal! Who cares?'

It had descended from there, shouting and cruel words, both of them saying terrible things to one another. Soon afterwards, Margie and her family moved out to California without them ever making up, and then Adelaide had her breakdown in Berlin. By the time she emerged from hospital, a year or so later, Margie's absence felt like a scab on her skin; superficially healed over, but raw and bloody beneath.

It wasn't until she embarked on her Darkness series, after losing Remy, that she finally managed to exorcise her feelings about Colin Copeland in a painting. The resulting piece – morbid, grim and incriminating – has still never been seen before, but it felt like something she had to get down on canvas, a means of release. Adelaide has often felt a squirm of guilt that the painting in question has been stashed away in her wardrobe like a ticking time bomb ever since. If she collapsed with a stroke or heart attack tomorrow, what would it mean for Margie? But a part of her has clung on to the grudge, choosing not to care about the fate of her former friend. *So what?* that part has always argued. *If we'd gone to the police when I said we should, we wouldn't still be in this position. It's her fault!*

Now though, having finally caught up with Coco, tanned and healthy-looking following her jaunt to Île de Ré, Adelaide finds herself having to rethink that final tempestuous row.

Because in the space of an afternoon, a whole new light has been cast over what happened. A light that changes everything.

They had managed civility pretty well, Adelaide and Coco, when they met for a drink at a classy bar in Saint-Germain-des-Prés. They even had a toast – *To surviving the bastard*, as Coco sardonically put it, a dark gleam in her eye. As soon as it was polite to leave though, Adelaide was glad to slump in the taxi that took her back to Place des Vosges, clutching the orange Le Bon Marché shopping bag the other woman had given her. What answers did it hold inside?

In recent weeks, Adelaide has become something of a regular at the brasserie nearest her apartment. She's not quite in Frieda's league yet when it comes to adventures, but having a place to go where the staff are welcoming and just the right amount of friendly, where you can sit and feel part of the world again – well, it's a start. Today it was exactly where she wanted to be.

'Madame Fox! Good to see you – please, take a seat,' cried one of the waiters, immediately hurrying to fetch her chilled water in a bottle, a glass, a menu.

Spending time with effervescent, friendly Frieda – several dog walks, another dinner, an enjoyable lunch – must be rubbing off on Adelaide, because she found herself bestowing a smile upon him. 'Do call me Adelaide,' she replied.

The waiter – blushing and looking thrilled – brought her a very good coffee and she sipped it, looking out at the square, at the tourists queuing back from Victor Hugo's house, the couples browsing the galleries, two elderly men playing chess at a shady pavement table. So many lives swirling in and around this spot. So many busy people going about their day, taking photographs, admiring the architecture, savouring a moment of togetherness. And her among them, apprehensive and not a little excited to have two unexpected posthumous communications from Remy.

Hands shaking, she reached into the bag for the painting first. Images before words, that's how it's been her entire life, after all. It was a small piece, six by eight inches, but as her eye fell upon its composition, the impact made the canvas feel mighty in her hands. Oh Remy! When did he paint this? It was a copy of her favourite photograph of her and Margie in their early twenties, the two of them sprawled on the same sofa, top to toe, heads and arms resting comfortably against one another, both utterly relaxed in their closeness. His painting was simple and beautiful, the white space around the image making it seem as if they were the only two people in the world. He'd always been so jealous of their friendship, dismissive even, but here he had rendered them both with such tenderness, it actually brought a tear to Adelaide's eye.

'Thank you, darling,' she murmured under her breath, deeply moved. She couldn't stop looking at the bright young faces of her and her friend, with an almost pained feeling. She even found herself thinking that it was a shame she couldn't send a copy to Margie – until she got a grip, anyway. *Don't get carried away, old girl.*

Now time for the letter. The envelope was yellowed with age and rather battered, and as she slid a finger under the seal, it released easily, as if it had been waiting to let go for some time.

It was dated May 1990, a year after they'd broken up, and her heart thumped at the sight of his familiar sloping handwriting. Okay. Here goes, she thought.

Dear Adelaide,

I'm writing this on the eve of my wedding, it began, at which point she nearly put the pages straight back down again. Oh Lord. If this turned out to be a letter raving on about how madly in love he was with Coco, it really would feel like a bad joke from beyond the grave. Or was this in fact some forgery cooked up by Coco as a means to have the last laugh? It had better bloody not be.

She took another breath and tried again.

I'm writing this on the eve of my wedding and of course I am looking back to the time I had with you. With fondness but also regret. We were a match of equals, a match of true love and passion, but perhaps so similar we ended up almost destroying each other.

Before I give my vows to Coco, I want to clear the slate. Confess to this page that I was not a good person to you. I was jealous. I was unfaithful.

There followed a list of examples of his infidelity that did not make for easy reading. Perhaps this was why he never sent her the letter, she thought, disheartened as the names went on and on. Couldn't he have talked to a priest about this instead? For heaven's sake, it was the last thing she wanted to read. She skimmed through the names, trying not to let them hurt her, but then one leapt from the page with a particularly hard kick: *Margie.*

Oh no. Please, no. Her hand clutched her chest as if her heart might break in two. Is that why Margie had always

388

hated Remy — or professed to, anyway? Was it, in actual fact, the guilty covering up of a long-standing affair? Suddenly the painting seemed to mock her, and she had to stuff it back in the bag so that it was no longer in her eyeline. Could she bear to know the details? Her fingers trembled on the paper, instinctively wanting to ball it up, abandon it, but then she sighed reluctantly. What makes a great artist is their unflinching ability to look the truth in the eye; she'd always prided herself on her courage. And so on she read, grimly dogged.

I must tell you also, with great regret, that I betrayed you with Margie. I was upset with you after the abortion and when I saw her at a party soon afterwards, I wanted to hurt you in retaliation. The worst thing I could think of was to undermine your friendship. I lied to her that you had gossiped to me about a dirty little secret — and then, when she looked back at me in alarm, I seized upon this and embellished further, announcing that I could tell the police about what she had done. Of course I knew nothing, I was lying, but she didn't know that. You never wanted to talk about her in later years (and, if I am honest, chérie, neither did I) but I apologise if my deceit played any part in your falling-out.

Writing this letter has been a sobering exercise. Should I even get married tomorrow now that I have reminded myself of my unkind, disloyal tendencies? Do I deserve love, a wife, a family? That is yet to be decided, but I feel, very strongly, that I did not deserve you. And I am sorry, Adelaide, for my weakness, and for how I have wronged you. I may not ever send this letter, but if you do happen to read it one day, I hope you will accept my apology.

With love,

For ever your Remy

PART THREE

Chapter Forty-One

'Well, this is unexpected,' Jess says with colossal understatement. Her heart pounds as she stands there in her doorway with Adelaide, Luc and Jean-Paul before her on the step. It's like being in a dream, only it's all too vividly real. What on earth are they doing here? 'Um ... Would you like to come in?' she asks, belatedly remembering her manners. 'You'll have to take us as you find us, I'm afraid, as—'

Eight-year-old Jake barrels around the corner just then, hotly pursued by the tickle monster (Polly), and Jess breaks off.

'Sorry if this is inconvenient,' Luc says. He's wearing a dark grey T-shirt and jeans, his eyes searching her face, and Jess feels her own features freeze in response, remembering their last awful phone call: the coldness in his voice, how he'd hung up on her. How she'd deserved it.

'We can come back another time,' Adelaide puts in, sounding uncharacteristically polite. 'If this is inconvenient.'

'Um ...' gulps Jess again, lost for words.

'Can we say hello to your dog?' Polly says, sidling forward before Jess can get any further.

'Yes, of course,' Adelaide says. 'His name's Jean-Paul and he's very friendly.'

'Jean-*Paul*! You're so *handsome*!' Polly croons, sinking to a crouch, one hand outstretched to fondle the dog's ears. 'Come on, Jake, come and say hello to him.'

'Do come in,' Jess says, feeling weary, even though her day has barely begun. 'We're making brunch if you'd like to join us. Kids, get up, you can have a proper fuss with Jean-Paul inside.'

The awkwardness eases somewhat once Luc and Adelaide are in the kitchen with everyone else, although the cat flap rattles violently as Albertine makes a rapid (and no doubt furious) exit. Jess busies herself with tea- and coffee-making, taking orders for pancake toppings, tasking Edie to run to the corner shop and bring back more eggs. She introduces Adelaide and Luc to her brother and sister-in-law ('They're *doctors*, don't you know?' she says, parroting her mum), and Owen and Deanna step up, making small talk with Adelaide and Luc about their journey and where they're staying, while Mia and Polly keep the boys entertained. Everyone seems to be on their best behaviour, impeccably polite, which only sets Jess on edge. What are they doing here? Why have they come? It's impossible though to launch into any kind of serious, heartfelt conversation while two little boys are charging about underfoot, squealing and laughing. Maybe that's not such a bad thing, she acknowledges, gathering everyone to the table at last.

After they've eaten, Owen announces that he and Dee will take the boys to the park to blow off some steam, and that there might be an ice cream in it, if any of their cousins want to come too. 'We'll give you a bit of space,' he murmurs to

Jess as they stack the dishwasher together, and although she's grateful for his tact, she's also left feeling a bit sick, wondering what on earth is in store for her now.

'Please can we take Jean-Paul too?' Polly asks Adelaide with her most winsome smile. 'I promise we'll take really good care of him.'

To Jess's surprise, Adelaide smiles back. 'That would be very kind of you, darling, I'm sure he'd like that,' she says, fishing around in her large handbag for doggy treats and bags. (*Darling!* Seriously? Jess has to try hard not to gape in astonishment.) 'Thank you.'

All too soon, the house has emptied, and Jess sits back down at the kitchen table with her unexpected guests. 'So,' she says guardedly. 'I'm guessing this isn't merely a social call.' She sighs unhappily because she still feels bad about how she left them both. 'Listen, I really am sorry about—'

Adelaide puts up a hand. 'It's okay. You said all of that in your email and ...' She hesitates, then meets Jess's eye, her gaze direct. 'And it's okay.'

'It is?' Jess looks doubtfully from Adelaide to Luc, who nods in confirmation, although his expression remains inscrutable.

'I don't know if other ghostwriters take their subjects *quite* so much to task as you have done with me,' Adelaide goes on darkly and Jess cringes, remembering all the terrible personal remarks she made in the heat of the moment. 'But I've always been a fan of the truth. And you telling me – what was it? That I'd given up on life and was lonely and vindictive—' Jess looks down, feeling her face grow hot. 'Well, I wouldn't say they were the nicest words to hear, but after a while, I had to admit that you'd made a pretty fair assessment of things,' Adelaide continues. 'I did rather give up on everything for a time. Being angry – yes, and somewhat vindictive too – it seemed as if that was all I had left.' She steeples her fingers together. 'But I've been feeling differently lately.'

Jess dares to look up once more. Her heart is thumping; she has no idea where this conversation might take them. 'Different how?'

'In part, I suppose it was talking to you about happier times,' Adelaide replies. 'Remembering that I *have* had a good life.'

'You've had an *incredible* life!' Jess puts in. 'You've done so many extraordinary things.'

'Yes,' Adelaide says, a tiny smile playing on her lips. 'I have, haven't I? But I had rather come to forget that side. Not completely, obviously, but I never thought much about those years of my life, back when I travelled and worked and had the greatest of friends . . .'

She looks faraway and then Jess stiffens, because she has the horrible feeling she knows what's coming. This is all driven by regret, isn't it? she guesses. Regret that Margie has died and Adelaide left it too late to contact her.

'So . . .' she says, but can't bring herself to ask the question.

'So I had a word with myself,' Adelaide goes on. 'Enough's enough, I said. What does pig-headedness achieve when your best friend might be seriously ill?' She looks down at the table for a moment and exhales. 'And so I got over my pride and did what I should have done a long time ago – I contacted Margie.'

Jess holds her breath. She's not sure she can bear to hear that Adelaide was too late. 'And? Is she . . . is she okay?'

'She's fine, Jess,' Luc puts in, as if he can tell what's on her mind. 'She's much better. What's more, she was very happy to hear from Adelaide.'

'Oh!' The relief is immense – followed immediately by sheer gladness. 'Wow, that's really great news,' Jess says, her eyes dampening at the corners. 'The best news, Adelaide.'

The older woman smiles briefly but there's something rueful in her face too. 'It *is* great news,' she confirms. 'Although I recently discovered that the huge argument we'd had . . .' She sighs, lips pressed together momentarily. 'Well, I discovered that it never needed to have happened. That the entire thing was founded on a misunderstanding. An outright lie.'

'No,' Jess groans, horrified for her. They've really spent the last four decades not speaking because of a *misunderstanding*?

'Don't get me wrong, we both said horrible things to each other the last time we were together, but fundamentally, the situation was not as we thought.' Adelaide sips her tea. 'Anyway, once I realised this, I emailed her to explain, and said sorry. Five minutes later, she called me up and then we spoke on the phone for two hours straight. We only stopped when her son told her off, saying she was getting overtired.'

'Oh, Adelaide!' Jess can see how much it means to her. 'I'm so pleased for you both.'

'Jessica – Jess, if I may – I can't tell you how pleased *I* am,' Adelaide replies. Are those really tears glimmering in her eyes? 'It's only now that she's back in my life that I've realised what a gaping hole there has been all this time. I've missed her so much.' It's obvious that she's struggling to control her emotions. 'I'm actually hoping to go out and see her in the autumn,' she goes on eventually. 'It's been too long, but we're determined to make up for lost time.'

Jess has a hand on her heart, deeply moved at the thought of these two fabulous women reuniting in person. 'Even better,' she says. 'Amazing. Good for you.'

'And it was through talking to her, and having Frieda, my new friend, badgering me about trying to get another exhibition on in Canada – and, again, spending so much time talking to *you* about my career and paintings ... Because of all of that, I have sort of ...' She hesitates then plunges on. 'I have sort of fallen in love with life again. With art again, too. I've been spending time in the studio with Luc, looking through everything. It's been a thrill, actually, the two of us trying to pull together a suitable collection of work for an exhibition. The Best of Adelaide Fox – like a greatest hits album by a band, if you like.'

'I think she should call it "Adelaide Fox: Staying Alive",' Luc puts in. 'Or, even better, "Fabulous AF".'

'Thank you, dear,' Adelaide tells him patronisingly, which makes Jess snort with suppressed laughter. 'As is the way of these things,' she goes on, 'I've lost many afternoons leafing through old sketchbooks and correspondence, immersed in nostalgia.' She picks up her bag from where it's been by her feet and pulls out a small rectangular object, wrapped in bright pink paper. 'Cutting a long story short: I found this and I think ...' She smiles mysteriously and passes it to Jess. 'I think it's meant for you.'

Intrigued, Jess takes the parcel and unwraps the pink paper. Inside is a framed sketch – an Adelaide Fox original sketch – of . . . 'Oh my goodness,' she says, hardly able to speak because there is suddenly such a lump in her throat. Her hand flies to her mouth as she peers at the figures in the sketch: two young women in chambermaid uniforms, sitting on a bench, leaning against each other laughing. 'It's . . .' Words fail her because there she is, captured in swift, sure ink-strokes, and there beside her is Pascale.

'It *is* you, yes? I remember you saying you worked around Faubourg Saint-Germain, and I think I even told you how I would spend time there, sketching, in the late nineties.'

'It *is* me,' Jess confirms. 'It's me and my friend.' She can't stop looking at the picture, overwhelmed by how emotional it has left her. 'Oh, Adelaide, this is the best, the nicest . . .' It's hard to hold back the tears. 'Thank you *so* much. You'll never know how much this means to me. I'm incredibly grateful.'

Adelaide looks delighted. 'You're very welcome,' she says. 'I was hoping you'd be pleased, because . . .' She glances at Luc and he nods. 'Well, because *I'm* sorry, too. Sorry I was so fierce to you. More than once, if I recall.'

Jess shakes her head. 'You really don't have to—'

'I do,' Adelaide interrupts. 'I want everything to be all right with the two of us again because . . .' She hesitates again then rushes on. 'Because if there's any chance you are interested, I do still need a writer for my book. I've tried recording audio files but it's not the same as having someone with me – having *you* with me – prodding me and poking me for extra content. Asking your nosey little questions.' She smiles at Jess, who smiles back. 'As for all my – how did you phrase it? – petty grievances . . . I've kind of got them off my chest now, you'll be glad to hear. Besides, I intend to be far too busy for me to waste any time being sued.'

'Obviously the writing can be on your terms, Jess,' Luc puts in, while Jess is processing all of this. 'We're going to stay in England for a few weeks now, so we can fit in with you.' He gestures around. 'We appreciate it's the summer holidays and you're busy.'

'Think about it, anyway,' Adelaide says. 'Take your time.'

Jess laughs because she doesn't need to think about it, and she doesn't need any time. This is the easiest decision she's had to make in a long while. 'I'd love to work with you and finish the book,' she says. 'Try and stop me. I'm in!'

Before the house descends into chaos once more, they set about booking in some days together over the next fortnight, and agreeing on a new work schedule. 'Also, while I'm in the area,' says Adelaide, suddenly looking flustered, 'Lucas has kindly offered to take me to a couple of places that have been important to me. You'd be very welcome if you wanted to join us.'

'Of course,' says Jess, her thoughts racing. Is Adelaide talking about Little Bower? Or does she mean ...?

'Yes,' Adelaide says, as if reading Jess's mind. 'Back to Margate.'

Chapter Forty-Two

On the day they arrive, it's as if Margate has put its best face on for them. The sky is vast and blue, with only a handful of feathery white clouds, and the beach is busy with holiday-makers. Holding on to the sage-green railing that overlooks the sand, Adelaide falls silent for a moment, taking in the scene. Down below, families have set up camp with colourful towels and umbrellas, alongside pairs of older couples with their folding chairs and Thermos flasks. Seagulls arc overhead with the occasional screech while the smells of sun cream, chips and seaweed mingle in a distinct seaside fragrance. In some ways, it's as if she's never been away.

Her eye wanders down to the shoreline, darting between the sandcastle-builders, the sunbathers, the paddlers. She's uncertain what she's seeking, until she finds it. There he is. A small boy with untidy brown hair and red trunks crouching at the water's edge with a bucket and spade. Be careful, little one, she thinks, but then there's a woman beside him, with a tiny blonde girl on one hip, and Adelaide watches as the boy shows them the contents of his bucket. It's too far for her to hear anything but she can read their body language – loving, affectionate, close. This boy will be okay, she tells herself. He'll have a lovely seaside holiday with his family. That'll do her right now.

She turns to see that Lucas is looking at her worriedly, as if expecting her to break down and start crying. Jess, too. She surprises them both by smiling back at them. 'Well, this is splendid, isn't it? Shall we wander along the front first? I'd like to get a look at the Turner gallery.'

The years have passed but the view from the promenade has barely changed since she was a girl, she notes as they begin a slow mooch following the curve of the bay. For so long, she's done her best never to think about this place and what happened, but with the sun warm on her face, and a holiday buzz in the air, new memories are surfacing unexpectedly. Her dad teaching her the names of seabirds, for instance – oyster-catcher, sandpiper, cormorant. Her mum gamely hunting out shells with her for long stretches of time. They went to the Shell Grotto too, she recalls suddenly, and has an immediate visceral memory of running her hands across the lumpy, shell-encrusted tunnel walls with a sense of deep awe. The days prior to Will's loss were probably the happiest of her childhood, with both parents content and amicable, everyone united in an unusual spirit of camaraderie. Before they go home today, she will make it down to the water again, she decides. She'll look out at the far indigo band on the horizon and say a final goodbye to her brother, to her childhood. She'll kick off her sandals, feel the suck and push of the waves on her old feet, and she'll stand strong. She's a survivor.

They've had a pleasant time in Kent so far, her and Lucas. Once they had cleared the air with Jess on that first day, they ended up staying the whole afternoon at the house, and then for dinner too, with Jess's brother and family. ('The more the merrier,' said Jess, who's clearly used to catering for a house full.) After Adelaide's quiet life in Paris, she'd found it over-whelming at first – so many people! So much noise! – but once the initial shock had passed, she found herself stimulated by the conversation and personalities around the table. She also enjoyed seeing Jess in this new light: as hostess, mother, sister; deflecting her daughters' attempts at mickey-taking with dimpled good humour and affectionate teasing right back.

And they're rather delightful, these daughters of hers. Mia was a little stand-offish at first, but, having been permitted a glass of wine with dinner, soon dropped the act, even admitting, wide-eyed, and in hushed tones, that she'd seen the painting concealed in Adelaide's wardrobe. 'Oh, really?' Adelaide replied, amused. 'Is this about to be a blackmail attempt? How thrilling.' Mia, embarrassed, had protested not, but confessed to being interested in the tale 'Ahh – a born journalist, just like your mum,' Adelaide said. 'Well, here's a deal, Mia – I've recorded the whole story on an audio file and when everyone relevant to said story has died, you can have the exclusive.' Then, as the girl gasped with excitement, she added, 'Although I'm not planning to die for a long while yet, so don't hold your breath.'

Edie, the middle daughter, turns out to be a keen manga artist and Adelaide, who has no particular interest in the genre, nevertheless asks the girl if she would give her a lesson on this

403

style of drawing, which earns her a look of gratitude from Jess as well as a blushing 'Sure!' from the girl. Heavens above, but Adelaide is turning into a soft touch in her old age, she thinks, as the two of them set to work coming up with a character together over a sketchpad. But what's even more surprising is how pleasing this is. How enjoyable. Who knew?!

As for Polly, she has poured a great deal of energy into teaching Jean-Paul tricks, with a level of patience that Jess says, in private, she never thought possible. To everyone's astonishment, in the last few days, Jean-Paul has learned to stand up on his hind legs and give a double high five, to 'speak' (the sweetest, politest of barks) and to leap through Polly's arms. Adelaide has left him in the girls' care today and her mind is already boggling, wondering what her faithful friend will be able to do by the time she gets home again. Put the laundry on? Sharpen some pencils for her?

Perhaps the most impactful thing of all has been a brief but illuminating exchange with Deanna, Jess's sister-in-law. After dinner that first evening, the children vanished off upstairs, and Jess made coffee for everyone. A rather boring conversation started up between Luc, Jess and Owen about the best route to drive back into town, while Adelaide zoned out a little and sipped her coffee. But too late she realised that her hands were shaking again, so much so that she narrowly avoided spilling the hot drink over herself. Setting her cup down, she hid her hands under the table, willing them to be still, but sharp-eyed Deanna had already noticed.

'Are you okay? Is that the caffeine making your hands shake?' she asked. 'The coffee's pretty strong, isn't it?'

They're doctors, don't you know! Adelaide heard Jessica saying again in her head, and perhaps Deanna's bedside manner was particularly on point that evening, because before she knew it, Adelaide found herself blurting out her long-held fear that she had Parkinson's and would soon be deteriorating like her mum before her.

Deanna listened intently before saying that Parkinson's wasn't necessarily hereditary. 'In fact, only fifteen percent of people with Parkinson's disease have a family history of the condition,' she said, 'and tremors can be caused by a number of things. Caffeine is one, smoking another, but also general stress and ageing. You should get yours checked out, but it could be something that's easily resolved with medication or lifestyle changes. And even if you do have Parkinson's, there have been some big breakthroughs since your mum's day – the treatments are hugely improved.'

What serendipity that kind, clear-eyed Deanna turns out to be a geriatrician, and knows what she's talking about! Adelaide has been so certain of her own diagnosis, it hasn't occurred to her that there might be other causes. Could it really be that her love of good French coffee is part of the problem? Hopefully she can find out before too long, because Jessica has contacted her GP practice, who have agreed to see Adelaide as a temporary patient. Whatever the outcome, she will deal with the problem properly, she's concluded. Better sooner than too late, as Deanna put it – and it's worth the effort, now that there is so much she wants to do.

Talking of which, she has been making plans galore in the last few days. She's lined up a meeting with the director of a forthcoming exhibition, Women of the Sixties, that's to be held at the Tate next January. Having spent many days in her archive recently, Adelaide has finally come face to face with her original Revenge painting again, the one of her beheading Simon Dunster, and feels that the time has come to show the piece to the world. *Adelaide and the Rapist*, she has called it, and intends to put the painting up for auction following the exhibition, with the proceeds to go to a rape crisis charity. Revenge is all well and good, but the practicalities of cold hard cash that will help other women ... that's even better. The exhibition director, foreseeing pages of publicity and a real scoop, professes to be thrilled. In truth, Adelaide feels quietly thrilled herself. How proud she is of the brave young woman who painted the gory scene, who refused to let the incident define the rest of her life.

Despite her earlier intentions, Adelaide has decided not to mention Dunster directly in the memoir. Partly because she doesn't want his name to sully her life story, but also because she'd always rather let her art do the talking. If people want to draw conclusions, then let them. 'A talentless nobody,' is all she'll say, if anyone asks about the identity of the rapist. If he happens to still be alive and hears that, it'll *really* piss him off. Good.

With the memoir rescheduled and her part in it due to be completed by the end of September, she and Margie are making arrangements for her to fly out to Pasadena in October ('The light in California is so wonderful for painting,' Margie keeps saying), and they're planning day trips together to the Norton Simon Museum and Eaton Canyon. Adelaide can hardly wait – and that's only the start of her travels. She's also been in touch with Frieda and Jim about possibly visiting them in Montreal next spring. The thought of being back in Canada makes her feel incredibly happy. Who knows, maybe she *will* look Brad up and see if he's free, at least so that they can go for poutine together again. Both Lucas and Catherine have offered to have Jean-Paul for her while she's away, although she has a feeling that Jess's Polly might also put in a strong pitch for the privilege.

Whatever, they're all going to be fine. *She's* going to be fine. There's a future out there for her that's full of good people and good times, as broad and boundless as the horizon before her now. As the waves rush into shore once more, she feels a corresponding surge of happy anticipation for what's yet to come. As the young people say: bring it on.

Chapter Forty-Three

Adelaide seems exhausted after her day in Margate, having taken in the Turner Contemporary gallery, a stroll along the harbour wall, a browse in the gorgeous independent bookshop, a nostalgic trip to the Shell Grotto and a very enjoyable wander around the old town with its pretty painted boutiques and smaller galleries. There are artists everywhere in this town – 'I'm in heaven,' Adelaide said happily at one point, buying yet another print and smiling for a selfie with the delighted young artist ('This is the best day of my *life!*'). She even had a paddle in the sea, staring out across the water with a wistful expression, while Jess and Luc hung back to give her some space.

Having returned to Canterbury, Luc picks up a similarly knackered Jean-Paul, who can now remove a giggling Polly's socks on command, and also play dead (helped, perhaps, by the smell of the socks), with the plan that he'll drop both Adelaide and dog at the rented flat where they're staying.

'What are you doing afterwards?' Jess asks, as they say goodbye. It's early evening and she is thinking ahead to what to cook the girls for dinner. 'You're welcome to come back and eat with us, or ... ?'

He looks shy, all of a sudden. 'Maybe I could take you out for dinner somewhere instead?' he suggests. 'You can choose where.'

Jess pretends to consider the suggestion coolly, even though her heart has started beating a little faster. They still haven't had a meaningful conversation, just the two of them, since his arrival in Kent, and she isn't sure how to feel.

'Let me think ... well, there's a *really* fancy and expensive place out past the university,' she jokes, if only to buy herself time. A giddiness is spreading through her; it's hard to keep her composure. 'Alternatively, we could go to my local for good old pie and chips?'

'Now you're talking,' he says.

She smiles and they make arrangements, only for her to come back into the house and realise that all of her daughters have been eavesdropping like crazy, and are now, to a girl, unanimous in giving her pursed-lip looks.

'What? What are those faces for?' Jess cries, marching through to the kitchen so that they can't see her pink cheeks.

'Mum's going on a *date*,' Edie says, sing-song. 'He really likes you, Mum, I can tell.'

'And *she* likes *him*,' Polly declares to her sisters with some glee. 'I told you. Didn't I say?'

'Let's hope this goes better than the evening with sleazebag Georges,' Mia puts in, as the three of them take up perches on the worktop and kitchen table, still eyeballing her.

'Blimey, it's like having my very own Greek chorus with you three commenting on my every move,' Jess says, amused. 'And it's not a date, anyway, more of a working dinner, I bet.' She opens the fridge door, staring blindly at the contents. *Is it a date, though?* she wonders. Would she *like* it to be a date? She had that strange physical reaction when he asked her, after all. Her tummy's still a bit fluttery even now. 'Although, to be honest ...' Shutting the door, she turns and stands against the fridge as if facing a firing squad. 'One day, I don't know when, I probably *will* want to go on a date again, you know. And yeah, I think that would be weird for all of us when it eventually happens but ...' She hesitates, wanting to choose her words carefully. 'But I'm telling you now, you three will always be my number one priority. Always. Okay? And even though it's been hard for everyone, me and your dad splitting up, we can make it work between us, all right? We're *going* to make it work.'

'Welcome to my TED Talk,' Mia says, in an impression of Jess, but it's not an unkind one.

'Can we have a takeaway if you're going out?' is all Edie has to say on the matter.

'Ooh yes, can we?' Polly chimes in, sensing weakness, and then they're all calling out suggestions – pizza, Nando's, Chinese.

Did they receive her message? She hopes it's gone in, despite their apparent indifference, but she'll keep on transmitting her love to them regardless. Recognise your child's feelings, she remembers pontificating in one of her parenting columns, and she plans to, even if, right now, she's mostly recognising

410

that they really *really* want a takeaway. 'Sounds like a plan to me,' she says.

Later on, she and Luc are in The Brewer's Tale, a cosy riverside pub with a large sunny beer garden. Sitting there in dappled evening sunshine, with a cold pint each and the satisfaction of knowing that your dinner is being cooked by someone else, Jess feels a rush of happiness. Life seems to be coming together better than she could have planned. The girls are upbeat. She has an enjoyable period of work lined up for the months ahead and, who knows, if this book goes well, she could even write another. Make a real name for herself. It no longer seems such a pipe dream any more, now that she's come this far.

'You sound cheerful,' her mum had commented on the phone the other night. 'It's not easy being a single mum, at times, is it? But it sounds as if you're doing a great job.'

Since Owen's stay, Jess has been thinking differently about her mother. Because no, it's not easy being a single mum, and yet Samantha managed it pretty well for years on end, after their father left when Owen was eight and Jess six. Disappeared off to Singapore, never to be heard from again – with not so much as a single letter, phone call or birthday card to show that he had ever thought about his wife and kids since. How did any woman carry on after that? But Samantha had, nevertheless; working twice as hard to keep the small family afloat. And maybe she'd felt she owed it to her children to make them tough in the face of a cruel world, fostering a competitive spirit in order to make fighters out of them. To hear her warmth, coming as it did so rarely, left Jess tongue-tied. Had Owen said something to her? she wondered.

'Thanks, Mum,' she said, then remembered the fond thoughts she'd had recently about go-getting Samantha, when compared to Adelaide's previous, more downbeat approach. 'I could say the same for you,' she'd gone on. 'You and all your friends and activities up there – you've made a really nice life for yourself.'

'I do wish we were nearer though,' Samantha had said. 'That's the only downside. Can we maybe arrange a time for me to visit? I've been so jealous, hearing about Owen staying with you.'

'Definitely! Mum, I'd love that!'

Now here she is with Luc, who's looking really handsome in a pale blue summer shirt and jeans. He's wearing cologne that has a grassy, leathery sort of scent – vetiver, is that the fragrance? she wonders distractedly as they talk. She's wearing a new dress that she picked up in the Zara sale and, for once, has managed a vaguely competent blow-dry. She feels good.

'I'm glad this is all working out,' he says. 'Are we okay, Jess?'

'What, after I reduced Adelaide to tears with my interfering, and you told me off and hung up on me?' Jess replies teasingly. 'Yeah, we're okay, Luc. All's well that ends well.' She nudges his foot under the table with hers. 'We're cool.' In the next instant, she imagines her daughters guffawing at that particular statement (*Er ... really, Mum?* they laugh in her head) and has to backtrack. 'Well – cool in the sense that ... You know what I mean,' she adds, flustered.

He smiles. 'Cool in every sense of the word, I'd say,' he replies, meeting her eye as he raises his pint glass in the air.

412

'Cheers, anyway, Jess. Good call coming here. Canterbury's great, isn't it? I can't believe I've never been before.'

'If you've got time, I'll take you and Adelaide around the sights while you're here,' she offers. 'You can splash out on a jazzy little Canterbury Cathedral key ring to remember us by, or go wild with an I Heart Canterbury T-shirt.'

'Don't tempt me,' he says, then picks up his discarded jacket and rummages in one of the pockets. 'Talking of classy souvenirs ...' He produces a small paper bag, sealed shut with a sticker of the Eiffel Tower, and puts it on the table between them. 'This is for you.'

'What is it?' she asks, taken aback.

'Believe it or not, there's a really simple way of finding out,' he says deadpan, gesturing at it.

Blushing, she laughs, then peels off the sticker, opening the bag and peering inside. 'Oh, Luc!' she cries, reaching in to retrieve a beautiful vintage snow globe. The pewter base is a circle of miniature Parisian landmarks – Sacré-Coeur, the Arc de Triomphe, Notre-Dame among others. Inside the globe is an Eiffel Tower amidst, when she shakes it gently, a blizzard of falling snowflakes. 'It's perfect,' she says, gazing at his face and then back to the snowy scene. 'And way nicer than the one I nearly bought in Montmartre. I love it, Luc. Thank you.' There's a lump in her throat because it's so thoughtful of him, so personal. He *remembered*, she thinks dazedly. He paid attention to me and remembered. *He really likes you, Mum, I can tell*, she hears Edie saying in her head, and feels her face heating up.

'You're welcome,' he says, his knee leaning against hers

beneath the table. Even though she was the first to initiate contact with her foot a few minutes earlier, there's something about him doing it back that sends a crackle of electricity around her skin. *I really like him too*, she finds herself thinking and blushes even harder.

'So,' she blurts out, just as he says, 'Anyway,' and then they both stop and look at one another across the table.

'You first,' he says.

'I . . . um . . .' she blusters, because the continued pressure of his knee against hers (how can the feeling of a *knee* be so sexy?) has meant that she's already forgotten what she wanted to say. 'Um. What are your plans, then, for the rest of the summer? I know you and Adelaide will be finalising arrangements for her exhibition, but after that, will you stay on in Paris, do you think, or go back to London?' Recovering herself, she raises an eyebrow teasingly. 'Or is it down to the nearest farm to start living your dream?'

'Funny you should ask,' he begins, but before he can get any further, the pub landlady Donna arrives with their food, and sets down a steak pie for Luc and a chicken one for Jess, both with fat chips and peas, and smelling divine. 'I might just move in here actually,' Luc says, inhaling the aroma.

'Ooh, fine by me, darling,' says Donna, who is a tiny tattooed seventy-something. She winks at Jess. 'Enjoy!'

Jess smiles, sprinkling salt over her chips as Donna totters away. 'Go on, you were about to tell me your plans,' she reminds him.

'Yeah. Well, turns out you were right,' he says, cutting into his pie so that the gravy floods out, dark and beefy.

414

'Of course I was,' Jess replies airily. 'About what in particular, though?'

'About Kent being a great place to study agriculture,' he says, which stops her breath in her throat. 'There's so much beautiful farmland, incredible orchards, some top-rated college courses ... I've been looking into it.'

It's hard for Jess to keep her composure all of a sudden because the air between them is charged with so much that's not being said. 'Right,' she manages to reply neutrally. 'Sounds good.'

'Although ...' He swishes a chip through the gravy and takes a bite. 'It would be pretty reckless of me, wouldn't it, to leave everything behind in London for a new start in Kent?' His eyes lock on to Jess's and she feels a frisson spiral down her entire body. 'Unless, of course, there was someone already living there who I liked so much, the thought of being anywhere else seemed ... well, like the most foolish idea of all.'

Jess swallows because the eye contact is so intense now she can hardly remember how to breathe. 'Are you saying ... ?'

'I'm saying ... I think I'm saying this,' he replies, and in the next moment he is leaning over and gently kissing her lips. It's only for a second but her body responds with such a surge of adrenalin – and passion – that her heart pounds like a jackhammer. 'I'm saying I think you're great, Jess,' he goes on. 'And I'd be mad if I didn't find out if ... if there's any chance of something happening between us.'

'Luc, I ...' She feels overwhelmed, as if her body is too small to contain all the big emotions it's currently experiencing. Her overriding instinct is to kiss him again, to put her arms around him and feel his body pressed against hers, but then she thinks of her daughters' sweet faces and is immediately conflicted. 'I've got to be honest, I don't know if I'm in the right place for a relationship yet,' she confesses.

'I don't know if I am either,' he admits. 'But we could find out, couldn't we? Between us. No pressure. Just have a laugh together. Hang out. See if anything comes of it.'

She feels as if she should keep a wall up, protect her fragile heart, but there doesn't seem to be anything fragile about it right now, thumping away in rude good health as it is. She finds herself unable to stop smiling at him – at this summer – at all the great and unexpected things that have happened to her in the last few months. 'I think I would like that, too,' she tells him. 'I think I would really like that, Luc.'

Epilogue

Adelaide steps off the plane feeling tired but also wired, with the excitement that comes from landing in a foreign country after a long flight. She's here. She's actually crossed the ocean, and arrived. A crisp October morning when she left Paris, the temperature in LA is apparently twenty-eight degrees, according to the pilot's final announcements. Twenty-eight degrees! 'Bring your bikini,' said Margie, who has a pool in her backyard. Adelaide had laughed at first, thinking *not likely*, but somehow or other, three different bikinis have ended up in her luggage. Bugger it, this might be the last time she's in California. Although, if the doctor she saw back in Canterbury is to believed, she could well have many years of bikini-wearing ahead of her yet. It's all about attitude, she tells herself, and hers has done a full one-eighty in the last few months.

It was a wrench leaving Jean-Paul with Lucas but she knows he's in safe hands. Having finished his work on her archive, Lucas had been toying with the idea of going back to college, but then, after selling his London flat quicker than expected, apparently changed his plans. The last she heard, he

417

was intending to bite the bullet, buy some land and learn how to be a smallholder on the job. Much to Adelaide's delight, he and Jess have been seeing a lot of each other recently, and he's currently renting a property in the sweet little town of Faversham, ten miles from Canterbury, while he looks for a suitable place of his own. They're taking things slowly, he assures Adelaide, but from where she's sitting, it looks as if they're both running headlong towards one another, beaming, arms outstretched. And good luck to them, she thinks, arriving at last at the baggage carousel. As long as he doesn't distract Jess from her writing deadline, they have her blessing.

Meanwhile, her exhibition is starting to come together. Having selected the pieces she is most proud of, and arranged for any loans from the owners in question, she and Lucas are in talks with the National Gallery, and others around the world, regarding dates and scheduling. The GP she spoke to prescribed some medication, that has, along with her new regime of decaff coffee, cleared up the tremors astonishingly quickly. As a result, to her great joy, she has begun painting and drawing in earnest again. In fact, she has spent the last month working on a couple of brand-new pieces for the exhibition. (She doesn't want to boast, but her painting of Jean-Paul in a chiaroscuro style is absolutely fucking magnificent.) After some deliberation, she also decided to entirely paint over her Furies piece with a watery white wash, renaming it *A New Beginning*. If you look closely, you can make out the shapes of figures beneath the white, where the original had been loaded with oil paint, but if anyone wants to know more about the piece, they'll just have to lump it, because she won't tell.

She has instructed Jess that any mention of the painting is to be left out of the memoir completely; let nobody say that Adelaide Fox can't keep her promises. As for the story about Colin's death, her lawyer has advised her that it's probably for the best if she sticks to the version that she gave the police at the time. That's okay by Adelaide though. Like any good piece of art, a memoir should always contain a few unresolved mysteries, in her opinion.

Here's her luggage now, a jaunty red suitcase juddering along the carousel. 'Excuse me, would you be so kind—?' she asks a rather attractive younger man, pointing it out. He immediately leaps to attention and hauls it off the belt for her, then sets about finding her a luggage trolley. 'Thank you, dear,' she says as he loads the case on for her, and asks if she needs any further help. 'No, I'll be fine from here, I think.'

The words echo in her head as she pushes the trolley firmly towards the Arrivals door. *I'll be fine from here, I think.* Yes. She will. She definitely will.

And then she's wheeling her trolley through Customs – nothing to declare but my genius, ha ha – and finally into the vast, brightly lit barn that is the Arrivals hall. There are faces everywhere. A tremendous amount of noise and bustle. Oh goodness, she thinks, scanning the crowd for Margie. It feels like half of America is here waiting for some arrival or other. How will they find one another?

But then – 'Adelaide! Adelaide!' – there is a white-haired lady, near the front of the scrum, leaning on a stick, her smile wide. It's like coming home, seeing that beautiful beloved face again.

'Margie!' she cries, her heart leaping behind her ribcage. She can't believe she ever thought life was over for her, she thinks, hurrying to greet her friend. In the next minute, she has thrown her arms around dear Margie's neck, and they're both weeping and laughing simultaneously. Life, thinks Adelaide joyfully, is only just beginning.

Acknowledgements

I really hope you enjoyed this novel – I think I enjoyed writing it more than any other book, not least because of the research opportunities it gave me! As well as a great summer Paris trip with my husband, taking in the delights of the city (including the sampling of many excellent brasseries, obviously – you can't rush this kind of fact-finding), I also signed up for the most wonderful History of Art evening class at Bath College with Andrew Foyle, who opened my eyes to incredible paintings week after week. Thank you so much, Andrew, for your inspirational teaching. As someone who is definitely not an artist myself (I wish), I may have made mistakes when writing about art and artists in this novel – please humour (and forgive) me if so.

Thanks as ever to Lizzy Kremer who steered me through this book with great patience and kindness. Thanks also to her colleague Orli Vogt-Vincent for excellent, insightful notes, and to the wider David Higham team, particularly Margaux Vialleron and Ilaria Albani for all the hard work you do on my behalf.

Huge thanks to everyone at Quercus – it's a joy to work with you all. Stef Bierwerth, Kat Burdon and Emma Capron – your combined editorial wisdom and attention to detail was very much appreciated. Ella Patel, Patrice Nelson, Katy Blott, Ella Horne and Ellie Nightingale, thank you for all the reviews, events, newsletter admin and creative flair – what a team. Thanks also to Dave Murphy and Izzy Smith for sterling work on the sales front, and to Micaela Alcaino for the beautiful cover. Thanks to Sharona Selby and Rhian McKay for fantastic copy-editing and proofreading too. Love and thanks to my wonderful foreign publishers – with a special hello to the Hachette Australia squad: can't wait to meet you all!

Thanks to Alexandra Heminsley who was kind enough to speak to me about the art of ghostwriting. Your generosity was much appreciated – and it should go without saying that Jess and Adelaide are entirely fictional characters.

Thank you, Sue Garrett and Florence Richardson, fabulous art consultants, for giving me helpful pointers on language around art. Again, all mistakes are entirely my own.

I'd also like to thank Therese Bonath, whose Facebook message inspired me to create Jean-Paul, as penance for some lazy stereotyping of mine around Staffies in a previous book! Thank you, Therese – I hope you like him.

Thanks to Hannah Powell who read the manuscript at an early stage and gave me really thoughtful, perceptive notes (plus a personalised playlist!), and who continued to discuss ideas with me for weeks afterwards. Much appreciated! Thanks too to Rachel Delahaye, another early reader, for your encouragement and enthusiasm. Our next lunch is on me!

Thank you to the Fort Road Hotel in Margate for the amazing hospitality while I was tussling with my first draft edit – I'm not sure I've ever worked anywhere that has a better view than your window seat of dreams. Hope I can come back one day.

Wishing love and great writing days to the Swans – Ronnie, Harriet, Cally, Jill, Emma, Rosie, Mimi, Kirsty, Kate and Victoria. Big love as always to the wonderful Milly Johnson for being such a pal.

Love and thanks to the booksellers who have been so supportive to me over the years, in particular Lindsay at Ledbury Books and Maps, Sarah at Mostly Books, Octavia at Octavia's Bookshop and the whole team at The Bookery in Crediton. Special shout-out to the brilliant booksellers at Mr Bs and Toppings in Bath too for helping me to spend my royalties within your wonderful book shops. I sincerely believe it's impossible to come out of either shop empty-handed.

Finally, lots of love to all my family, especially Martin, Hannah, Tom and Holly. You're the best – thank you for everything.

Discover more from *Sunday Times* bestselling author

Visit www.lucydiamond.co.uk for:

About Lucy

★

FAQs for Aspiring Writers

★

And to contact Lucy

To sign up to Lucy's newsletter
scan the QR code here:

Follow Lucy on social media:

 @LDiamondAuthor

 @LucyDiamondAuthor

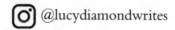 @lucydiamondwrites